THE GRID

THE GRID

JEREMY REED

PETER OWEN
London and Chester Springs, PA, USA

PETER OWEN PUBLISHERS
73 Kenway Road, London SW5 0RE

Peter Owen books are distributed in the USA by
Dufour Editions Inc., Chester Springs, PA 19425-0007

First published 2008 by Peter Owen Publishers

Inside cover: Detail of *Jonathan* by Marco Livingstone
(2004, oil on canvas)

ISBN 978-0-7206-1303-5

Printed in the UK by CPI Bookmarque, Croydon, CR0 4TD

For Toyoko

'I went in search of myself and never did a day's work I regret.'
– Derek Jarman

'Every man that writes in verse is not a poet; you have the wits that write verses, and yet are no poets: they are poets that live by it, the poor fellows that live by it.' – John Daw, 1592

'Your laws are not mine.' – Keith Richards

1

Whoever they were, the three men Kit had seen getting away from Deptford that night in a black state-of-the-art vehicle – with halogen lights bright enough to cause temporary blindness, grenade launchers and high-voltage door handles – they left in a hurry, creating a thick wall of exhaust to cover their getaway. SmarTrucks were principally the prerogative of the city's tsars, and as a footnote to its escape the vehicle had released an oil-and-tack slick to prevent pursuit. The armoured car, based on Ford's F-350 pick-up and looking like an inviolable Hollywood 'fortress' limo, accelerated into the night like a Boeing blasting off into the busy skyways.

Kit watched it go, sure that it signalled some form of urgent catastrophe in or around the city. Ever since he had taken up the option to write a screenplay on Christopher Marlowe he had made Deptford, with its unreconstructed tower blocks and container yards looking out over the Isle of Dogs and close to Rotherhithe and Jacob's Island, the industrially littered and dystopian precinct that he visited at night. At the risk of being set upon by marauding gangs of inner-city refugees he derived a perverse thrill in communicating from Deptford with his laptop to a Marlovian cult scattered across the Anglo-Japanese capital. The migration of Japanese people to London had begun in the late twentieth century, the two auto-destructing digital cultures fusing into a mutually dependent society. If Tokyo had been emptied in part of its workers, and in particular of its youth, then a London subjected to the autocratic rule of its militant Commissar had readily adopted the invasion of Japanese immigrants drawn to its increasingly apocalyptic ethos.

Kit had no doubt that Marlowe had been murdered at

Deptford Creek on 30 May 1593. His job was to research and write screenplays for a production company with an eye to biopics about the lives of a number of gay men who had become cultural icons. Kit's commissioning editor there, Scott Diamond, was obsessed with the lives of gays who had been posthumously sainted, such as Oscar Wilde, Jean Genet, Jean Cocteau, Piero Pasolini, Michel Foucault and Derek Jarman. That Kit had a research project out on Marlowe not only fed a personal enthusiasm but helped deepen his links with the Elizabethan playwright by allowing him the freedom to re-create his life.

Most lights were out in the surrounding towers, and at night the place looked brain-damaged and uniformly alien. Kit could smell the river's skin as it sweated pollutants. He turned up the collar on the black cashmere coat given him by his friend Yumiko and listened to a boat making tracks downriver. The tide was coming in; he could feel it push through his arteries like a drug. Even in summer he couldn't get rid of the river's creepy chill in his system or be free of noting its ebb and flow. He was even conscious of it when fucking some epicene Japanese boy in an underground foot tunnel or behind a corporate office tower at Vauxhall.

For no apparent reason, other than that he was saturated by the Marlowe plot, Kit fantasized that the three men in the getaway SmarTruck were the notorious quango named as Marlowe's killers: Nicholas Skeres, Robert Poley and Ingram Frizer. They were underworld figures, inseparable from his life and the place by historic association and the river's toxic passage through the Deptford badlands. Through his research and recent regression hypnotherapy sessions at the Grid, he felt he knew their history as intimately as his own, for they were all connected in some inextricable way through Marlowe's blood. It was, according to the official story, at Eleanor Bull's closed house on the Creek, on the evening of Wednesday 30 May 1593, that Christopher Marlowe had been stabbed through the right eyeball, the blade penetrating the superior orbital fissure

at the back of the eye socket and taking that route into his brain. Kit placed a defensive hand over his eyes. The SmarTruck's headlights had left him burnt by their power, as the vehicle with its retractable weapons system had veered full on at him before being touch-screened towards the A2 and New Cross Road and disappearing in a blaze of roaring torque and 1001 b.h.p. get-away.

It was starting to rain, a furry drizzle reaching in from the surrounding marshes haloing a nearby complex of container yards. Kit knew without doubt that he should get a train back to Charing Cross and return home to his top-floor apartment at Colville Gardens, Notting Hill, the fugitive base from which he worked, looking out over Hammersmith and the constellating lights on the sonic drone of the Westway flyover in the distance.

He felt instinctually he needed somehow to break his habitual pattern. He'd hung out here at night too often and too long, consumed by a morbid empathy with his subject. He knew if he didn't catch that train then he risked going back in a reversed space–time all the way to 30 May 1593 and the undoubtedly homophobic murder that formed the basis of his story. After the killing Marlowe's bloodstained body had been carried to burial by drunken sextons from a house on Deptford Strand, through the dockyard streets to the Church of St Nicholas, the steeple of which he could just make out through the increasingly fuzzy pixels of rain. Marlowe's body had been unceremoniously dumped in an unmarked grave near the north tower of the church as a gay outlaw, a man who went in behind and made that place of entry the gateway to his poetry.

Kit kicked his way along Church Street in the direction of the station. An orange-and-white *Evening Standard Metro* delivery van had been overturned and left on its side, after having been torched by one of the nuke gangs who frisked the south-east of the city on an axis between Greenwich and Dartford. On several occasions he had narrowly missed run-ning into a fired-up local gang uniformly dressed in sloganed sweatshirts, combats and with their grizzled hair shaped into a swastika stamped on the skull. He could see from the trashing given the neighbourhood that the gang had passed through a matter of hours ago. The pavements were diamonded with littered glass, and the gang had spray-painted their iconoclastic DNA-shaped vocabulary over an enamel-scratched line of Audis, Toyotas and Nissans. Car doors had been torn out of a conspicuous black Jaguar X-Type and black sacks slashed open and discharged across the road.

Kit hugged the shadows like a fugitive. An X-Hawk flying car went over very slowly, its front and back housing propellers that whirred like a helicopter's rotor blades. Urban air traffic had increased in recent years, and the Israeli-built craft pursued a rooftop reconnaissance before going off in an arc towards Greenwich. Kit assumed from its white panelling, logoed with a red cross, that it was a Medicare team searching for a disaster site in the endlessly disruptive inner-city estates.

Amongst the nuked Fords, Vestas, Fiats and a Cherokee wiped for its saleable gizmos, Kit's eye picked out a discarded inkjet cartridge from a desktop printer. He didn't know why, but something made him stop and retrieve it. He could see from the printed label that this was no ordinary cartridge but most likely a tube that had contained living tissue. He had read about such tubes being used illegally in tissue-engineering. By washing out the cartridge and refilling it with suspensions of cells contained in a thermo-reversible gel it had become possible to print complex tissues and whole organs with a view to biological repair. Kit had heard rumours in his circle of the tube being used to effect on people with Aids, where secondary infections proved immune to anti-retrovirals. He had a half-interest through the Grid in biotechnological breakthroughs, particularly where they touched on longevity. The printed label on the tube was clearly in code, and he pocketed the item, thinking he would show it to a friend in the know.

Kit hadn't eaten all day, and the bottle of Merlot he had drunk by the river had left him feeling spacey and hyper. He couldn't remember a time when he hadn't drunk or relied on alcohol as a trigger to altered states. Red wine was his poison – anything from the Bordeaux, St Emilion or Croz Hermitage selections – and the bottle, once drunk, usually ended up thrown into the muddied river.

Kit, although he preferred ordinary reds, would drink almost anything as a stimulus to writing the poetry he published with small presses. He saw poetry as a total commitment, an all-or-nothing, do-or-die occupation that the writing of screenplays helped finance. He had little time for compromise in his art and didn't easily fit into – or tolerate – the corporate trend towards celebrity publishing. Writers, to his mind, had come to look and think like their accountants, and his way round this was to go underground and publish his work fugitively. He was a cult to a small readership and his books hard to find. You had to be linked to a network to own them or be prepared to pay optimal online prices. It matched his idea of the historic Kit Marlowe who had, in his imagination, cottaged his way across London in the late sixteenth century, using the theatres where his plays were staged as notoriously reliable cruising grounds. Gay channels hadn't really changed and were, despite activism, still part of a marginalized community connected to the underworld.

A surveillance helicopter blustered over in the direction of New Cross, causing him to look up through a gap in the clouds. Its reverb coshed the air as a wall of sonic feedback. What had once been a familiar late-opening high street, was now only functional in the day – its lock-ups presenting a metal face to the neighbourhood after dark. Most of the nuking was random and directed at the corporate ethos, its anti-war coalition directive aimed at outing investors associated with WMDs and World War III.

Kit knew the dangers involved in hanging out there but kept returning to the place for its topographical links with Marlowe. In Marlowe's time plague had menaced the city like a pathological cluster bomb; if the modern equivalent was Aids, then he had played safe and taken every conceivable precaution.

Marlowe would have cruised the naval yards, drunk hard with his passive conquests and coming back at dawn heard the queen's buckhounds howling in their kennels on the outskirts of town. His dodgy reputation as a 'roaring boy' and as someone who stood for tobacco and boys had been established then, his bad name being whipped up like cappuccino froth wherever he went. It was common knowledge to his contemporaries that Marlowe was a professed atheist and someone who delighted in ripping into any received notions of moral truth, an offence punishable at the time by thumbscrews, the rack or by having his ears sliced off under torture. In fact, it was the anti-Christian bias of his play *Tamburlaine* that had contributed to the suspicion under which Marlowe was viewed as a punkish enemy of the State and as a dangerous inciter to free thought. Kit was only too well aware that atheism in Tudor times was associated with homosexuality and that similar charges levied against George Gascoigne, Nicholas Bacon, John Caius and the Earl of Oxford had together carried the smear of a gay witch-hunt. Kit knew from his research that Marlowe had promoted the image of himself as a bad boy, his celebrity known to the lowlife who attended his plays on their circuit of provincial stadia. In his prologue to *The Jew of Malta* Marlowe had written, 'I count religion but a childish toy / And hold there is no sin but ignorance', a statement as provocative for the time as the Sex Pistols' snarlingly intransigent 'Pretty Vacant' or 'God Save the Queen' was to the DIY garage-band dissidents of the mid-1970s. Marlowe's sister Anne had also shared her brother's propensity for tearing up orthodox beliefs, her flaming geranium-red hair banged out like her temper when slashing the idea of monotheism to verbal shreds. Marlowe would have cross-dressed as a child, as was customary with Elizabethan boys, but his sister's evident same-sex attractions were known to her brother as an extension of his own aberrant gene. Kit had discovered through his research that Anne, on her occasional visits to her brother in London, had provoked further controversy by defiantly smoking in company, and she had resoundingly slapped the face of a man coming on to her at a party given by one of her brother's patrons, Henry Wriothesley, the Earl of Southampton. She had slapped him not just once but three times in stinging succession, then disdainfully gone back to her place at the table and lit a pipe, tamping the black pungent tobacco with a user's expertise.

Recklessness had stuck to Marlowe like a slogan on a T-shirt. Gay, liberated in thought, anti-religious, a lowlife-mixer, precociously gifted and indifferent to his gift, his attitude had marked him. His reputation as a degenerate had accelerated with fame, something that had provided him with a platform for his subversive ideas. The liberation of Tudor Britain into free thought was a hard one, the resistance hard as the brick walls against which he had pissed his fizzing urine after nights of getting wrecked along Hog Lane. Liking to shock, he had chewed and smoked marijuana, and the substance had increased his acute sense of paranoia and the uninhibited free association of his intellectually subversive ideas. The notion that poets were often demonstrably lawless and answerable to no other state than imagination was written into him like a blood type.

London's underworld had proliferated like a cancer during the time that Christopher Marlowe had known it. He was familiar with the whole subterranean topology – the area of the Savoy along the Strand was already one hotspot, so, too, the no-go complex of alleys inhabited by criminals and prostitutes called Alsatia. He was also familiar with such evocatively named places as Devil's Gap and Damnation Alley, inner-city zones where he had encountered money launderers, hit-men, convicts, negroes – whom he fucked for their anomalous colour – thieves, rent boys, pickpockets, contract killers, junkies, every form of outlaw that had the Mayor of London writing to the Privy Council complaining about stage plays, and in particular Marlowe's, as inciting social disdain and political unrest. He was, in addition and more dangerously, a government snoop, a double agent engaged in espionage, monitored by the secret police and its chief, Lord Francis Walsingham, for his access to sensitive data.

Kit's mind chewed on these things as he walked towards the station, the rain lifting to reveal a great doughnut ring of luminous cloud overhead. Homophobia, he knew, was harder to decommission than the stockpiling of nuclear weapons and more virulent in that it had proved to be the rogue cell poisoning history by the misguided conception of a straight supremacy. He imagined that Marlowe's experience had differed little from his own sense of belonging to the marginalized in society.

As Kit picked up pace along the shattered high street, part of him thought of turning back and taking refuge overnight in the Church of St Nicholas, sharing that space with the winos who were doubtless oblivious that particles of Marlowe's body were compacted under the church's Elizabethan remains.

There were so many dead in his life – faces he remembered in the instant of love, of suffering, turning in the street to go – young men who crowded into his memory, touching on the moment and alerting him to a sense of inconsolable loss always in excess of the loss of something in particular. Uppermost in his mind was Nick, the reformed Dilly boy with whom he had formed a lasting relationship before Nick had disappeared clean out of his life. To this day Kit had no idea if Nick was still alive or had been torched off his bones by the virus. Nick had followed the classic rent-boy route: running away to London at seventeen from a good family in Buckinghamshire, his ambitions fuelled by the desire to succeed in music as well as to opportunistically meet the perfect stranger while hanging out in front of Boots at Piccadilly Circus. Nick was a pretty boy who hadn't watched out for himself and who was desperate to attract the attention of the music industry. With his blond hair, gold earrings, white T-shirt and sprayed-on jeans he had looked irresistibly cute the first time they had met at First Out in St Giles' High Street behind Centre Point. For some reason it all came flooding back to Kit now. Kit suspected that he must already have been damaged goods when they met, the virus working undercover in his cells. He was vulnerable, feminine, hurt by the world but determined to succeed at any price. He had got his act together with a number of musicians, set up rehearsals and through an agent started to get gigs in small clubs. It was his voice that Kit remembered, largely for its sensitive register of pain. There was always a point in the song when the woman in Nick took over, if you listened for it, and the lyric opened out from that genderless axis. Nick's wound was his strength as a performer, although his critics were quick to exploit the trait as a weakness. Not that he had cared. He was strong like that, and if he had provoked antagonism then he had always been prepared to go back for more. Kit had loved him for his resilience and known love in return.

Their relationship had broken down because of the usual habit of taking each other for granted and the unintentional neglect that resulted. Nick was the boy you saw on every corner, the one somehow marked out as rent, but to Kit he was different because he had known and loved him. He had lived with the unsettling image of Nick in his head, day in and day out, and tonight, a year after his total disappearance, the signal seemed even stronger as he reconstructed him in his memory.

He remembered bringing Nick to Deptford Creek one September afternoon and how the most overwhelming and disorientating sense of *déjà vu* had hit him on arrival. Together they had walked down Evelyn Street in the honey-coloured light to the Creek, taking in the church where Marlowe had been buried on 1 June 1593 after a rapid service conducted by the Revd Thomas Macander, who had written in the parish register 'Christopher Marlowe slain by Francis Frizer'; even the name of the suspected killer misspelt in the hurry to dispose of Marlowe's body as well as the evidence of a homicide pardoned by the queen. Kit had so often returned to the site of the crime and hung out near the 'Armada gate', where anonymous men dressed like today's homeless on the Charing Cross Road, in hoods and rags, had carried Marlowe's blanketed body to rest, drunk and swearing in their slow progress. Together they had made their way through a network of sidestreets to the river fronted by Palmer's Wharf, Borthwick Wharf and the landing stages looking out over the Isle of Dogs. It had seemed to Kit then, as it did now, that London as a city was made up of a sequence of space–times that dissolved the past into the present and that it was possible to cross from one zone to another just by doing a little neural adjustment in consciousness. Kit remembered experiencing a heightened sense of familiarity with his subject, as though he had accessed the password to Marlowe's past like a driver entering a code into his dash panel for entry to an underground car-park. Nick had wanted to fuck that afternoon, and Kit remembered the hurt carved in Nick's face as he had rejected his ravaged come-on and how later Kit had playfully picked up Nick's emaciated body and carried him for a way along the empty street, as a weird re-enactment of the ritual Marlowe had undergone all those years ago in the same streets. Kit wondered now if it had been raining when the drunken sextons had shouldered Marlowe's body into the ruinous churchyard, the stone wharfs and the king's yards fogged out by a fine saturating drizzle. He had looked into every aspect of Marlowe's murder and had studied contemporary forensic reports on the state of the body after death. According to William Danby's official inquest at the time, Marlowe's body was viewed in a state of rigor mortis in the back room of an inn in Butcher's Road, a room the poet would have known for the access it gave to sailors and sex. Kit knew from research into the subject that stiffening of the body usually starts within five hours of death, so that beginning with the jaw and the eyelids the muscles would have contracted, with total rigidity taking up to twelve hours to achieve. Kit knew that in Marlowe's time an inquest was ordered not only to ascertain that a crime had been committed but also in the belief that in the presence of the killer the victim's wounds would reopen and bleed, despite absence of circulation. Kit's obsession with detail had led him to discover that the exact proportions of Marlowe's wound were given as a depth of two inches and a width of one inch. Knives were in as common usage then as amongst inner-city youth today. This one had been purchased for a shilling, and the one-inch blade had been measured to see that it fitted exactly the dimensions of the wound. The forensics were crude but formed the documentation necessary for the coroner William Danby and his jury to acquit Ingram Frizer on the grounds that he had acted in self-defence.

Tonight Kit couldn't get Nick out of his head. His puckered lips, the sparkling catchlight in his blue eyes, the acerbity with which he shredded his music contemporaries, the contagious enthusiasm he imparted to his likes, the tantrums he threw if crossed, his awareness of each nuance of his appearance, the appealingly soft inflections in his voice – Kit remembered these to the point of meltdown. There was no getting away from him, alive or dead. Like Marlowe, he had got him inexorably under his skin.

An armoured truck – a skull and crossbones logoed on its bonnet, no headlights on and with the horn ground down by an irate fist – roared into view, coming directly towards him. Kit dodged into a Starbucks entrance for cover. The van burnt through in the direction of the Creek without checking its speed when cornering. The horn persisted, the driver recklessly pressurizing the airbag as a militant alarm pounding into the airwaves. Kit recognized the van as belonging to the Pirates, a Peckham gang that illegally body-bagged the victims of street fights and roadkill and sold the bodies for the value of their organs to rogue surgeons. Wherever there were casualties the Pirates attempted to pre-empt the emergency services by arriving at the incident first and stealing the body. The hardened gang had been known on occasions to raid the understaffed intensive-care and mortuary departments of south London hospitals in order to boost their lucrative trade in donor organs.

Kit was certain the truck was heading towards whatever business had brought the blacked-out ministerial SmarTruck to these parts and accounted for its urgent getaway. London had been blasted into anarchic chaos by conflicting gang rule and the proliferation of terrorist cells. To those in the know, the *realpolitik* tags of graffiti canned across the city provided a regular update to state-of-the-art terrorism. Each gang had its own colour and contended for propagandist rule. There were, amongst others: Black Wolf, a biker cult from Vauxhall; the Pirates; Search and Destroy, whose speciality was nuking; the Bloods, who took on contract killings; the Pinks, who were a gay-activist cell; and the Bottleheads, who terrorized the Underground.

Kit kept on going in the direction of the station, afraid as he went that he would find it gated, the line made dysfunctional by some undisclosed atrocity. This happened with increasing regularity now, with whole areas of the line closed, sometimes for days, because of the ferocity of alcohol-fuelled Bottlehead raids.

Kit was glad of his memories in the outlawed dark. He still had Nick in his head even if he couldn't hold him in his arms, a virtual Nick, who persisted in invading his memory on a deep level. It was Nick who had had the gift of fine-tuning gossip. Working as a rent boy he had encountered everyone on the stairs down to the Piccadilly Underground – the lost, the lonely, the famous, the notorious, the Whitehall coterie, the married, ambiguous pop stars, bankers, drug-giant execs, all of them representing factions of the socially outlawed. Nick had met them on the way up and on the way down, the twinkle in his eye catching them out in the crowd. He had called them his family, the ones who searched for love in the city's underground corridors. Tonight, for no particular reason, Kit remembered Nick ironing a stack of black-and-white T-shirts, his hair streaked with highlights, his attention to detail so concentrated that the exact lines of his thought seemed visible as he worked. It was the memory of these little moments that sustained Kit, their poignancy rounded at the edges by time.

Kit stood outside Tesco on the high street and saw on the opposite side of the street a light on in a barred window above an off-licence. Through it he could make out the profile of one of London's solitary inhabitants, busy doing some small domestic thing and risking attracting voyeuristic attention in the process. People living in no-go zones such as Deptford had taken to blacking out their windows, something that didn't apply to Kit's own part of town but which added a dimension of terror to the districts affected. Whole areas of north and south-east London had red danger crosses superimposed on them in the atlas, and Deptford was one of those districts. By visiting it he knew he was taking his life in his hands and that he would be without protection if he was set upon by one of the marauding homophobic gangs. So far he had survived his random nocturnal forays into Deptford Creek, but he knew there would come a time when his luck ran out. He had fucked other fugitives in the yards, deepening his empathy with Marlowe in this way, risking all in his attachment to faceless pick-ups. It was something he couldn't let go, this impulse to commission anonymous sex, no matter that the aftermath left him broken.

Kit pocketed his hands and continued to busy himself with thoughts of Nick to fire up his courage. Nick's chutzpah, combined with the sensitive underside to his street savvy, had made him the ideal foil to Kit's introspection. Nick could be loud as oranges or instinctively adapt himself to Kit's mood. Kit remembered him singing 'Johnny Remember Me' with an impassioned coloratura that left the song scored in his memory. He had fallen off the stage performing the song as a surprise encore to a tightly packed Borderline, been helped up and insisted on finishing it to a crowd suddenly made aware of his vulnerability. It had been his last performance before he had disappeared. Nick with his arms and legs as thin as the microphone lead had turned his wasted defences on the crowd.

Kit kept going over in his mind some of the reported sightings that had grown in proportion to an escalating cult interest in a singer who had vanished like Richey Edwards without leaving a single clue as to his whereabouts. There were rumours of him having reappeared at the Dilly, a Nick miraculously cured of illness and about to go into the studio with a major deal. Kit had discovered a rogue obituary on the net only the night before, stating that Nick had been found dead in a Soho alley and that he had been body-snatched by a wealthy, obsessed admirer who had been tracking him for months and had subsequently been deposited at great expense in a cryogenic tank. It was hard to live with the sort of sensational factoring that had Nick singing in a drag bar in Marseilles, dead and cremated at Golders Green Cemetery or living on a cocktail of retrovirals somewhere in Earls Court.

The surrounding tower blocks had mostly observed the blackout. They looked to Kit like fall-out from the architectural dream of building upwards into the sky. While the majority of skyscrapers constellated round the Docklands grid were now deserted, inhabited only by isolated fat cats still clinging to a belief in the vertical dimension representing power, these devastated vestiges of community towering over the south-east were homes to asylum seekers, spammers, Yardies, the mentally ill and the dispossessed. They had their own raging in-tower wars, internecine arson and lootings. Nobody was safe, and the new architecture had been forced underground, with the rich taking refuge in smart reinforced bunkers built into the warren of expanding tunnels underneath the city. Kit disliked the new gated subterranea with its SAS guards attached to each cell and avoided going there. The wealthy Londoners and Japanese were its inhabitants, and he instinctively kept away, remained above ground and looked out for himself.

It was 11.15 on his watch, which allowed him ten minutes if the trains were running on time. The river felt excruciatingly cold in his spine, and for once he found himself anxious to get away from the place. The nagging visceral fear of being attacked that tightened his gut reminded him of how Marlowe must have felt on that oppressively thundery afternoon in May 1593, when he had made his way here along London Street, towards Eleanor Bull's closed house at Deptford Strand, where he had an appointment to meet three lowlife fugitives, namely Ingram Frizer, Robert Poley and Nicholas Skeres. Kit imagined the noise of the docks as Marlowe would have heard it reverberating across the precinct. A hard masculine noise one got from sweat, taut muscle and the remorseless conversion of the body into rigorous labour. He, too, picked up on that energy like a drug whenever he encountered docks. It was something absent from his present life as a writer, but the thrill of the docks lived on in his blood like a persistent hammering between heartbeats. It was something that never went away and caught him out each time he was near working yards along the river's green toxic ooze. As he made his way towards the station he felt doubly sure that the three men he had seen getting away in the bullet-proof armoured SmarTruck were Marlowe's murderers. He wondered for a moment if their continuing existence was contingent on his and if they had rematerialized to signal an impending crisis in his own and the nation's life.

There was nobody on duty at the station, the automated ticket dispensers were out and the platform deserted. The monitor indicated that the Charing Cross train was due in at 11.25. He sat down and waited on alert. He wrapped himself in his black coat and watched a bristling sewer rat make a reconnaissance of the platform. It interrogated a discarded McDonald's carton, the Big Mac only partially consumed, wedged its head into the contents and began eating. Kit stood up as he heard the train's audible groove in the distance, its headlights powering through the dark. When it came in he activated the compression door and jumped into an empty carriage. As the train pulled out and headed towards London Bridge he repeated the refrain 'London Bridge is falling down, falling down, falling down' to himself like a mantra, closed his eyes and slept the short journey to Charing Cross.

2

When Nick woke up there was thunder in the air, the spooky reverb cooking like a guitar figure played in the sky. He could tell by the light streaming into his Islington flat and by the register of traffic outside that it was probably round noon. The city's noise built to a sustained wall of sound at that hour, a constant roar that seemed to come from an imaginary centre but which was dispersed uniformly throughout the city's circumference.

Even on good days the fact that he had officially died was the first thought with which he connected on waking. Terminally ill with Aids but in possession of the tube from the Grid, he had gone to the Grid centre in Bloomsbury and spent a month there recuperating from chronic pneumonia. That he had survived was extraordinary, as was the regressive journey he was in the process of making back to the unconsciously stored data of an earlier and only partially completed life.

He hadn't been disciplined about taking his anti-retrovirals and had left off them for weeks at a time because of the debilitating side-effect of nausea and his refusal to acknowledge his illness. He simply wouldn't subscribe to the pathology of the plague, seeing it as something that belonged to the viral epidemics of earlier centuries rather than to the present. His last concert at the Borderline had marked a turning point in his decline – and it was then that he had decided to call his close friend Robert and make the necessary break with his past.

When Nick had gone missing a year ago he had found it essential to forget Kit. The undercover agents tracking his immune system had switched to a programme of virulent cellular genocide, leaving him without the energy to focus on anything but the virus and the total exhaustion that it had brought. He had left his flat in Marble Arch without notifying anyone, walked out on his band, broken his appointments at St Mary's Hospital and completely disconnected. He had the money he had saved from his good years as a Dilly boy, and what's more he had the tube that Robert had given him.

As Nick sat up and blinked into the bleached August light, he heard the storm going off in diminishing basslines across the river. He was reminded of the fact that Robert was due soon and that they were to drive over together to a Grid meeting in Coptic Street near the British Museum. It was close to there that Nick had first seen Robert one winter afternoon, standing outside the Dominion Theatre, as he and Kit had crossed over Tottenham Court Road on their way to the gay café First Out in St Giles' High Street. His attention had been drawn to a conspicuously unusual young man, hunched into a black great coat, who had stopped to read something in a free newspaper before going down to the Underground. He would simply have been another face in the crowd, anonymous and strained by big-city alert, only that he must have sensed he was being observed, for he had looked directly at Nick and made immediate eye contact. 'He's one of us,' Kit had said authoritatively, but at the time Nick had attached no importance to the statement, only looked back one last time to find that Robert had disappeared into the station.

Nick's rehabilitation had been slower than he expected – not physically but in terms of the psychological adjustment needed to accept his regression. He was still Nick, but his attachment to an earlier life was so powerful that at times it seemed to him as if he had never died. He still wasn't confident of his own status, and sometimes out walking in the crowd, hidden behind widescreen Jackie O sunglasses, he would stop dead, blown away by the realization that, through what he had experienced, he almost certainly differed radically from almost every one of the city's 17 million inhabitants.

The regressive side was often too much for him to take in,

despite the fact that the Grid was there to offer psychological support. He received a monthly allowance from the Grid under the alias John White, and his flat was owned by the organization.

When the entryphone sounded Nick got out of bed in his little black tanga briefs, instinctively raking his hair back to give it a spiky, slept-in feel, checked it was Robert on the video screen and let him in. He hurried into the kitchen to grab a carton of orange juice out of a fridge he had painted shocking pink, an image of Monroe postered to the door, and quickly set about making coffee. He should have been up hours ago but had worked late into the night on some demos he was recording at home. It was the first time he had felt sufficiently confident to risk singing since his encounter with the tube. He had been relieved to find that he had lost none of his individual tone, and the reminder that he could still sing injected a euphoric rush into his mood as he opened the door to Robert.

'Hi,' Robert said. He was wearing a skinny black T-shirt and bottled jeans. 'Thought it was going to rain on the way over,' he added, coming inside and throwing a glance out of the window at a confection of mauve clouds parked overhead like surveillance. 'I take it you're up to the meeting today.'

Nick busied himself pouring a frosty cone of orange juice into a tall glass and, knowing Robert's preference for coffee, added hot water to the meniscus of coffee grains in two white porcelain cups.

'Yes, of course I'm coming with you,' Nick replied, 'but I'm running a bit late. I was up last night working on demos on my laptop. It's been the first time for ages.'

'I'd like to hear something,' Robert said, taking his coffee over to the window and looking out at the city's complex architectural modem as if it was a film set. 'I never told you that I came to hear you sing once at the Troubadour. It must have been three years ago.'

'I'd no idea,' Nick replied, his voice inflected with surprise. 'Was that why you looked at me the way you did when we first saw each other outside the Dominion Theatre?'

'Partly. I thought it was you, and I knew also you were one of us. It was obvious to me that you were HIV and that you needed the tube. I knew the guy you were with also.'

'You mean Kit?' Nick replied, his voice air-pocketing into panic.

'I've seen him hanging around the centre. Some people say he's dodgy and that he's obsessed with the idea that he's the poet Christopher Marlowe. I used to see him in the bars under Vauxhall, always solo and moody. As I see it, we're all – through the help of the organization – growing into some sort of awareness that we're linked.'

'How do you mean?' Nick asked, feeling his spine freeze.

'I'll tell you one day,' Robert said, attempting to make light of it. 'Play me a new song. I'd love to hear what you're doing.'

Nick felt confused and resentful to learn of aspects of Kit's character that had remained concealed in their relationship. He didn't like what he was hearing and still felt protective of the lover he had walked out on. When he retrieved the CD labelled 'Nick Demos' from a litter of papers and jewel cases cluttering the table, he felt the unexpected sense of hurt deepen.

He fed the disk into the CD drawer. He had rough cuts of three new songs: an achingly heart-stopping ballad, blue-mooded to a predictably layered chorus, called 'St Giles' High'; a catchy excursion into trip-hop that relied on drag-strip instrumentals, given the working title 'Dress Rehearsal'; and the pop-friendly, bright-as-an-orange 'Veuve Clicquot'. He was sufficiently philosophical to put his current elation down to the fact that he was still heady from writing them and on a rush. They were rough sketches, unmixed and still little more than home recordings, but he felt certain the vocal on all three was an up-front talking point.

He put on the velvety 'St Giles' High' and, not liking to listen to himself, withdrew into the kitchen to fix a sandwich. Nick was a confirmed vegan and almost pathological in his dislike of meat and dairy. In between applying architecture to a tofu and rocket sandwich, he caught phrases of his ballad roofing the flat's interior with the new authority he sensed in his voice:

> It's winter on St Giles' High Street
> I huddle in your black great coat
> I'm stamping out fires with my feet
> The café's like a sinking boat . . .

he heard himself sing in rainy-blue colours for Kit. It was Kit again who had triggered in him the impulse to write the song by historically associating the church St Giles-in-the-Fields with the burial of plague victims in its grounds during the sixteenth and early seventeenth centuries, the place having served originally as a hospital for the chronically diseased. The plague had started in this parish, and remnants of it remained in the homeless and the methadone addicts who had made the area into a druggy zone that still reeked of the underworld. He both did and didn't want to hear the song, as he hid behind his defences on emerging from the aqua-blue kitchen that Robert had emulsioned for him during a low. The room was his chill-out space for those days when his mood zeroed in on loss.

'Fantastic,' Robert greeted him. 'The best thing you've done. This has got to be a hit . . .'

'I doubt it will ever be released,' Nick said in a self-deprecating tone. 'Not unless I put it out myself. I can't see accountants endorsing this.' He let the chorus fade on a reprise before zapping the sound. He suddenly felt the need to withdraw his work, to keep it on hold and, perversely, deny himself the critical feedback he needed. 'I'll play you the other two later,' he continued, directing his attention to the plate of symmetrically proportioned sandwiches he had cut.

'Your voice has really opened out,' Robert said. 'Who are you listening to these days?'

'Old favourites and Momus. He's a neglected and inventive songwriter, a chameleon who always reinvents himself. Nobody to my mind has got his ear for melody or writes such quirky songs about taboo.'

'High praise,' Robert said as Nick refilled his glass with juice so that it looked like an orange traffic-light.

'I've been thinking about what you told me earlier. You're right. Kit used to tell me that he was the poet Christopher Marlowe and remembered everything he had done in Elizabethan times. I used to put it down to the fact he was a poet and the amount of time he spent alone. You know, he was always full of such convincing stories that seemed not so much memories as realities, like they do with a lot of psychos.'

'Like what?' Robert asked.

'Well, he told me in detail, for instance, how in a previous life he had lived in the London suburb of Norton Folgate, not far from the insane asylum at Bedlam, and that he found inspiration for his plays in the mad. He had it all mapped like it was yesterday. He explained that his neighbourhood was one of several "liberties" that ringed the City of London and were outside the law. He told me how you could pay to see certain types of madmen at Bedlam and that a man led out to him on a long chain had claimed to be Edward II and that he had adopted the man for a week, cut off his long red hair and got details from the man for his play. It was all crazy stuff. He claimed that the theatres like the Cross Keys, the Belsavage, the Bull, the Boar's Head and the Red Lion were really brothels and that sex workers were far more of an attraction than the plays put on there and that the public toilets were cruising areas. Who knows?'

'What's remarkable', Robert said, 'is your memory, and how you remember things, right down to the names of the theatres Kit told you. I'm the same. Therapy at the Grid seems to instate total recall. I don't know, but I have this weird feeling that we all share access to a linked past and a particular time and place that we've suppressed in the interests of the present.'

Nick suddenly remembered Kit's bloodshot right eye, the one that turned as scarlet as a canned tomato at times, and wondered against all reason if his ex really was some sort of update of the notoriously queer playwright Christopher Marlowe or whether Kit's obsession with Marlowe was as much an identity crisis as that of Mark Chapman, the man who had shot John Lennon under a similar pretence.

'I used to see him in pubs like the Fallen Angel,' Robert said. 'I found him decidedly odd. He drank too much. I remember how he used to make outrageous claims, not only that he was Christopher Marlowe but how he and Shakespeare, during the time they were briefly an item, used to challenge each other to drinking sessions that would last all day and night. He used to make it all sound so credible. I was so impressed with his stories that, like you, I started to read books on the period because his facts were also starting to become mine. I always thought that he was on to the tube.'

'Not to my knowledge. He never said anything about it when we were an item. You've never told me much about your illness, not even when we were close,' Nick said, picking out a blush-cheeked Pink Lady apple from the bowl and looking up in response to the rumble of Boeing engines overhead.

'I was like you, Aids,' Robert said, 'although I kept on denying it. Combination therapy made me too ill from the side-effects. I was in diamonds and had to travel on a regular basis to Antwerp. I just couldn't keep up. I'd started to look the part, too, wasted and plagued.'

'Diamonds?' Nick said. 'You never told me that before. Not that any of us ever came straight.'

'It sounds more romantic than it is. I had to fly to Antwerp three times a week. The security's so tight it can take thirty minutes to get through the door of the diamond office, and then you have to hand over your passport.'

'So you were buying?' Nick said, raking his hair into the ideal of the windswept beach-movie star.

'Yes and, believe me, you've got to be absolutely certain the stones don't carry hidden flaws. I'd arrive in my Armani suit, and the guy who specializes in coloured diamonds would bring out two hundred sacks the size of a crisp packet with twenty stones in each.'

'I didn't realize there were coloured diamonds,' Nick said, obsessively rearranging his hair.

'The rare diamonds are blues and pinks, reds, greenish blues, browns, oranges, even black. You'd be amazed at the variety. They've all got their individual properties, from sleepy to hyperactive, introspective to flaunt-it.'

'Don't you miss it?' Nick asked, savouring the aromatic top notes in his coffee.

'I still dabble,' Robert said, 'despite my work with the Grid. Of course, there's the dodgy side, too. I remember once going to a council flat in Hackney where an Indian family showed me a 140-carat diamond that they'd clearly smuggled out of India. I could have cheated, but I got out of there fast.'

'How did you keep your nerve when buying? Or does it come down to being naturally dodgy?' Nick asked, trying to imagine the fault lines in a big flashy rock.

'It's what they call a sophisticated gamble,' Robert replied, looking at him surreptitiously with foggy grey eyes. 'I bought a stone once that was seventy carats, a blue from South Africa – an inch and a half, man – and the workshop ended up with five diamonds out of it. If the stone is suspect it can crack down the middle when you cut it. It's an expensive risk.'

'I'll put this on before we go out,' Nick said, retrieving Momus's 'Slender Sherbet' from a CD tower and programming in the song 'Closer To You'. He left Robert with Momus and went into the bedroom to find his leather jacket. Travelling into the central Anglo-Japanese zone involved not only carrying ID cards but also having to give iris scans by way of security. Nick instinctually kept checking his lymph glands for the tell-tale sign of lumps as he fished for the black-leather skin that Kit had given him one birthday. It had become his second skin, an extension of himself in which the incessant wear and tear of his own and city life got mapped in the creases. He had worn it everywhere, including on stage, and had adopted it as a familiar

Presley-like epidermis, with a referential nod to Elvis's famous 1968 comeback television appearance.

'I'm ready,' he called out, as he came back into the living-room to find Robert concentrated on Momus's semi-spoken, bittersweet reflections on sex and death. Nick searched for his keys and a CD of his decoded DNA that he had to take into the Coptic Street centre so that his genes could be screened to predict and prevent future illnesses. The Grid medical team wanted to ascertain, this time through hard science, whether the tube had effectively repaired the molecular kill-off of cells on a permanent basis.

Together they went out into the charged London air, hazy with toxic petrocarbons.

Nick's zone was still officially a Grade 2 in terms of safety and hadn't yet been persistently invaded by the gangs that had erupted across the south-east. The antiques market struggled on in nearby Camden Passage, the reconversions were taken over by rainmakers and slickers, and the rest of the community was the ubiquitous multinational mix that occupied London's redundant tower blocks.

Robert had parked a couple of streets away in Gerrard Road, and there was a brief flurry of thundery rain as they headed past the newsagent's in search of his car.

'I've gone conspicuous again,' Robert said. 'It must be the legacy of my diamond days. I've got a Nissan 3502. Mean anything to you?'

'Not really. I've never been a car buff, but I like them big and flashy.'

The rain had given over by the time Robert pointed out his slick holly-green Nissan. 'It's got everything,' he said. 'I won't bore you with the finer details, but it's fast. It delivers its power without a turbocharger.'

Robert had automated the doors, and Nick was about to get into the passenger side when a young man with bleached hair and wearing black aviator Ray-Bans came walking towards him at a fast lick. For a moment Nick thought they were going to collide, but the young man kept on going and with his head down shot at him in passing, 'I know who you are. You're from the Grid.'

Nick harnessed himself into the passenger seat shocked by the incident. He had never expected to be confronted with his secret identity in the street, and there was a note of hostility in the stranger's voice that left him feeling threatened.

'Who was that?' Robert asked, fitting his shoulder belt. 'Do you know him?'

'I've never seen him before. He came straight at me out of nowhere and said, "You're from the Grid." He must be one of us.'

'That's crazy,' Robert exclaimed, his voice going up an octave as he scanned the satellite navigation. 'There're so few of us. Surely we would have seen him at the centre.'

'But *we* met by chance,' Nick said, trying his best to account for what had just happened. 'I suppose it's possible we attract each other, even in a city this size.'

'Who knows?' Robert replied, firing the ignition. 'What about that? Can you hear the low-rev torque response?' He smiled. 'It can do nought to sixty miles per hour in five and a half seconds and a hundred and fifty-five flat out. Better than Audi, Honda or Porsche. When I was really ill I had to give up driving. I'm trying now to make up for lost time.'

Robert negotiated an L-shaped sidestreet and came out on Upper Street to be frozen by a red light. 'Couldn't he be a snoop?' he asked like someone delivering a question from gut instinct. 'I mean, knowing what we do about the past and genetics, somebody's going to be curious.'

Nick looked out at the shower twinkling in from a mono-chrome urban sky. The rain was stop and start and went off again as they finned into a tailgate. Nothing was moving. They sat behind the fat lollipop-shaped rear of a tanker, while parallel to them a girl in a tomato-red Toyota Corolla was laughing as she talked into a hands-free. Nick felt uneasy about Robert's intimation that the stranger was possibly a snoop. He had heard enough about spying from Kit, who claimed that Marlowe had been a projector in Elizabethan times – an intelligencer whose case officer was Sir Francis Walsingham. The name Walsingham had started coming up in his own regression therapy recently, but his chief recollections were of Thomas Walsingham, someone who had not only served as Marlowe's highly duplicitous patron but someone with whom he had been involved personally on a criminal level. Snooping was their world and presumably always had been. And operatives, in order to survive, required a faculty of corruption that would match their employer's as well as keep them one step ahead in terms of spin. Blocked into a temporary gridlock, churning pollutants, and with Robert impatiently waiting for the break, Nick found his thoughts largely polarized to Kit.

When Robert kicked the Nissan back into the traffic stream Nick was forced to rethink the question. If his own status, like that of all Grid members, were discovered, then the organization would be investigated and doubtless become the subject of media disclaimers. Nick still had no idea how the tube worked or why certain individuals were chosen to be part of the process. He liked still less the idea of being tracked into revealing his true identity.

Robert had put a Bowie CD on the car stereo, and the singer was shaping a dramatically curved vocal trajectory on 'Station to Station', with the particular epicene dynamic he had possessed in 1975. Against the dissonant jet-hanger squeal of Adrian Belew's guitar, Bowie's strained falsetto issued from an endlessly extensible fixed moment in time.

'Do you really think we're being snooped on?' Nick said, against the Thin White Duke's cokey, hysterical undertones.

'Yup,' Robert said, as he tucked in behind a blacked-out Grand Cherokee, his face taking shine in the rainy light. 'We're bound to be,' he added. 'We're reinvented. Isn't death the big mystery for most people?'

They had just got on to Pentonville Road, tailing a white Omega Express Ford Transit van, Robert's feet beating time to

Bowie in the car's footwells, when Nick saw two of the Black Wolf biker cult in action. Segueing through the traffic like police outriders, the two bikers mounted the pavement and trapped someone busy using a Lloyds cashpoint. Hemmed in between two Triumph Daytona bikes, with their aggressive aerodynamic bodywork, the front mudguard of one prodding his femur, the dark-suited man was forced at gunpoint to hand over his cash and keep on punching in his PIN number for repeat withdrawals. Nick stared impassively at the de-clued passers-by, who either pretended the hold-up wasn't happening or simply didn't want to know.

They were still glued to the tailback when the two bikers backed off from the hole in the wall, 'Black Wolf' lettered on their leather jackets, injected fuel and roared off on their bikes, using the pavement for a fast getaway.

'What about that?' Nick said. 'Nobody dares stop these gangs.'

Robert nudged the car forward at walking pace towards the Ford Transit while Bowie phrased 'Wild Is the Wind' like a studied operatic diva, only better. 'We're all meant to believe it didn't happen,' Robert said. 'It's called disinformation.' He upped the volume to let Bowie loose like a rock Maria Callas in the car speakers and checked his hair in the driver's mirror.

'Are all the members of the Grid gay?' Nick asked, shifting his attention away from what had just happened.

'I'm not sure,' Robert replied. 'They're big on confidentiality. You could ask one of the doctors.'

They were approaching King's Cross now, duelling with a conspicuous BMW and the solid paramilitary pretensions of a swamp-green Range Rover. Nick felt his vulnerability return like peach fuzz on his skin. It was Kit, he knew deep down, that he was missing, and even though he had found it necessary to make a clean break with the past he was still dominated by an overriding sense of loss. Kit's defences had always succeeded in keeping him out, but that, in part, was the continued attraction he felt for the man he loved. His armour was like the Citroëns, Porsches and Volvos competing for the lights as they negotiated the St Pancras complex. Nick felt suddenly afraid of his reinvention and of the whole desperate underside to living brought out by the anonymous warehouses fronting York Way. The urban decay paralleled his emotional state, making him think of platelets furring his arteries and free radicals ripping his cells.

'How's your retro going?' Robert asked, his eyes slaloming right as they passed a pretty Japanese boy in white vest and jeans headed in the direction of the station.

'It's almost too much,' Nick said, still uncertain about the whole concept of regression hypnotherapy and the neurotransmitters used to speed up the process. 'I mean, I get confused about what's real and what isn't. Sometimes it feels like the past and present are fused, and I can't separate them.'

'It left me a bit fazed at first,' Robert said. 'Certainly, while I was in diamonds I had no idea of my past life. Money, regular blow and clubbing were my entire world. But now I'm not sure.'

'What do you mean?' Nick asked, hoping for reassurance that he wasn't going insane.

'Well, what's come up in the sessions seems so convincing that I, too, start to wonder if I'm not still this character from the past called Robert Poley. I've never told you that I went to prison for a period for fraud – six months in Pentonville. Nasty, I can tell you. Well, according to the regression, I had, as a snoop in 1586, been responsible for the death of a Catholic priest named John Ballard. It was all part of something called the Babington Plot. All the horror of the man's execution came back in the session. He was one of seven dragged on sleds to the open square of St Giles' in Holborn. There he was hanged until he lost consciousness, was cut down alive, his genitals hacked off, and disembowelled before being quartered by horses. Recollecting all this left me badly shaken for days. Anyhow, it seems, as a consequence of my snooping, that I was sent to the Tower for two years as one of the fall guys who needed cover.'

'Weird that you should be able to recall it all in such detail. I'm the same. Do you think we're crazy?'

'I got so shocked over the details of that session,' Robert said, 'I found it necessary to go on to Seroxat for a while. It really shook me up. And then getting sentenced three years ago seemed like a link with something I hadn't resolved from the past.'

'I suppose it's all speculative. If you don't mind me asking, who gave you the tube?'

'You know as well as I do that we're supposed to keep donors secret,' Robert replied, as the in-car satellite instructed him to take the first left in three hundred metres. There were robosoldiers positioned by the traffic-lights, wearing computerized helmets with whisper-sensitive radio implanted in the ear. FIST – Future Integrated Soldier Technology – had been introduced into the Whitehall zone by the Commissar, and Nick felt continually threatened by the potential firepower of soldiers equipped with thermal-imaging guns that could fire round corners. He was always glad to get away from their ubiquitous monitoring presence as the reminder of an autocratic leader who largely lived in his customized nuclear shelter.

'Scary,' Robert said, as though accessing Nick's thoughts as the car pointed into Camden Road. The district was full of Japanese, many of them with English partners, the mixing of the two races having created a strong Anglo-Japanese community in London. Nick looked out at a number of Japanese manga-type cyberpunks with confetti-coloured hair grouped round a quad bike. With the collapse of Tokyo's international technology conglomerates the corporate sector had relocated to London in a joint programme aimed at targeting the exhausted financial market. For Nick it had brought the added advantage of an influx of Japanese youth from Tokyo and Yokohama into an otherwise imploding, samey gay scene.

'Going back to regression,' Robert continued, as they looked out at the fizzy Camden Market crowds, 'I'd go for it if I was you. I'm back to what they call my core incarnation and seem to know almost everything about my existence in the seventeenth century.'

'I'm finding much the same,' Nick said, backtracking again through a complex of dark neural corridors through which he made continuous retrievals.

'I've no doubt that in my previous life I also agented diamonds,' Robert said, as they sat in heavy traffic watching a raft of retrodressed miniskirted Japanese girls headed for the market in the high street. 'I was always in the Low Countries in my previous life on dodgy business with friends in high places. It sort of fits,' he added as they squatted behind a red bus displaying ads for Japanese theatre. 'But there's something much more significant I haven't told you.'

'Go on,' Nick said, 'tell me.'

'Well, something came back almost too clearly in my last session. I can remember being involved in a contract put out on Christopher Marlowe in 1592. The man I paid to set Marlowe up and kill him – and I remember this exactly – was a tailor and musician called William Corkine, who waited for Marlowe in Mercery Lane, off the Bull's Inn. He knew Marlowe would be drunk and came at him out of an alley. I was there, watching from a floor above. They fought viciously with knives, and Marlowe gashed Corkine's cheek before chasing him off. I can see it now. There was a red zigzag of blood all down the alley, like a demented central marker-line painted by a drunk. Both men were arrested by two rough constables. The incident didn't do me any favours at the time, as I had mismanaged it.'

'It's amazing you can remember it all with such clarity,' Nick said.

'We'll just about get there on time,' Robert said anxiously as they continued to do traffic meditation in a blue halo of petrochemicals.

'It's strange,' Robert reflected. 'All these people out there started as somebody they've forgotten and will never know. We've been given the tube, and that puzzles me, baby.'

'Are you quite sure we're the first?' Nick asked, the nervousness in his voice filtering the question.

'Yup, as far as I know,' Robert said, suddenly liberated from the ponderous tailback as it padded towards Gower Street.

'Quick. Look over there,' Nick said. 'That's the blond guy we saw earlier. I'm sure of it.' Nick pointed Robert's attention to a slim blond boy, peroxide hair, black shades, stripy sailor's vest and black jeans, moving through the crowd as though acutely aware he didn't belong. He walked fast and appeared to look at no one, picking his way round the body-shy Japanese with quick deliberation.

'He's got to be one of us,' Nick said, as though suspicious of the bond he shared with this stranger. 'I know it would sound crazy to anyone but you, but there's something about him I recognize. And if I've known him before, then most likely you have. There's something about the line of the face and the walk that reminds me of someone who used to be in our lives, if we believe all that, called Ingram Frizer. Does the name mean anything to you?'

'Yeah,' Robert said. 'It's come up in regression quite often. He was the person who was supposed to have been responsible for Christopher Marlowe's death. He was reputedly a dealer who started out in Basingstoke and who, because of his lowlife contacts, was ideally placed to work as a double agent. I suspect the motives were homophobic, but we'll never know. He's probably coming to the meeting. He's certainly in a hurry to get somewhere.'

'From my understanding of events, which is quite crude,' Nick said (a lot of his information had come from Kit), 'if Marlowe had intended to kill Ingram Frizer in that room at Deptford he wouldn't have beaten him on the back of the head with a knife but would have stuck the blade straight in his neck. He certainly wouldn't have allowed himself to be pinioned to the bed before being stabbed through the eye. Marlowe, Nick knew from Kit's obsession with the subject, was a desperado, who, like Shakespeare, was so cool about his lyric spontaneity that he didn't even bother to correct his proofs. He wrote largely to shock and because the books he liked simply didn't exist unless he wrote them. Even with the little time he had to give to the case he often found himself speculating on questions rarely asked by Marlowe's biographers, such as what happened to his clothes, his belongings, his books and his papers after his death – if, in fact, he owned any possessions after the summer he had spent at Walsingham's manor and living, most probably, in rooms above pubs. Nick liked to imagine Marlowe writing, stripped naked to the waist, at a wooden table, like someone possessed.

Nick watched the alarmingly conspicuous youth cross over at the lights outside Borders, his emaciated body and bottle-blond hair having him stand out in the crowd. He really wasn't sure about the boy and felt split. It was a case of natural fascination overcoming the instinct for caution that had him feel sexually attracted to the youth, as though his libido had been triggered by imagining the possibilities of having sex with someone who seemed to be the epitome of the modern archetype in London's hybrid community. Nick felt as though entering this man from behind would be like penetrating the times. There were always certain people, he reflected, who were so much a part of the present that they were inseparable from it and seemed themselves to be responsible for managing progress. Nick had the fantasy that this wired blond was shaping the August day in which they were all windowed, and that sex with him would somehow resolve everything that seemed inexplicable about being alive here and now in the accelerated burn-out of the West End.

Nick lost him in the crowd as they headed towards the subterranean car-park in Bloomsbury Square. They found a space in the oily dark next to a decommissioned hearse converted into a revamped limo – with red-leather upholstery, shocking-pink carpets and a faux leopardskin dashboard, its customized registration plates reading FCUK DEATH – and came out blinking into the strong afternoon sunlight.

Coptic Street was a five-minute walk. Nick felt unusually paranoid as they made their way through a neighbourhood largely overrun by junkies and the overspill of illegal immigrants, its good side still maintained by bookshops as the spin-off of the British Museum. Nick couldn't get Kit out of his mind. Kit's face, Kit's eyes, Kit's nose, Kit's voice, Kit's smell, Kit's navel, Kit's cock – the images pursued him all the way to the centre. The Authenticam camera at the door scanned each of them with iris-recognition biometric software, photographing their eyes to identify members. Once inside the reception area they were subjected to a second ID test and touch-padded to verify fingerprints. Nick went through first and waited for Robert. As he did, he saw the emaciated blond guy sitting in the recreation area reading a magazine and drinking coffee. He got up almost immediately and joined the other members heading for the briefing-room. He was still wearing his shades. He turned round once, looked directly at Nick and made his way ahead of them into the meeting.

3

Kit's Marlowe project drove him hard. He had returned home the previous night to find Yukio waiting for him and had forgotten completely that he had given him the keys to the flat. Chilled by the night river's sinuous crawl and its shimmying silver-top hum, Kit had been grateful for the green tea Yukio had immediately made him and for his warm presence in the bed. Too tired for sex, he had dreamt that he was standing on a platform waiting for a train, and Nick had been on the other side, only a deep channel of water separating them. In the dream Nick had been holding a knife and had pointed it directly towards him.

Kit knew from the drone in the air that it was a Saturday and that the early crowds of inquisitive tourists were starting to wedge into Portobello Road for the market. Yukio had left a note to say that he had gone off early and would be in Brighton over the weekend staying with a friend. Their arrangement was a casual one, something that suited Kit, who had no wish to dub the mistakes he had made in his previous relationship on to a new serious commitment. Things were easy with Yukio. He was uncomplicated, domestic, sunshiny and was taking a year out and filling in with part-time jobs in the Old Compton Street bars.

Kit could feel a dull, but significant ache behind his right eye, its slow-burn intensity having him search for the Nurofen he used as a means of temporarily zapping the pain. He was only too well aware – and uncomfortably so – that his particular vulnerability was located in the ocular site in which Marlowe had been stabbed. Nothing over the years had relieved the demobilizing pain when it came up, not even having the powerful neurotoxin botulinum toxin type A jabbed into his palm a hundred times in half an hour.

Kit drummed down three capsules with a pull on an Evian bottle and scanned the poem he was reworking before preparing to search the net. The poem was about the need to carry a survival kit in London, both as a protection against bioterrorism and as a customized mini-pharmacy designed for his personal needs. His way of treating poetry was to blast it with his oomph and fuck the consequences. There was no other option. The thing worked and went stratospheric, or it crashed. Nobody cared in the end anyway. He had Marlowe's attitude. Why should anyone want to be read after death? The deluded conceit of writing for an illusory posthumous legacy was like trying to live your life backwards. He had no time for careerism and saw little point in writing if you weren't going to up-end convention. A poem, he believed, should have the same burn as an F1 Ferrari driven towards vanishing point.

As Kit occupied himself with making tea he remembered the tube he had found in the street at Deptford the previous night and how he was convinced it had to be linked to somebody who visited the Grid. He had originally been alerted to their website by an Aids link when doing research on HIV replication in relation to the film-maker Derek Jarman. The Grid site, devoted to redesigning humans, had made no mention of the tube but provided data on the link between specific genes and specific diseases. Looking for information on antiretrovirals Kit had been attracted by the information given on DNA-improved destinies and recent advances in reproductive biology through gene manipulation. It was then that his association with the place had begun, and the optimist in him had been alerted recently to the possibilities of Nick receiving a cure by using the centre. He had never given up on the hope that Nick was alive. If on several occasions, hanging out at Piccadilly, he had hallucinated Nick into existence, then he had experienced a charged shock to discover the faces in the crowd were simply lookalikes. He had had other disconcerting sightings, transient flashes in and around Leicester Square, as though his brain was documenting the elusive chase from the overproduction of noradrenaline. Piccadilly had become Nick's operative grid in his mind, and in his afternoons, killing time there, he had come to associate each building and street around the Boots radius with Nick and the possibility of finding him. He searched for him in Glasshouse Street and Sherwood Street, half expecting to find him sitting disconsolately in a café window, looking out on the rainy cosmopolitan street like he was participating in reality television.

Kit planned on going up to Piccadilly later, in the early evening, that blue hiatus between afternoon and twilight that attracted him as a time in which to hang out in the teeming precinct. He believed, irrationally, that if he tried hard enough he would have Nick materialize as the embodiment of his thought. In his set of beliefs poets were not only adept at dissolving the boundaries between imagination and reality by tweaking neural hardware but they should, by extension, be able to recast dream imagery as reality.

Kit switched on his laptop and clicked on his Deptford file. Scott Diamond, as his agent, was insistent on dramatizing the gay aspects of Marlowe's murder and of the need to establish a homosexual connection between Marlowe and the three men implicated in the putatively premeditated homicide. The Elizabethan homosexual underworld was a complex one, closeted, paranoid, ambiguous, electrifyingly alert to snoops and layered in its documentation with rhetorical *double entendres* aimed at concealing the truth. The attitude towards the subject in authoritarian Tudor politics, governed by a woman who remained unmarried, was, to say the least, ambiguous. While there was no discernible underground subculture of gay literature, there were undoubtedly clubs in Southwark where unsanctioned gay sex took place. If sodomy was outlawed, as Kit had discovered in his reading, it was because it was perceived as a moral offence rather than a sexual aberration. Part of the Baines report compiled on Marlowe in the months before his death – much of it including information extracted from his friend, the playwright Thomas Kyd, under torture – claimed that Marlowe referred to Jesus Christ as the lover of John the Evangelist and to his disciples having homosexual leanings, a notion considered at the time to be so outrageously offensive as to be punishable by death. Marlowe had further enhanced his notorious gay celebrity by taking Edward II, a king renowned for his homosexual relationship with Piers Gaveston, as the subject of one of his crowd-pulling plays. That the politically prominent Bacon brothers, Francis and Anthony, were gay was something tacitly known to their contemporaries, but Marlowe's suspected relationship with his patron Thomas Walsingham and the existence of shadowy figures in his life such as Lord Strange were all open to potentially scandalous interpretation. Kit didn't doubt for a moment that Marlowe was sexually involved with his killer, either directly or through contention over a third party. Whether he was set up by his case officer or had exploded in a drunken rage into a knife fight, Marlowe's death contained all the components of a classic gay murder in the tradition of Pier Paolo Pasolini, Joe Orton and Ossie Clark, in which acute jealousy or pathological self-hatred was, in part, the motivating force behind the killer's ferocity.

Kit did his best to rewire himself to Marlowe's conception of reality, even though he was separated from it by four hundred years. He knew he couldn't shift blocks of time around and get back to his source. The past, if it existed at all, was only there in the concrete mapping of things, and the inaccessibility of its subjective contents remained one of his obsessions. His theory was that all gay murders were essentially one murder, motivated by the killer seeing what he so disliked and feared in himself evident in another. Marlowe, he felt sure, hadn't been killed by a straight because he was gay but had been knifed by another gay. A rival, a blackmailer, a casual encounter, someone who didn't want to come out: the options were somewhere in the mix. His feelings were that traces of Marlowe's DNA still existed somewhere on the road to Deptford Strand, overhung by the derricks that project beyond Convoy's Wharf and Fairview's Millennium Quay, its signature written into the foundations of African-fabric shops and ubiquitous kebab houses.

In his obsession, Marlowe for Kit was a character for a potential biopic, whose lugubrious underworld, shut out from light like the canted floors of a high-rise car-park, had come to occupy most of his working hours. Marlowe, who was renowned for his love of boys and partying and his uncompromising agitprop, was still on the loose as a punk archetype whose attitude got channelled into rebel causes. Kit liked re-creations, reinventions, character makeovers, and so did Scott Diamond, who was only too happy to have virtual stem cells injected into a celluloid Marlowe. And whoever was going to play the part – Jude Law, Johnny Depp, Tom Cruise or Brad Pitt – none of them was good enough to get under Marlowe's skin. Kit had become overprotective of his subject to the point of obsession. He had sat in the Ku Bar listening out for clues to the murder he was researching, as though he really expected some cryptic allusion to be dropped between two leather guys, before alerting himself to the fact that Marlowe's death belonged to Tudor times and that the papers relating to a contract put out on him had been declassified by Walsingham's agents.

Kit found himself drawn deeper into his work. What troubled him was the feeling that came up in him at times of total identification with his subject, as if he had direct access to Marlowe's past. The connection had begun during regression hypnotherapy at the Grid and had never gone away. Kit knew all about personality disorders and delusional states but was sure he had no pathological symptoms. His association with Marlowe, while it was troubling, was none the less containable. It worried him more at times that he accepted so readily that he was possibly the living reincarnation of the subject he was researching. That he offered so little resistance to the idea was, on reflection, disquieting and rather like waking up to find that a dream had become a reality. His compulsion to keep returning to Deptford was equally disturbing, a habit he was attempting to kick, albeit with little success. Like a shaman or obsessed psychogeographer Kit felt himself physically extended across Marlowe's London, and he had drawn up a map in which his brain was located in the Globe at Southwark, his heart in Shoreditch, his liver in Damnation Alley on the Strand, his kidneys in the Devil's Gap by the Savoy and his cock and balls in Deptford.

Kit settled to his work, half wishing that he was giving fins and tail to a poem lifting nose up from the page like a Boeing, and he promised himself he would meet up with friends later in the day and chill out in Soho. For the moment he was trying to establish links between three figures central to Marlowe's life: Nicholas Faunt, Anthony Bacon and Thomas Walsingham. All three, despite their various layers of defence and the spin used to doctor their policies, were almost incontrovertibly gay. Nicholas Faunt, like Marlowe a Corpus Christi man and a discreet agent provocateur in the employment of the Secretary of State Francis Walsingham, had in his Paris years become a close friend of Anthony Bacon's and had been included in the ambassador's gay circle. Nicholas Faunt, an ex-scholar of Benet's College and an undercover snoop, existed as a fugitive in the Marlowe plot like a drug foil slipped beneath the tongue for oral trafficking on Rupert Street. That it was Faunt who first commissioned Marlowe as an intelligencer for the secret service while he was still at Cambridge again hinted at ties between the two men that were most probably sexual. Faunt had clearly seen in Marlowe a pretty boy who came from a poor background and who was in need of sponsoring. This was how the Elizabethan gay network functioned. It took people who were already potentially criminalized and sent them underground to report on other fugitives. It was a form of political homoeopathy favoured by the Walsingham quango. Gay men made good spies because they themselves were constantly under scrutiny. This was all part of Kit's theory that homophobia was a virulent reaction to being found out in ways that were compromising to masculinity. Snooping was more invasive than Big Brother because it brokered a person's sexuality.

Kit's initial research into the life of Anthony Bacon had linked him to Faunt but not, as yet, directly to Marlowe. It was documented fact that in the summer of 1586 Bacon was accused, while monitoring the political situation in Béarn, of having sodomized his houseboy Isaac Bougades, who was probably rent in the local town of Montauban. Bacon's letters to Faunt were the exchange of two men who shared a propensity for rough trade. The case brought against Bacon, punishable by death, was dropped as a consequence of bribes and intimidation of witnesses. Bacon had been a snoop for too long not to be expert at airbrushing his tracks. The dissolve between doer and wronged, perpetrator and victim, never clear at any time in the history of gay convictions, had obscured all trace of whether Bacon's boys were complicit in the sexual act and motivated by blackmail, or unwilling partners genuinely seeking revenge. Anthony Bacon had also entered history from the back way like a car crossing the river through the Blackwall Tunnel. A London under London existed in a ziggurat of mazes, not so different, Kit was discovering, from the ambivalent sexual dialogue of Marlowe and his contemporaries, in which same-sex relations existed as a transgressive parallel. A language every bit as colourful and inventive as the palare used by Piccadilly rent boys and their punters in the 1950s and 1960s had existed in Marlowe's circle as an indispensable code of secrecy. The idea of subverting language into a series of closed but highly flamboyant signs was all part of the Marlowe signature.

As he shifted search engines Kit's mind was suddenly full of Nick and the belief that he was out there somewhere in the city doing tricks, fishing a pair of Levis out of the dryer, looking out for eye candy or flipping through the new releases at HMV in Oxford Street. Kit felt his cock stiffen in the constriction of his jeans. If Nick was dead, then, oddly, it didn't lessen his desire. Masturbation was a tool that could be directed as easily towards the dead as the living. He thought, too, of Yukio in Brighton, doubtless wearing a cerise V-neck jumper that signalled like a Kandinsky slash of colour. Yukio in contrast to Nick was so open he concealed nothing. Even his personal letters were left out on the kitchen table.

Thomas Walsingham, on the other hand, was decidedly dodgy and was another key projector in the Marlowe plot, made additionally so by being one of his patrons. The cousin of Francis Walsingham, the acting chief of police who presided over the secret service, Thomas was Marlowe's age and, like him, engaged in espionage. He had inherited the family home at Scadbury, where Marlowe worked on his unfinished poem 'Hero and Leander' and was almost certainly, given their mutual attraction, his lover. Walsingham was a well-heeled man of property, and in addition to the family estate he owned local manors at Dartford, Cobham, Combe and Chislehurst – like Shakespeare he had an acquisitive flair for acquiring property. That Walsingham employed Marlowe's reputed murderer Ingram Frizer as a real-estate hawk and gofer supplied still another possibly criminal link between the two men. Frizer seems to have been on good terms with Walsingham's wife Audrey and to have been a frequent visitor to their country house near Chislehurst in the weeks before Marlowe was killed. Frizer was a businessman, expert at property scams, and successful, too, in that he had, amongst other acquisitions, purchased the Angel Inn in Basingstoke in October 1589. There was something between Walsingham and Frizer, given their contrasting backgrounds, that implied duplicity. To Kit's mind theirs was an unequal relationship, the sort of corrupt bond that exists between two men, each of whom recognizes the potential for crime in the other. That Walsingham and Frizer had come together possibly as part of a same-sex coterie suggested to Kit that Marlowe's killing was a gay insider's job. Marlowe had too much on all of them: Walsingham, Bacon,

Faunt, Lord Strange, Poley, Skeres and Frizer. And, what's more, he talked when fired up and drunk.

The fact that Marlowe's life story was now sourced from unreliable intelligence data and speculative biography, and that it been reduced to the boards and paper of the *Complete Works* (edited in two volumes by Fredson Bowers in 1991), made him seem four centuries more elusive than Nick, who had disappeared comparatively recently. There was something about Nick that was somehow integrated into Kit's Marlowe work, and it constellated round the irrational belief they had been involved together on a deep level in an earlier life. It wasn't something he had ever properly discussed with Nick, but it had grown over the past year to be a constant in his mind. Meeting someone in a big city, he told himself, wasn't luck or simply being in the right place at the right time; it was undoubtedly intended. He was convinced from his research that Marlowe's relationship with his killer was no less accidental than his own with Nick. People met because their electrics attracted, and it was even possible that Marlowe had first met his murderer while imprisoned in the Tower, the two men sniffing each other like dogs and both protected by a security apparatus that kept them inside, without conviction, for their own safety. London and its spillover into wooded suburbs may have had a population of only 250,000 in Tudor times, in contrast with Kit's city of 17 million, but Marlowe and his killer still had to find each other out in a way that left no doubt as to the resolution.

On the day Kit had met Nick, and it fitted with his theories of synchronicity, he was intending to be somewhere else. A cancelled appointment on his voicemail had taken him into the First Out café with the idea of killing a bonus hour. He wasn't looking for anyone, but his eyes had almost instantly made contact with a young blond guy sitting in the corner reading the freebie paper *Boyz*. To anyone watching it would have looked as though he had come there to meet Nick as he walked straight over to his table on impulse. And no matter how tentative each may have been at first about the improbability of their encounter, it had worked. What had appeared random, opportunist and impetuous had sobered into a reverse chemistry. Something between them had matched like the pink socks fitted to the foot pedals of a Steinway grand. After the mutual formality of intros and the initial search to colour-code interests, they had found themselves genuinely at ease in each other's company. If Kit had entertained worries about Nick being rent, then these had dissolved in the context of their instantaneous attraction, and by the time Kit had gone off for his rescheduled appointment he was high on the feeling he had not so much met someone new but reconnected with somebody he had always known.

Independent of his work for Soho Media, Kit was determined to follow his own line of enquiry into Marlowe's death, the event having about it something of the great legendary disappearances in history, like the unacceptable deaths of Byron, Oscar Wilde, Hart Crane, Billie Holiday, Marilyn Monroe, Elvis Presley and Jimi Hendrix.

But today Kit wanted to head into town early to visit his friend Alex, who lived on Archer Street in Soho as a sitting tenant of a top-floor flat that was now a prospector's target worth a cool 800K.

Kit shut down his laptop and hurried off in the direction of Notting Hill Gate station. Down there the air fried with the potential for bioterrorism and gang nukes. He boarded a Central Line train and held on, eyes speed-reading a copy of William Gibson's *Pattern Recognition*, as the train accelerated through synaptic stations on its rush. He exited at Tottenham Court Road in a wedge of Anglo-Japanese medical students, all excitedly talking about stem-cell research and football. An attractive Japanese girl, probably a trainee doctor, her hair dyed red, was standing to the side, evidently preoccupied with trying to link her VR phone to her computer. Kit was glad to get out of the station, and as he ran up the steps to the street under a dull, white afternoon sky his mind was obsessed with the hope of encountering Nick somewhere in the maze of Soho alleys.

Kit cut a fast line down Old Compton Street, crossed over Wardour and Rupert Streets and headed for Alex's flat overlooking Ham Yard. Alex almost instantly let Kit into a building that was made up offices apart from the top floor in which he lived with Sam. The entire street apart from a few remaining clip-joints had been converted to accommodate the food chain of expendable companies on short-term leases. Alex's flat was done out in loud orange, silver and blue, fine-tuned with a run of gold-painted bookcases stashed with fascias of CDs. Kit caught sight through the open door of a minimally spaced bathroom, a number of goldfish doing qigong in a globular bowl. There were photographs of icons on the walls – the divas Judy Garland and Shirley Bassey, Francis Bacon podgily frozen into Soho history by John Deakin's lens, the histrionic gravitas of Maria Callas, and everywhere the accumulative slew of Sammy's records, the twelve-inch vinyl he spun on the decks as a DJ.

Sammy was out, and Alex, who had the permanent look of someone who had stepped abruptly out of a dark room into the light, busied himself with tea things, his twenty-eight-inch waist anorexically bottled into pre-damaged jeans. He was a blade of flesh with irregular, but refined features, who, like Nick, had proved resilient to the period in which he had worked as rent. Alex methodically brought in tea and frangipane slices on a tray, and Kit recognized his scent as Opium, a cocktail so evocative of Nick that it hurt.

'I suppose you're looking for Nick,' Alex said, reading Kit's mind, the concern in his voice routing above the quiet expression. 'Well, as a matter of fact, I was going to call you. Of all things, Peter Worth says he saw him last week in Leicester Square. Said he looked up for it and tanned, as though he'd been away.'

'Can you really believe that?' Kit asked. 'And what about the fact he was ill. Has the virus just gone away?'

'That crossed my mind, too,' Alex said. 'But it wasn't like I was looking for the facts. Peter called me about something else and right in the middle of the conversation dropped it in. Said he'd met up with Nick and that it was like old times. Apparently he's got a deal with an indie label and has been writing new songs.'

'Did Peter say where he's living?'

'No he didn't. I'm just trying to remember if he said anything else about Nick. If he did I can't remember.' Kit watched Alex search for connections like a satellite dish picking up signals. 'I'm trying to think,' he said, regressing. 'What else was it Pete told me? There was something . . . I know, that he was attending meetings somewhere.'

'What sort of meetings?' Kit asked. 'He didn't mention a place in Coptic Street, did he?'

'Not that I remember,' Alex said.

Kit stared out of the window over Great Windmill Street. It seemed weird, almost extraterrestrial to be this close up to Soho and to live at the disquieting epicentre of the fault lines running across the West End. The place would have been fields in Marlowe's time, a treacled quagmire from winter rains, and in the summer a wasteland bristling with muggers, thieves and unscrupulous outlaws. Kit knew without being told that there were bookshops Marlowe had once used at St Paul's Churchyard and Paternoster Row, pubs selling Rhenish and Gascony wines and eating houses he had frequented, such as the Oliphant in Southwark and Marco Lucchese's in Hart Street, all part of a vanished London. He remembered these things with alarming clarity, the free concerts held at the Royal Exchange on Sundays and always the pervasive reek of the city where endemic plague sweated from its diseased organism. The river, as he remembered it, had been shallower then but equally toxic and often yellow with the coagulated pollutants it carried downstream. He had seen hospital supplies dumped in the turgid water and a raft of bloodstained bandages pushing sluggishly along towards Southwark and saw it again now in a lividly sustained flashback. Now the precinct throbbed with transients, Eastern European sex workers, movie producers, music industry pundits and a few last surviving live-in Soho residents like Alex and Sammy, living under the threat of escalating rent and eviction.

'I'll find out as much as I can for you,' Alex said. 'I'd like to see Nick myself, but so far he hasn't shown up on my beat. He could be anywhere, if he's alive.'

Kit left Alex, who was planning to Tube over to the Fallen Angel in Walthamstow, to get ready for his journey and made his way slowly, deep in thought, down Denman Street towards Piccadilly Circus. He was on Nick's patch, sniffing for his scent, although a deeper consensus of feelings told him that even if Nick was alive he was unlikely to be back on the scene as rent. He made his way to the corner of Glasshouse Street and stood off at a distance from the landmark Boots, taking in the whole scenic curve of the black railings on the Regent Street side where Nick had hung out selling sex. The sonic roar was urgent there, like a polluted ecosystem of unmixed sound, coaches, BMWs, a liquid-nitrogen truck, black cabs gunning to get away, an urgent clash of conflicting energies reverberating in a West End traffic studio. The tourists came at him three deep, a multinational exodus armed with Nikon and Sony digital cameras housed in Body Glove ballistic nylon and neoprene fabric cases. They seemed drawn to the Piccadilly circle like one of the concentric diagrams of Dante's Inferno. What they encountered were the corporate façades of Boots, Burger King, McDonald's and Caffè Nero, the homogenized chains that were invariably repeated in every high street.

Kit stood with his back to the wall and looked across the road, urgent with traffic, through a shimmer of haze. For a moment he really did think he had hallucinated Nick into existence and could see him standing outside the subway steps opposite, dressed as he imagined him to be, in jeans and a black T-shirt. He steadied himself and searched the endlessly mutating crowd. His eye scratched a Japanese guy's, but he let him go, cancelling the signal immediately. He refused to be distracted from his search and waded into the slow-motion crocodile of urban backpackers looking for Nick's blond highlights to show. He was about to round the corner by the pizza house on Shaftesbury Avenue when he thought he saw Nick back over his shoulder to the right, heading for the Underground. The person crossed over at the lights, the red freeze momentarily computing the traffic to a regulated halt, and walked over quickly to the Regent Street entrance to the subway and, with a flick of his hair, disappeared. The fleeting experience was so intense that to Kit it felt like a flashback transmitted over hundreds of years to the present, in the way that bad acid sometimes reconfigures images that have never properly cleared from a trip.

Kit took off in pursuit, unsure if it was Nick or a look-alike he had seen. He segued his way rapidly through the crowds, jockeying for breaks, was rewarded by the lights reverting to red and headed for the subway. He ran down the steps into the main concourse but was stopped in his tracks by the congested swarm of arrivals coming through the ticket barriers. Nick was nowhere to be seen. He checked the impulse to buy a ticket from the dispenser and pursue the chase underneath the city in the suffocating dark. He stood there on the tiled mezzanine searching the crowd, hoping the improbable, that Nick would reappear, then gave up, went back to the street and lost himself in the impacted West End jostle.

4

ick wasn't sure about the enigmatic blond boy, Ingram, he had met at the Grid. Ingram Frazer or Frizer, he couldn't be quite certain of the pronunciation or the spelling. The name sounded to him like an alias. Ingram was somebody who spoke from behind the iris-free screen of dark glasses and made no concessions about the social disdain implied by his cool. From what Nick could make out in their meeting after the group, Ingram had been in real estate, and from the paralegal criminality of brokering stucco-fronted houses in Thurloe Square he had graduated to being a dealer with expensive clients. Ingram's coke habit had encouraged him to feed other dependants. Somewhere in the chain of multiple addictions in his life he, like Nick and Robert, had become positive and done nothing about testing. The rest was the familiar story of how he had been given the tube by an undisclosed source and had taken up with the Grid.

Nick felt attracted to Ingram, despite the fact that he couldn't trust him as a leftfield trickster looking to exploit any advantage. But at the same time the trickiness was the fascination. He had, right from childhood, been drawn to those who had the power to corrupt, a perverse Gestalt that had encouraged him to run away from home, take up life as a rent boy and, ultimately, place his trust in the ambivalent motives of punters. Even with Kit he had never lost the feeling that he was using and being used, rather than being in an equal relationship. The attractive side to Ingram, his quietly inflected voice, the imperturbable cool that seemed to exist behind his shades and the feeling that they were partly bonded by reason of their extraordinary rehabilitation, had partly won him over. He felt

he liked and disliked the man in equal proportions, was perversely attracted to him sexually and repulsed by the habitual
payback mentality that governed his exploitation of others.

Regression hypnotherapy was making big inroads into
Nick's life, and as he headed towards Leicester Square's
Coventry Street to meet Robert and Ingram at a Starbucks he
felt extraordinarily confused by many of the discoveries he had
made about himself. He had come out of the Underground
drenched and wedged his body into the chaotically direction-
less crowd, the air reverberating with a reconnaissance helicopter bugging the Whitehall Precinct. A suicide bomber had
narrowly missed blowing up the Commissar in a direct one-to-
one kamikaze a week ago, and security was tight. More robosoldiers had been moved into the Westminster Precinct, and
Nick could feel the tension in the hot polluted air like static.

He made his way through Little Newport Street where the
crowds were thinner and mostly Cantonese, Vietnamese and
Japanese, drawn to the Chinese herbalists and mini-markets on
the street. Nick felt unduly vulnerable as he played back in his
mind some of the markers that had come up in the previous
day's therapy. He was frightened inwardly of regressing to what
seemed like unfinished business, still demanding attention,
stemming from his life as an underworld figure in Tudor
London. The process of retrieval was still in its formative
stages, and as he hurried in the direction of the Swiss Centre
some of the previous session's vividly memorable signposting
rushed into his mind. What troubled him were the detailed
specifics of memory. The precision with which he could
remember that he was born in March 1563, a Londoner, and
had lived in a house near the river between Dowgate and
Coldharbour in the parish of All Hallows, was particularly
unnerving, given that he wasn't up on the topology of
London's rivers. According to what he remembered, he had
been for a time a law student at Furnival's Inn in Holborn, a
training that had provided him with the baseline for his future
career as a moneylender and extortionist. Although he had

made light of the facts as random associations, exploited by hypnotherapy, he was no longer sure. The details he was in the process of retrieving and piecing into a biography seemed too composite, too concrete to be dismissed as a gratuitous movie projected by his unconscious.

As he walked up Little Newport Street a cortège of three black stretch limousines finned into view on Wardour Street, blacked out and closed to all scrutiny. He had heard via media reports that Michael Jackson had relocated to London, drawn to its dystopian theme of anticipated apocalypse by a fascination with self-destructive endgaming. The biologically reinvented Jackson with his restructured features was apparently in town looking to relaunch his career. Nick watched the three Cadillacs manoeuvre for space in the narrow Soho streets – two for Jackson's security and nomadic entourage, he had read, and one for himself and his Botox specialist. The tabloids had sensationalized this ostentatious triumvirate of sleek cars crossing the city, but actually seeing them at first hand brought the times up close like a reality cosh.

Nick dodged his way along Wardour Street into the crowds massing towards Piccadilly. There were two roboguards positioned outside the Trocadero as part of the robotic policing of the precinct. Robokillings – the guns were equipped with voice controls and a radio link enabling them to be fired remotely from several feet away – had become a regular feature of the Commissar's London, and Nick kept well away from their sensors.

He was about to cross the road when, to his alarm, he saw Kit standing, hands in his pockets, on the corner opposite. He was just standing there, eye-surfing the crowds, intensely, as though looking out for someone. Nick instinctually recoiled, hurriedly put on his shades and, trying his hardest to dematerialize on the spot, incorporated himself into a slow-moving raft of Japanese. Part of him wanted to rush over and spontaneously declare that he was alive and well, while the other resented Kit's continuing presence in his life. Detaching himself from cover when he felt safely out of view, he hurried on, quite certain that he hadn't been seen and that he was no more than an indistinct feature in the crowd. It felt odd hurrying away from the man he still loved, like a store thief beating a fast retreat from the vicinity. He didn't dare look round for fear of being seen but instead moved in and out of the congested Japanese, all of them, he guessed, coded into Biobank, with its national database of DNA samples linked to forensic and medical records in an attempt on the part of the government to politicize the human genome. As he hurried on he had a song unconsciously cooking in his head, the fragments of a lyric and the catchy hook demanding he pay attention to their rhythm.

Nick was slightly late for his appointment, and when he arrived at the Starbucks in the Haymarket Robert and Ingram, whom he hadn't anticipated knowing each other quite on this level of intimacy, were already there, sitting moodily together and not saying much. You could never tell with Ingram if his taciturnity was deliberate and used to secure advantage or if it came from a purely solipsistic source. What Nick had noticed was that Ingram's diffidence rubbed off on Robert when they were together, so that the two seemed inseparably conspiratorial, bonded by bits of a pattern that left him feeling excluded.

As usual Nick came up against the impenetrable black screen of Ingram's aviator glasses. They were as defensive in their total black-out as the windows of Michael Jackson's limo he had just seen slinking down Wardour Street. Ingram nodded implacably, as though taking Nick in, and left it to Robert to say an obligatory 'Hi, how are you?' in a way so nonchalant it half implied he had broken into their conversation.

'I'm sorry I'm late,' Nick said. 'There were delays on the Tube. It's frying down there. We were all evacuated at one point because of a bomb scare.'

'We've only just got here,' Robert said, his tone implying that he had arrived with Ingram. Nick noted, too, how Robert was sitting with his right knee projected against Ingram's left, the point of contact visible, like they were an item.

Nick got himself some herbal Refresh tea and a cookie and came over to join Robert and Ingram, who had requisitioned two plum-coloured armchairs, leaving him to a more utilitarian wooden upright.

'How's the regression going?' Robert asked out of the blue. 'I think we've all been having a hard time of it lately.'

'Personally, I find it draining,' Nick replied. 'It's like a long-haul flight into the past. Most of the time I feel psychically jet-lagged.'

'That's a good way of putting it,' Robert said. 'Those sessions have something about them, I agree, like the exhaustion of coming back economy class from Tokyo.'

Ingram said nothing and played at being dumb. Nick couldn't tell if he was listening or totally preoccupied with his own thoughts. The glasses prevented him from knowing. They were mood cancellers.

'I'm way back in the past in my sessions,' Nick said. 'It's weird. I've never felt any affinities with the period until now. But the deeper I regress, the more composite the character. I've definitely been there all right.'

'We all seem, for some reason, to be in the same space,' Robert said. 'My regression, as you know, has taken me back to life as an Elizabethan gofer. Ingram's, too. I don't know whether to believe it or not, but it's certainly convincing – so, too, how little my character has changed seemingly from the person I was supposed to have been in the past.'

'It's like going home, man,' Ingram said defiantly from behind his defences and instantly shut up.

Nick was acutely conscious of the risk of breaching confidentiality and didn't want to get too far drawn into road-mapping comparative regressions. Robert and Ingram both looked overstretched, as though the drug they were doing was still coming up in their chemistries.

'It's all part of our work,' Robert said. 'Without the Grid we'd all three of us be dead.'

'Sometimes, though, I still can't believe I'm here,' Nick said.

'All I know is that the virus had at one time penetrated my blood barrier, and now there's no trace of it in my body.'

'In an odd way I trust the regressions,' Robert said. 'They're markers to something important that the three of us need to know.'

Ingram directed his attention to his espresso, staying with it as a focal point to the exclusion of all else. The roots showed through the bleach in his hair. His torso was bamboo thin, and the waist tapered to a concise triangle. Nick felt simultaneously aroused by this modified human and repulsed by Ingram's lack of emotional give.

'What I don't understand,' Nick said, 'is if we're exempt from reinfection.'

'Don't know,' Robert said. 'According to the Grid we're redesigned humans. At the moment I'm more interested in my past than in my future. I've rediscovered I was a sizar of Clare College, Cambridge, at one time. It was somewhere around 1568 according to my regression. God knows where all this comes from, but there's some deep core that we're all sourcing.'

'What's a sizar?' Nick asked, as Ingram massaged a bony knee against Robert's, while refusing him eye contact.

'I'm told it was someone who did menial tasks for richer students. If you were university standard but poor it was a means of getting by.'

'My grounding seems to have been in law,' Nick said sceptically. 'I suppose if you know the law it's easy to bend it.'

'I'm starting to get drawn in like reading a page-turner,' Robert said. 'Some of it I don't like, but I recognize the possibilities in myself to have been and done certain things.'

'Like what, if you don't mind me asking? I'm curious,' Nick said, suddenly aware of the feeling that he had known Robert for a lot longer than the relatively short time in which they had been acquainted.

'Well, I know from my recent sessions that I left Cambridge without taking my degree, most likely because of the prejudice against Catholics. All sorts of strange things came out. I seem to have been married for a couple of years to someone called Jane Watson and to have had a daughter called Anne, who was baptized, if you believe this, at St Helen's Bishopsgate in August 1583. I was a Catholic so had to marry secretly. I'm not sure I like the idea of marriage,' Robert laughed. 'But I deserted them and ended up in Marshalsea prison in Southwark as a snoop for my case officer, Francis Walsingham, and with a chest of money to purchase intelligence. It sounds crazy, but equally it could be true.'

'From what I've read on the subject you can't take anything of the Elizabethan network at face value,' Nick said. 'It was all about pretending to be someone you weren't and double dealing. It seems, and I'm talking about the underworld, that people were mostly into being their opposites. God knows, I met enough of those when I worked at the Dilly.'

'I can see you've done your research,' Robert said. 'Most of the dealers were duplicitous in my old profession of buying and selling diamonds. I suppose most people are bent like a banana's back. The problem with being intelligence, as we were all supposed to have been at one time, is that you can so easily be accused yourself of committing the very crimes you are in the process of unearthing. It's a weird contract.'

'Tell me,' Ingram said, directing his skewed voice over the lip of his coffee mug before instantly retreating into silence.

'If I understand it right,' Nick said, 'we were all, for want of a better word, spies or snoops. It's certainly an interesting theory. I'm not sure I relate to it. It was too long ago, even though the idea's convincing.'

'I don't agree,' Robert said. 'I think you can move time around like building blocks. I learnt that doing all those air miles. Things went on happening in the place you'd left behind, even though you weren't there. And, likewise, when you arrived back home you were missing out on things going on back there.'

'So what you are saying,' Nick said, 'if I get it right, is that the past doesn't exist other than in how we re-create it in the present.'

'Something like that. I need to think about it more. I remember reading Derek Jarman's book *A Saint's Testimony* on a long-haul to Washington and being struck by a line in which he talked about the telescoping effect of death and how, try as we might to get a framework on it, we'd all be dead in the time it took to boil a kettle. And, I suppose, relatively speaking he's right.'

'Dead right,' Ingram said monotonally, appearing to look out of the window from behind his black-outs.

'What about music?' Robert asked, sounding notably friendlier. 'Are you recording?'

'Yes, I am actually. I've written three or four new songs since the ones you heard. I've got enough for an album. As I'm supposed to be dead I haven't done anything about looking for a deal.'

'I'm sure you'll be back soon. The Grid, as I understand it, will reintroduce us slowly to normal life, but only after they're sure we're medically sound.'

'Makes no difference to me, man,' Ingram said. 'I've always liked being incognito. If people don't know who you are they can't get anything on you.'

Nick wondered about Ingram and whether the criminality he constantly alluded to was real. He was all attitude, a redoubtable hostility coloured by social disdain, but the under-side to his sunglassed 'fuck you' façade was that of a gay man who had been irreparably hurt by having to live dishonestly. It was to Ingram's concealed wound that he was attracted, believing somehow that if you stripped him of his layered defences the man at the core would be sympathetic.

Nick kept dreading that Kit had seen him coming here and was waiting somewhere outside. The paranoid feeling induced by having seen him wouldn't let up, having him believe for panicky moments that everything was watching him – the passing cars, the buildings opposite, the photons arriving at 186,000 miles per second, the Boeing crossing the sun, the whole impacted complex that was Piccadilly, digital floor on floor lit with computer radiation.

As he sat there he was increasingly anxious to be gone. Today Piccadilly seemed brutally deromanticized of his past as rent in its heyday as a pick-up centre. He felt he had been deselected from its memory, his signature wiped from its streets. He decided he wanted to come back another day and rewrite the place according to how he had once known it.

'Are you coping all right?' Robert asked, clearly wishing to express some personal concern before they went their separate ways. 'I'm sorry if I appeared abrupt earlier on. These sessions are starting to do me in.'

'I'm fine,' Nick replied. 'I've got off drug management now. I couldn't sleep on the prescribed antidepressants.'

'I was the same,' Robert said. 'I don't like the implications of what the Grid call "biological happenstance". I like to think we're still humans and not part of a process.'

'Let's quit,' Ingram said abruptly. 'I've got business.' His Motorola phone flashed with orange and blue lights like a spaceship, something Nick associated with the hyperactive communications of a dealer who delivers crack cocaine consignments across town.

'I'm coming with you,' Robert said, as Ingram did a lateral take on the place, seeing everything without himself appearing to be seen.

When they got outside Nick observed how transparently brain-faded and physically wasted Ingram appeared in the daylight. He looked virtual rather than real, and although he professed to be free of the virus he still had the distinct lipo-atrophied look of a carrier.

'Let's meet up again soon,' Robert said. 'I'll give you a bell.' He was clearly anxious to be off with Ingram, who nodded cursorily as the two hurried off in the direction of Regent Street, conferring, as though cooking a plan.

Nick found himself loose again in the Piccadilly crowds,

and despite the fear of encountering Kit he decided to briefly remap his old territory. Even though the scene had shifted, and boys who'd run away to London no longer took up their station outside Boots, he could still smell chance in the air. Nick liked to think of those who had made it good there and taken up with benign patrons or wealthy sugar daddies. He knew the stories from the boys who had worked there and had rehearsed them like street myths: Ray, who had been adopted by a politician and sent to university; John, who had been partnered by a rainmaker; someone else who had taken up with a pop star; someone else again retrieved from the black end of the corridor and drugs by a closet actor. It was in part the possibility of being redeemed by a meeting with the perfect stranger that had boys of his generation risk the inevitable downside of hanging out there.

Nick promised himself he'd only stay for five minutes to feed his nostalgia and then be gone. He kept an anxious eye out for Kit as well as signs of a Bottlehead gang surfacing from the Tube on a random nuke and took the stairs down from the street on the Shaftesbury Avenue side. He was relieved that he no longer worked the place and had sorted himself out with his work at the Grid and his continued interest in music. Now that he had some remove on selling sex, he saw its dangers and the vulnerability to which he had been exposed. He had lost his health here to big-city exploitation and for dirty money, and he was glad that he was only passing through and had a purpose on the other side of the corridor that connected with Regent Street. He took the stairs slowly up to the street, the light flooding back with its sonic overload, adjusted his glasses and felt a stranger draw up beside him, parallel his step and talk him up with his eyes. Nick could see that the man was in his forties, blond-haired and dressed in a menthol-green V-neck and ubiquitous bleached-out blue jeans.

'Do you have a moment?' the man asked, his quiet voice used in a way that was kept flat and could have been directed at somebody else.

'What do you want?' Nick said, irritated by this sudden invasion of his privacy.

'You're Nick, aren't you?' the man said as they stood at the top of the stairs in the chemically mixed sunlight. 'I saw you perform once at the Monarch and thought you were fantastic.'

'I think you've got the wrong person,' Nick said, acting cool. 'I'm John. I'm sorry I'm in a hurry . . .'

'I've been wanting to sign you for ages,' the man continued, the hesitant catch in his voice causing Nick to stop and stare up directly into the sun, his glasses turning the sky the colour of an airport runway.

'I'm not here picking up, if that's what you want,' Nick said, stopping in his tracks at the same time to meet the man's quizzical green eyes.

'Don't worry about that,' the man said. 'I'm Richard. I have a label called Black Sun. If you have a moment I'd really like to talk to you about some ideas.'

Nick bit on his dilemma. He wasn't yet ready to go public, and the Grid had advised him against doing so, but at heart a record deal was what he wanted more than anything in the world. He told himself he could just listen to the terms and, if the man became too inquisitive, walk away. He'd heard it all before anyway, the empty promises, the industry-speak, the AOR coke-fuelled enthusiasms that evanesced overnight, the harnessing of stardom to a superficial image. He'd listened to it repeatedly and always as somebody who saw through the whole illusory package.

'All right,' Nick said, reluctantly, 'but I really don't have much time. I'm not the man you want. Try somebody else.'

As Richard fell in beside him Nick could sense that he was gay by the manner in which his eyes gave dramatic expression to his thoughts. It was often a giveaway, and Richard used his eyes to effect, as though they were registering a gorgeous colour moment.

'What about the Café Royal?' Richard said, pointing to the place. 'It's all on expenses. We can talk there.'

'OK, but it will have to be quick, and I mean that. I'm busy.'

'The court of St Oscar,' Richard said, as they went through the entrance into the bar area, alluding to the outrageous celebrity Wilde had brought to the Café Royal during his sex-addicted years of excess.

Inside, they chose the Edwardian Room, and Richard ordered tea and sandwiches and two glasses of champagne. Nick felt uncomfortable and displaced, as if he shouldn't be there, his preconceptions of disappointment interfering with whatever recording proposals Richard had to offer.

'If *Fallen Angel* had come out on a major, or even a slow-burner like One Little Indian, it would have sold well,' Richard said, trying to win confidence by showing he was wised up on Nick's past.

'I thought the artist was dead or missing,' Nick said. 'According to the music papers he hasn't been heard of for a year or two, if I'm right. Didn't he just disappear and clean vanish – if we're talking about the same person?'

'That's your story. The cult interest in your apparent death has generated quite a following and will help sell the next record you make big time. We'll finance it. We'll reinvent you as the living dead. What about all the Elvis sightings?'

'But I'm not even owning up to who you think I am,' Nick said. 'Hasn't it occurred to you that I'm probably a Nick Hebden lookalike, someone emulating his style. Isn't that what image is about?'

'Your voice gives you away,' Richard countered in a manner that was reassuringly friendly. 'You needn't worry. I'm not going to let on that I've found you. Legends need to be nurtured and marketed and not outed.'

'I'm John to you. OK?' Nick said decisively as he struggled to suppress a natural antipathy to commercial greed. 'I've got Nick's record, and I'm a fan. That's all.'

'Well, John,' Richard continued undeterred, 'I'd like you to think about signing with our label with a generous advance and a two-record contract. We'll look after you and give you complete artistic freedom.'

'I'm sure artists are told that all the time,' Nick said evasively, unable to quite let the proposal go, despite the obstacles in his way to signing.

'You don't have to decide today,' Richard said, savouring his fizz. 'Think about it. You put out a record yourself that was critically acclaimed. We could quadruple your sales in the first month and build from there.'

'But I read that the record sold because of the mystery surrounding the artist's disappearance,' Nick said. 'The fact is, he's probably dead, but it's more romantic to say he isn't. It was his death sold him, not the record.'

'It's irrelevant. Bringing someone back from the dead is the ultimate PR scam. We can pull it off. Imagine if Hendrix turned up playing guitar again in a small club in Minehead.'

'But Hebden's not Hendrix,' Nick said. 'He's a tiny cult. Only a few fans know of his existence.'

'Cults can cross over, you know, and enter the mainstream. Being a cult means you're defined by its limits. It doesn't mean you can't transcend the limitations.'

'What about loss of integrity?' Nick argued. 'At least artists with some sort of vision can self-express.'

'Nobody's going to sit on you. Your coming back to music will be weird enough in itself to sell anything if we get the story right.'

Nick felt instantly confused. He was still inwardly unable to accept his virus-free status let alone contemplate the idea of being marketed as a post-human pop star. It all seemed unreal, sitting in the Café Royal on Regent Street, refusing to admit to his identity and being coshed by a blatant PR stratagem aimed at selling into the mainstream his perverse individuality as an offbeat singer. But singing was his life, and while he felt afraid of alienating himself from the Grid he was reluctant to blank the offer totally and continue to go it alone.

'Give me a couple of weeks to think about it,' Nick said

as a compromise. 'It's not something I can instantly rush into.'

'Cool. Don't think I'm trying to probe into your past or anything. Whatever's happened to you in the missing years is your affair. We'll spin our own marketing story anyway.'

For all his inveterate industry speak, Nick felt a degree of sympathy for the man he was confronting. He warmed to the evident vulnerability of the person beneath the artificial perma-tan, the exaggerated Shirley Bassey chutzpah that so obviously lived buried in him as exaggerated camp. Nick knew his sort only too well and had so often seen the woman in a man come out in dramatic moments, like a singer walking on to a dark stage to be picked out by a filtered spotlight.

'I'd better be off soon,' Nick said cursorily, feeling compelled to look round anxiously, 'but by all means leave me your email.'

'I suppose you've been writing new material in your time away,' Richard said. 'I'd love to hear whatever demos you have. Send me anything.'

'That's assuming I am really Nick Hebden,' Nick said, still maintaining his ambiguity. 'Don't people who disappear usually give up on their previous existence and reinvent themselves? I mean Rimbaud went off into the desert and never wrote again. A lot of people go missing permanently, you know, and leave no traces. If Nick had really walked out on music, wouldn't he be busy doing something else?'

'You'll have to tell me,' Richard said, his eyes suddenly sparkling with 25-carat rocks. 'I have another theory, and I think that's why we met by chance today. I'm here to reinvent your image.'

'I'll see you in two weeks, then,' Nick said coldly, casually pocketing the man's card.

'Call me to confirm.'

Nick walked outside into the Piccadilly day with his head exploding. Everything he'd dreamt of happening for years was suddenly being offered him, and he was unable to commit. All his scepticism about AOR scams had instantly dissolved in the heady endorphin rush of being wanted. The sulphur-dioxide emissions in the air were lit up radiantly, the curved arm of Regent Street looking like it was cut from blue opals. Nick suddenly found it hugely exhilarating again, to be dead centre to life as the world turned beneath the Piccadilly axis. He felt better than he had at seventeen, when the dirty money earned from selling sex, crumpled in his pockets, was a gateway to hotels like the Dorchester and the rich clients they provided.

Caught up by memories he stayed above the entrance to the Underground, deliberately delaying his journey back home. He had worked this site in order to pay for his music, gone with strangers in the hope they had access to the music industry, and now, after a year's disappearance in which it was assumed he was dead, he found himself wanted. It all seemed too much to take in. The weirdest things were happening in his life, but this offer was by far the best. Putting his sunglasses back in his pocket the sky seemed violet, the colour of Elizabeth Taylor's eyes. A boy who could have been him when he had started out here was standing over on the opposite side of the street, trying his luck. *Pas de chance*. Nick made a last visual take on the place, prepared himself mentally to go under the city and contemplatively took the steps down into the scorching dark.

5

For days now Kit, after his sessions at the Grid, felt unnerved by his discoveries as to what he assumed was his true identity. The conviction had steadily grown on him contemporaneously with his research, so, too, the certainty that Marlowe and Shakespeare were cottaging rivals, hanging out under the pavement at Eastcheap, their sexual radar beamed to syphilitic rough trade. Marlowe, it seemed, had Thomas Walsingham as a patron; Shakespeare, Henry Wriothesley, the Earl of Southampton. But there was the distinct possibility, he was starting to realize, that all four men were sexually involved at some stage before pairing off as rivals. There was always a price to pay for patronage, and Kit suspected both Marlowe and Shakespeare of being used in ways that turned them into predatory users. It was the Elizabethan pattern. Nobody was straight: every thought process was coded into a secure file; every physical favour demanded a return of the favour. Words, as he was starting to rediscover, conveyed the rich ambivalence and ambiguity of spin. The eloquent rhetoric used in speech or letters of the period was largely semantic froth – a doubling process that alluded to but rarely delivered the truth. Marlowe's poetic line, in comparison with that of his contemporaries, was relatively streamlined and had the sort of flex that kept it modern and pumped full of vitamin B6.

Kit had always preferred Marlowe to Shakespeare, and now there was a clear reason, almost an obsession, to support that singular preference. There was, too, more purchase in his big line and more risk. And the life was far more controversial and undeviatingly resistant to the establishment. There was an element of conformity to some aspects of Shakespeare's character, of a caution aimed at instinctual self-preservation that Kit mistrusted, preferring instead Marlowe's profligacy and reckless daring. And if Marlowe had cared little or nothing for money and possessions, then Shakespeare had developed a natural facility for business and property speculation that suggested an acquisitive capitalist ethic, quite the opposite to Marlowe's anti-establishment leanings. Kit had even begun to entertain seriously the notion that Shakespeare, if he wasn't Marlowe's killer, was certainly a part of the plot. If the Deptford murder conspiracy was, as he believed, factored by the coroner to doctor the truth of what really happened and to acquit the obvious conspirators, such as Sir Francis Walsingham and Lord Burghley, of involvement in the plot, then Kit was open to the idea that Marlowe, far from being an alias for Shakespeare, may have been killed by his colleague out of jealousy. It was a controversial angle he intended to discuss with Scott Diamond. If Shakespeare were cast as the homicidal co-star of the Marlowe biopic, the story would radically rewrite the events of that Deptford riverside evening.

Booting up to do a search on Marlowe links Kit realized how possessive he had grown of his subject. He had even stopped telling Yukio of his exciting re-edits of the past and of the fizz he experienced in making those discoveries. He had come to identify so totally with Marlowe that he felt it was his own past he was retrieving rather than that of a character intended for a movie. None of the biographies of Marlowe, with the exception of Charles Nicholl's masterful re-creation of the Deptford killing, *The Reckoning*, provided him with anything but academic theory. Facts didn't help, largely because they were substitutes for the emotional content of what had really happened. He was searching for rogue clues, ones more likely to be tracked by imagination and revealed by his sessions at the Grid than those located in biographical research. There were so many fugitive connections in Marlowe's life – for example, his closeness to the network of printers and book smugglers in Holland, where Dutch printers at Middleburg produced clandestine editions of unlicensed texts aimed at the English market. Marlowe's relations with the bookseller underground had given rise to the persistent rumour that he himself wrote a lost book attacking religion as a manmade product devised to suppress free thought.

Kit lost himself totally in the search. Derek Jarman's film adaptation of Marlowe's Edward II was precisely the sort of imaginative re-creation of history that excited him. On the other hand, the latest update from the Marlowe Society was harnessed to convention. Of more interest to Kit was a detail found in Peter Ackroyd's *London: The Biography*, to the effect that a real devil was supposed to have appeared at a performance of Marlowe's *Doctor Faustus* at the Belle Sauvage Inn on Ludgate Hill. At such times Kit felt Marlowe under his skin. In his mind he could see the acne craters, scar tissue, sexually transmitted diseases, the whole profile of a youthfully disabused poet. Marlowe was an enigma, like the Bob Dylan of *The Basement Tapes*, who had walked over to a pink house each day to deliver an impromptu stream of free-associated lyricism to the musicians, loosely calling themselves The Band, assembled in its basement. Marlowe's pink house was a rank urinal in Shoreditch, a constricted arena of sexual conflict, marble-slabbed like a mortuary. Kit, who, like his namesake, loved to shock, relished the idea of doing an al-Qaeda on the literary world by having Shakespeare join Marlowe in his compulsive networking of London's underground toilets. In his mind the animosity between the two could have started over a mutual crush on some pretty thing that had escalated into jealous rivalry. In any Marlowe biopic he would like to have Kit hold a sweating Shakespeare at knife-point against a wall, air-cut a stab at his throat, laugh directly into his eyes and then walk away leaving him a wide-eyed wreck surfacing into the foggy Shoreditch night.

Kit kept the idea in mind like a dance groove reprising and went back to Jarman. It was Edmund White who, in his review of *Caravaggio* for the *Literary Review*, had signposted the way for Jarman's Marlowe obsession by writing how the film put him 'in mind of Marlowe – the glowing intensity, the ramshackle structure, the pagan sensuality and violence, the highflown rhetoric, the meaty fascination with men and the rather abstract admiration of women. Jarman really should do an *Edward II* one of these days.'

According to Kit's initial search Jarman had deepened his bonds with Marlowe in January 1987 by writing a script called *Sod 'Em* in one of the large notebooks into which he also pasted photos of beautiful young men. A vitriolic reaction to the endemic paranoia surrounding Aids – Jarman had already tested positive – Jarman had imagined a warrant was out for the arrest of Edward, the young actor playing the lead role in Marlowe's play. Jarman's counterterrorist response to 1987's Clause 28, recriminalizing homosexuality, had about it a temerity that was like Marlowe speaking from the dead. Jarman had hardwired himself to Marlowe's outspoken intransigence by suggesting that Clause 28, in its targeting of Aids carriers, 'was pivotal, like Kristallnacht, or the burning of the Reichstag; it fixed itself in the imagination'.

It was imagination and the freedom it offered to live in the visionary present that interested Kit to the exclusion of all else. The gateway to Marlowe was through how others had imagined him, and, in doing so, they partially re-created something of his character. Imagination for Kit shaped the universe like subatomic particles. It was like quantum stuff, an electron able to spin clockwise and anti-clockwise at the same time. Jarman's breakdown of Marlowe's epic into eighty-two short sequences was not only in the interest of converting language into film but of moving time around, so that the linear conception adopted by Elizabethans was denarrated and compressed into Jarman's individually speeded-up, hyperanxious investment in Marlowe as a twentieth-century icon. He had exchanged Marlowe's risk of getting diseased for his own virulent update of the virus, and he kicked it into the usual hum of controversy that his work consistently generated by giving the text a metaphorical transfusion of infected blood.

As a brief distraction from the intensity of his research Kit checked his phone for emails. There was, amongst others, a message from Yukio saying he had decided to stay on a few days in Hove and would not be back until the weekend. Kit felt oddly liberated by the message, as though he was free now to explore not only his theories about Marlowe but his equally weird hunch that Nick, too, was part of a network pointing back to the murder at Deptford in 1593. Nick, for some reason, after Kit had caught sight of him again near Leicester Square, had taken on the role in his imagination of a key player. He conceived of him as implicated in a plot that was fast turning into an obsession. In his mind they had met because of unresolved business, some deficit that had brought them together again in the way that strong attraction is often conditioned by associations from previous lives. Nick had been ill – acutely so – but appeared to all accounts well and virus-free in Kit's brief sighting of him.

Kit had to resist the impulse to stop working and head off now to the West End in search of the elusive Nick. He had to keep reminding himself that he was being paid to research and write the first draft of a screenplay for a film that was likely to prove hot property for gay enthusiasts. Nor was it without significance that Marlowe himself had first taken to disappearing while still a Cambridge undergraduate and that during the first years of his MA course he had begun to leave his college for weeks, then months, at a time. His absences were so notorious that he missed at least half of the academic year in 1584, and Kit assumed his periods of extended leave were sanctioned by his employment as a spy and that the faculty were familiar with his status as an operative. Kit desperately needed a new angle on Marlowe that was both historic and contemporary. The Shakespeare theme, the idea of one great dramatist killing another over a spotty bit of rent, later elevated into the unnamed recipient of the sonnets, seemed daring enough as controversy, but he was still searching to establish, as much for himself as for the film, a chain of Marlowe links to Shakespeare and his killers and flash-forward the action into the present as Jarman had done with his *Edward II*.

At one point Kit conceived the idea of a text message arriving extra-temporally on someone's phone, dated 30 May 1593, and accurately recording the details of the murder as a possible way of re-creating the past in the present. In his script Marlowe's murder would be confessed to now, as though it had just happened, the text and digital images of the murder received by an apprehensive leather-coated Shakespeare hanging out at the sweaty bar in Comptons. It was an idea to be pursued that fitted with his belief that somebody could be apprehended in the present for a crime committed in a previous life. He played with the notion that certain people repeated things on a behavioural loop. If he really were Christopher Marlowe, then he would have to make do with inheriting Marlowe's legacy, dark as the Thames Pool and menacing as a graffiti-slashed foot tunnel under the river. According to Francis Meres, writing of the event in 1598, Marlowe 'was stabbed to death by a bawdy serving man, a rival of his in his lewd love'. Thomas Beard had claimed in the same year that it 'so fell out, that in London streets as he purposed to stab one who he owed a grudge with his dagger, the other party perceiving so avoided the stroke, that catching hold of his wrist, he stabbed his own dagger into his own head, in such sort, that notwithstanding all the means of surgery that could be wrought, he shortly after died thereof'. William Vaughan, writing a few years later, assembled the facts with more forensic accuracy in presenting the reader with a highly plausible scenario: 'It so happened, that at Deptford, a little village about three miles distant from London, as he meant to stab with his knife a man named Ingram, that had invited him there and was then playing at tables . . . he stabbed this Marlowe into the eye, in such sort, that his brains coming out at the dagger's point, he shortly after died.'

Kit fastened on to the lurid death rites, the brains spilling out at the dagger's point. It was Samuel Tanneaum who had objected to this detail, claiming that death would not have been instantaneous from this wound and that the blade would have had to go in horizontally to the depth of six or seven inches to achieve this, something that would have been technically impossible if Marlowe and Ingram Frizer were locked in the position described by Vaughan.

In other accounts, equally apocryphal and distorted by prejudice, Marlowe had not died instantly but, bleeding heavily, had made his way from the house into the nearby churchyard, dying there hours later in a pool of tomato-coloured blood. What seemed most glaringly obvious to Kit was the absence of any record of questions put to any witnesses. The coroner, Sir William Danby, a personal friend of Burghley, was clearly appointed by the crown authorities in this instance to obscure the facts and authorize no convictions. Danby's lack of integrity was reflected in the choice of the jury, which largely comprised small local businessmen, such as Nicholas Draper, Wolston Randall and William Curry, none of them qualified to sift the real facts of the murder and all of them ignorant of Marlowe's poetic genius. The emphasis throughout was placed on Marlowe's infamous celebrity and that his reputation for mixing with the underworld and brawling had inevitably led to him being involved in a knife fight in which he had been killed by someone acting out of self-defence. That Frizer went to gaol for two weeks before being acquitted was simply a formality that was part of espionage.

Of more interest to Kit, as he put on Radiohead's *Hail to The Thief* and listened to its tight sonic collage directed by Thom Yorke's voice, was a strapline of information provided by John Aubrey in his classic biography of eccentrics, *Brief Lives*. Referring to the poet and playwright Ben Jonson, a contemporary of Shakespeare's, and having placed Jonson as living in contemporary seventeenth-century Holland, he laid claim to an extraordinary and neglected fact: 'then he came over into England, and acted and wrote, but both ill, at the Green Curtain, a kind of nursery or obscure playhouse, somewhere in the suburbs (I think towards Shoreditch or Clerkenwell). He killed Mr Marlow [*sic*], the poet, on Bunhill, coming from the Green Curtain playhouse.'

The unapologetic nature of Aubrey's controversial claim seemed never to have been questioned by Marlowe's camp or disputed for its possible historic inaccuracy. Bunhill, EC1 – *A–Z* reference: 4D, page 62 – situated between Clerkenwell Road and City Road, was another precinct possibly stained with Marlowe's contentious blood. According to Aubrey, it was now an inner-city killing, random, opportunistic and individualized, rather than a notorious dockside one involving lugubrious spies and sailors. The unashamed naming of Ben Jonson as Marlowe's killer was the pointer Kit needed to investigate further Shakespeare's part in the murder. He believed that Aubrey may have had scent of it but lacked the swipecard necessary to access Shakespeare's closely guarded double life. Instead, he incriminated the hard-drinking outlaw poet Ben Jonson in order to cover for the scheming and constantly net-working real-estate bandit Will Shakespeare, whose reputation was already established.

Kit's usual method of doing historical research was starting to do quantum tricks with his head. Desire, unease and an innate gravitation towards death as the ultimate sex-rite came up again in him, as though he was being pushed downriver towards an inevitable end clean as an assassin's bullet. It wasn't enough that he published small-press poetry books under the name Kit Marlowe – he felt increasingly now that he had adopted the poet's personality in addition to developing a fix-ation with every recordable aspect of Marlowe's life.

He took Scott Diamond's incoming call and agreed to meet him at his Soho office in an hour's time. Scott wanted to discuss the Marlowe project in depth as well as project his usual atomized rush of ideas constellating round *Funeral Roses*, a gay epic intended to cast Jean Genet as the criminalized saint of the dispossessed. Scott spoke in multichannels, never letting up on his rush. His ideas overtook him in the fast lane and were reconfigured by others but rarely himself. Kit thought of his mind as being like fibre optics.

The advantage was that Scott knew everybody worth knowing in every walk of life, and Kit was anxious to have the tube he had found in the street decoded. With a view to passing it on to his agent in the course of their meeting Kit took the Tube over to Tottenham Court Road, reading on the way about a random gang nuke in Bloomsbury. The fiercely territorial bandits were moving closer in on a radius of operation that had seen them torch a Sainsbury's on Theobalds Road, the closest they had come yet to an organized West End reprisal. Kit knew it was only a matter of time before robosoldiers and robopolice were deployed all over London in a pathologically dehumanized programme aimed at cleaning up the city through fear politics.

He got out of the overheated Tube at Leicester Square, dehydrated, and headed up Romilly Street in the direction of Wardour Street, where Scott had an individually designed loft with convenient access to a roof garden. He'd managed to grow boxes of herbs up there – rosemary, basil and thyme together with summer try-outs such as heliotrope, splashy striped petunias and Bordeaux-red geraniums. That Scott had been a personal friend of Derek Jarman's during his lifetime heightened his always ambiguous mystique in Kit's eyes. Never having known Derek, it was like he met a little bit of him each time he saw Scott. He knew deep down that the Jarman connection was why he put up with Scott's violent mood swings, his abrupt changes of plan, the inability to focus on a project and the multiple schemes he attempted to instruct on a daily basis.

Let in on arrival, Kit went upstairs to the office floor and up another flight to Scott's duplex. Scott was lying on the faux-fur throws on a revolving bed with the colourwash lighting creating a blue mood. Both artificial light and natural daylight had been harnessed and controlled in the penthouse. On winter days yellow cold-cathode lighting added artificial sunrise to the interior, although most of the time Scott opted for indigo.

There was no clutter on the bed, just the laptop and phone that comprised Scott's studio and office. He waved Kit into the living-room as, with gesticulating hands, he short-fused a conversation in which he had rapidly become uninterested to an abrupt, nose-diving end.

'Glad you've come,' he said impassively to Kit, simultaneously switching off his phone. 'There's real interest in the Marlowe project. It could be a big seller. I've meetings arranged with development companies next week. It looks set already to get the green light. Where are you with the screenplay?'

'I'm still researching it,' Kit said, blown away by the wind tunnel of Scott's energies. 'I'm working on a first draft, but it's rough. Naturally my direction keeps changing.'

'Cool,' Scott said. 'We need a selling point. Derek would have scripted it in three days and shot it in a month on a shoe-string budget.' He took up a deliberately angular profile on the bed. He invariably looked to Kit like someone who found it impossible to get comfortable no matter how he arranged and rearranged himself. His ideas cooked too fast to find a physical correspondence.

'My problem is that I'm somehow involved in the plot,' Kit said. 'I'll explain later. I'm also hung up on the murder.'

'What about the murder?' Scott said, resisting the impulse to field a call. 'Who did it? That's the question.'

'Shakespeare,' Kit replied, coming right out with it like a pathologist certain of his microbial analysis. 'He's my suspect at present. There are plenty of other options, and don't laugh at the idea, but I've come to seriously suspect the culprits are still around. Or at least I think so.'

'What substance are you doing?' Tony asked. 'Are you mad? How can they still be alive? Marlowe lived four hundred years ago. You're clearly losing the plot.'

'I know it sounds crazy, but I know I'm on to something

84

profound. People's pasts stay around, and I'm convinced all the main characters involved in the Marlowe murder are living in London today.'

'Including Shakespeare?' Scott quizzed, his drawl thickened by years of smoking.

'Possibly,' Kit said. 'I know you think I've lost it, but I'm on to something. I've got the smell of it. I've started to develop the belief that some people never really die. To me, it's quite conceivable that I am Christopher Marlowe and that I meet up regularly with Shakespeare on the Soho scene.'

'Whatever your beliefs, keep them out of my screenplay,' Scott said, his voice dropping an octave. 'I'm not buying scams.'

'But it's true. I just know that what I'm writing about I owe to personal recollection rather than facts. I know more than I read. I can remember perfectly, for instance, travelling to Brussels in 1587 and finding there a copy of the German history of John Faust, the scholar-magician who struck a bargain with the devil and who inspired the play *Dr Faustus*. I can remember the bookseller drinking Rhenish wine and pulling out this black book for my reference.'

'Are you really serious?' Scott said.

'It was Faust's attempt to fly at Venice that fascinated me – you know, the idea of the human flying, like at the end of J.G. Ballard's novel *The Unlimited Dream Company*, when a village community migrate over the Thames.'

'You've always had too much imagination,' Scott said, attempting to earth the conversation.

'What about the Ben Jonson or Shakespeare angle?'

'That's cool,' Scott said, 'but Jonson's not a big enough name. Go for Shakespeare. What's your evidence?'

'Jealousy over a boy is how I read it. It could be made into a cottage death like Pasolini's, only right in the bowels of the city.'

'Or drag it into *Funeral Roses*,' Scott shot. 'That bitch is dragging its heels. I want Beanie to re-edit the part where

Cocteau comes out of the sea in a gold dress, unzips it and hands it to Genet to wear before fucking him to ensure the chain continues. What do you think of them having sex in a circle marked out by flaming torches?'

'Great,' Kit said, 'only it's Marlowe we need to discuss. What I want to avoid is the faked-death theme. You know the sort of redundant argument that the body of the recently executed John Penry was snatched and substituted for Marlowe's.'

'This is the Marlowe–Shakespeare conspiracy theory, isn't it?'

'It can't be ruled out. There are always conspiracy theories. Look, Marlowe at the time was in deep trouble with the Privy Council. His friend Thomas Kyd was under torture and in the process of cracking. Whether Marlowe was wise to the fact or not, two agents, Baines and Cholmeley, were on his case. Marlowe was known all over Europe to the world of espionage, and if he was to be shipped out of the country, possibly with Walsingham's help, then the only way to get the police off his back was to fake his death.'

'It doesn't hold up,' Scott said dismissively.

'Not totally. If it was a way of saving Marlowe from torture and death it worked. Think of it, Scott. Why were there three people present? If the killing, assuming we are to accept the facts, was done in self-defence, then that provided a killer and two witnesses. All three men were professional liars, pimps, snoops, whatever, and if they'd had to face a jury would have been discredited.'

'Tell me more,' Scott said, clearly interested.

'Well, you've got to remember that two of the witnesses, Ingram Frizer and Nicholas Skeres, were a firm. They were unscrupulous loan sharks already under scrutiny for attempting to defraud someone called Drew Woodleff of Aylesbury, Buckinghamshire, of the little money he had inherited, in return for commodities. The commodities, in this case guns stored at Tower Hill, were impossible for the debtor to convert into cash except by selling them back to the lender or some accomplice of his at a reduced price. They were racketeers like the Krays and every bit as ruthless. Marlowe may have dipped in and out of the firm, but we'll never know.'

'I still don't go for the post-death theory,' Scott said. 'The man was clearly seditious. They wanted his balls for atheism. He drank, same-sexed and got knifed.'

'He was one of us,' Kit laughed. 'He was in addition, it seems, a graffito.'

'What do you mean?' Scott asked, checking his glass of water, as though expecting to find micro-organisms visible in the glass.

'Well, what really accelerated Marlowe's end was something known as the Dutch Church libel. The graffiti tag was painted in red on the walls of the Dutch churchyard on the night of 5 May 1593. The document reeked of Marlovian contempt and was signed "Tamburlaine" – a signature further incriminating Marlowe by alluding to his propagandist sympathies. My research shows from the full transcript of the manuscript made in about 1600 by a Cambridge man, John Mansell, that the title of the poem was "A Libel Fixed upon the French Church Wall in London, Anno 1593".'

'You really have done your research,' Scott said, again scrutinizing his water with the fixed concentration of a snooker player.

'I certainly have,' Kit agreed. 'But it's not research. It all comes from memory. The poem's author was clearly obsessed with Marlowe and could even have been a stalker. He was clearly fixated and adopted his style, even to the point of labelling predatory businessmen 'infected with gold', the anti-capitalist denouncement linked to the idea of disease – plague or today's equivalent, Aids. The notion tied in strongly with Marlowe's notorious anti-Semitic views. Marlowe was a punk, Scott. He was out of town at the time the graffito appeared, so Thomas Kyd was arrested as the fall guy, even though it wasn't his style to be so openly subversive and up front.'

'And who was Thomas Kyd?' Scott asked. 'You'll have to remind me.'

'The author of the hugely popular *A Spanish Tragedy*, Kyd,

like Marlowe, was a drunk but much easier to break. He had an interest in atrocity but not quite in the visceral sense that Marlowe uses it in his play *Massacre at Paris*. Anyhow, the graffito libeller, in wanting to further his own racist message, used the sort of hot-blood imagery associated far more with Marlowe than with Kyd.'

'Your deadline is four weeks for a first draft,' Scott threatened. 'Then I want you back on *Funeral Roses*.'

Kit looked around the cubist-clean space. All the cabinets were illuminated from within and glowed like a single light filament. The place could have been a loft in a moon hotel, only it was Soho. It was extraterrestrial, all the surfaces made from reconstituted glass, the door open on a glass bathroom, a pair of red Manolo Blahniks discarded at the entrance to create a diva flourish, a number of DAR metal chairs with Eiffel Tower metal-rod bases grouped around a blue-glass table supporting an antlered Gaudí of pink gladioli. Kit thought of the place as a neural studio occupied by nothing but Scott's ideas, nerve-sheathed and electrified in their patterns.

'It's a tight schedule,' Kit said. 'As I say, I'm as much living as writing the thing. I feel I've really got to Marlowe. There's a story that Marlowe once coaxed a rat into sitting on his lap in the Spotted Dog and stared it into submission so that he could stroke its saturated fur like a cat.'

'Stick to the facts,' Scott said. 'It's a biopic. We can colour it up later. If you want a glass of lunar water there's a bottle in the fridge. They've got very limited supplies at Planet Organic.'

'There's a favour I need to ask you,' Kit said at a tangent. 'I found this tube last week in Deptford. It's the sort from which biomaterials are printed using modified inkjet printers.'

'What's this got to do with Marlowe?' Scott grilled.

'I'm not sure,' Kit said, 'but, given your network, I thought there might be a chance you'd know someone who is a tissue engineer.'

'It's not my world,' Scott said, 'but I've read about the Aids link. What do you want?'

'Just the data on the label decoded and nothing more.'

'I've got a friend called Vladimir Mironov at the Medical University of South Carolina,' Scott said. 'I can email him the code if you like. But get on with Marlowe. I want to smell him, honey, like a river rat. You're not him, but keep living under his skin. Now get back to work. I've got another appointment.'

Kit made his way back down the glass-and-steel staircase, as though negotiating a re-entry corridor. He felt like he was descending a cortical groove in Scott's brain and, in the process, found himself ejected from a glass hypothalamus into the parallel space–time that was Soho. Outside, the sunny glare of a traffic-corridored Wardour Street seemed too much a part of real time to be included in Scott's virtual ecosystem. He somehow couldn't imagine Scott Diamond doing something as ordinary as flipping over the road to Prêt à Manger to buy a hummus wrap. Out in the street Kit felt the adjustment signal to urban reality come on in his brain. He immersed himself with the pushy, clubby Soho crowds and knew without even having to think about it that he was instinctually headed for Piccadilly Circus in his search for Nick. It was early evening. A glowering orange sun microwaved the ozone barrier. London was dusty, megabyte-loaded, and it seemed to him ready to blow. Kit, for some reason, felt like a member of an apocalyptic post-human species as he joined the crowds along Brewer Street and headed off decisively in the direction of Piccadilly Circus.

6

New digital-recording methods had made the process so much easier since Nick's last studio sessions. He'd decided to go in simply with his home demos, insisting that only Richard and a sound engineer were present. He still hadn't committed himself to signing, but the excitement of tentatively signposting a way forward with label support pushed adrenalin buttons in his system. He felt surprisingly hyper again, as he did before he used to go on stage, the excitement roaring through his veins like a superbike.

Richard was already there when Nick arrived at the tiny underground studio by London Wall. He was wearing a cerise-coloured Liberty's cashmere V-neck, the sort of jumper Nick was able to label instinctively after years of being sexually targeted by soft-sweater forty-something men on Piccadilly. Harrods, Liberty, Jaeger, Burberry, Pringle, agnès b, he knew the exact quality of the designer as well as the price by the wearer.

Nick felt unduly stressed. He'd taken to dyeing his hair again for attitude and was living dangerously on his nerves. He was still frightened of breaching contract with the Grid and of the inevitable payback if he was found violating trust. He needed to sing again and this time become a star, although part of him didn't really care. He had grown accustomed to the financial benefits of belonging to the Grid, but at the same time he longed to be independent. The whole confused cocktail of conflicting emotions came up in him as he nervously sipped the tea he had requested. His voice felt dry and on the blocks, as though a combination of panic and air pollutants threatened to kill his expected performance. Part of him wanted to walk out of the studio now rather than risk the possibility of failure.

Richard, without preliminaries and with a mug of tea in his hand, introduced him to Yong, an engineer in his thirties, long hair caught in a silvering ponytail, a T-shirt sloganed with 'Liquid Nitrogen', his naturally quiet manner fused to a tech-head's programmatic mindset. They weren't going to try for blue-sky writing today; they weren't going to do very much at all except listen to Nick's demos through the monitors. Nick had the feeling there was something going on between Richard and Yong, a subtext of sexual discourse that had him feel edgily excluded. They were alive to each other like the imperceptible temperature changes on heat-sensitive film.

'The computer has the most ferocious and instant power in music now,' Yong said immediately on meeting Nick and as a way of introducing himself and his ideas. 'The computer's the instrument: it edits and manipulates. Basically, I collect sounds from TV, records, 1960s free jazz and improvise a texture. I'd like to put some of your songs to an off-kilter palette of sounds. We can introduce live instruments if you like and phase the fragments or keep to a laptop. Whatever you're happy with as a means of production.'

'I need a sound that's very different from *Fallen Angel*,' Nick said. 'I don't know how to describe it but something more choppy and urban.'

'I'm open to ideas,' Yong said. 'Things that fuck up by spontaneous accident can be as valid as what you intended to do. It's often when things seem to crash that something important happens.'

Nick found himself warming to Yong and to his mixture of innate quiet and keyed-up creative intensity.

'The song that I think has real chart potential is "St Giles' High",' Richard said. 'But it needs a dance anthem on the chorus.'

'I'm more inclined to go for trance,' Yong said. 'Put the vocals over a four-to-the-floor beat and have the drums disappear, while the melodic elements carry on, then kick back in again on the groove. It's just an idea. We could also mix up zydeco with contemporary urban beats and make it into an accordion-driven dance tune.'

'Sounds great to me,' Nick said, excited by the available menu. 'Before, I just did it at home on a laptop and brought in musicians for live dates.'

'I'll set up a mike if you want to sing,' Yong said. 'Just concentrate on warming up your voice for a while.'

Nick listened apprehensively to his voice in the monitors. His try-out of 'St Giles' High' surprised him with its vocal register, even though he busied himself with self-critically analysing the phrasing and listening for obvious edits. He was struck immediately by how much his voice had improved. The lover in the song was ambiguous – it could be a woman or a man – and that didn't matter. Those already in the know would, of course, reference First Out as a same-sex meeting point, but the song benefited, to his mind, from the ambivalent lyrics. He liked the fact that the lyrics were essentially genderless – you never heard an allusion to he or she – and that it wasn't made up of scrambled *non sequiturs* like so much of today's pop. His minimal keyboard figures allowed the voice to be showcased up front so that it was the dynamic filling the studio – its inflections sounding filmic, despite their primitive home origins. The associations in the song inevitably brought Kit back, and the experience hurt. He'd walked clean out on him and his life, and the song was a part of the remains.

'Great,' Richard enthused. 'The hook needs building on, and it requires a dance mix. We can morph it around. I like it stripped down and edgy, like you've got it.'

'Want to hear one more through the monitors?' Yong asked. 'What about "Veuve Clicquot"? Are you ready?'

'OK,' Nick said. 'This one's more upbeat. I think of it as my orange song.'

Hearing the song again Nick was able to stand up to it without feeling unduly self-conscious. It was his rebirth song, catchy pop about getting high but not wasted after a visit to Heaven. He'd gone out clubbing one weekend to celebrate being virus-free and drunk nothing but champagne until his head was expansively spacey. Leaving the club and coming outside at 3 a.m., he'd looked up to see a big orange moon over Charing Cross Station, and the memory of it had triggered the song.

'Wacky,' Richard said after the fade-out. 'It's as breezy as Morrissey in the eighties, when he had something to sing about. Pure pop.'

'It's textbook sixties pop,' Yong enthused. 'I wish people still created songs with a running time of two minutes fifty-eight. Sixties guys will always tell you that music soaked into them like suntan and that they remember their youth by the pop songs they heard on the beach.'

'I'm seventies,' Richard said. 'But even then music was a way of life. It was the big event. It still made something happen in a social context.'

By comparison, and because he was so much younger, Nick felt liberated by having so little music history. He'd compensated by listening to a retro palette and by doing his own thing. He put it down to being gay that he beamed in on torch music, with its emphasis on personal tragedy in the singer's life and its overblown coloratura. Garland and Bassey were in his genes as archetypes, but so, too, were Bolan and Morrissey, Björk and Radiohead, Tricky and Moby. Pop, he had discovered, was a sound collage in which every strain of music was assembled and reassembled to reflect the studio integration of its various sources.

The three of them took a break and chilled with cans that Yong lifted from the in-studio fridge. Nick was still apprehensive about doing a number cold, but as Yong had fixed up the backing track to 'Halloween Party' he decided to give it a try. He walked slowly over to the mike and did a preliminary sound-check. The playback in the monitors sounded surprisingly good to his ear – the voice passably controlled and emotionally charged – despite his misgivings. Something had connected, and he felt confident again. He wanted to show them that his talent was up for it, even if he still equivocated over taking up their offer. At twenty-six he had a few years ahead of him in which to peak before going on ice. 'Halloween Party' was pop with depth and a song that brought out the compelling choke in his voice at sadness. He wasn't a song stylist in terms of phrasing, but he worked instinctually with his feelings, having them inject raw emotion. He gave it his best over the scratchy trip-hop rhythm he'd programmed into his laptop. The cathartic release that came from singing was his way of being totally himself; it was unlike any other experience he knew. He was wrung out by it, and his whole body shook from giving so much in an untutored way.

'Fantastic,' Yong said. 'It's really powerful, man. You sound like you're possessed. Let's try another take.'

Nick returned to the song, trying less hard this time to dramatize emotion and inflecting it with a more understated phrasing. He liked going down a notch in intensity and listening back to compare. Both takes had their individual merits, and Richard stuck with the first, Yong the second.

Making it a last for today, Nick did a take on another new song, 'Dress Rehearsal', a gay-themed number with drag-strip instrumentals that gave it a hint of Weimar cabaret. He sang it as though he was performing in a 1930s Berlin nightclub, leaning against the piano, his face caked and a red feather boa draped across his shoulders. If the song hinted at Brecht as an influence, then it was iconoclastic in a new sort of way, the gender-bending taking place in a bar built into a nuclear bunker. He tried to give his take a touch of smudged lipstick, leather and topically depleted uranium. He imagined himself singing it in a bunker as the lights went out for good.

'Great stuff,' Richard said. 'I'll book the studio proper in a couple of weeks so we can lay the songs down.'

'I still need to think about it more,' Nick said, suddenly anxious to get away and abruptly declining Richard's offer of a lift.

'If you feel like dinner one night I'll book the Ivy,' Richard said. 'We can talk about possibilities of your signing over some good food.'

Nick made a quick exit from the studio and was relieved to be off by himself. He needed to be alone after singing, and Richard would have pushed his boundaries. It had rained while he'd been in the studio, and coming back outside from a compressed space was always like a re-entry into real time. He walked aimlessly in the direction of the City, observing the green-mirror wadding of corporate towers spectacularly inter-facing each other's glass fascias, a passing jet mirrored in a façade like a hallucinated 9/11 flashback.

Nick headed vaguely towards Moorgate Tube station, his paranoia about the Grid leaving him edgy and convinced he was being followed. In his head he imagined a film-noir gun-burst from a passing car aimed at him and his body crumpling on impact.

Dreading the Underground journey he got on the Tube, thinking obsessively for some reason about Robert and Ingram, the one's connection with the diamond trade and the other's with the dodgier aspects of real estate and selling to Box Hill aristos. He was coming to feel that he really didn't like either of them and that they were friends forced on him by circumstance rather than through choice. Their collusion smacked of corruption. Since meeting the two at Starbucks he had lost all belief in their integrity. He had the feeling that Ingram was dealing and that Robert was an extortionist. If they were an item, then very clearly they were bad news.

Nick remained busy with his thoughts as the train main-lined down its central artery. He hadn't given much attention to the two Japanese girls sitting opposite in low-slung Miss Sixty hipsters, exposing their midriffs and busy with headsets. But, rather more significantly, someone he took to be gay (arts exec? forty to forty-six? wiry, grizzled hair; single, by the slightly hunted expression; working at home for the afternoon? thirty-inch waist in Levis, shaving nick under the left jawbone, Paul Smith floral shirt; nose job; passive?

Pisces?) was running his eyes over him from the other side of the carriage. The man made only a slight concession in turning away for a moment after their eyes briefly met before quickly resuming his persistent attempts to make and hold eye contact.

Nick, who hadn't let himself be picked up for a long time, at least not in this way and for the obvious purposes of a sexual encounter, felt the old thrill of random sex flash up as a possibility. He liked the man's slim, slightly angular body and foggy-grey eyes. Nick felt reassuringly good in himself for having returned to singing with such emotional oomph. He thought about taking his high that bit further and remembered picking up on the Tube in the past, converting a look into spontaneous provocation, getting off at the same stop as the interested stranger, conferring with him on the crowded platform before going off with the man into the big city. He'd had sex like that on impulse in West End hotels, apartments that resembled movie sets or in the backs of buildings, often for the thrill of proving to himself that he could take a straight man away from a woman by his desirability.

He hoped secretly the man signalling to him was straight. He got more of a kick out of it if they were, knowing very well that a straight man doing gay was gay all along. He looked over this time directly into the man's eyes. Now that Nick had made contact they shared a tentative chemistry. But there was more to it than that. Nick felt sure he knew this man from somewhere deep in his past. It seemed crazy to him, but someone called Lord Strange – or, more familiarly, Ferdinando Stanley, fifth Earl of Derby – came to mind, for no other reason than that he was someone who had emerged lately in his regressions, and the two men bore slight hints of facial similarities. By the time they reached Euston, and from the stranger's fixated expression, he was certain the man would exit with him at Tottenham Court Road. He could feel the old excitement of pulling a stranger out of the crowd road-mapping his groin. All of his old sense of peaking on risk had suddenly returned. He didn't know what the man wanted, only that they shared an opportunist attraction under the city and had set up a communications system between themselves. A lot more people had got on at Euston, and Nick secretly enjoyed the fact that they knew nothing of the coding he had established with the stranger. A Japanese girl showing the red T-bar of her G-string above the waistline of her low-slung Lees, stood between them, mobile in hand like a snouty gun, but he wasn't worried. They were wired now; their rapport existed like a drug. Nick took a deep breath at Warren Street as the central aisle filled in to suffocation. He knew the man wouldn't exit until he did, so losing eye contact made no real difference. The train accelerated towards Goodge Street, a short jolting rush under Tottenham Court Road, the deceleration sounding like jet whine. Nick prepared to get out at the next stop. Either the stranger followed or he didn't. It was a game he had played so often and hadn't thought to again, only this time he wasn't doing it for money.

Nick stood up early so that the man had advance warning of his intentions. As the Japanese girl standing between them backed into his seat he was able briefly to meet the man's eyes again and re-establish a signal.

When Nick forced his way out on to the asphyxiatingly crowded platform at Tottenham Court Road, the man was five or six deep behind him, wading to catch up. The station was like a sauna. He waited for him at the entrance to the escalator and he was smaller than Nick had imagined, probably only five foot six, wirily constructed, and he had clearly done this before, chestnut-leather shoulder-bag serving as a portable office, his iPod connected to Bang and Olufsen earphones. He was wearing candy-pink sneakers and an expensive scent that Nick recognized as Creed's Vetiver. In a blinding flashback Nick remembered that he had experienced the same sensation on first meeting Ferdinando Stanley and that he, too, had projected a false impression of height. Nick had learnt as rent that dodginess of character was often translated into a similar faculty of physical deception. Something about the man's inherent self-confidence as he came up parallel on the stairs told him that he had a partner and was most probably married. His studied appearance, the casual-but-moneyed signature of his clothes, the self-regarding cool in going for a trick, all seemed to stem from someone who had emotional back up and wealth. Somewhere in this man's life Nick scented money as a secret index coded into the man's genes. It could have been earned, but it was more likely inherited. He had known men like this before. The scent of money clung to them like tobacco.

They hardly spoke on the escalator going up; rather it was taken for granted that they were together. When Nick met the man's eyes his pupils were messaging sex. Nick had gone off once with a pop singer to a flat in Brewer Street in similarly random circumstances, who had ended up throwing knives at him after the act. He wasn't totally sure about this man and the unnerving calm he projected.

When they emerged through the exit turnstiles into the jostling mezzanine the man stayed at his shoulder as Nick vectored a way towards the graffiti-slashed underpass with its lexicon of Anglo-Japanese icons spray-painted across the fissured concrete walls.

'I'm Ferdinando,' the man said casually after a time, 'but you can call me Ray. I suppose you know what I want?'

'Sex,' Nick said outright, as though putting a bullet through Ray's testosterone receptors.

'I've got a workspace in Soho,' Ray said. 'We can go there if you like. It's quite safe. How much do you charge?'

'I'll decide on the way,' Nick answered, feeling instantly unnerved and unwilling to commit. 'Do you do this often?'

'Not really,' Ray said as a hesitant disclaimer, clearly thrown by Nick's incisive questioning.

'My advice is don't,' Nick said as they took the steps up to the street with its huddle of resident methadone junkies grouped round the entrance. 'If you value your health, stay away from people selling sex.' Nick, from experience, wanted to take control of the situation right from the start rather than be manipulatively tooled by a man who was probably indiscriminately sex-addicted. Ray's cool, as if he lived on remote, reminded him of types he had met at the Dilly, whose clinical detachment from him as a person was repeated in Ray's almost sociopathic chill.

Nick let Ray map out the way to his place. It gave him time to access Ray's mindset better and to develop a general feel of the stranger. The man took the back way into Soho, through Manette Street by the side of Foyles bookshop, where the vandalized body of a white stretch limo with black shatterproof glass was parked outside the Chapel of St Barnabas. The car's convex roof had been repeatedly tracked by a carjack and sprayed with lurid lime-green graffiti post-mortems. Nick read it as an endemic sign of the times, a gestural outrage on the part of the dispossessed against the fat cats of outmoded capitalism.

Nick, with his fine-tuned intuitive radar, noted Ray's familiarity with the place. He seemed to have Soho mapped like a car pilot. He wondered, as he walked parallel with him, about going through with it. He didn't need the money, and, what's more, he didn't in their short acquaintance like the man. He had proved to himself that he could still pull somebody out of the crowd, and that was enough. Ray didn't speak or make eye contact in the street. Instead, he crossed over Greek Street authoritatively and headed for the narrow, urine-stained alley called Bateman's Buildings. Nick followed cautiously, smelling money and evident duplicity. He'd noticed the wedding ring from the start, a thin gold band worn into the epidermis of the man's finger like tissue.

In the end curiosity got the better of him. He wanted to know and see for himself how Ray lived out his dual existence. His life as rent had given him intuitive infrared sensors for going in on someone. Ray wasn't physically violent; he sensed that. His compulsion was probably with numbers and keeping a tally of his anonymous sexual conquests.

Ray adeptly fingerprinted entry to an aircraft-blue security door in a residential building. Once inside, Nick followed him into the lift, and they went up to the third floor. They came out next to the stairwell, each floor comprising a single office space. Ray, it seemed, had no direct neighbours, and it clearly fitted fine with his lifestyle. Nick followed him after opening the door to the flat into a neutral space occupied principally by light. The walls had been painted eau-de-Nil, and there was a turquoise 1960s chair arranged as a kitschy central exhibit, a Mac Cube on an aluminium work table and not much else. The door to the adjoining bedroom was partially open on what looked to be a green-and-white striped rug, and the place had the unlived-in feel of being a showcase for opportunistic sex. Nick suspected from Ray's evident sleaziness that the Mac was loaded with porn, his eye noting the Canon Digital Ixus 400 camera sitting next to the computer as the ready four-megapixel accomplice to zeroing in on mortuary-cold porno meat, if that was Ray's fetish.

'Is this your place or a friend's?' Nick asked, unnerved by the flat's clinical identity-free interior.

'It's mine,' Ray said. 'I use it to chill when I'm in town. I can be alone here with the camera.'

Nick felt brutally overexposed in the impersonal surroundings. Even words had the impression of coming out self-conscious in this atmosphere and of hanging around on delay. He wondered if all the words spoken here became part of a collective, a semantic configuration stored in the light, the walls and the studio's memory.

'I find it spooky,' Nick risked saying, intending to turn negative on the man's thesis. 'It's as though nobody lives here.'

'It's central and convenient,' Ray replied. 'It serves a purpose when I'm here.'

'I'm not probing, but you're married aren't you?' Nick angled.

'So what if I am? It's none of your business,' Ray said defensively, visibly disconcerted by Nick's questioning. 'I prefer men, if you want to know. What's it got to do with you?'

'I think I know your wife,' Nick sneered defiantly. 'I met her at your country stack in Knowsley once, a very long time ago.'

'Don't try and put the creepers on me,' Ray said, deliberately dropping his refined accent and hinting at a ruthlessness of character existing as a subtext to his controlled surface veneer. 'It won't work.'

'What are you looking for?' Nick asked outright, reconnecting with the rent boy formula he had grown conditioned to, quite sure in his mind that he wasn't going to have sex with the man. His excitement at the casual encounter had peaked back on the Underground like a drug rush and subsequently left him feeling flat. He had no interest in Ray as a person or in going through the obligatory motions of a blow-job to the accompaniment of a porn movie.

'I want to take some photos of you first,' Ray said, 'before I fuck you.'

'I'm not into either,' Nick said, through waves of suppressed hostility. 'How do I know what you'll do with the photos?'

'I can upload the images to the PC,' Ray said, 'so that you can have the option of viewing them and asking for deletions.'

'Not my scene,' Nick replied. 'I don't get off on digital meat. If you get done at some stage I don't want to be on your hard drive.'

'What makes you think that will happen?' Ray said, clearly nervous. 'Are you undercover?'

'No,' Nick replied. 'I don't know anything about you, but you're certainly not going to photograph me or fuck me.'

The situation booted up tense. Nick could smell the man's scent coming on like an alien strain in an otherwise odourless zone. Ray's smile lines had disappeared. He looked like he wasn't used to rejection. Nick sensed that if the man's habit was porn then he needed cold hits. The PC, he didn't doubt, was loaded with high-resolution images, a pathological software library of rent-boy genitalia morphed to accommodate Ray's particular index of fetishes.

'Why'd you come here then?' Ray asked provocatively. 'Nobody forced you.'

'That's not the point,' Nick argued. 'I object to having to fit your menu. Aren't gay people allowed to have some choice, some discernment?'

'Not if they're rent,' Ray said dispassionately, his eyes looking flat like computer icons.

'I don't see any point in continuing with this,' Nick said, looking for a way out. 'OK, it was a case of mixed messages. Let's leave it at that.'

'But you're the missing link,' Ray said enigmatically.

'What do you mean? What missing link? I don't get it.'

'In the Marlowe plot,' Ray replied self-referentially. 'You're needed in the chain to complete the pattern.'

'I don't know what you're into,' Nick said, 'and I don't want to. I'm going, right.' He stood facing the man with the light between them driving in at the speed of thought.

'You're number 1063 in my scheme of things. Have you forgotten your old intelligence code? You were agent 1063 to Lord Burghley and employed at one time to track Christopher Marlowe, the playwright, who had offended the government. Don't tell me you've forgotten. Just let me take a few photos.'

'The answer's no,' Nick said emphatically, shaken by the man's retrieval of an espionage number that suddenly rang so true he wondered how he could ever have forgotten it. Nick wanted to be out of the flat before his resentment turned to anger. He could see Ray's size coming up big in his pants, but it was the silence that unnerved him. Even though they were in the middle of Soho's media network, the soundproofing in the flat created the effect of being inside a web page. Nick suddenly had the mad idea that he was trapped inside Ray's consciousness and not his own. It wasn't his brain map with thirty billion neurones and a million billion connections that he was in, it was Ray's branching patterns of axons and dendrites that he had inexplicably entered.

Nick knew he had to continue to establish the upper hand.

The possibilities of harming Ray were a mental option that he wasn't going to entertain unless the man turned violent.

'Let me out of here right now,' Nick demanded. 'If you keep me any longer it's kidnap.' He beamed his menacing signal right into Ray's eyes and watched it impact.

Nick didn't hesitate. He turned his back on Ray and headed for the door. He could hear his heart change rhythm and shift up on adrenalin as he walked authoritatively out of the room. He knew he was already there. He was that calm. The door was on a heavy Yale lock, and when he got it open and stepped outside he sensed immediately that he was safe. He took the fire stairs at a run, hit them two at a time and knew he wouldn't be followed. Each floor was an L-shape, a sealed workplace behind anonymous security doors. He arrowed down the stairs' DNA helix-shaped spiral and out through the blue-painted fire door to the alley that was Bateman's Buildings. Ray's image was still inside his head like a virtual psycho. In his imagination Nick could see the emotionally shut-down eyes and the unlined face like masking tape staring at him like a humanoid. He didn't attempt to run for fear of drawing attention to himself. Instead he walked fast down the alley and out into Soho Square. Michael Jackson's convoy of ostentatiously sleek black limos was negotiating the square, retractable pepper-spray dispensers and laser-guided machine-guns ready in their state-of-the-art proficiency. He watched them fin off like a sign of the times, a displaced Hollywood cortège conveying a cos-metically restructured fallen star round and round on the dystopian London circuit in search of a contract. Jackson's last hit record, 'Blood on the Dance Floor', had grown into a reality as Nick conceived it, only the self-destructing star was the victim of a deliberately managed media vendetta aimed at demolishing his credibility as a person and hypnotically con-tagious performer.

Nick was aware that he had to be at a hypnotherapy session at the Grid in less than an hour. As a way of dissolving the memory of the unpleasant encounter he went and lost himself listening to loud music in Comptons. He wanted to shut every-thing out but the music and to forget his renascent identity as Nicholas Skeres, undercover agent, in the sweaty leather crowd with their sex-addicted libidos coming on like summer heat in a space geared to reckless abandon and the pursuit of sex as the ultimate confrontation with death.

7

Kit simmered with temporary feelings of euphoria in his loft. The sex he'd had with Yukio after his return – who liked to dress for it as a samurai – had left him on an up. Yukio, whose hero was the writer Yukio Mishima, became totally uninhibited during sex, and if his prototype had fed on a menu of homosexuality, Yomeigaku and emperor worship, then Yukio had adapted this erotic cocktail to his own individual needs.

Standing at the window, the full-on London sun with its light-polluted glow zapped Kit with its irritant glare from the direction of Shepherd's Bush. The UV index was right up, according to the news, and he did all he could to avoid direct skin contact with the light. His mind was still preoccupied with sex as he looked out at a sky like a nuclear lab. When he fucked Yukio it was partly in the belief that he had adopted Marlowe's character and that his spermatozoa had made tissue contact in the past with the likes of Shakespeare, Anthony Bacon, Francis Walsingham, Lord Strange and any amount of Elizabethan sailors in the riverside docks. Marlowe, he was aware, had contracted countless STDs, whereas in the interests of practising safe sex Kit used the protective of micro-thin Japanese condoms, their teats shaped like the nose cone of a Boeing.

Kit was having problems in meeting his deadline. As his sense of being Marlowe deepened so he found it increasingly hard to accept the historic facts presented through biographies of his subject. Marlowe, he knew without any historical back-up, had fucked Thomas Watson, his accomplice in killing William Bradley in Hog Lane. Marlowe's wrist had been badly slashed in the fight, and Watson, driven to the edge of a ditch at the northern end of the lane, had desperately forced Bradley back and ripped him open. Both Marlowe and Bradley were adept at street fighting and used a technique that included tripping, kicking and shoulder-barging, as well as the various components of fencing, integrated into their offensive. He saw himself engaged in student protests at Cambridge, as one of a gang who would go into town and fire guns in the street, wreck themselves on excessive drinking, smoke black tobacco in the pubs and fire up controversial ideas pulled from Giordano Bruno's *The Heroic Frenzies*. Bruno, the famous Italian occultist and magician with whom Marlowe had developed a fascination as a student, had spent two years propagandizing in Britain and, as a self-styled 'mad priest of the sun', had aspired to mystical knowledge derived from solar worship.

But Marlowe's Cambridge friends – less interested than him in the likes of Bruno – kept horses and greyhounds, had the smell of landed money and were almost exclusively interested in women. He remembered the afternoon they had had a girl with them in town, who had demonstrably wanted group sex. Fascination, false bravado and the inability to back out had brought him to a crisis in the hired room where his young friends had gorged themselves on the elastically compliant girl. To save himself embarrassment he had exaggerated his drunkenness and gone out on the pretence of fetching another bottle, drinking himself into a state of hallucinated coma in a ditch near a public house rather than risk failure in front of his friends.

Day by day Kit's personality felt increasingly invaded by Marlowe, as though the Elizabethan playwright and he were in fact the same person. The possibility of doing the film as reality television, even if it meant the prospect of living out the murder all over again on an inexorable time loop, had come to be a new and persistent obsession. He couldn't rid himself of the idea that Nick was somehow implicated with his past in a way that was still unresolved. It was only a feeling, but it was one that persisted. Nick had something on him he didn't like and which he felt was reciprocated by his own sense of suspicion that his character was slightly out. He knew that most rent boys were thieves, and in his regression the name Nicholas Skeres, as someone vital to his past, had come up along with the likes of Staring Robyn and Welsh Dick as men who were on the London police records as housebreakers and fences expert at the disposal of stolen goods.

He reflected on the notion cold, trying as he did to separate the possibilities of fantasy from fact. No matter how incongruous the union seemed, he was convinced that he and the playwright Christopher Marlowe were the same person, and that he carried deep inside himself the psychic scar of Marlowe's death, the residuals still programmed in his memory. The occasional intense pain in one of his eyes was indicative of this. At times his visual field turned into fractal components before it righted, the blinding intensity of the experience leaving him feeling like a pilot in a climb-out towards the sun. He reached for the usual packet of Nurofen to disperse the pain and popped three capsules with water in an attempt to knock it on the head.

After working for a time on his screenplay Kit checked his messages. Amongst the proliferating rafts of spam and the thirty-four new messages was one that demanded attention, even though he suspected it was nothing more than a timesink. The message was from 'raybans' and he clicked to open. What he met with wasn't the anticipated spam with a virus attached but a personal communication written with what seemed like forensic detachment. Kit quickly scanned the contents, feeling immediately disquieted by what he read.

Dear Kit
    We're due to meet. We share a body in common. Nick. Nick who? Ingram told me about you. Ingram who? He got it from Robert. Robert who? We're all linked. Sex is at Ray's. Ray who? You'd better find out? Who?

Despite his impulse to delete the message Kit reread the contents. The threatening assumption 'we're due to meet' and the reference to sharing Nick's body – there could only be one Nick – put him on alert. It didn't take him any time at all to figure out that Ingram and Robert were allusions to Ingram Frizer and Robert Poley and that Nick must be Nicholas Skeres – the three criminal snoops who were all witnesses to the Deptford murder.

Kit assumed that Ray had got his personal email details from the habit he had of supplying it on the title page of his books. Most of the messages he'd received about his books had been in relation to the weird grab of the work itself and the often startling individual language he used to hype the fast-track method in which he wrote. On the contrary, Ray's message had nothing to do with his poetry and read like a rogue stab at a part of his sanity he was starting to question.

His inbox was additionally loaded with prompters from Scott Diamond, who fired off one- or two-liners each time a relevant thought was generated by his naturally manic sensibility. The usual scrambled stabs at incomplete sentences and fragmented ideas left in disconnect comprised the majority of Scott's messages, all of which underlined the need to deliver urgently. Kit knew he wasn't going to be given any latitude with this one; the agreed deadline was being repeated like a mantra.

Still unnerved by Ray's message, Kit went back to road-mapping ideas for the screenplay. That both Marlowe and Shakespeare had competed for the patronage of Henry Wriothesley, Earl of Southampton, whose name survived in London's traffic-congested Southampton Row in Holborn, provided Kit with still another possibility, that of creating a love triangle or arguing that Shakespeare's sonnets 78–86 were addressed to Marlowe rather than Southampton. History came alive only if it was reinvented, its building blocks reconfigured, its stories injected with testosterone. There were numerous other points he had discovered in common between Marlowe and Shakespeare. Not only were they both writing for Lord Strange's company in the early 1590s but there is evidence of their collaboration in parts of the *Henry VI* trilogy, performed at the Rose Theatre in 1592. And Shakespeare was most certainly in London during the early summer of 1593 when Marlowe was killed, as his poem 'Venus and Adonis', registered at the end of April, was then being printed at Richard Field's shop in Blackfriars. Kit's personal belief was that the past was largely a media rewrite that factored events according to the ideological spin of the times. It was rooted in power, corruption and lies. It was a distorted fiction, invariably aimed at vindicating the oppressor. Sir Francis Walsingham's seventeenth-century hierarchy was re-created in the likes of Stalin, Hitler, Milosevic and Blair – discredited autocrats vacuum-sealed from reality at exhaustive cost by State security. That both Marlowe and Shakespeare were undoubtedly gay to his mind meant that whole chunks of their civil rights had disappeared as individuals and been rewritten to fit with a predominantly straight view of history. It was something that Kit had discovered in researching the lives of such gay icons as Wilde, Genet and Cocteau and how in each of their cases biographically invented lives had often been substituted for truth. The right to be gay was conceded as the differentiator in the work, the possible genetic aberration allowing for its existence, but the person's differing emotions were airbrushed, their private lives invariably consigned to a rapport with the deviant and criminal. Marlowe's personal needs for understanding and tolerance as a gay man in the context of his times had rarely been discussed, and so his behaviour was typically seen as aberrant and socially transgressive.

Kit wanted to do something to redress the issue and to over-turn it like a dictator's torched limo. Ray's message continued to needle him as he attempted to turn over the whole question of truth and the lack of it. To accompany his thoughts he put on REM's *Reveal*, the band's summery sound of blue-skyline pop acting as a temporary palliative to his growing sense of unease.

It occurred to him that if he rewrote history and had

Marlowe as the recipient of Shakespeare's sonnets – and undoubtedly Shakespeare's head at the time of writing them was full of his streetwise rival – then he also had a credible new angle on the conspiracy theory. Shakespeare's attempts to keep the object of his love permanently young, through supremely lyrical and often profoundly elegiac poetic expression, would carry more purchase if it were directed at Marlowe rather than at ambiguous claimants to be recipients of the dedication, such as Southampton. What Shakespeare had avoided in the sonnets directed to a youth, and precisely because he was addressing a man, were the precise details that would have personalized this individual and lifted him out of the abstract. There were no descriptions given of the shape of the face, the colour of the hair and eyes, the skin tone, the body weight, shape of the fingers, choice of clothes, shoe style, smile lines, lip contours, voice inflection; nothing was approved or individualized about his looks. The lover remained undifferentiated from the figure of poetic ideal. He could have been any bright young thing who had captured the poet's attention – a pretty boy in an age that cultivated but disapproved of same-sex relations.

With Ray's message still uppermost in his mind, he decided to email him on the spot with a view to meeting and to use a phrasing that was equally provocative in the ambivalence it implied.

Dear Ray

Ray who? Of course it's time we met. You name the place and time. Where? Who will you bring? Who? Nick who? Robert who? Ingram who? I'm who to you? Who are you?

Kit baby who?

He clicked on 'send' and returned to his thesis. That Shakespeare was the dark outrider in Marlowe's life was to his mind a given, and that the two men had met in back rooms and in corridors under the city he didn't doubt. Marlowe's real killer may have been let go under the usual methods of MI5 blanking, but was killing Marlowe and bonding himself to him through blood what Shakespeare had meant in the dedication of his sonnets by 'All. Happiness. And. That. Eternity. Promised.'? Was that really what he meant? Kit questioned.

> For such a time do I now fortify
> Against confounding age's cruel knife
> That he shall never cut from memory
> My love's sweet beauty, through my lover's knife.

There was no evidence of Shakespeare having had any proficiency with a knife and no crimes listed against him in the way of Marlowe's criminal record as a repeat offender, but there was every possibility to Kit's mind that Shakespeare had received a detailed account of the knifing within hours of the event or even within minutes if he was a party to the murder at Southampton's instigation.

Kit ignored his intrusive ringtone. He couldn't face Scott's verbal pressure at present or the way you could cook an omelette on the heat of his rayed-out ideas. Instead he wanted to pursue the theory, no matter how crazy, that if Ray in his association with Nick, Robert and Ingram was a part of the fugitive quango responsible for Marlowe's death then his identity fitted with the part played by Lord Strange in Marlowe's historic scheme of things. Strange, after all, had been a member of the School of Night as well as a scientist and free-thinking intellectual in sympathy with Marlowe's radically deconstructionist views on religion and politics. That Marlowe was a follower of Walter Ralegh's professed atheism, even if not, as far as Kit knew, a member of the federation of occultists who met at Ralegh's house under the moniker of the School of Night, was sufficient to smear both men and lead to their being scrutinized by Walsingham's and Burghley's agents. Lord Strange – a.k.a. Ferdinando Stanley – was still another clandestine figure that Marlowe and Shakespeare had in common and whose company of players regularly toured the country.

According to Kit's research some of Shakespeare's early works, including *Titus Andronicus* and the *Henry VI* trilogy, were first performed under Strange's theatrical patronage. Strange's double life, the man behind the man, conformed to the duality at the core of Elizabethan politics and sexuality. In the movie Kit would have Strange cross-dress and would feature him at the great house at Knowsley, gorgeous in drag on the dance floor, assiduously correct when the occasion demanded, despite the generically arched eyebrow and the inflected lisp in the speaking voice. He would present him sunning himself indolently in a gold-sequinned dress on the manor steps, his domestic life one of pampered excess, like the sluttish Mick Jagger in the role of sybaritic rock star in *Performance*. And, in a very real way, he remembered it as having been exactly like that with Strange. The imperious Ralegh, he seemed to recall, had come and gone at these occasions; so, too, the likes of John Florio, who attended soirées in the company of such poets as Sir Philip Sydney and Fulke Greville and the radically free-thinking scientist Thomas Hariot, all of them kept under the scrutiny of watchful agents such as himself.

He had nothing of substance on Ray as yet but his message. Was Ray the matrix, he questioned, reconfiguring a plot in which he, Kit, was a pivotal player? All sorts of possibilities flashed up in his mind, as he refreshed his memory and research tools on Lord Strange, who was, it seemed, descended from syphilitic blood on both sides. His father's great-uncle was Henry VII, and his mother was the daughter of Henry VIII's niece Eleanor Brandon. His dubious celebrity placed him in the grid of a Catholic figurehead, with a direct, if remote, claim to the throne. He was another classic example of a devious snoop being monitored by other snoops, the two conflicting forces dissolving seamlessly like the modality of consciousness in which there is no differentiation between subject and object.

Lord Strange, or Ray as he suspected him to be in his current identity, was the most enigmatic of entrepreneurs. When he thought of him Kit, for some reason, repeatedly retrieved the image of late-summer sunlight sitting on tobacco plants. The scent of a sixteenth-century garden in Cheshire plotted with roses, sweet william and nicotia came instantly to mind. The scent remained with him, heavy in its associations of indolent summer days spent sitting writing under giant oaks, while next door someone was turning up the volume of a Radiohead album. He recognized the stand-out track, 'We Suck Young Blood', with its low handclaps and turbulent pianos – an off-melody stab at postmodern pop that he admired for its textural abstraction and oblique referencing of a world headed towards as catastrophically violent an end as its musical dissonance.

From his research menu Kit had come to link Lord Strange's name with intelligence like Bruno, Florio, Ralegh, Thomas Hariot, Henry Percy and, of course, Marlowe himself, in that his interests were decidedly leftfield. All of these men had suffered inwardly and politically for their beliefs: Strange had died a slow and agonizing death from poisoning a year after Marlowe, in April 1594; Bruno's astronomical beliefs had led to him being torched; Hariot was unable to publish his scientific writings in his lifetime; and Henry Percy, the Wizard Earl, was imprisoned in 1606 over his alleged involvement in the Gunpowder Plot and was to remain caged in the Tower, without appeal, for sixteen years. Walsingham's inscrutably efficient police had used spin to effectively subvert the judiciary. His hired gofers had consistently intimidated those who showed the least subversion in their ideas, attempting, under threat of torture, to bleach out their philosophical beliefs – or, in some cases, their aberrant sexuality. Walter Ralegh – at one time the favourite of the queen – whose occult cell, the School of Night, was acclaimed by Marlowe, had his head cut off in 1618 after a lifetime spent fomenting controversy by his outspoken political views.

The headache Kit felt coming on was garaged in the right hemisphere of his brain. He hoped the disturbing light show accompanying it wasn't the prelude to a migraine attack with its acute visual disturbance. Within minutes Ray had responded with proposed details for a meeting:

7.30 Bateman's Buildings. 7a. No name on the door. Who? Sex included. With who? Nick? Robert? Ingram? Ray? Ray who?

Kit felt as if someone he didn't really want to know or have any associations with had succeeded in invading his neural hardware. The scary prospect of meeting Ray felt in its disturbed undertones like the anxious wait for a pathologist's blood profile to come back from the lab. Kit knew Bateman's Buildings only too well and its location right in the heart of Soho. An alley of floors recently converted into prime office space that ran between Soho Square and Bateman Street, it was old Soho made over by money. It was right in the core village where floors were sold for seven hundred thousand. He was aware also of the possible dangers implied by getting involved with Ray and that the suggested meeting could be a trick, a dodgy hoax designed to set him up.

Deep down, though, Kit didn't really care. He had always got fired up by the prospects of danger, and any lead that appeared to give him access to Nick and the two friends he was clearly hanging out with was, he knew, a step further to establishing his improbable identity as the Elizabethan playwright and bad boy. In his imagination he saw himself as the indestructible one, the Marlowe that taxis had stomped over in Hoxton and whose body had lain drunk in the middle of Clerkenwell Road. He had been found shot by a crack gang in a Rupert Street alley, burnt alive on Clapham Common, but he was, despite every effort, unkillable. He had been knifed in Deptford Creek, and, north of the river, he had risen as a gay desperado on Hampstead Heath, searching the oak woods for sexual encounters in the pitch dark.

If Kit really was, as he suspected, Christopher Marlowe, then it occurred to him that the same blood had been circulating in his arteries for more than four centuries. The idea didn't bear thinking about.

Before meeting up with Ray Kit decided to do a Google search on 'raybans' to see if his net-voyeur regularly used any of the popular gay dating sites. He went initially into the ubiquitously popular site Gaydar to see if Ray had created a profile there and, using the advanced-search tools available to him as a member, browsed through the database but drew a blank. He then tried the equally popular Gay.com with its extensive network connecting the gay community globally through personals, lively chat and engaging content. With over one million profiles and high-speed technology facilitating access, Kit was reasonably confident of finding Ray amongst its members. Again using his membership package to search the database, he quickly drew another blank, however. It occurred to him, though, that Ray, like so many other members, probably used any number of chat-room aliases to disguise his true identity.

Disappointed, he decided to access the upmarket, stylish JakeTM online community for London gay professionals to which he subscribed each month. The payback had been in the form of work contracted through other members, and as a bonus he had entry to a real-time meeting place called the Jake Bar. It was just possible, he thought, that Ray could belong to this more elitist creation of Ivan Massow's, with its exclusive Jake events and privileges, including weekly parties in London and Manhattan. Kit instinctually searched companies and, to his relief, came up with his man. He clicked on the appropriate icon and waited for the page to open:

7a Bateman's Buildings, Soho, London W1. Photographer. Home studio. Models wanted who also sell sex. By appointment only. Fees discussed. Explicit rent.

For some reason Kit immediately connected the fact that Ray photographed rent with his vanished lover Nick. If there was, as he suspected, an association between the two, this was it. And if Ray, or Lord Strange, was somehow part of the ongoing Marlowe plot, then the original Lord Strange, a claimant to the throne, had been suspected at the time of a duplicity that extended to actively conspiring against the crown. What still wasn't clear to Kit in the increasingly complex network of move and countermove was whether Strange was directly implicated in Marlowe's murder or whether he himself was poisoned a year later precisely in order to shut him up. Men in espionage worked on each other with all the insidious cunning of the HIV virus. The mutations always happened subsurface. There was never a clear interface between the two connecting issues. The invisible ink in which Elizabethan intelligence wrote their findings was like the blank cube of a computer switched on but still not booted up. You couldn't, try as you might, get at the facts. They were, as Kit knew only too well, like declassified papers. Thomas Kyd had called the relationship between Marlowe and Strange a strictly professional one, whereas Marlowe had suggested more by claiming to be 'very well known' to Strange. Either way Strange had a dodgy history. Although accused, like Marlowe, of being an atheist he held the office of Lord Lieutenant of Lancashire, and on a level of local government his duties included the identifying and charging of recusants, an ambivalent role that made him into a magnet for Catholic conspiracy. It wasn't impossible that Marlowe's relations with Strange had extended beyond those of patronage and that he had perhaps served as a government listener in the Northumberland circle. Strange had attracted support as a Catholic pretender to the throne and had drawn to him a cell of militant exiles – Stanley, Persons and Owen – all of whom were busy in Brussels and Madrid, plus another cell of devotees in Prague. His history was one of intrigue, and, like Marlowe, he had a propensity to shock his contemporaries by expatiating on the subject of free thought and, in his case, of a tenuous but indisputable claim to the throne.

Kit wondered if there was a selective omissions system and if history was full of recorded events still waiting to happen. Nobody could know as he walked casually down Oxford Street to pick up music and DVDs at the HMV store that he was, in fact, the living embodiment of Christopher Marlowe, being tracked by a cell contracted to kill him and dispense with the clues. The idea that Marlowe, as the nefarious Elizabethan gay outlaw, whose lawlessness had shocked his contemporaries, could be brought forward in time with the speed of an Apple computer continued to fascinate him as a central thesis for his screenplay.

Ray's message had, in addition, alerted him not only to the distinct possibility of Nick's continuing existence but to the fact that he appeared to have re-established contact with the other two criminal outriders in the plot, Robert Poley and Ingram Frizer. Although there was no mention of it in Leslie Hotson's seminal 1925 reconstruction of the murder, *The Death of Christopher Marlowe*, or for that matter in F. S. Boas's life or Charles Nicholl's brilliantly investigative reconstruction of the murder in *The Reckoning*, a book so amazingly authoritative in its detailed analysis of all possible avenues leading to Marlowe's murder that the presentation of facts seemed irrefutable, it seemed likely to Kit that Robert Poley and Ingram Frizer were most probably queer. Nick had never hung out with straight company in his past or present lives, and it seemed unlikely he would begin now.

Kit was confident that he had accessed sufficient data to establish a tentative connection between the past and present, between the putative evidence of a murder committed four centuries ago and the potential for it to be re-created now. At first the idea that he himself was central to the plot had appeared as alien as a transplant organ rejected by the body's cells, but already he was learning to tolerate the notion of his rogue identity. The image that he kept on retrieving in his dreams and waking life was that of a knife – the one that had taken four hundred years to find an entry point from the murderer's hand? The whole suspended action reminded him in an offbeat way of Lou Reed's classic drug song 'Heroin', which seemed musically to evolve out of some non-equatorial time zone and decondition the listener's expectations of the normal process of linear time for its duration.

Despite facing the uncomfortable prospect that he had to Tube over to central London to meet Ray in a short while Nick felt surprisingly calm. His initial apprehension had begun to dissolve, leaving him excited by the imminent prospect of meeting the man he suspected was in reality Lord Strange.

He took a scattershot call from Scott who, as an aside from his Marlowe directive, claimed to have got his friend's read-out of the information on the tube. It had, he claimed, to do with a molecule called RAD51D, which is generically instrumental in cell death, but he was still waiting for further information from his friend.

Kit played an REM song while he dressed. Michael Stipe's voice seemed impregnated with alienation, the experience of overdosing on global touring, too much desert light, too many depersonalizing hotel rooms – he sounded dusty, off duty, the vocal equivalent of a space–time.

He left a hurried Pentel-scribbled note for Yukio in lipstick pink, put on a Topman grey pinstriped jacket over his bleached jeans and single-mindedly hurried out into the ozone-saturated London air.

8

Regression always hit Nick hard in terms of nervous exhaustion. Playing around with blocks of missing time invariably left him feeling jet-lagged and temporarily displaced from reality. Nick always got a sensation he imagined comparable to the gravity-free buzziness that lunar tourists reported after time spent at the moon hotel, despite the fact that the space hotel revolved at exactly the right speed to counteract weightlessness.

Nick's excursions in therapy into inner space in the attempt to reclaim his identity as Nicholas Skeres were as unnerving as they were illuminating. He, too, for the duration of an hour appeared to occupy a zone that, like the moon, had no atmosphere, no living organisms or fossils. The sessions took place in a white room at the Grid HQ in Coptic Street. What came up involuntarily and at the prompting of hypnotherapy appeared neither random nor accidental but acutely selective in its detailed focus on the particular life it seemed he had experienced in the sixteenth and seventeenth centuries, a period to which he had paid little or no attention in his current life. History had never been his forte – on the contrary, he expressed nothing but indifference to the past, seeing it rather like a deleted car, a used-up model continuously succeeded by technological update. To his way of thinking, history lacked on-board ergonomics and recreational aids, such as hi-fi, reclining upholstered seats and television. It had never occurred to him that its leather-hooded gearstick could be in his hand right now. Regression hypno-therapy was, it seemed, like a DJ remix of the past. He was learning that he could mix it himself outside therapy and make it into his own sound. By accessing different brain areas he was discovering the respective qualities of each menu as it related to memories of a past life that spilt over into the present. The continuity in his life seemed to argue for the incongruous fact that he had never died or that there had been no proper extinction of his personality, no die-off of individual characteristics in the transition from one state of reincarnation to another. His therapist joked about it being the big sleep and how he had woken up four centuries later, to find his personality intact as Nicholas Skeres, intelligencer for Sir Francis Walsingham, dodgy broker, someone who had been a member of a cell called Smart's Key, a financier who had eluded conviction and whose criminal sexuality had taken him into yards, back rooms and cottages by the river and who had been implicated in Christopher Marlowe's murder, making the tabloids as one of the three principal suspects, none of whom had been cross-examined at the time for the part they played in the death of a public figure.

Nick was always acutely nervous before sessions at the Grid, the adrenalin racing round his system like hydroelectricity. He'd go in as a sweating rag on the Tube, his pores sweating four centuries of neurotoxins.

The therapy cell was a minimally furnished white cube. It was a safe space, presided over by his hypnotherapist, in which he regressed always to the same life, the same pattern of variant memories and the same undifferentiated identity. He was Nicholas Skeres, an Elizabethan outlaw, and in this respect he had work to complete, an interrupted life in which there were major issues to address. He was also a singer with the over-riding belief he could harness his marginalized voice to the Top 40. His recent studio session had proved that he could still cut it with catchy, vitaminized pop and that his talent was, against all the odds, commercially marketable. But, increasingly, when he went into regression his highly dubious past fitted him like a black banana skin.

Most of his current life he had gravitated to the under-world, starting out at Piccadilly Circus as a spotty renegade teenager, despite his conventional middle-class education. He had found it natural to be in the company of rent boys. His money dealings had always been illicit. Ironically his father had wanted him to read law, and for the duration of a number of school holidays he had worked in the family practice. He had read something of property law in the belief, at first, that this would have to be his career – that it was his designated groove in life – only to do a brainstorm against it at seventeen. His defection had grown over number of months of escalating defiance, and it had coincided with his first gay experiences. Living a double life at home had no longer proved possible, and suppressed anger at his efficiently road-mapped future had steadily built to the point of explosion. One afternoon, cramming his belongings into a single case – mostly CDs and a few books and clothes – he had taken the train to London knowing he would never look back. He regarded the moment he arrived at Euston as his first. He had covered himself with a note left on the kitchen table, so that he wouldn't find himself posted as a missing person, and gone. He had promised to call from time to time but made it very clear that he was in control of his life and wanted to go it alone. Because of his looks he'd been lucky from the start. He'd met a man that same day at Piccadilly, spent the night at his Russell Square flat, stayed on there for a few weeks as a base and gradually made his own way. London had quickly become the modem into which his energies were plugged and the dynamic source not only of his ambition but inevitable ruin, given the nature of his profession.

That was his immediate story, but there was another equally valid one pulled from his sessions at the Grid, and that was the part he had played in witnessing the murder of the lover of Thomas Walsingham, Southampton and Shakespeare – the poet Christopher Marlowe. It was a story digitally recorded by his therapist, an autonomous piecing together of facts that related to a homicide which still occupied contemporary awareness. It involved a past spent with the criminal underworld in the area of the Savoy along the Strand and in the

gangland known also to Marlowe and his lot as Alsatia, as
well as in such hard-drinking, lawless zones as Shoreditch and
Bankside and the piss-stained network of alleys constellating
theatreland in Southwark. But, more specifically, his regression
radar, after a series of repeatedly panicked attempts, had
beamed in on the evening of 30 May 1593 when he had gone to
the naval boomtown of Deptford, with its expansive shipping
industry, as part of a State-hired package of lugubrious contract
killers who had persuaded Christopher Marlowe to meet them
there at a closed house. His recollections of the event, fragmen-
tary at first but little by little pieced together, were coded into the
confidentiality CDs given him by his therapist to help prompt
further recall. They formed the incriminating record of someone in the process of personally confessing to an involvement
in the murder through an unconscious anthology of memories
based on concrete facts. It was often so traumatic to recall the
part he had played in the events of a still-unresolved crime that
sometimes he wished he could walk away from it all and refocus the world as somebody else.

When he went in today Josh, his hypnotherapist, was
already waiting for him in the cell, its minimalism accommodating little else but a chair, a couch and recording equipment.
A sensitive mike was clipped to his cheek, and while the
recording process appeared analytically clinical its cumulative
effects were ultimately therapeutic. It was simply, according to
Josh, a matter of getting back in touch with himself as the
moneylender Skeres – one-time resident, in the early 1580s, at
Furnival's Inn along Holborn and friend, amongst Marlowe's
acquaintances, to the poet George Chapman – and letting
things come up spontaneously. Already, as he waited on the
couch for Josh's cue, he could feel almost instantly the unconsciously organic fusing of his current identity with his
recollected life.

JOSH: Last time, if you recall, we settled on 30 May 1593 as
the date most crucial to you in these sessions. The place was

Deptford. You were going there to meet somebody called Christopher Marlowe at Deptford Creek. What happened there?

NICK: There was thunder in the air. I remember it being hot and sweaty. I'd gone over there earlier in the day. No, I'm wrong. I remember arriving the previous night and staying over at the Black Dog. There were sailors everywhere cruising the yards, a lot of them stoned on Chinese black. Marlowe used to go there for sex. It was one of his hunting grounds. We'd been casual lovers on and off for a few months, and we were both employed as snoops. I mean, Marlowe was on my case and I was on his, Frizer on Poley's, and Poley on Frizer's. Frizer and Poley were both on Marlowe's who was on both of theirs. It was that complex.

JOSH: What happened there?

NICK: I hung around for a while in the town and, not wishing to make myself conspicuous, met Kit alone at a bar called the Three Pirates. There was a back room there, and Kit immediately started exploring it and going down on sailors. I was jealous and couldn't help feeling excluded. Although we weren't partners – we couldn't be at the time – there was a bond. I don't know what it was about him that attracted me: his recklessness, his humour, his hot blood, his blue eyes? If I told him I loved him he would laugh in my face. It was his way of pretending he didn't care. I didn't want sex with this guy called Yukio – that was the sailor's name – but he and Kit seemed to be getting it on, and it was going to happen. The owners of the place, I remember, were called Reggie and Ron, like the Kray brothers. Reggie encouraged the two of them to fuck and took my place in the threesome. I stayed at the bar drinking, not wanting to show my hurt. I loved Kit deep down, and although I couldn't make an issue of it he was sort of betraying me . . .

JOSH: Go on. What happened next?

NICK: I stormed out after a time and went down to the river.

I needed to be alone. Part of me wanted revenge. I was waiting for a word from Ingram Frizer as to why we were all meeting up, and I imagined it was to extract information from Marlowe. With Walsingham, sometimes you didn't know right to the last minute what he intended. I never liked Ingram; he was Robert's friend. He was shifty and had something on the other Walsingham, Thomas, Kit's patron from Scadbury House.

JOSH: What did you do walking by the river?

NICK: I was in a desperate mood at the time and didn't want to live. I thought about drowning myself, but the smell of the river turned me away. I knew I would have to face Kit later, and I still hadn't decided what to do.

JOSH: Did you think of killing him?

NICK: I was cut up inside and didn't like myself for that. I couldn't believe he was that up front. I thought I counted for something in his life. As I remember, I met up with a group of sailors and shared their bottle for a while. They were planning to desert ship and getting drunk for courage. I got wasted with them on rum.

JOSH: Where did you go then?

NICK: I don't know, only I robbed a sailor stretched out dead drunk on the ground and got into his pockets for pay. I never got my money smoothly for being a snoop. We had to hassle indefinitely before payment arrived. Being late was all part of their policy of keeping us hanging on.

JOSH: You mentioned two individuals, Ingram Frizer and Robert Poley. Where did you meet them that day?

NICK: We met before our appointment with Marlowe in a pub called the Ship. You'd get messages from Poley in deep-yellow oxidized ink. Invisible ink. He was the better of the two but tricky. I learnt with them to keep to the business in hand and never tell them anything personal. First thing Frizer noticed was that I had money on me and that it was theft. Frizer could take you apart just by looking at you. I was so paranoid that he had seen me frisk the sailor that I came out with it and confessed. It was his method. He made you feel guilty, so you'd confess and hand over what was stolen. Poley had a bad reputation. He was a snoop and had also poisoned someone. He was supposed to be married, but Frizer was his item. Most of Walsingham's secret police were gay. We were so used to being watched that we could turn the experience round and project it back on to the watcher.

JOSH: Tell me what happened at the Ship?

NICK: They'd got it in for Marlowe and started taking him apart. They were jealous of his success as a poet. They bitched about most writers being faggots and how Southampton was uptight about Kit making it known that he and Shakespeare were lovers. Nobody had come out with it yet, but I had the feeling there was a contract out on Marlowe.

JOSH: How long were you at the Ship?

NICK: There was an hour to spare before we were due to meet him at Eleanor Bull's place, an address used by intelligence. We all knew the place. People got grilled there. Eleanor was in Walsingham's pay. I was hoping that neither of the other two knew that I had already met Kit earlier at the Three Pirates.

JOSH: And this Eleanor? Tell me more about her. She's clearly important.

NICK: Red hair, as I remember. Discreet. Maybe thirty-five or forty. She was related to one of Kit Marlowe's enemies who schemed against him, Lord Burghley. She wasn't just anyone. She was the widow of a court official. I never liked her, but there wasn't anything particularly to dislike. She kept to herself and was in the same pay.

JOSH: So you went there after the Ship?

NICK: Things started to get edgy at the Ship. I sensed trouble. We were all armed. You had to be in our world. It was then that Poley told us that Shakespeare, the poet who was Kit's rival, was also due to meet us later in the evening at

Eleanor's. Ingram Frizer, I remember, had a knife tucked into his waistband. Poley was in the mood for trouble. He always went along with Frizer's mood. They kept on doing Kit down.

JOSH: You're getting tired? Do you want to stop?

NICK: No, but it's a tough one. I need to be strong to go in there because it's still happening inside. I am, like it or not, as I've discovered in these sessions, Nicholas Skeres, who was once involved with the Earl of Essex, carrying the Earl's letters from Exeter after the Portingale voyage of 1589. I had already, in the Earl's service, been arrested in dangerous company at Edmund Williamson's house in Philip Lane. I was no stranger to prison.

JOSH: You're certain of that identity, of your association with the past?

NICK: Of my association with the present, more like. There no longer seems a distinction. In many ways I don't seem ever to have cut free of my past life.

JOSH: You know you can stop the session at any time.

Nick: Yes, I'll tell you when. I kept wondering at Deptford, as we waited at the Ship, if it was me they wanted rather than Kit or the both of us. When you're that involved you get paranoid and can't trust anyone.

JOSH: And Eleanor Bull's house. You all went on there?

NICK: We walked there through the streets in the heat. I can't remember much except I knew something bad was going to happen. She wasn't just anyone, I can tell you. I'd checked her out, naturally. She was born Eleanor Whitney, a member of an ancient border-country family whose seat was at Whitney-on-Wye, near Hereford. The Whitney's history can be traced back to the thirteenth century. They provided, even as bad blood, generations of county knights, MPs and pistol-shooting sheriffs. A generation or so before Eleanor, James Whitney held minor court office as a Server of the Chamber to Henry VIII. I'd more than done my research before going there. My life depended on it.

JOSH: Go on.

NICK: Nobody could touch these two guys, Poley and Frizer, when they were on the case. They were a firm. You had the feeling they would turn up wherever you were, at any time. That's why they're still in my life. That's why we all come here to the Grid. It's because we're connected through blood.

JOSH: We're not going to go into Eleanor Bull's house this time. That will be for another session, when I've prepared you, little by little, to re-create the murder. Do you remember anything else of significance about what happened on your way to the house?

NICK: Yes. There was some sort of heated discussion going on between Poley and Frizer about money and who should get the biggest cut. We stopped on the way for Poley to take a leak against the wall. It was then that Shakespeare's name came up – or Billy the Rainmaker as we called him.

JOSH: Who was putting up the contract money?

NICK: Southampton, or Wriothesley as we knew him – I'm certain of that – and not Burghley or Walsingham. I really need to stop now. I've gone as far as I can for today.

JOSH: That's fine. The session's at an end anyhow. I'll see you on Wednesday, as usual, at three.

When a nervously exhausted Nick went to recuperate and have a coffee in the recreation space he was just in time to catch sight of the peroxided, sunglassed Ingram, implacably cool behind his shades, checking out from his individual session and making his way towards reception. He looked to Nick as he always did, indifferent to everyone and everything around him, his emotions bleached of all traces of humanity.

Nick sat quietly at a table with his espresso. The Grid, with its ubiquitous databank of pharmacogenetics, looked like an off-limits genetic laboratory – a decommissioned space shuttle morphed into a Bloomsbury conversion. He knew little or nothing of its commercial infrastructure other than that its major clients comprised the indomitable drug giants, such as GlaxoSmithKline. The space-age chairs littered around were recognizably Philippe Starck. Everything was minimal right down to the cube-shaped coffee table at which he sat. Space was intrinsic to the design theory – and it was aimed creatively as much at the architecture of the mind as it was at the custom-built building. The place, in every respect, was designed seemingly to encourage blue-sky thinking.

Nick chewed silently on his latest dilemma. In terms of the short commercial career offered by music, he couldn't really afford to sit out the time stipulated by the Grid as necessary to his character rehabilitation before going public. His mind was fired up with ideas for new songs – slow, aching ballads that were like deep pools of still water and dance grooves with infectious hooks and contagious choruses. He had taken to using all his spare time to write. He had written twenty new songs since going into the studio and was working on another two at present. The lyrics to 'Gutted' were coming up like dot-matrix boards in his mind:

> You stripped my white shirts off the rail
> trashed suits and jumpers on the floor
> airbrushed my photo by the bed
> hung my snakeskin loafers on the door . . .

The memory of being humiliated early on in this way by his Greek lover George, the first man to take him in on his arrival in London, still stripped him naked of defences when the memory came up.

Nick stayed on at his table with his coffee and memories. Even though the past was like a river in his bloodstream he liked the fact that his time was his own, except when he was required to report at the Grid. There was something exhilaratingly liberating about being out in the city in your own time, free of the commercial targets and routine hours imposed on the workforce by their corporate employers. It was the sudden availability of unconditional time that didn't have to be accounted for that was making him, he felt, unduly prolific as a songwriter. He had never experienced this degree of freedom before.

He came outside to the blinding-white afternoon light still feeling disorientated from his session and made his way aimlessly into the complex of small streets constellated round the British Museum – the bookshops, the cafés catering to tourists and the inevitable gift shops contingent on the latter. For all its closeness to the West End the area was unpredictably quiet, as though soundproofed from the surrounding city's regulated noise corridors. Bloomsbury had its own immutably time-warped ecosystem, and Nick liked to hang out there after his regressions at the Grid, imagining that he was about to encounter a flash-forwarded, delusional Virginia Woolf, hair banged out, shoplifting in her black negligée before being retrieved by her sister Vanessa and discreetly escorted back home through the sidestreets.

Nick had, despite an initial resistance, picked up a bit of interest in books from the years he had lived with Kit, and he found himself drawn to the first editions on display in Ulysses' window in Museum Street. True to the shop's name, there was an aquamarine-covered first edition of James Joyce's *Ulysses*, published by Shakespeare and Company, in the window, doorstep thick – a very good copy in almost pristine nick – and next to it copies of the British editions of Paul Bowles's *The Sheltering Sky* and *Let It Come Down*, in their bright, highly collectable Keith Vaughan dustjackets. Nick monitored the books on display, one eye on his reflection in the window, broken into fractals as if he were seeing himself underwater. Behind him he could see the constantly changing street footage as it came up on CCTV – the millions of faces as facts in the city, almost instantly vaporized on recognition into anonymity. He stayed for a long time, face glued to the window, before a sudden disconcerting impulse had him check on someone coming out of the shop that he was certain beyond all question was Kit.

Nick stayed gummed to the window, absorbed in the stranger's reflection, and watched the person he took to be Kit, dressed in a black jumper and jeans, go into the Ruskin Café on the corner of Little Russell Street. Nick felt like the blood had been blown out of his head, his past and present meeting in an impacted collision. Part of him wanted to pursue Kit into the café and the other to get away from the area fast. He could have walked off abruptly if he wished in the direction of New Oxford Street and headed straight for the Tube. Instead he purposefully delayed, his emotions unzipped all over again by seeing the man who had for so many years been his lover. He approached the café hesitantly and, unable to go through with entering the place, turned back. Playing for time he headed right into Little Russell Street. He was completely thrown for the moment. The stringy egg-white clouds overhead didn't seem real as they finned over in calligraphic trails, nor for that matter did the dark-blue cellulose parallax of a Toyota Land Cruiser as it burnt urgently down the narrow street. Nick continued to delay, stopping at the top of the street by Bull's Yard, looking anxiously over his shoulder, half expecting to find Kit staring at him from the corner, before retraining his steps in the direction of the café. Curiosity, if nothing else, forced him back. It wasn't just seeing Kit again that triggered his confused state of conflicting emotions; it was more the certainty that their relationship had continued to evolve over the centuries. If they had been separated by the bust-up that appeared to have regained momentum after an improbable four centuries, then they were suddenly back in each other's lives again, this very moment, in the same light-polluted London street.

Nick should have gone off, and he knew it. He told himself repeatedly that he wouldn't go in, that he wouldn't confront Kit out of the blue and risk it all going wrong again through impetuousness. Standing there, equivocating, not knowing what to do, he toyed with the idea of waiting and following him or of going in and pretending he'd never seen him before in his life, looking at him stone cold with eyes hard as a titanium laptop. Instead he hung out on the street corner and waited. He felt shy, like an offended teenager twisted into self-denial through hurt but hard, too, as though his newly reclaimed identity as Nicholas Skeres had prepared him to confront Kit with attitude.

Nick stayed put on the street corner outside the café where some wooden tables had been placed for customers. A number of Japanese students, clearly fresh from a seminar, sat outside talking. At that moment he suddenly became aware of the sun pointing through cloud like the orange nose cone of a jet. The ray of light, projected through the gap in the clouds, touched him as if it had travelled all that way specifically to seek him out.

Overtaken by curiosity he threw a brief look through the café's open door. He could see Kit sitting reading with his back to him, looking up from the book occasionally to become involved with eating what looked like a Danish pastry. Feeling acutely self-conscious, Nick, who pretended he was looking for someone who wasn't there, went off again and hung out lower down the street, debating his next move. There was so much missing time between him and Kit, he realized, that he didn't know where to start by way of a meeting point.

He finally, after much debate, made the decision to go in and approach him. He walked back quickly to the café only, to his surprise, to be confronted by an incredulous Kit who was on his way out. There was no way of avoiding him. Shocked into disbelief by confronting one another in this way, each spontaneously froze as if paralysed by an atomized nerve spray, before the bewildering recognition hit.

'Nick, it can't be you?' Kit said, standing back from the encounter.

'This can't be real?' Nick replied, flashbacking and flash-forwarding simultaneously to try to find some purchase on reality.

'But I thought you were dead,' Kit said, still looking thrown and upping his dark green shades to see Nick better.

'I don't know. Maybe I was,' Nick said. 'But you can see for yourself I'm still here. In fact, I've been thinking about you a lot lately. Are you still living at the same place?'

'Yes, I'm still at the old flat in Colville Gardens. Some things don't change.'

'I'm in Islington now,' Nick said. 'I'm trying to sort myself out.'

'What are you doing? Have you gone back to singing?'

'Why do you ask that?' Nick asked suspiciously.

'I don't know. It's my natural assumption. This is all so strange, the fact that you're still around. I can't believe it's really you.'

'We'll have to meet and talk about it,' Nick said spikily and deliberately keeping it brief. 'I'll give you my new mobile number.'

'I'd better give you mine, too, it's changed,' Kit said, as he punched Nick's details into his Nokia, the light hitting his hand at that moment from the same star that had touched Nick earlier.

'You're off somewhere?' Nick asked.

'I'm meeting a friend in Soho,' Kit replied, sounding deliberately vague.

Nick observed Kit's black baseball boots with their purple laces. His lack of strong emotions for his old lover was confusing and something he attributed to shock.

'I don't have much free time these days,' Nick said defensively, warning Kit that he couldn't walk into his life like someone just stepped out of the crowds at Arrivals.

'I'm the same,' Kit said, acting cool, as though the purpose of language was to freeze emotion to a watermelon granita.

'I thought I saw you a while ago in Leicester Square. I was in a hurry and couldn't be sure if it was you.'

'It could have been me. I'm always around,' Kit said, trying to stay under the question.

Nick knew without any doubt that Kit had been there looking for him, but he wasn't going to force the issue. He sensed what he had always known, that the two of them could never be entirely rid of each other. They would always somehow be pulled into the same gravitational field, wherever they were.

'Give me a call then,' Nick said. 'It feels like it's been a lifetime. There's a lot of catching up to do.'

He opened up a space between them, as if he was being tugged in another direction, one foot pointed to go. Kit's baseball boots, he noted, were perfect. So, too, were the bows tied from the purple laces. He found himself fixed on that one detail amongst the millions of options the city presented.

Impulsively, he decided to split and, turning his back on Kit, made off quickly in the direction of the British Museum. Two red-haired Japanese girls were in his near line of vision, bare midriffs, low-slung jeans supported by broad 1960s retro belts, black T-shirts proclaiming 'Tokyo Mars' as a planet conquest slogan. He didn't know where he was going, nor did he care; he knew only that he needed to get away. He turned right into Great Russell Street and headed up Holborn way, guessing that Kit would take off in the direction of New Oxford Street and Soho. There were fins in the sky, a 727 nosing south through a white cloud the shape of China and that same light he had noticed earlier doing a hologram on his skin. He tried not to think about it. If he started to get paranoid that the light was watching him he'd really be in trouble. He took a turn into the quiet of Bury Place and slackened his pace. He threw his head round once to make sure he wasn't being followed. The street was empty and lividly defaced by state-of-the-art graffiti. The two Japanese girls he had passed earlier entered the street, occasionally consulting an open A–Z. Beautiful, reinvented Asian mutants – he slowed down as they approached. One of them must have recognized him. 'Look, it's Nick,' she exclaimed excitedly to the other.

'Excuse me are you the singer Nick Hebden? Nick . . .' they screamed with girlie adulation as he hurriedly, and in a state of irrational panic, took off down the street, as though his true identity really had been found out.

9

Kit was running a bit late for his appointment. He could have stopped one of the armour-plated black cabs policing the West End, been scanned for weapons and jumped in, but the traffic tailback choking New Oxford Street in a chemical haze of pollutants was held in indefinite cryonic suspension. The fastest way across the city that he knew was to walk.

Most of the city's youthful community had picked up on this, and he cut a fast pace in the direction of Centre Point, its thirty-five storeys mirroring the empty sky stepping away with its low clouds to Marble Arch. He knew that every step he took was on CCTV, his image, like all street footage, coming up grainily on monitor screens in security control rooms.

He was still shocked by his unexpected meeting with Nick and the edgy aftertaste it left. Nick was a sweet poison in his nerves. He could hear Martina Topley Bird on an open convertible's stereo, her 85 per cent cocoa sensuality worked into the gospel groove of 'Soul Flood'. Nick was in the song if Kit wanted him to be – you could place your lover in pop – and he was also somewhere back in town, undoubtedly circulating in the city's underworld. Either way, he was real again in Kit's life and out there on the streets. All the rumours, the lookalike sightings, the infobites snatched from friends had been confirmed by this opportunistic meeting.

Kit hurried in the direction of Soho for his appointment with Ray at Bateman's Buildings. Centre Point sucked him in with its bad aura, its wind-corridored underpass stacked with a vinyl sculpture of uncollected black sacks and the white van parked on its St Giles' High Street side dispensing carriers of sterilized needles to junkies. Two or three users were grouped by the van's open window, and one of them was arguing over his supply. The precinct throbbed with palpable tension. People were living in the windowless, fire-gutted upper floors all along the high street. The district, noted for its quasi-dereliction, had been taken over by smackheads, the homeless, floors converted into a drugs warren. There was a billboard ad up for the Japanese rock band Melt Banana's new release. Kit was a fan of their idiosyncratically bizarre sound, the rhythm section maintaining a sustained, accelerated forward thrust while simultaneously finding spaces to dismantle and reassemble songs in mid-flow. But the real hook for him was the singer's piercing squeal slicing through relentlessly unpredictable guitar noise.

Soho Square, as he crossed it, was buzzing. People were sitting in groups on the dehydrated grass – the borders planted with a chorus of red geraniums and purple petunias. There were gay clones sitting on benches, and the area's slip into ghettohood was palpable. Young Japanese men were particularly prominent in the racially hybrid culture that now characterized the city.

Kit hurried through the square towards Bateman's Buildings. The entire alley was a series of conversions aimed at accommodating corporate technologies. There was an office worker standing outside an anonymous black security door injecting himself in the thigh. The new cult of injecting in public had come to replace smoking as attitude. People did it on buses and the Tube or confronted strangers with their habit. The man stared directly at Nick as he depressed the plunger into a vein, as though conscripting him as a witness heightened the dopamine rush in his brain.

Kit wouldn't be drawn by the man's perversity and kept on his way. He could hear his own brain noise coming up loud as he searched for 74a at the far end of the alley. When he finally came across the blue-painted reinforced door with a large combination dial he couldn't find any reference to the name Raybans. There were three names posted up – Nico, Pink Express and

Sohohighs. He took a quick guess the unnamed buzzer was probably Ray's. He stood there for a while, holding off from announcing himself but undeterred in his mission. He could hear the generative force of London somewhere behind him, its ambient roar filtered into a diffused drone. He placed his finger on the buzzer tentatively, realizing at the same time how sometimes the city appeared to go missing for intervals, only to come back on the senses all the more powerful for having been away.

Almost immediately a voice said peremptorily, 'Come in. It's the third floor. Use the lift or the stairs. It's marked "Raybans" on the door.'

Once inside Kit found himself in a neutral-coloured rectangular space prefacing the stairwell. He decided, instead of the lift, to take the stairs that, as far as he could make out, went up in a series of L-shapes to the third floor. When he arrived he found himself confronted by an anonymous blue fire door, a video camera monitoring the floor. The silence came at him like the empty space inside sleep. He caught his breath and rang the entry bell, which was almost immediately answered by an intensely blue-eyed, off-blond-haired man, slim, white shirt, pre-damaged jeans and candy-pink sneakers. The man's inscrutable face gave nothing away: no smile lines, no pronounced lived-in indications of age. He could have been anything between thirty and fifty by Kit's reckoning: his largely unblemished skin had failed to signpost the biological changes along the way.

Kit was shown into a spacious floor, its walls painted mint-green, with a Mac Cube prominent on an aluminium work table and a kitschy turquoise chair arranged ostentatiously central to the room. Like Ray the place exhibited no visible flaws or apparent wear and tear. It looked like a space unslept in, unlived in, uncooked in; it could still have been on the market, newly converted and repainted to minimally anodyne effect.

There wasn't anywhere to sit apart from the one arty chair,

and Ray motioned Kit to a large mauve cushion on the floor. Kit sat down opposite the Mac, the Venetian blinds drawn on the street side. The Canon digital camera placed next to the Mac was the only possible indication he could find of Ray's profession. He didn't know, in his state of confusion, quite why he was there on a stranger's floor, the axis of power so evidently Ray's in the strained preliminaries. But, oddly, something in him didn't really care, didn't quite connect with the potential danger that could come of this meeting.

'Sit down,' Ray said. 'You probably don't recognize me. It's been a long time since you were my guest at Knowsley.'

'Excuse me?' Kit said, taken aback by the reference.

'You don't remember? You used to like the roses and gilly-flowers in the garden, and the lavender and sweet william. You'd sit out under the beech trees behind the house and write so fluently that it was obvious you were a natural, even though you were the son of John Marlowe, a self-made shoemaker from Canterbury. You were nine years old when Queen Elizabeth visited Canterbury and stayed there for two weeks displaying her pageantry. You never forgot her remarkable talent for self-deification. That's what you told us at the time. The incident, you said, coloured your writing, as did the story of the Duke of Guise, who, if you remember, slaughtered three thousand Protestant citizens of Paris, leaving rafts of their bodies to choke the Seine and turn the river red.'

'What are you talking about?' Kit asked.

'Nothing but your past, of course. By the way, Nick's been here,' Ray added coldly. 'You do know Nick. Nicholas Skeres, as he was, although now he uses the name Nick Hebden.'

'How do you know Nick?' Kit asked, shocked to hear this calculated disclosure about his ex. 'Let's say we met,' Ray said with deliberate ambiguity, 'and, like you, I've known him a very long time. Far too long, in fact. Is it four hundred years now that we've all been acquainted?'

'I still don't get you,' Kit said, not wanting to assist Ray in coming clean about his identity and feeling at a disadvantage to the man's inscrutable composure. The cool between them was like dry ice as Kit fidgeted for time.

'I think you do,' Ray said. 'I'm Ferdinando Stanley, Lord Strange, your one-time patron and theatre promoter, and you're none other than the notorious Kit Marlowe. We've come a long way to meet up like this.'

Kit found himself looking directly at the Mac Cube, its blank rectangle sleeping. He felt his entire past had converged on this blinding light-bulb moment, but he still wasn't willing to let on. There was too much to fit into words, there were too many associations, and he preferred for the moment to remain silent.

'If I'm right,' Ray continued, 'you must have known about this all along on some level. My meeting up with Nick, as another member of the Grid, was the missing piece in the pattern I needed to reach you.'

'I don't know what you're talking about,' Kit persisted, continuing to stare at the Mac rather than make eye contact with Ray, whose extreme economy of movement had left him standing in exactly the same position and spot he had taken upon first conducting Kit into the room.

'You've forgotten your code?' Ray questioned. 'Your mind was always the fastest, the trickiest of its kind. What's the speed of this computer, do you think? I'll tell you because I like facts: 3 GHz and able to use up to 8 GB of RAM and address 1 TB of disk space. You're much quicker.'

'And your pretender's blood?' Kit turned on him viciously. 'Do you still feel royal platelets swimming through your arteries?'

Ray laughed as quietly as he spoke. He altered the position of his left pink sneaker fractionally and shifted axis. The woman buried in him showed up now, visibly brought into play by the sudden conflict between wounded vanity and the need to hit back. 'My claim is legitimate,' he said calmly. 'Intelligence has proved it. I always had high standing in the order of succession. I was the son of Henry Stanley, fourth Earl of Derby and, with royal blood on both sides, a contender for the throne. You've checked all that out at some time. The issue has been on slow-burn for centuries. But, don't worry, my time will come.'

'If you really are who you claim to be, then I never trusted you,' Kit said, 'and I don't now, even though you were once my patron. But let's be clear about what we want from each other. I came here because I thought you could put me in touch with Nick. That's all.'

'Nick Skeres?' Ray questioned. 'I assume you're referring to Nick Hebden who wants to be a pop star.'

'Yes,' Kit said, deliberately not letting on that he had encountered him just minutes ago by chance.

'Your boy,' Ray said. 'He was always your bit of rent, wasn't he? The one you kept quiet about.'

'And your double life? I bet you're the same now as you always were. Married and keeping up the usual pretence. That's why you've got this place, isn't it?'

Ray shifted his other foot to counterpoint the movement he had made earlier. The smile he attempted remained suppressed. He was too clever to be drawn.

'You met Nick on the way over here,' Ray said, taking the advantage from Kit with his direct thrust.

'Your methods haven't changed. And neither have mine.' He was starting to feel uncomfortable in the presence of the sleeping Cube that dominated the room. The contact with Ray was too close, too sneakily reminiscent of a past in which they had both been double agents reporting on each other.

'You can be of use to me,' Ray said dispassionately, as though he had planned all this out in advance.

'In what way?' Kit asked, suspicious, naturally anticipating a trick.

'By doing something for me,' Ray said, deliberately stalling on the option.

'What?'

'It's information I want,' Ray said, his mind working with an idea he had clearly been tweaking for a long time.

'Who are you on to now?' Kit asked, his voice adopting the neutral tones of intelligence.

'Somebody you can reach via another mutual acquaintance of ours, Ingram Frizer. The man I want tracked is Wriothesley, who used to be known to you and me as the Earl of Southampton, a patron like myself, to you and Shakespeare. He's living somewhere in Eaton Square, and he's regularly in touch with Frizer. It's a small world.'

'This is madness,' Kit said. 'Do you really expect me to believe all this brainwashing from the Grid that you're clearly a part of, too?'

'It's the truth. It's quite obvious that none of us has ever died. The pattern will go on until somebody breaks the chain.'

'I don't follow you. What do you want with Wriothesley?'

'Let's say he contests my claim to authoritarian power,' Ray replied, cold as a gun snout.

'I see,' Kit said, getting a metallic taste in his mouth, like swallowing vitamins. 'Is the used-up monarchy still worth anything today?'

'Everything. I've been waiting a long time to assert my claim, and I'm totally legit. Don't forget I was poisoned for the danger I represented to the throne. It happened a year after your reported death, from a poisoning so virulent that my vomit was corrosive enough to strip the gloss off metal.'

'If I was taking this from anyone else but you I'd think you were crazy,' Kit said, feeling a freeze notch up his spine.

'There's a lot you don't know about, surprisingly. For instance, your friend, the poet Matthew Roydon, who was in Prague in 1591, was there specifically to carry letters from Sir Edward Kelley to Lord Burghley in England. It wasn't just that Roydon was part of the intelligence network relating to the Prague conspiracy but that those letters carried sensitive information about our particular relationship, suggesting not only that we were lovers but that you were a part of the "Strange plot". The Mac's loaded with images of Dilly rent boys,' Ray continued conspiratorially, suddenly switching track. 'I have to do something to amuse myself. Old habits, I suppose, just get updated. Do you want to see Nick on all fours, chained as my slave?'

'I'm not in the least interested,' Kit said, longing to be gone and looking for a way out.

'Get on to Wriothesley, or James Waters as he calls himself, straight away,' Ray said. 'It's the only way you can save yourself. You'd better act fast, in your own interest.'

'What do you mean by that?' Kit asked, experiencing the onset of familiar panic.

'That you had better watch out for yourself. It seems impossible to me, given your underworld contacts, that you don't know there's a contract out on you,' Ray continued with disconcerting cool. His mobile was ringing, but he let it go. 'Get back to me in a week,' he said, without the slightest give in his emotions. 'I'm expecting a model at any moment, so you'd better go.'

'Don't worry, I'm going,' Kit said, feeling relieved and conscious as he got up from his mauve cushion on the floor of the intended hostility projected by Ray's indomitable entrepreneurial pressure. He had never really got a hold of the conversation and felt ruthlessly manipulated. What he remembered of Lord Strange from his past was a similar facility for breaking people by the most insidious means, and what he was experiencing now seemed little more than the continued refinement of those characteristics.

Kit was only too glad to leave an increasingly tense situation and in using the stairs on the way down to the street, came almost face to face with Ray's expected model – a rough-diamond Soho stereotype, eighteen or nineteen, post-acne spotty, blue, roughed-in Levi jacket with matching jeans and Reebok trainers, dodgy hazel eyes and black hair cut short with an incisive side parting. Kit knew his biography from a single glance – model by profession, street drugs, petty crime, fucked up, broken home, looking for a break, depression – he was a type he had known so many of in Nick's circle of friends.

He watched as the boy mechanically depressed the blank buzzer, like it was all too familiar. The user and the used, he had seen it so often, and their unbreakable pattern of exploiting one another.

Kit didn't hang around. He walked quickly down the alley and out into Soho Square where the lawns were still compact with men stripped off and sunning, despite the aggressive light pollution and the air zippy with Japanese pop.

He went and sat down on a bench in the shade, facing on all sides a rectangle of corporate technologies. There were robo-security guards on every floor to protect the staff crouched over their monitors like long-haul pilots. The precinct was now a money zone, an Anglo-Japanese merger of drug giants, research-ing programmes targeting highly lucrative longevity projects. The rich and the powerful had dispensed with the idea of biological ageing, and the drug giants were growing fat on chemicals designed to facilitate the idea of resistance to natural death.

Kit sat on a bench in a corner of the square and endlessly replayed the contents of his meeting with Ray, whom he knew to be particularly dangerous because of an ego that bordered on megalomania. Outwardly, Ray wasn't the seventeenth-century aristocrat any longer, rippling in gold braid, jewels and expen-sive fingerwear; his clothes now accommodated the Soho scene, but he had the same tightly structured intelligence, his mind given to networking with the trickier echelons of the London underworld.

A surveillance helicopter went over like a black cyberwasp monitoring the zone and turned back on a vigilant arc to the bomb-proofed high-security Whitehall complex. Next to him a cute Japanese boy dressed in a black sloganed T-shirt and white Gaultier jeans was busy with a laptop. Kit caught the corner of his near eye and saw the momentary lapse in con-centration he had triggered before the boy refocused his text. With his blond hair and stick-thin body, he was a 21st-century Aryan–Asian, his hybrid aesthetic almost indistinguishable from a girl's. A mixture of punk, manga and Aryan, to Kit he epitomized the new conception of blond ambition.

Kit sat in the quiet particular to London squares, feeling unduly guilty about not working on his screenplay. He badly needed the injection of money due at the next stage of completion and was, additionally, in debt to Scott's agency. A group of mostly blonde and pink-haired, tartan-miniskirted Japanese girls were sitting drinking Starbucks coffee in styrofoam cups under one of the giant plane trees. Their excited laughter reached him in snatches, broken only when a delegation of four black guys in hoodies sauntered through the central aisle, fists bunched into their pockets like rap gangstas, eyes scanning the lawns, inscrutable with their concealed weaponry. Kit relaxed only after they had gone. They were urban guerrillas creating panic, a Yardie cell toting guns and knives as a streetwise vocabulary.

Kit left a voice message for Yukio that he would be back by nine and that he intended to work late on his Marlowe to compensate for lost time. He was sitting there lost in his thoughts, when to his alarm he saw Ingram Frizer enter the square. Ingram just stood there immobile, obligatory shades, bleached-white hair, black clothes, his emaciated arms crossed, clearly scanning the crowds for somebody. His look drew people by its intensity. Kit, too, couldn't avoid staring, as though polarized to the one person in the crowd he didn't want to see.

Ingram must have seen him or have been looking for him, for he nodded and cut diagonally across the lawn in Kit's direction.

'I might have guessed you'd be here,' Ingram said dismissively, as he stood staring directly at Kit.

'Why's that?' Kit asked, thrown by the assumption. He hadn't anticipated meeting Ingram and resented the invasion of the little space he had been busy creating for himself after the shock of meeting up with Ray.

'Dunno,' Ingram said, with his usual economy of phrasing. He was clearly wired. Kit knew from the look that he was on

H, as well as from the nonchalant but meticulously cultivated image of a drug-wasted casualty he projected.

'Been to the Grid?' Kit asked, looking to build some sort of bridge between them.

'Nah,' Ingram replied in an adopted street drawl. 'I was looking for you. I thought we should talk.'

'What about?' Kit asked, feeling acutely uncomfortable at Ingram's tone.

'We're two of a kind,' Ingram said enigmatically, upping his shades fractionally as a protective shield.

'I don't follow you.'

Ingram sneered, pulling the emotion back inside to keep it private. It was his habitual method of canning what otherwise would be shared.

'When I'm doing drugs, when I'm on, I know who you are,' Ingram said. He flicked his shades up for total protection as a compensation for having broken cover.

'I still don't get what you're saying,' Kit said, trying to remain calm. He wanted to be alone after his disquieting meeting with Ray and felt needled by Ingram's presence.

'Still snooping I suppose,' Ingram said after a pause, in a voice extracted from the freezer.

'I'm not with you,' Kit said, trying hard to sound detached.

'Intelligence,' Ingram capped, as though blowing apart the pretence of a game.

'If you know my game I know yours,' Kit replied, matching Ingram's coldness to a zero.

'Has Ray told you that Wriothesley's in town? I believe Nick's seeing him.'

'What's that got to do with me?' Kit asked, trying to keep his cool.

'Plenty.'

'Like what?' Kit asked, pretending indifference.

'Wriothesley always had it in for you. Don't tell me that's news,' Ingram sneered. 'As the Earl of Southampton he may have been fascinated with you as a poet who was also cheap

144

rent, but that's where it ends. I know for a fact, man, he once gave Shakespeare a thousand pounds outright to help with the purchase of a property. You got nothing but his end up you.'

'That's the past. Why do we keep going back there? I'm busy living now.'

'So is he,' Ingram said with chilling counterpoint. 'Not too far from here either.'

Kit took a deep breath. The whole scenario was turning into the equivalent of psychotic architecture, only the construct was too brutally, coldly schematic, and he was, somehow, because of some unbroken link with the past, a part of it.

'What do you want?' Kit asked outright, hoping to strip the layers of hostility from Ingram's skin.

'Out,' Ingram said with a marksman's precision. 'An exit, man.'

'And don't you think I want that, too?' Kit levelled.

'Someone's got to go, and fast, to break the chain. Otherwise we're all stuck with identities from the past.'

'You sound like Ray,' Kit said, unconsciously deepening the plot by referencing the man he had just visited and feeling increasingly anxious around Ingram, who showed no signs yet of going.

'You get around,' Ingram said, flattening the innuendo in his voice and again fidgeting with his eyewear. 'Ray's bad news, man. He wants blood, and it's probably yours.'

Kit had the sudden feeling that he was, in some way, through his past and present connections, plugged inextricably into London's underworld and that the bond was unbreakable. He was irrationally afraid that very moment of reverting, in an accelerated timeshift, to a sixteenth-century London he remembered only too well, leaky with poisons, muddy and contaminated underfoot and networked by cut-throat alleys.

'Hadn't we all better meet up and talk?' Kit said. 'This whole thing is getting out of control.'

'It's not that easy,' Ingram quipped. 'These guys, you should know, don't just get together and talk.'

'But we all need to find a way out of this,' Kit said, desperate for a solution.

'Speak to Nick. He's the one who'll put you on to Wriothesley.'

'What's Wriothesley's present name?'

'James Waters,' Ingram replied, slowly accentuating each syllable and getting up at the same time from the extreme corner of the green wooden bench on which he had perched. Without saying a word he made his way off casually across the square in the direction of Greek Street – a neural laser impervious to everyone, trance-walking with heroin as his chemical guide through the city.

Kit watched him go: a standout in the casual crowd, someone who lived, it seemed, without real friends or ties. Ingram was a species of one, and Kit was thrown by the possibility that he, too, displayed these characteristics and stood out to others as an alien. He looked up on impulse to see a Boeing show its tail fins dangerously close to Centre Point, as though simulating a terrorist run that the BA pilot would return to at a later date. Kit could sense the undertow of turbulence in London's collective psyche. The city appeared to be documenting its own apocalypse, its core infected by the power-mad tsars and their entourage of druggy, discredited celebrities who hijacked its privileges. Kit could sense the build towards catastrophic burn-out. He was amazed at the complacency he experienced everywhere, as if the Anglo-Japanese community was desensitized to the possibility of its own imminent destruction. On the bench next to him two Paul Smith-suited city types wearing black leather Chanel trainers – the double-C logo visible like a DNA helix – were openly showing each other the guns they kept locked in their cases. They were joking about management rivals, their casual adoption of lawlessness through possessing weapons simply a sign of the times.

Kit inwardly flinched from the prospect of reacquainting himself with Wriothesley, a.k.a. James Waters. Even the man's anodyne name seemed to him like a virused attachment posted in his nerves. If he really was the notorious Kit Marlowe, from an uninterrupted previous existence, then he was involved with a bad lot all over again, and Wriothesley, an intimate friend of Lord Strange's, from whom he had stolen Billy Shakespeare as a lover, was, at heart, despite his patronage of the arts, a fat-cat gangster with networks reaching into organized crime.

Kit looked up quickly to see another airliner banking in suspiciously low, turbos blasting at rooftop level as the pilot shaved Oxford Street, as if searching a landmark target to ditch his plane.

Deciding to act fast on Ingram's advice, Kit punched Nick's numbers into the keypad of his mobile and caught his breath. He heard the tone ring five times before Nick answered.

'You didn't waste much time,' Nick said by way of answering. 'Did you see that Boeing bounce over Oxford Street just then?'

'Scary,' Kit said against a background of unmixed white noise. 'That's the second today. I'm sorry to press you like this, particularly as we've only just met again, but do you happen to know someone called James Waters?'

'Why's that?' Nick asked, his manner turning suddenly defensive.

'We're all in this together, aren't we?'

'In what?' Nick said, deliberately blunt and conceding nothing.

'The Grid, of course. I don't know quite how to put it – it's too complex – but it seems we're all linked by connections to the past. We've all got some major clearing to do, and some of it looks very nasty.'

There was a sustained pause, leaky with street noise, before Nick said, slightly apprehensively, 'We'd better meet. This isn't something to discuss on the phone. I'm outside Zavvi in Oxford Street. I've got things to do, but I could be at First Out in half an hour.'

'Fine. I'll be there.'

He got up from his bench feeling wrung out and looked over in the direction of the 20th Century Fox building, its shatterproof windows blacked out on the square. Michael Jackson's ostentatious, black stretch limo was parked outside, like a customized hearse transporting the discredited celebrity across a semi-lawless London.

Despite the rooftop fly-over of the two Boeings, the crowds in Soho Square continued to chill, insulated from reality by their headsets and videophones. The chemical sun, red as a squeezed orange, lit up the West End like a spotlight on a nuclear city. Kit stood looking directly into it, half expecting an aircraft to fly out of its core into a nose-diving kamikaze over Whitehall. It seemed unreal, like everything else in his life, that after all this time he should be meeting Nick again at First Out. The place carried such associations for him – Nick, the partially reformed rent boy, sitting in there looking for all the world like trade, and he himself, hunched over a notebook at a table writing or hoping to turn a trick in a way that would have pleased the Kit Marlowe who had hung out there at St Giles' with Shakespeare in the plague years.

His natural impatience had him arrive at the café, with its familiar charcoal-grey fascia and windowed front, early. He got a table by the window upstairs and looked out at the busy street scene as if watching a movie, until eventually Nick hurried into view, burning calories, the fast pace of big-city life written in his eyes.

'Hi,' he said. 'Sorry I'm late. I got distracted in Zavvi. Eye candy is one of my therapies.'

'No worries,' Kit said, looking up from the copy of *Boyz* he was reading and suspicious at the same time that the man he had loved was a makeover for the altogether more devious prototype concealed beneath.

Nick spoke to a French girlfriend, Jacquie, who was serving, came back to the table with a cappuccino and sat down, the rev counter switched on in his blood, a prominent blue vein standing out like a highway cut into his temple.

'I'm sorry to eat into your time,' Kit said, 'but I need you to help me make sense of crazy things that keep happening in my life – and yours, too, I suspect.'

'Is that why you want to know about James Waters?' Nick asked, like someone conversant with the whole ramified and extraordinary plot in which Kit found himself a central player. 'I'd be careful. He's a powerful man.'

'In what way?' Kit asked, his curiosity fired.

'Arms, if you want to know. He's part of Ruag Munition Warhead Division. Very dodgy stuff, I can tell you. The MOD and all of that . . .'

'You mean a gay man working for an arms company?' Kit queried, biting on the apparent contradiction.

'If I was you I'd keep away from Wriothesley – or Waters, as he now calls himself. Let Ray do his own dirty work.'

'So you know already that I've met Ray?' Kit said, amazed at the perfection of Nick's insight.

'It's a small world. Watch out. Ray's sold on a power trip. He's never forgotten the fact that his claim to the throne was conceived as illegitimate and rejected outright.'

Kit pulled on his bottle of Stella. This was the real Nick talking – not the rent boy with aspirations to be a pop star but the insidious snoop Nick Skeres, who had always got into the darkest corners of Kit's life.

'It seems like we're all somehow living double lives, and none of us can get clear of our past. I don't know what's happening, other than that it leaves me feeling wrecked.'

'It's a game for the strong,' Nick said emphatically and without the least trace of sympathy over the agonized phrasing of Dusty Springfield singing 'All I See Is You'.

'What exactly do you mean by that? That some of us don't make it to the other side?'

'You could put it like that. The Grid would call it in their terminology, "reconfiguring the pattern".'

Nick appeared, like Ingram, to be as dispassionately cold as a bottle of Smirnoff lifted from the freezer, and Kit, no matter the attention he paid his ex-lover, felt ruthlessly exploited by his programmed objectivity and deliberate hard front.

'It's important I see Wriothesley,' Kit said. 'He was once an important figure in my life, a patron, even if he demanded sex in return.'

'It's probably better to go and see him before he visits you,' Nick said in an admonitory tone. 'He knows where you are, you can be sure of that. I'll give you his details. They're on my phone.'

Kit was suddenly made alert to the wall of sound created by an approaching aircraft's engine rumble, the rush of adrenalin in him anticipating another rogue pilot defying the computer by coming down level with office towers, risking putting the nose cone through the mirrored cladding of a corporate slab. This time, to his relief, the pilot, while flying dangerously low, levelled out before re-enacting the mock kamikaze tactics of the two runs that he had witnessed earlier.

Nick peremptorily flashed his eyes at his watch and said abruptly, as a means of terminating the conversation, 'I'd better go; I'm running late. Call me sometime if you want.'

Nick got up quickly, shouldered his expensive Camper backpack and made for the door with the same hurried, determined air he had entered with ten minutes ago, beating it out to the ozone-fried crowds massing along Tottenham Court Road.

Kit was left with no option but to stay on with his unfinished beer. The boy sitting alone at the window seat opposite was trying to catch his eye with a series of provocative stares. He reminded Kit of Nick as he was five years ago, the same rough-diamond twinkle, the same exploitative, streetwise mindset. The café, popular at this hour, was beginning to peak with regulars there to meet friends or eat vegetarian, and without being asked the boy took it on himself to come over to join Kit, his white T-shirt as clean as his skin smell. 'Mind if I join you for a bit? I'm Chris, by the way. I'm waiting for a friend who's late. Have you got any coke?'

Kit looked at the boy's thin lips, his dark-brown needy eyes already busy with the prospect of contemplating yet another rejection. He knew instinctually he didn't want to get involved in this, even on the most casual level. It was Nick all over again, with the same level of duplicity, and he didn't have the time. 'I'm sorry. You've caught me at a bad moment. I'm about to leave. I've got to meet somebody, and I'm running late.'

He got up immediately and smiled at the boy. There were already too many repeat patterns in his life – corridors opening up to the wrong underground car-parks in the city's endlessly labyrinthine subterranean world. He deliberately made himself appear busy, headed for the nearby door to the street and hurried off, determined not to look back.

10

When Kit awoke the next day he knew intuitively that something catastrophic had happened. He picked up the lightweight handset from the bedside table and, using the FM radio facility, tuned into the news that the British Commissar and his wife had been reportedly assassinated by a suicide bomber on their way to Chequers in an SAS-driven 'fortress'. From what Kit could make out from media reportage, early stages of the investigation pointed to the driver as the chief suspect – the bomb furnished with an acid-capsule trigger having been concealed in the car's customized ergonomics.

Kit slowly took in the gravity of the news and its social implications, suspicious at the same time that the event was still another instance of ubiquitous spin. The Commissar, surrounded by his suited thugs, was awaiting the serving of international papers indicting him as a war criminal, and he had unapologetically conducted an illegal global-intervention policy for over a decade, characterized by unlawful and genocidally enforced regime changes. The Commissar manifested all the stereotypical characteristics of the psychopath, right down to the asymmetrical structure of the face and the dissociation from any responsibility for his actions, and his assassination had always been simply a matter of time. The man's psychopathology had existed throughout the duration of his autocratic rule, like an oil stain leaked on to the concrete floor of a high-rise car-park. The legacy of his political DNA was to be found fingerprinted on the killing fields of Kosovo, Afghanistan and Iraq and not only on the concealed mass graves of the dead but on the millions of shattered, maimed post-genocidal survivors of wars conducted for no other objective but oil.

Kit got a carton of orange juice out of the fridge, wondering at the same time why there was no message from Yukio. He realized his personal-communications radar was starting to rely more on happenings generated by synchronicity than real-time arrangements, and the conscious lapse in conducting his more intimate relations had him feel anxious at his friend's silence.

Over a period of time Kit had grown used to the familiar soundtrack of sirens chasing across the city, and today's volume of urgent white noise was no greater than normal in London's persistently stressed-out soundscape. He went and stood by the window pillar, looking out at the skyline towards the Westway towers, sensing the urban apocalypse he could feel growing at the back of Paddington Basin, like a guitar storm building by figures to mega-burn-up-and-out.

Uppermost in his mind was the knowledge that it was today he was due to meet the redoubtable Wriothesley, the lover he had once shared with Shakespeare in a vicious triangle of jealousy and competition for favours. Aspects of the past that he had tried so hard to suppress were starting to resurface and seemed no less distressing now than when they had first occurred. Wriothesley's politics were predictably built into a sexuality that, because it was considered aberrant, was equally dependent on money and power to sustain its fugitive existence.

Kit methodically got himself ready for the day and, ignoring a series of texts from Scott Diamond, flicked an eye over the print-out of his late-night input into the screenplay. It was always his habit last thing at night to free-associate on the computer and read back the spontaneous expressions of his drunkenness the next day. Some of it would seem genuinely inspired and the rest junk – the product of alcohol, over-excitability and the inevitable brain-fade of fatigue.

What he looked at today, sober and refreshed by coffee, were two pages he had written the previous night on exactly what he could remember of his relations to Shakespeare and Wriothesley in their period of rivalry. He knew the pages were never likely be endorsed by Scott, but he intended to keep them as a true record of scandalous sexual intrigue. He believed that he alone had witnessed the young Shakespeare tunnelling into his patron, whose face at the time had been buried deep in the pillows. His only option, after encountering the two having brutal sex – and he remembered it clearly – had been to leave Southampton House fast, slashing a portrait of the young earl with a blade on the stairs, and when Wriothesley, dressed in a white shirt, had come running after him, he had, out of a temper that matched his patron's, pushed him aside and rejected him in a way that was never to be forgiven.

He stood, recollecting the incident and how the nature of his hurt had been confused at the time with the realization that he had something potentially scandalous to use against Wriothesley. The windows, as he looked out in the direction of Portobello Road, were full of gold September light. He put on a dark-blue floral shirt over a Yumisuke T-shirt and Vanson trousers and checked himself in the mirror. His look was casual, but the pieces fitted.

When he went outside the day was the usual big-city film. Everyone was a stranger in London – a person you didn't recognize and would probably never encounter again. Kit liked it that way, despite the vulnerability attached to being alone in the crowd. He had, like everyone else, learnt to face-read instinctively as a method of survival.

Stopping off for a paper at the local newsagent's, he read that a dirty bomb had gutted the YMCA baths, killing twenty people and injuring another eighty. The anti-gay cell, the Pink Panthers from Hackney, had claimed responsibility for the bomb in the interests of gene cleansing by eliminating minorities. The tabloids were full of pictures of the dead or injured being stretchered from the disaster site by emergency services.

Kit didn't know quite why, but he felt immediately panicky. The London–Tokyo around him was turning into a war zone, a precinct of escalating catastrophe in which the baseline for revolution seemed to have been lifted from a J.G. Ballard novel.

As Kit headed into the Underground he was aware that the vision of the nuclear future that had infected the city's pathology for most of the twentieth century was most probably about to be realized. The constituents of apocalypse were programmed deep into its inhabitants, who had come mostly to accept the inevitability of thermonuclear destruction. It was, he knew, just a question of time.

After cooking in the Tube for twenty minutes, deep in the city's constricted arteries, Kit came above ground at Sloane Square and cabbed it the short distance to Wriothesley's place in Eaton Square. Weapon-scanned on entrance to the cab, he watched the jumpy driver dressed in combat gear negotiate the avenue as if he was handling an army reconnaissance vehicle. Kit could see the man's heavy Glock pistol resting beside him in the cabin. An oxygen mask was suspended above the driver's seat, and the man's jerky, paranoid movements seemed a reading of the city's index of terror.

When Kit got out of the armour-plated vehicle and paid, the driver had one hand involuntarily placed on his gun. With CCTV cameras tracking his movements, Kit approached the front door of Wriothesley's mansion block and waited apprehensively for an answer from the entryphone. His earlier conversation with him had been brief, but the imperative was that he should pay him a visit at noon. There wasn't a voice response to his signal – Wriothesley would have known it was him from the security video camera – just an electronic click, telling him the door was open. When he stepped into the voluminous reception area a uniformed security guard fingerprinted him as part of procedure before pointing to the lift with instructions for the fourth floor.

Kit went up in a mirrored lift and came out into a red-carpeted corridor silent as a Ritz interior in the mid-afternoon. He made his way apprehensively to the door of apartment number 24 and rang the bell. He could feel the silence compacted in this moneyed space push at him like a restraining hand.

The door was opened almost immediately by a blond-haired young man with impossibly high cheekbones, who looked twenty but was probably thirty. Something about the unnatural spacing of his eyes gave Kit, as a first impression, the notion that he was undergoing facial reconstruction.

Kit was shown into a cherry-red hall hung with showy frocks that glittered with Swarovski crystals that could have been picked up from an auction of Shirley Bassey's discarded stage gowns. He was taken into a large lived-in sitting-room with a high gilded ceiling, two of the walls shelved with a crippling tonnage of books. When the young man disappeared out of the room without saying anything, Kit started to feel uneasy. He regretted coming here so impulsively, and the suspense of waiting for Wriothesley to appear didn't help. He had the feeling, all the time, that he was being watched. There was no such thing as a reformed snoop – experience had taught him that – and technology had enhanced methods of intelligence in ways that he knew were there to be utilized to advantage by Wriothesley's inveterately duplicitous nature.

When Wriothesley, after a considerable delay, walked into the room and introduced himself as James Waters Kit could still pick out the Elizabethan in his features. He was taller than his sixteenth-century counterpart, but the oval-shaped face, the deep-brown eyes and the scar tissue above the nasal bridge were all instantly recognizable. So, too, was the quiet voice inflected with an arrogance that bordered on cruelty. He had never forgotten how, to Wriothesley's indignation, the queen had commented on his political aspirations, that he was 'one whose counsel can be of little, and experience of less use'.

'It's been a long time,' the man said with cutting irony, before dropping into a comfortable chair.

'I'm not sure I'm with you,' Kit said, still on his guard.

'It depends on how you see time,' James said, 'as a forwards, backwards or circular loop. I feel like we met last a couple of days ago.'

'I'm not so sure I do, but you have it your way.'

'You know who I am, don't you, Kit? You can't have forgotten the sex we had, my patronage and, more to the point,
certain secrets we shared.'

Kit looked up to see the young man who had answered the
door staring at him from the hall. Found out, he simply dusted
his blond fringe and continued to stare.

'Don't mind Billy,' James said. 'He's curious, that's all.'

'I think I know who you are,' Kit said reluctantly, struggling
with the idea. 'Henry Wriothesley, the Earl of Southampton.'

'A.k.a. James Waters,' the voice came back at him perfunctorily. 'I knew you had a good memory.'

Billy stepped right into the room this time, both hands
behind the back of his head in an affected pose and stood looking directly at Kit. He didn't speak, just stood there, immobile,
until he was ordered out of the room.

'It depends on what you want me to remember,' Kit said,
acting cool as the man confronting him in a green chair.

'Would you like a drink?' James asked, pointing to a tray
stocked with bottles of spirits and mixers. 'You were always a
heavy drinker – we all were at the time, but you were the
worst.'

Kit asked for a large Isle of Jura scotch and sat nursing its
amber eye in a tumbler. He had the weird presentiment that
Billy was still looking at him with surround-vision.

'There's a reason we've all met again,' James said, 'and I'll
come to it slowly. Billy keeps staring at you because he's got
something important to tell you later, but I'll leave that to him.'

'I'm still not totally sure what I'm doing here,' Kit said.
'Nick told me to come and see you in connection with a man
called Ray, who claims to be your old rival and acquaintance
Lord Strange. Like you, at one time he was my patron. I never
liked the man – not then, not now.'

'I'm glad to hear that,' James said, his downturned smile
creased at the corners. 'The photography, Bateman's Buildings,
they're a cover for something else, of course. You know very
well it's connected with drugs. And the person's mania for

power. Ray's wealth comes, not surprisingly, from PMK, smuggled into the European Union every year to make ecstasy tablets. The gay-club scene's the world's biggest consumer.'

'I'm not totally with you.'

'PMK is piperonyl methyl ketone, better known as the synthesized derivative of the sassafras tree. It's transported in drums meant to contain acetone. These go to ecstasy factories in Benelux to process piperonyl into MDMA powder, which is then formed into tablets. Dealers will pay £50,000 per kilogram of MDMA and convert it into 10,000 pills. Ray uses his wealth derived from drugs to maintain his country stacks in the north and uses his Soho base for rent.'

'You always used intelligence to compile case histories, and I can see you're no different now.'

'Are you?' James asked. 'Old habits, depressingly, never die.'

'What if I told you Ray sent me here to kill you? Would that make sense?'

'Totally,' James replied, his response streamlined like a bullet.

Billy had decided to come back into the room and proceeded to open up his laptop on a deep-pink sofa. He looked intensely across at Kit, as though expecting something of him, before focusing his attention on the keyboard.

'He writes all the time,' James said by way of explanation. 'It's an obsession. It always was. Most of it's brilliant. He won't publish it, though. I met him by chance at Heaven. He would hardly speak then, even though he was attending the Grid and attempting to come to terms with his suppressed identity.'

'I keep thinking I've seen him somewhere before,' Kit said. 'The face is familiar despite its reconstruction. I've an idea who it is from my past, but I can't be certain.'

'He'll introduce himself to you when he's ready. He's shy and a bit dyslexic. But, believe me, he's a genius.'

Kit looked across at Billy in profile, his black Jamie Mcleod

T-shirt sprayed on his body with the same consistency as his D&G jeans. One shoulder appeared to be slightly lower than the other, as a genetically flawed mismatch, and the eyes seemed to him incapable of closing. They were spaced too wide and were too attentive. He seemed, as much as Kit could follow his direct input on the laptop, to write without revision, naturally, compulsively.

'Cute, isn't he?' James said. 'But, as you can imagine, he comes at a price, rather as I imagine you would if we were to enter into a contract.'

'It's not my sort of job,' Kit said immediately. 'You should know me better than that. I'm not a contract killer, and I never was.'

'Think about it,' James said with implacable cool. 'Somebody needs to be killed in order to break an established pattern. It's the only way any of us can be free of the past.'

'But why should murder be the price necessary to liberate us?'

'It's a blood law,' James replied emphatically. 'Ask Billy about it when you get to know him.'

Kit could feel the whisky heating him inside. He hadn't eaten all day, and the alcohol went straight to his head. But he remained inwardly resolved that he wasn't going to be the one responsible for a killing in cold blood, of the kind that he himself had once been a victim of at Deptford Creek.

'I'll need time to think about all this,' he said. 'I'm finding it difficult enough already to come to terms with who I am. You should know yourself that the Grid doesn't make it easy.'

James laughed sardonically. He gulped on his scotch like someone wanting to deaden a nerve signal, emptied his tumbler and threw his head back for the volatile hit.

'Give me a break to think about all this,' Kit added, anxious to play for time and go.

Billy, he noted, was totally focused on his writing, oblivious to the conversation. His hands moved at the speed of thought, and his eyes followed.

Kit risked getting up in mid-conversation and looked out of the window at the black Jeep parked on the opposite side of the street, which was obviously monitoring his movements. It looked to him, quite clearly, like intelligence substituting for a mobile biological van.

Without once looking up from his work Billy continued typing, as James involuntarily conceded that the meeting was at an end, got up from his chair and accompanied Kit to the hall. Kit had the indomitable feeling that he knew Billy on a deep level from somewhere he couldn't immediately place. Through Nick he had met so many rent boys over the years that he had forgotten their names and faces, and for a moment he assumed that Billy was one of their number. They formed an anonymous stereotype, all of them without exception in love with the idea of striking it rich.

James made no effort to try to detain him. Kit walked unobstructed to the front door – expecting at any moment to feel a pistol snout fitted to his back – and lifted the latch, hardly turning round even to acknowledge James's presence.

When the door finally clicked shut behind him Kit found himself out in the red-carpeted corridor once again and made his way directly back to the lift. Despite the couple he could hear, the woman's voice screaming her way to orgasm behind a locked door, the building had about it an air of complete desertion, like a government HQ emptied by the threat of a dirty bomb.

Tracked all the way by cameras, Kit went down four floors to the reception area and found the security guard occupied on his videophone. Kit flashed the man a smile and watched the Jeep take off immediately he stepped outside. The timing was the perfect signal to the watcher that he was being watched in his turn.

When he stepped outside into the street, out of instinctual curiosity he looked up at the fourth floor, and he could see Billy standing staring out of the window, his white hair contrasting dramatically with his black T-shirt.

Kit had no intention of waiting around, and he headed off in the direction of Sloane Square to look for a taxi. A desert-camouflaged cab gunned out of nowhere towards him, but the oxygen-masked driver wouldn't stop, and the cab burnt on like a military vehicle leaving civilian survivors abandoned on the road. Only a week ago a number of cabs had been hijacked by a psycho who had held three successive drivers at knife-point, brutally disarmed them and physically abused them after ordering them to drive to a yard near World's End.

Kit felt alarmingly overexposed in this part of town, despite the abundant CCTV cameras mounted at every vantage point. Gated estates and expensive apartment blocks were the new targets for London's increasingly anarchic cells. The balance of power had shifted, so that now it was the secure neighbourhoods who were the most vulnerable to violent robbery – and the poor inner-city communities that had made themselves into the new inviolable élite. Eaton Square, once the sanctuary of the privileged that counted the neurodegenerative autocrat Margaret Thatcher amongst its fat-cat residents, was now in the front line of attack.

Kit walked hurriedly and on his guard towards Sloane Square, increasingly aware that the apocalypse he had once imagined had become a reality in his own lifetime. The city was literally starting to burn with carbon-monoxide pollution, and the Japanese clubs were already staging endgame nights, in which Madonna dance remixes were played to video clips of a London in flames, with packed mortuaries and fighter jets cruising the city's skies. Endstate was the new popular culture, and clubbers were doing drugs to kill. The whole city was in danger of becoming a crazily partying nuclear bunker in which champagne exploded temporarily as a substitute for radiological bombs.

Kit found himself getting off on the weird, exhilarating thrill of danger. It was like chemical fall-out in the blood. He knew he was walking towards the possibility of a terrorist strike at any moment – the roof blown off Chelsea and the explosion surfing through the streets as a lethal cocktail of radioactive dust, uranium, potassium and botulinum.

Kit assumed, as he walked in the direction of the Tube, that men like Wriothesley, with his arms interests and government associates in the corridors of power, had, with the increase in technology, been building towards this catastrophic finale for decades. He remembered only too well their sixteenth-century equivalents – the Cecils and the Walsinghams – as being equally demonstrative in their power-politics and limited in their capacity for genocidal potential only by the unavailability of WMDs. For no clear reason at all, the figure of Sir Robert Cecil, member of the Privy Council responsible for assessing the suitability of plays for court, came into his mind. Kit had worked as an agent for Robert Cecil, a small, fastidious, complex man, physically deformed with a hunchback, probably as a result of scoliosis, but who made up for his disability with a formidable intellect and natural ability to scheme his way to the top. Cecil, Kit remembered, had served his political apprenticeship in France, where he had consorted with the adventurer Parry and run dodgy errands for the Secretary of State, Sir Francis Walsingham. Groomed by his father for political office, Robert had been knighted in 1591 and incorporated into the Privy Council. Eaten up by an inexhaustible appetite for intrigue and surveillance, Kit knew at heart that Robert Cecil from Hatfield House had been one of the key government players instrumental in endorsing the contract that had resulted in his carefully planned murder. It wasn't that the greed for power amongst the likes of Cecil, Walsingham and Burghley had been any less, or had become an expansive pathology over the centuries, it was simply, Kit realized, that leadership was directly linked to the available weaponry for world domination given to the ruling despot at the time.

As he watched the grey wash of clouds parked over the King's Road Kit's head was full of these things and the scheming characters who had come alive again as part of his reinvention at the Grid. He wasn't sure if it was the same one, but a black

Jeep, identical to the one he had seen earlier, passed by him slowly, its halogen lights on full despite the fact that it was broad daylight. The driver ignored a red light and coasted imperiously through as an act of lawlessness.

Sloane Square, as the aorta to the King's Road, was busy with rafts of Anglo-Japanese shoppers. A Japanese girl walking in front of him provocatively showed the diamanté twinkle of her black G-string, the glittering T-bar visible above the waistband of her bleached hipsters. Kit always picked up on the particular roar of the place, and he recalled his years of illicit cottaging in the toilets beneath the square, just by the taxi-rank, before they were sealed up in the late 1980s. The extinct site was another dark hole in the city's subterranean network that had become airbrushed by progress.

Kit stood at the entrance to the King's Road, taking in the sniff of the real as a burst of toxic petrocarbons, and he decided to look round the place and kill time there before training it back to his loft. When his mobile went off, interrupting his stream of thoughts, he could see from the display that it was Nick.

'You've just seen Wriothesley, haven't you?' he said abruptly and without introduction. 'I'm over this way with friends and wondered if you'd care to meet for a coffee.'

Kit hesitated. Nick had caught him off guard, and he didn't know quite what to say. He suspected immediately that Nick had been watching him all the time.

'OK. Where are you?'

'So close I can see you,' Nick replied, the suppressed laughter evident in his voice. 'We're in Caffè Nero on the corner of the square. I'm looking directly at your back. If I was a marksman . . .' He laughed.

Kit turned round slowly, apprehensively, and he could see Nick sitting in the window, blond hair licked over one eye. He was too shocked by the twist in events to change his mind and backtrack. He admired Nick's method. Wriothesley had clearly told him what time they were meeting and had phoned him after Kit had left.

Kit took his time, careful to stake out his independence and not be intimidated, his eye alerted to a splash of cerise roses at the nearby flowerseller's stall. When he walked in to the café, quite casually, he realized Nick had company. Ingram was sitting there behind his black-out Jackie Os, his shoulders pinched into a black leather coat, and seated next to him was a dubious-looking young man with short black hair, dark eyes and a thin sculpted nose.

'Hi,' Nick said casually, putting their conversation on pause. 'You haven't met Robert for a time,' he added, immediately introducing the dark-haired young man. Ingram appeared his usual incommunicable self, busy shutting out the world.

'Good to meet you,' Robert said, extending a hand with a conspicuous blue diamond worn on the index finger.

Kit did an instant time check to see if this was someone else from his past he should recognize. It hit him straight away that this was the young man he had seen waiting that time with Nick, reading a paper on the corner outside the Dominion Theatre on Tottenham Court Road.

Kit deliberately took his time at the counter and sat down after having got himself a double espresso. He needed the caffeine hit to psych himself up. He felt gunned into submission by three lanes of intensely scrutinizing eyes.

'Seen Wriothesley, have you?' Nick asked, injecting contempt into the name. 'Hasn't changed, has he? Money, power, boys – the usual recipe for corruption.'

'Arms, you mean,' Robert commented with authority. 'He's right in with Whitehall. He's a screaming queen who wants to be a king.'

'Let's not pretend. We're all in this together, right. Doesn't matter who's paying you. You do both parties.'

'I live from writing now. I'm no longer part of intelligence.'

'You mean you're still sucking on patrons,' Robert said cuttingly.

'Look,' Nick said, evidently the leader of the conspiracy. 'We can work this out. We need you as a go-between to snoop on both Wriothesley and Strange. Or James and Ray if you like.'

'Fuckers,' Ingram interjected, then went back to being catatonic.

Kit had the sense of being mentally autopsied. The past kept returning with insidious jabs, and he knew from experience that once a bit fitted the rest followed.

'It's like stroking snakes, dealing with these people,' Nick said. 'You have a way with them, Kit. Always did. Shaft them both . . .'

'Motherfuckers,' Ingram said contemptuously, the tight skin on his cheekbones looking transparent.

'This city's fucked,' Nick said. 'The monarchy's up for grabs, the Commissar's dead – or is supposed to be. These two, they've been waiting their time.'

'Have they got the tube?' Kit asked, catching Nick unawares. 'Have they been genetically redesigned like you and me?'

'Is that what you talked about?' Nick cut in, looking troubled, his face suddenly breaking up into worry lines.

'Why, of course not. The subject never came up,' Kit said, conceding nothing, and seeing in Nick's defence a person he didn't like or really know, someone who was clearly ruthless.

'Better not,' Ingram sneered from behind his black-outs. 'Talk to those guys and you're a goner.'

'And Jacko?' Robert asked. 'Did Wriothesley mention him? They're in touch, naturally, as they share the same sort of mindset.'

'No,' Kit replied, feeling stun-gunned by the incisive and unexpected questioning. 'Not a word. I've seen the black-limo fleet round the West End like everybody else, but I had no idea they were friends.'

'You'd better wise up,' Nick threatened. 'The loser in this game pays a heavy price.'

Kit threw a glance out of the window. He wondered if everyone knew about the events that so preoccupied his circle.

The whole city seemed hardwired to apocalypse, and it was a fact that people would never shop again without the knowledge that it could be the last time a particular store or street would remain standing. He didn't like the questions being fired at him or the baseline assumption that he was one of their number, a fellow conspirator.

'It's rather like old times,' Robert said. 'Meetings in the back rooms in pubs at the Savoy, the Strand, Shoreditch, Alsatia, and, of course, you remember Eleanor Bull's . . .'

Kit froze at the mention of the name. He could feel the nerves jump to attention behind his right eye as though swarming to attack.

'We're the unkillables,' Nick said coldly. 'We're as odd in our world as Chinese or Japanese blondes. That's why we're all still here. We're reinvented specifically for crime.'

'Stick to the point,' Robert said. 'It's info we need, not speculation.'

Kit drew his shoulders up instinctively and tensed. He looked outside again, contemplatively, at the indifferent orange October light. The time, place and century didn't really matter. He could have been observing a post-human world in that instant, one that had regrouped after being blown apart by hypersonic drones or one that was still awaiting the imminent catastrophe.

As he watched the crowds stream by, two black Jeeps opened fire on each other at the entrance to the King's Road, machine-guns bristling, before one accelerated away behind a black smokescreen, leaving an oil slick on the road to prevent pursuit. Nobody made any attempt to intervene. People looked on dispassionately or ran for cover as the remaining Jeep manoeuvred out of the square and took off in the direction of Victoria pursued by a green police car.

'Man, see that,' Ingram said, coming clear of his narcoleptic daze.

Nick and Robert looked out, clearly bored by events, like casual spectators of an ongoing scenario of gang warfare that was by now so commonplace it didn't merit attention, then transferred their attention to a gay Japanese boy who had just come into the café with a Sloaney girl, wearing a sequinned mini and a slash of red lipstick.

'You still go back to Deptford, don't you?' Nick said out of the blue, turning his eyes on Kit.

Kit didn't answer. He looked away as though preoccupied with the action outside, where police were busy marking off the incident with red-and-white crime tape.

'I thought we could all have a reunion down there,' Robert said.

'Don't wind him up,' Ingram warned before reconnecting with his chemical haze.

Kit wasn't sure where this conversation was going, only that the undertones were turning scary. It was their uniformly shared remove from all emotions that he found most disconcerting. It seemed to him that Nick's motives were only too apparent in their threatening undertones, like a bass figure in a register so low it made the ground vibrate.

'I'm only suggesting we get together and party,' Robert said, trying to make light of it and flashing his blue diamond.

'We're not suggesting anything,' Nick said, pushing a bony knee against Kit's thigh as a sign of reassurance.

'I didn't think you were,' Kit replied, looking at his watch. 'If it's all the same with you guys, I need to get back. I've got work to do.'

'Get on the case,' Nick said. 'There's big money there.'

'There's Jacko, too,' Robert said, refreshing his diamond with showy gestures. 'You might look him up at the Dorchester.'

'Support the androids,' Ingram said. 'We're the new species.'

'We'll send you the case details,' Nick added.

Kit was suddenly reminded of the real Nicholas Skeres in this admission, the Skeres whose authority had always spoken for the rest. It was the same now. Nick was the insidious frontman, Robert the back-up and Ingram the deep probe who worked obliquely on the subject by upending him through lateral thinking. They all three met in a pivotless centre, where there was no vestige of shared trust as a resting point.

Kit finished the bitter residue of his espresso and got up to go. There was no camaraderie amongst the men he faced. He could see them properly now in their vulnerability and scheming. They had made corruption their own, like bacteria in the gut.

'Be seeing ya then,' Ingram said dismissively as a postscript.

'I've got your number from Nick,' Robert said. 'I'll be in touch.'

Donna Summer's 'I Feel Love' was being played as Kit made his way out of the café into a swarming, panicky Sloane Square. There were police everywhere in the glowering light, the sunset doing red-and-shocking-pink dramatics over World's End. He was shocked, as he surveyed the gathered crowds, by how much Nick had changed in their time apart. His feelings for him had instantly gone cold. Nick, more than anyone in the group, seemed to have reverted to his original character. As Kit remembered him fingering dirty money from his latest extortion racket he realized Nick was every bit the clone of his scheming, dodgy sixteenth-century counterpart.

Kit had no intention of hanging round the crime scene. He sensed that Chelsea, as a rich precinct, would be lit if not today then tomorrow in the systematic torching of London's moneyed zones: Kensington, St John's Wood, Holland Park, Knightsbridge and Mayfair, they had all been burnt at the edges by urban terrorists.

Kit walked to the station, bought a ticket from the automatic dispenser and stood at the entrance to the Underground. The hot air down there was cooking. He took a long, deep breath, drew his shoulders in and disappeared into the solid dark.

11

Back home Kit worked on his screenplay with renewed energies. He felt now he was no longer in the process of inventing a character but had become the participant in his own story. If his life as the poet Christopher Marlowe had been hijacked over the centuries by speculative biography and redundant academic commentary then he was, for some reason, being given the chance to redress the issue. The work in hand was now dependent more on personal memory associations than it was on accepted facts. The transition in approach had been rapid, but he had grown to accept it.

When Yumiko stopped by to collect the black coat she had loaned him, Kit was amazed to find that she had bought him an almost identical one in Brick Lane market. A black woollen double-breasted coat with the label ripped out, which, being a small size, fitted him perfectly, moulding itself to the slim line of his body.

He made a show in the mirror for her, collar turned up, hands slouched in the deep pockets. Yumiko, whom he had met as a friend of Yukio's, was studying fine art and photography at Goldsmiths, and she was so shy she rarely made sustained eye contact. She was dressed all in black with red highlights in her straight shoulder-length hair; her eyelids glittered with a frosty diamanté sparkle while her small mouth was sealed with black lipstick.

Kit knew nothing of her private life. She visited him and Yukio occasionally, and today she had brought the autumn light inside with her, its cool air polishing her skin. That she was lonely he guessed from her inveterately busy schedule of courses. Her leopardskin boots came up to her black mini, as part of her adopted goth-punk aesthetic. She was fragile and overprotected by her ageing and possessive parents. He knew that she found it difficult to function away from home, that she relied on her parents to finance her degree and pay for the upmarket flat she rented in Islington.

Kit enjoyed seeing her from time to time, partly because she was beautiful to look at, also because she gelled with some of his own interests in the arts. They both liked Genet, Burroughs and Ballard, writers who worked with a subversive vision, and they shared a common interest in their rock/pop/classical music tastes. It was written tacitly into the reserves of their friendship that both had a shadow side about which neither enquired – a dark side of the moon that remained alluringly dark.

Yumiko stayed only briefly for a cup of tea, her black lipstick leaving its signature imprint on the cup. She talked quietly, her eyelids lowered so that the subject of conversation always appeared to be sighted below her. She spoke downwards, as though Kit was seated at a slightly lower level. It was her way. She was going on to meet a friend in Soho, she said, to catch a movie at the Curzon cinema on Shaftesbury Avenue and, after making apologies for the brevity of her stay, left traces of a designer scent behind her as a footnote to her brief visit.

After she had gone Kit went back to writing, but his mind wasn't fully on the work. The compulsion to visit Deptford always came on with the night, pulling him as if the place was a gravitational centre. No matter how he tried to resist he always found himself going back there, remapping the streets, visiting his past like a retread, the place forming a detailed psycho-geography in his mind.

Kit agonized over the decision of whether to make the journey there and risk the hazards of opportunistic street violence or to stay put in his altogether safer neighbourhood. A part of him was for staying at home and giving his undivided attention to his work. Yukio was due back later that night, and if Kit decided to be there for him they could watch a film together or go somewhere locally to eat. He stood at the window and looked out in the direction of the Westway – its film-set gantries, dot-matrix boards and cellular towers swimming into view as the sky deepened to cerise and navy blue. The Westway was part of the city's brain, housed in London's cerebral cortex. It connected all over town with parallel architectures and the corresponding shine on water-vapour particles and dust pollution. London, he realized as he stood watching at the window, wasn't a home any longer but a digitally networked grid, a place invaded by conflicting terrorist cells conspiring towards urban apocalypse.

Taking a pull from the neck of a bottle of wine, he decided, against his better instincts, to go. He needed to be out there in the dark, drawn to the centre of things. It was as if the city would suddenly give up its subterranean secrets if he persisted in his nocturnal searching.

He put on the black woollen coat that Yumiko had brought him, scribbled a hasty note for Yukio and hurried out on his way to the Underground into a street gridlocked by corridors of traffic. At this hour the city always seemed to comprise a single coagulative tailback, frozen into immobility under a killer toxic haze.

When Kit, after making his way quickly through the streets, entered the subway, members of a black Kensal Rise cell, known locally as the Black Outs, were spray-painting graffiti over the subway stairs and walls – an indecipherable noodle-bed of purple slashes littering the concrete surfaces with the tag PANSPERMIA standing out central to the lacerating scrawl. In hoods and wearing orange wraparounds they attacked their targets like kung-fu fighters armed with spray cans.

Kit got his black coat atomized with paint as he hurried through the subway entrance to the main concourse and the ripped-out ticket dispensers. London Underground was critically understaffed because of the violent raids made on the system each day, and robosoldiers had been brought in to police key stations such as Victoria, Euston, Paddington and King's Cross.

The escalator was out, and Kit was forced to join the queue of commuters running or shuffling down the semi-vertical gradient of metallic stairs. People were waiting twenty deep on the platforms below. A packed train pulled out, passengers gummed up against the doors, faces flattened like snails to the steamed-up glass.

Kit stood his turn in the crowd and waited, feeling twitchy with paranoia. People kept arriving in increasing numbers until all the exits were blocked. The dusty air and the non-functional CCTV cameras added to the feeling of terminal dystopia in the air. He wished now he had stayed at home in the safety of his flat, a bottle at his elbow and pop creating an orange sunshine glow on the airwaves.

When he finally got on the train he found himself glued to a wedge of Japanese, their Anglo-morphed features and blond hair creating the mutant look of a hybrid species. The girls had blue lenses and bleached hair and wore neo-geisha makeup with Top Shop clothes. They were laughing amongst themselves, extending a joke that grew steadily more contagious. The boys in the group had Aryan hair and were in designer suits with unlinked shirt cuffs and candy-coloured ties.

They trawled along the Central Line with long delays in between stations – the pauses amplified by the cooking heat. People looked resigned to the indignity of being grilled alive, impacted in airless carriages deep under the city as they jolted across the unreconstructed network.

When Kit, to his relief, exited for the overground line at Charing Cross, he felt wasted by the heat. His shirt was wet on his back, and he was washed out. The same inert masses crowded the main concourse, waiting for delayed services, and gathered there like a nation at the end of time. People didn't seem to know any longer why or for whom or what they were waiting.

Kit joined the crowd waiting for the Greenwich train. It was late, and when he boarded he found he had to stand near an open window in a side door. As they pulled out of Charing

Cross London, to his eyes, looked like a series of high-rise death camps, illuminated concrete blocks lit by blue flickering televisions and monitors. Stoppages caused by faulty tracks occurred every few minutes to a feedback of dissonant brakes. The sky outside, Kit observed, was a dusty scarlet smudge eyebrowed across the galaxy. His cock was already hard in anticipation of cruising and pointed towards his destination and the slow mapping out of the tide in Deptford Creek.

When he got out at Deptford the last of the sunset was like tomato juice slashed across the sky. The high street was buzzing with locals shopping after work and grabbing burgers. There was a hearse parked up outside a local Tesco, a coffin badged with red carnations in its rear. Kit wondered at the black-suited driver reading a glossy magazine behind the wheel and the unlikelihood of a funeral being conducted in a local cemetery at night.

He stopped off at an Oddbins to buy a bottle of wine and have it uncorked. He slipped the bottle of St Emilion into his coat pocket after taking a liberal gulp, and already somewhere on the air he could smell the river's chemical skin. He grew excited, for his life would start to reverse each time this happened, and the London he remembered as the notoriously subversive street-fighting playwright Kit Marlowe, stalking its fetid alleys for poetic inspiration, would come up again for retrieval. At such times his old impetuosity would return and with it the characteristic intransigence written into those who create their own imaginative reality, rather than passively inhabit the existing one. He cared nothing for convention and never had – it was simply a framework of received ideas for those who were too frightened to shape their own laws.

As he walked inquisitively along Church Street he felt himself consciously entering deeper into the true nature of Marlowe's character. He had a friend who could film the past using a camera with a stand-by mode in which images are continually recorded in RAM. The memory stores a few seconds' worth of data and continually overwrites it. He wondered if the mind did the same, so that what was captured was saved before deletion.

Of his historical existence there existed only one likeness, that which had come to be called the Grafton portrait. The portrait – believed to have been salvaged when General Thomas Fairfax's New Model Army gutted the royalist Grafton House in rural Northamptonshire, in December 1643, and subsequently stashed in the nearby house of Anthony Smith – was put forward by Thomas Kay as late as 1907 as a putative painting either of Marlowe or his declared rival Will Shakespeare. He had checked the portrait, now hanging in the gallery of his old college, Corpus Christi at Cambridge, and without doubt recognized himself as the ambiguously featured young Elizabethan with auburn hair, a distinct blush on the cheeks and the perfectly defined pencil-line moustache and beard that was fashionable then, but, above all, he remembered the superbly glamorous gold-and-black taffeta doublet with padded shoulders and bronze buttons that he was wearing in the painting. Shirt slashed open to lend style to his attitude as a bohemian poet – he was tall and rangy in the portrait – he remembered the fashionable top he was wearing as his one pricey clothes purchase, a piece of ostentation that had ended up stained and ripped from days of reckless bingeing.

There was a chill in the night air, an October note of invasive damp off the river. He continued on his way to the Creek, sniffing at his territory, and through heightened olfactory associations succeeded in bringing the fetid Elizabethan London he had known, with its constant discharge of raw sewage, into play with the heavy-metal toxins of the current century. His brief encounter with Wriothesley/Waters had reawakened the snoop in him, and already he had succeeded in uncovering intelligence about the man's highly lucrative arms dealing. The facts came to mind as he paced his by now familiar personalized territory. Wriothesley's wealth, he had discovered, was all part of the illegal sale of surface-to-air missiles, from which people of his dodgy leanings and government associations profited. Posing as a representative of a fictitious Gibraltar-registered company, Kit had approached Wriothesley's company by email with a request to buy two hundred missiles. Claiming to be acting on behalf of the government of Rwanda, he had supported his request with documentation bought for £150 from a corrupt official in Kigali. Wriothesley's company had promptly, and without any reservations, offered to supply him missiles from Eastern Europe for £32,000 each. With a range of 10,000 feet the shoulder-mounted Igla missiles offered for sale could be used by terrorists to bring down aircraft during take-off or landing. Wriothesley's company had agreed to supply the weapons for £6.9 million. They were to be handed over to a Rwandan government representative in Kigali. Wriothesley had, in addition, offered anti-aircraft missiles, a range of Iranian launchers and rocket-propelled grenades. With such supporting evidence, this time Kit knew he really had something significantly incriminating on Wriothesley/Waters, and he suspected he had only scratched the surface of the man's lugubrious criminality.

The Creek was becoming an increasingly popular cruising area, a place in which he had no difficulty picking up – and, as Kit knew of Wriothesley's particular liking for anonymous sex in public places, it was in his mind that Wriothesley might try his luck there himself one night. Outwardly a city slicker, in his Jermyn Street suits and his purple leather lace-ups made to measure by Berluti, Wriothesley was also a man adept at dissolving into the fugitive world of cemeteries, heaths and wooded parkland where gay outlaws congregated and came out of the trees at night.

Kit stopped dead in his tracks as a man came out of the Rat and Parrot – blind with liquor, solid in a black leather jacket – and segued dangerously across the road, bringing a blue Audi to an impacted halt. People were openly out of it all over London, day and night, doing drugs and alcohol to excess, and this man, built like a fridge, might mean big trouble if confronted. After the man had zigzagged his way towards his parked car Kit continued on his way to a yard off Copperas Street, which had become a hot cruising area. He could smell the river strongly now, tracking along Greenwich Reach before muscling into the Creek all the way to Deptford Bridge. It nosed in as far as Church Street, a dark-green snout nuzzling the shore, smelling of chemicals, and it ran almost parallel to Norman Road on the other side. He and his sailor friends had in the past pissed all over this precinct as part of his territorial history. Time never quite succeeded in erasing the past, he told himself; a residual signature always remained like a DNA trace of oneself.

Kit could smell sex and danger in the air. A white Ford Transit came out of an alley and roared off in the direction of Creek Road. The whole complex behind Church Street and the works had become the monopoly of arms dealers and East European-operated drug mules. But at night a gay scene had located the precinct and quickly established tribal rights to the place. He liked the way this was a given in all major cities and nowhere more so than in London, where specific parks and public places had been unofficially declared gay territory. The yards had become precisely that – a gay colony – a same-sex community mapping out a new vision of the future, in which the childless outlaw would take precedence in society over received notions of family.

A man came out of the gloom, materialized as though composed of dark matter, just the reflection of his leather jacket distinguishing him from the solid night as he circled Kit and made off again in the direction of the Creek. Kit stayed put by a pile of ferroconcrete blocks, the reflected light from the street hardly reaching him there. He knew only too well that in watching he was also being watched. It was the law of the fugitive. There were others out there in the dark, aware of his presence as much as he was of theirs. It was all done extrasensorily, like watching the letters E and F moving out of a fax machine upside down and not knowing which one was coming out until the fax got to the end. He got off on the build-up of tension. He drew on his bottle again – the wine burning in as an exhilarating sugar hit. Despite the obvious dangers inherent in his pursuit, he felt oddly relaxed and at one with his territory. He was out there at night in the city's endocrine system, and he wanted to burn, to turn on the IGF-1/insulin receptor controlling the ageing process and beat them all – Nick, Robert, Ingram, Wriothesley, Strange and all the vital players from his past who were still alive.

He knew from long habit that waiting eventually paid off. The cold brushed him like fur as he pulled repeatedly on the wine. He heard a train's whistle over on the Greenwich side signal something of the alienation and vulnerability he felt when exposed to London's dangerously compromised travel network. Trains were no longer a safe means of transport and were, as much as cars in the present lawless state, the targets of rogue gangs that derailed services and robbed passengers at gunpoint.

Kit froze, sensing someone coming at him out of the night. There was a yellow tipper truck parked behind him, the elevated canopy above the gridded diesel engine giving him the weird impression he was being monitored by heavy machinery intelligence. The man was somewhere back of that in the dark. He couldn't see him, but he was on his radar.

He tensed at the light skitter of footsteps as the stranger repositioned himself in the yard. The man was playing cautious and kept dissolving back into the dark. Kit shifted position into reflected light and waited. The stranger was moving in on him now. He could hear police sirens tracking the night before it went still again. When the man came out at him Kit saw he was shielded by a beret and dark shades, his collar pulled up high to the cheeks. He could have been a boy or a man by the slim angularity of his body, and he signalled for Kit to follow.

Without any regard for his safety Kit went in pursuit of his athletic guide, whose breath sparkled on the cold night air. His rapid movements told him he was young and had mapped out the territory in advance. They dodged round the back of what looked like a hydraulic shovel, and he could see a silver car parked outside in the road that he took instantly for a silver-bullet Ferrari, too ostentatious, too superquick for the down-graded neighbourhood. Kit, who had some knowledge of cars, knew it was a model that took off like a panther through a sea of torque. It was serious money – 200,000K he told himself, as he followed the man in its direction. The man waited for him to come level before remoting the door open. Kit took the risk and lowered himself into the car's Bordeaux-coloured interior. The overhead light was on as he manoeuvred into a bucket seat and glanced across at the suede steering wheel and leather-trimmed roll bar. The car smelt of money and limited-slip differential. It wouldn't have been stolen, he knew that for sure; the model was too outstanding to evade detection.

The man sat quietly for a few moments, his hands placed in his lap. He didn't say anything at all, but his signals were clear. There were racing harnesses and a phallic gear lever, and the aircraft-cabin smell of supercar ergonomics. Without any intro-duction, the man started kissing him, taking it for granted that he had that right, feeding Kit with his slippery tongue. Kit found himself forced back against the headrest and pushing for air. As he struggled for control, he partly dislodged the stranger's beret, and a blond spill of hair escaped.

The man broke off the kiss, backed off and lifted the glasses slowly from his face, revealing himself as Wriothesley's blond trick Billy. Kit went wide-eyed with shock. He couldn't believe that Billy, whom he had assumed to be part of Wriothesley's proprietary Eaton Square package, was the man who had cruised him in the Deptford dark. There was something about his evidently Botoxed features and dissolute mouth that upset Kit. Somewhere in his past he had known this person before, and he was anxious to block the memory. He thought of get-ting out of the car on the spot and running for his life in case the boy turned dangerous.

Billy must have sensed this, for he placed a restraining hand on Kit's arm and said, 'Don't go. It's all right. He doesn't know I'm here.'

'Who doesn't?' Kit asked.

'Wriothesley. You remember me, don't you?'

Kit stared hard at Billy in the car's filtered light, noting the blood vessels floating like egg yokes in the whites of his eyes. The face was a restructured makeover for someone older – his own age perhaps – the contourless features creating the look of an alien. Billy leant forward and tried to kiss him again, then threw his head back petulantly and stared out of the windscreen.

'Don't you know who I am?' he asked again. 'I know I've changed to fit the times, but you must have an idea.'

'No,' Kit said abruptly. 'I haven't a clue, and I don't want to know. I've had the past up to here. All I want to do is live now and forget.'

He felt Billy's hand on his arm, and this time it was comforting. With a quick gesture Billy killed the overhead light, and his blond profile stood out as distinctly film-noirish in the blue, grainy light.

'We used to be rivals,' Billy said emphatically. 'And sometimes lovers, too, in a brutal way. You must know.'

Kit fitted himself to the red carbon-fibre bucket seat and tried, despite his racing heart, to relax. Confronting Shakespeare in the shark-shaped body of a silver Ferrari parked up in a Deptford works four centuries after their last meeting was something he didn't want to own to. He knew without having to be told that the slightly scary Aryan youth sitting in the driver's seat, visibly erect, was none other than a remodified Shakespeare, adapted like him for the times.

It was starting to rain, a light rap knuckling the hood as an autumn reminder and quickly gone again. It was all part of the night, the big-city night going through permutations of climate like changes to cells in the body.

'I was Shakespeare,' Billy said, 'if that seems credible. At least that's what the Grid tells me, and experience seems to confirm it.'

'That's as weird as me saying I'm Marlowe,' Kit said. 'How does either of us prove it?'

'I'm sure you've got sufficient proof, haven't you?'

'No more than you. Let's say I've been that person.'

'But there are so many conclusive facts,' Billy said, placing his hand nervously on Kit's cock. 'It's not like we're alone in this. The other members of the Grid remember, too. You must know that better than anyone. You're in touch with them all.'

Kit stiffened under Billy's raking fingers. He didn't want to concede his excitement but felt powerless to control it. There was something communicated by Billy's touch that he knew on a deeper level. That hand had been there before, and yet he didn't know why or how he could distinguish it from all the others.

'What do they remember?' Kit asked.

'That's a big question,' Billy gasped. 'Unresolved business I suppose, relating to your death. It seems that none of us has properly completed our lives.'

'But why us? Why should we be singled out to relive our lives from all the billions of people who have lived through the centuries?'

'I suppose, partly, because you and I shone like no others. We were imagination at a time when there was none. You and I, by our writings, shape-shifted language into a durable living organism and got ourselves written into history. But, more than that, we were tainted. We all used same-sex as a swipe card. I don't have to tell you . . .'

Billy forced the zip on Kit's jeans and ran his hand inside to explore. Kit was still vaguely on his guard and didn't fully respond, suspicious that he was being set up by Wriothesley. He resisted Billy going down on him and fought his way upright again in the seat.

'Don't you want me to?' Billy asked, the possibility of rejection showing in his troubled eyes.

'I'm not sure if this is right. You and I, we shouldn't be doing this. It belongs to the past.'

'Nobody will ever know. It's a way of reuniting.'

'I'm not so sure. You and I, although we're convinced of

our identities as Shakespeare and Marlowe, could be anyone. Let's leave it at that.'

'But we're not just anyone,' Billy said. 'Some misguided academics claim you wrote my books, that your death was faked so that you could elude charges from the Privy Council and disappear into Europe for a time, and so our identities are somehow linked for ever in the public mind and interchangeable. In a very real sense we're cloned.'

'What are you trying to say?' Kit asked, his triggered erection still signalling desire.

'That we're one person,' Billy said. 'We're clones in a weird sort of way – a mind-fuck that can't be separated. We were, after all, lovers and collaborated on plays, most of which have gone missing.'

'Where does that leave us?' Kit asked, his mind reframing the Shakespeare he had known, Wriothesley's intelligent rent with his muddy complexion, black tangled curls, effeminate mouth and gold earring, every bit the scheming Elizabethan youth with a clear hazel-coloured eye fixed, unlike him, on establishing a secure future.

'Knowing that only by one of us dying – and I mean that quite literally – can the other live. The rest are here because they're drawn superficially to our celebrity and, on a much deeper level, to their involvement in the murder that occurred here in Deptford all those centuries ago. They can't let go. Their existences depend on us resolving the issues that were left undone by the murder of genius.'

'That's your interpretation,' Kit said, 'not mine. We're here, to my mind, because of the tube, the Grid, genetic engineering.'

Billy laughed. 'You'll see,' he said dismissively. 'You'll learn the hard way.'

The rain opened up again, tracking the car's cellulose sheen. Billy came down on him relentlessly, and Kit let it happen. Billy took him in deep and resurfaced for air, tooling his cock against his cheek in the pause. He swallowed him whole with a facility Kit had rarely encountered. He abandoned himself to the rhythm, his width pushing against the constricted interior of Billy's mouth, as though he was going through changes in the gearstick's gates.

Billy pulled himself back for a moment to kiss Kit hard on the mouth. Kit tried to avoid his incongruously wide-spaced interrogating eyes. He didn't want to see himself in their reflections or be reminded that the man going down on him had once been, if only for a short time, the inseparable brother to his creativity.

Billy kept whispering, 'Let's fuck. I want it deep', but Kit was determined not to surrender his body completely to someone he didn't trust. Billy wasn't safe property to handle, nor was this the sort of sex Kit had counted on finding tonight in his habitual search for other outlaws in the complex of riverside alleys. He didn't want to be fucked by a kept boy whose rich come would be like caviar.

'Look at me,' Billy said, turning desperate. 'I can't live without you or you without me.'

'Speak for yourself,' Kit said. 'Posthumous fame doesn't interest me. What's recognition for one's work without being able to claim it?'

'But we're still read universally,' Billy protested. 'Isn't that something?'

'It's what I'm writing now that matters. Past achievements don't interest me. Books are ultimately just paper and glue stitched together, with a name on the spine.'

Billy looked hurt, as though Kit's willingness to deny the past in some way undermined his achievement. He placed his right hand on the suede steering wheel, like the car was his assurance.

'Doesn't it mean anything to you that our books are on all the syllabuses, that we're constantly taught, that writing books about our work and lives has grown into an industry and that editions of our works are in every bookshop?' Billy asked incredulously.

'Nothing,' Kit affirmed.

'You're wrong,' Billy claimed, his hand tightening its grip on the wheel. 'What we've done will always remain. Part of why we're here is to acknowledge the work. One of us has to continue . . .'

'Never,' Kit said, turning deliberately perverse. 'You've got to let go of what the Grid tells you, Billy. The past's not important. It's like telling me the universe is coloured magnolia because of the heat remaining in deep space. You get me? Facts aren't important, but the underlying emotions that give rise to them are.'

Kit watched the tremor in Billy's left cheek as he eyed the sculpted centre console with its luminescent display in the main instrument cluster. He could see that the offended and indignant Billy was waiting to burn. The modified racing car, he guessed, was one way for him to jump the centuries. Paid for by arms money, as Kit suspected, its conspicuousness in a city dominated by ubiquitous paramilitary off-roaders made it a potential target for urban terrorists. It was ostentatious, like its platinum-haired driver, the hybrid Billy Shakespeare re-focusing the world after his lapse into regression.

Kit heard the electronic door lock released on his side – an unspoken invitation to go. Billy was sitting there impassive at the wheel, staring straight ahead through the windscreen into a night filling with smoky fog from the Creek.

Kit had no intention of staying or of asking for what would have been a convenient lift back into town in the silver bullet. As he manoeuvred out of the passenger door he could see that Billy was still flashing anger. Simultaneously with the door snapping shut, the bullet-nosed 550 WSR burnt off with precisional acceleration – the sort of firepower that Kit knew went from 0 to 60 mph in 4.3 seconds, like a missile blasting off.

He stood there on the road, grateful to be free, the fog at his throat, and hearing a ferry wail downriver. The cold white vapour of the fog stuck to him like candyfloss. He heard a man cough in the dark and knew on instinct that he, as a sexual predator, should follow. It was, he assured himself, Marlowe's night, and it had only just begun. Shakespeare was on the road back to London, doubtless flooring the car's accelerator. Everything had its time and place, and his was now, out here in an urban wasteland near Deptford Creek, rooting for a stranger in the foggy autumnal night.

12

The Grid was rapidly expanding. Kit knew it was not only an organization specializing in regression hypnotherapy but also a supplier of global technology. By linking digital processors, storage systems and software on an enormous scale, Grid technology was poised to transform computing from an individual and corporate activity into a general utility.

He wondered if there were others outside of his group – out there in the polluted hassle of Regent Street or amongst the congested crocodile of Oxford Street tourists – who were like-wise possessed of the same disquieting knowledge that they had never died and were aware, detail by detail, of their past lives. People who not only knew they had escaped death but were trying somehow to account for their continued existence in the present.

He had fielded a surprise call from Robert earlier in the day and had arranged to meet him on the Boots side of Piccadilly. He wasn't quite sure why he was doing this, other than that he retained a strong centuries-old attraction to danger and sexual kicks in meeting up with proven lowlife characters. Robert Poley – and it was by his seventeenth-century name that Kit preferred now to think of him – was, he guessed, attached to both Wriothesley and Strange and adept at supplying both with information in keeping with his trained duplicity. Robert looked and smelt dodgy as a Paul Smith-suited estate agent, mobile bricked to his ear, standing outside a cheap makeover in Queen's Park and looking creased.

Kit fished his jeans and black cashmere D&G jumper off the debris of the bed where he and Yukio had fucked the previous night. He took, as he often did, when the occasion required, a number of over-the-counter analgesics to silence his headache.

Racial tensions, together with anti-gay hostilities, were progressively invading the city, and many of the rival factions had largely dissolved their individual differences in the interests of collectively targeting the major banks and corporates. Robo-guards could now be seen all over the Square Mile, where office towers were now as empty as the skyscrapers at Canary Wharf. There were too many rogue airline pilots, some of them affiliated to terrorist cells, doing drug cocktails in the London skies. What Kit had witnessed at rooftop level above Oxford Street had been repeated several times by pilots whose aircraft he had personally seen approaching the Heathrow corridor and performing random free falls over Richmond and Twickenham before levelling out at five hundred feet to cabins of hysterical crew and passengers.

Kit, as was his custom, went out hurriedly into the busy, choking London day. People carried their own portable fuel cells now on the Underground, in case of black-outs. The size of a briefcase and weighing around twenty-two pounds, they worked by combining oxygen with hydrogen to generate an electric current. Some of the Japanese suits negotiating the subway entrance at Notting Hill Gate were carrying these as Kit ran down the permanently dysfunctional escalator to the Central Line platform.

The journey to the West End was the usual unremitting ordeal. The Tube was suffocating, and someone had emptied a canister of liquid confetti in a calligraphic blur over the windows to his carriage. The Pollock-like fragmentation of colour had created random maps across the pollutant-grimed windows, atomized whorls of manufactured colour, celebrating the marriage of the Underground with its new graffiti warlords. Two blue-haired Japanese girls dressed in Miss Sixty tartan miniskirts sat holding hands, sharing an iPod as the train lurched into Lancaster Gate, to be further filled by bodies packing into the already asphyxiating aisle. Kit kept on air-writing his Marlowe screenplay – a facility, despite his alert, paranoid jumpiness, he had developed to keep it all going in mental space until there was time to write it down. Free-associated clusters of imagery came up in his mind and hung there like objects in weak gravity. Quite out of the blue he was overtaken by a flashback in which he saw himself as the money launderer he had temporarily been while staying on State business at Vlissingen in the Netherlands in January 1592. He had lived there with two other Englishmen in the little seaport at the mouth of the Scheldt river. He remembered the town as overcrowded and insanitary, full of deserters, spies, wounded soldiers and the traffic of war, including supplies and military personnel on their way to the front. He had seen the place as ideal for profiteering and had set about money-laundering. The scheme had gone radically wrong, and he and his two accomplices, Evan Flud and Gifford Gilbert, had been ignominiously deported in irons at the order of the governor of the town, Sir Robert Sidney. The humiliation came back to him now as a series of shock waves, and he felt himself compressed like a baked bean in a can under the city. The offence was punishable at the time by hanging, but as a government snoop he had documentation that he was there on important espionage work. Lord Burghley, for whom he had periodically worked as a spy, had personally interrogated him in the Tower, but the case was a sham, and all charges were dropped on the grounds that he was only testing out the professionally dodgy goldsmith's skills as a curiosity and had no intention of criminal activities.

The incident replayed itself in his mind as the compression doors opened to a wall of bodies at Hyde Park. The faces stared in at the occupied space like urban nomads. Londoners had developed the desperate look of evacuees caught in transit. They panicked across the city's grid in a state of confusion. Some of the on-board Japanese were wearing oxygen masks in the sauna-like heat. Kit hung on desperately, in his survivor's ecosphere of imagination. He remembered acutely how

Burghley's face, when he had interrogated him, had been shot with acne craters and pits from some form of virulent STD. He was so close up to him in his mind that it seemed like he was standing there opposite him across the centuries, arrogant and conniving, sweating in the Tube.

The Japanese boy crushed against his left shoulder was wearing a menthol-green jumper and combats, the soft wool contrasting with the cooler utility wear. Kit flicked an admiring eye over his greased-back hair and youthful androgyny – the long feminine eyelashes, the porcelain skin and the sensual fullness of the lips. He was thin as a Pentel pen, as though he lived permanently on neutroceuticals and bottled water. Kit would have liked to have dated him and explored the delicate architecture of his psyche as much as the taut contours of his body.

At Marble Arch there was the same colonization of the platform. It was as hard to get off as on, and Kit planned to get out at the next stop and walk the remaining distance from Oxford Circus down Regent Street to Piccadilly. He needed air after the intensely hot, confined space. It was scary to have strangers up that close, skin-to-skin in a deoxygenated carriage, and when they got to Oxford Circus Kit had physically to force a passage through the solid mass of bodies to finally get access to a wedged platform. He was soaked through as he took the cranky escalator up towards the street.

He stood for a while, recovering from the journey, outside Liberty on Regent Street, and took in the high, blue October sky, empty of clouds and open like a window on space.

Kit had switched his meeting with Robert from outside Boots to the Royal Academy restaurant, the unlikely venue providing the neutral space he felt necessary for the occasion. He knew he was marked wherever he went and that he was part of a small circle of mediated survivors which depended on the Grid. He wondered if Billy was flicking back his white fringe right now as he sat writing at Eaton Square or if he was out somewhere in the London crowds, illicitly cottaging in

Broadwick Street or even behind him this very moment in the crowd.

Kit swung round on instinct to confront the human stream. Its transience was too confusing to take for more than a few moments at a time. One stranger's face rapidly succeeded another's in the endless food chain of individual destinies hurrying across the city. He was one of them – but he felt separated by the fact that his life was discontinuous in its split between past and present.

He joined the momentum, contemplative, hands thrust in his pockets as he caught his reflection in a shop window. Robert had already sent him a text with the agreed code, 'sweet Robyn', to say that he had arrived. Kit segued round tourists carrying Jaeger and Burberry carriers – Euro-Japanese addicted to endgame shopping, some of whom might have checked out of the lunar Hilton in recent months, as enthusiasts for the increasingly popular space-tourist industry. The poet in him fed on the idea that people who had moonwalked across the Spitzbergen Mountains also vacationed in the world's major capitals, their periodic space hops as quasi-astronauts appearing as commonplace as a transatlantic long-haul.

As he cut through the Burlington Arcade, Kit noticed a security guard nursing a Taser stun-gun; the man returned his stare with the trigger-happy contempt of someone who resented having his authority questioned.

Kit had little doubt that he himself was being tracked. A snoop never gained ascendancy; he knew that whatever he had on Robert Poley would be matched by counterespionage, as though the fundamental dishonesty in all humans made the accuser as impeachable as the accused. His real world of poetry existed independent of that system and fought free of attempts by the corporate world to lock imagination into its factored remit. Imagination wasn't part of moral conditioning any more than it was part of the retail market. It was his space – and no Robert, Nick, Ingram or anyone could get in there and undermine his vision.

Kit turned into the broodingly quiet courtyard of the Royal Academy without bothering to check what exhibition was showing. Frisked by the ubiquitous security in the foyer, he made his way directly to the restaurant and saw Robert sitting alone at a table in the corner. Wearing black shades like Ingram and with the collar of his leather jacket turned up, he was doing something on his phone while asserting a bad-boy image to keep the table free. The place was filling up with the exhibition crowds looking for places to sit down, but Kit noted how people instinctively avoided Robert's table.

Kit noticed, too, how Robert had pushed the jar of three pink carnations in a jar to one side and that there were two used coffee cups beside the large espresso he was drinking. He was visibly wired from caffeine and probably coke, too, and Kit, in sitting down, straight away noted how Robert's fingers shook.

'You're late, aren't you?' Robert said, still not taking his eyes off his phone display.

Kit sat down feeling on edge and took in the weird electrics Robert transmitted. 'Four centuries late, if you like,' Kit replied, trying to make light of the fact he was unnerved. It struck him immediately that Robert still had the lean, hungry look he would doubtless have had at Clare College, Cambridge, in 1568, where he had been a factotum to the more privileged students. He was someone who had never forgiven the world his initial social disadvantages, and he had adopted malice and cunning as a form of revenge.

Robert finally pocketed his phone and turned to look at Kit through black screens. 'I thought it would be good to meet,' he said. 'We don't really know each other. I don't think we ever did.'

'I suppose we're acquaintances rather than friends. What have you been doing over the years?'

'You mean since the Grid?' Robert asked. 'Or do you mean post-Deptford and your murder? Diamonds. At least for a time. It's a dodgy trade. You've got to be careful.'

'Why's that?' Kit asked, pretending ignorance.

'Largely because the profession's full of cheating crooks playing games with big rocks. It's a professional secret that there are distinguishing marks put on some diamonds, like the hallmarks on gold. You've got to know how to polish these off, otherwise cut diamonds are traceable. We call them "hot stones".'

'I see,' Kit said, faking interest. 'I read about a recent heist in which a fleet of motorbikes cruised down Greville Street in Hatton Garden, smashed the window of the Ace of Diamonds jeweller's, I think it was, and took off with a tray of diamonds worth half a million. Were you part of that?'

'What makes you think that?' Robert laughed in a way that seemed reflex-defensive. 'Do you think I'd take the risk?'

'Yes, I do.'

'You're right,' he said, lowering his shades and turning his eyes full on Kit. 'Of course I would. Diamonds are light and easily hidden and can be traded for cash. They're the underworld's currency of choice.'

'So you were part of the recent raid?' Kit asked, refocusing his question.

'You're still a snoop, aren't you? Old habits don't die.'

'It's a secondary thing with me. Poetry comes first.'

'I go for money,' Robert said. 'I've got a habit, but diamond heists are risky. Too many informants, too much gossip. You know what I mean. There's a whole new network, for instance, connected to Bin Laden's former personal secretary Wadih el-Hage. He was the key figure in al-Qaeda's African diamond-and-gemstone-trading network. The Americans took him out of circulation. He's been replaced now by Abdullah.'

'And arms?' Kit said, suspicious at how easily Robert was opening up and putting it down to the coke.

'That's Wriothesley's game,' Robert said. 'But it's all linked. Abdullah's behind the embassy attacks. It was he who negotiated a deal with President Charles Taylor, the ex-Liberian leader, in order to buy diamonds from rebel groups he backed in Sierra Leone. In return, they helped his forces to obtain the arms they needed.'

'And Wriothesley was part of that?' Kit asked, impressed by Robert's speedy eloquence on the illicit aspects of his trade.

'He's scored big on it. That's why Billy drives a Ferrari. I know my facts. Global Witness reported that a bank account of one of the diamond dealers in Sierra Leone had a billion routed through it last year, a huge amount of money for a mid-level dealer, and a big chunk of that was Wriothesley's.'

Kit looked at Robert's speeded-up movements. It was the coke in his brain that was talking with such manic enthusiasm. He was made suddenly aware of just how much sensitive information this insignificant-looking individual in an overly lived-in leather coat carried in the databank of his memory cells.

'I've heard that Wriothesley wants to buy up the vacant monarchy,' Kit said.

'You've heard that, too? He and Strange are obsessed with heredity. They always were; we know that. Both are contesting rights to the throne through their lawyers. Billy tells me that Elizabeth won't settle for less than twenty billion, and there has, somewhere, to be a bloodline.'

'So that rules Jacko out?' Kit said, reminded of the fleet of black Cadillacs that had become a familiar sight in central London.

'Not entirely. There are loopholes, and Jacko's legal team are looking for them. It'll end up as a blood coronation.'

'And what about your regressions at the Grid?' Kit asked tentatively.

'I keep going to the Grid, but, as you know, you change with it. I'm more accepting now of who I really am and what I'm doing.'

'And can you accept the facts of your past identity?'

'My past is the present. That's what they teach you there, don't they? I mean, although it's a hard one to come to terms with, I feel all right about being Robert Poley? And you?'

'I'm Kit Marlowe, without a doubt, or the man you knew once as Christopher Marlowe, but I'm still fighting it.'

'What do you need to be sure? Another blade stuck through the eye?'

'Hardly,' Kit replied, laughing to deflect something that was intended seriously, and simultaneously feeling a jab of pain needle his right eye.

'We never died. Don't you understand?' Robert said, rapping out his message by beating his right hand on the outspread fingers of his left. 'We're a group, and there are probably others of us out there. We've got to come to terms with it. We're the living dead.'

Kit looked round the restaurant at people engaged in animated post-exhibition conversation. Their world, he assumed, was normal, unlike his own. He looked at Robert's interrogative stare and said, 'When I come to believe in this fully, I'll act. But not until then.'

Robert fixed him with his eyes and replied, 'If you leave it much longer it'll be too late. Better join us now.'

'Join who? I can't be sure that we've all been so conveniently resituated. What does it all mean?'

'That's what we're here to discover,' Robert said perfunctorily, 'so you'd better wise up.'

'I see no reason to continue with a past life, no matter how invasive or apparently real it becomes.'

'Then you'll have to find out the hard way. Nick, Ingram and myself, we're all comfortable with who we are. You could benefit by learning from us.'

'In what way?' Kit asked, immediately suspicious.

'Well, there's the Strange–Wriothesley affair, and there's Billy's involvement with arms . . .'

'You're suggesting I get involved? Why?'

'Because you've done it before,' Robert answered with impeccable cool. 'You know their vulnerabilities. You're second to none as a spy.'

'It's not something I want to remember. People are all corrupt. It's just some are more adept at hiding it.'

'Think it over. And think hard. You wouldn't want somebody knocking on your door at night, would you?'

'Is that a threat?'

'No,' Robert replied, adjusting his shades. 'It's just something that happens to people who don't cooperate.'

'I still think you're threatening me. You want me to revert to who I was in the past so that you and your friends from the Grid can justify killing me.'

'That's your version,' Robert said, looking strained and re-concentrating his attention on his drained espresso.

Kit glanced over at the Japanese girl at the opposite table, engaged in using a lip-brush to meticulously repair her bruised-mulberry lipstick-line, and at her friend who was equally meticulously dissecting a piece of lemon cake. They were discussing the Bill Viola catalogue, and they seemed to Kit's estranged sense of reality to occupy a parallel dimension.

'All you've got to do is cooperate and we'll leave you alone,' Robert continued, looking tight-lipped and angular. He lowered his voice, aware that someone at an adjoining table had shot him an inquisitive glance.

'What is it you want to know?' Kit asked, again trying to pin Robert to a specific answer.

'I want more on Wriothesley. By that I mean his connections to al-Qaeda. Billy likes you. He always did. He's your source. What's more, he's a pushover.'

'Why do you need me to do this?' Kit asked. 'Why can't Ingram or Nick or you do the intelligence?'

'Don't keep asking dumb questions,' Robert said. 'There's a huge pay-off in this. We've all got our specific roles.'

Kit felt worn down. 'All right, I'll do it,' he said reluctantly. 'I'll work on Billy. I'll get the information you need.'

He got up almost immediately, anxious to be gone. One of the Japanese girls had taken a shoe out of a Camper box – he knew the make well – and was showing her friend the scarlet sole that made it special, together with the eye-catching detail of a shocking-pink inner sole. The two were, as Kit watched, totally concentrated on the enduring workmanship of this Majorcan family that made such individual shoes.

He took a last quick look at Robert, who seemed, in his shades and leather, to be cloning Ingram's cool image. He knew without doubt that the two of them definitely had something going together and that Nick was a part of it, too.

'See you,' he said to Robert, who was once again concentrating on his phone in the way that it had come to constitute a person's virtual DNA in terms of the data it stored. Robert looked up for a second but was too preoccupied to make eye contact.

Kit was glad to get out of the room and out of the building. The old-world hierarchy of Fortnum and Mason opposite looked oddly incongruous with the armour-plated black cabs gunning towards Piccadilly. The London skyline was fast becoming dominated by helipads, the baronial mansions once occupied by embassies deserted and used to draft street junkies into methadone projects. Only a week ago one of the deserted embassies had been fire-bombed – the rush-hour crowds running in panic from the rehabilitated psychopathology of neo-apocalyptic terrorists.

Kit's mind raced with a speedtrack of hallucinated imagery. There were so many conspiracy theories relating to his death and to those of countless celebrities that they had come to form a taxonomy incorporated into an alternative history. There was the theory that Lee Harvey Oswald shot and killed US President John F. Kennedy with a mail-order rifle from an upper floor of the Texas Book Depository in Texas. There was September 11; the death of Princess Diana; the equally controversial deaths of Elvis Presley and Marilyn Monroe. There were the perennial stories of alien encounters, cures for Aids and cancer, explanations for which the human psyche, in its attempt to rationalize the unaccountable, demanded closure. The conspiracy theory surrounding his own death was still another unsolved mystery in the narrative of all the greats who had disappeared, he reminded himself. It seemed to him that nobody ever really got the causes of these deaths conclusively right and that when big things happened they resisted simple explanations and invariably demanded the invention of a myth to accommodate their theme.

In the meantime he busied himself with imagining what it was like to have a post-human life. There was a silver Lexus stalled in the traffic. He could hear Lou Reed singing 'Satellite of Love', and he wished suddenly that he could clear the entire programmed matter of his past out of his head. As he walked along he was obsessed with re-visioning the legendary deaths of the famous.

Kit, as usual, headed towards Piccadilly Circus, a hub that seemed over recent years to have lost its propositioning edge of sleaze. Kit couldn't feel excited today by approaching the black railings, where rent boys had hung out as the evening came on in soft-tempo blues. Above all, it was Nick he needed to see, not out of any misconceived attempt to restructure the past but out of the necessity to talk honestly about the Wriothesley situation before he undertook the serious step of making renewed contact with Billy.

Arriving at Piccadilly, he stood outside Zavvi and looked across at the Boots mezzanine. There were the usual news vendors selling the *Evening Standard*, the curious who appeared to be quite literally killing time in standing there, an out-of-place rent boy trying to sell attitude and the urgency of commuters relentlessly tracking towards the Underground. Outwardly, nothing appeared to have changed. Regent Street was still a solid precinct of corporate investment, its emporia linked to the international money markets and its fascias lit up with chic-designer window displays. He could feel London's concentrated energies move through his arteries. The Haymarket, Leicester Square, Cambridge Circus, Shaftesbury Avenue, they were all indomitable landmarks that were coded into his cells. It was a city he felt certain would disappear in his lifetime from massive terrorist reprisals. The fault lines had already started to show in its matrix – its tower blocks were fissured, its light polluted with kerosene, its air toxic with the build-up of carbon emissions.

As he stood there taking in the crowds, the now familiar sight of Michael Jackson's limo fleet and outriders came into view. It was like a Hollywood mafia funeral staged in London, an all-black cortège commandeering the road. For a brief moment he caught sight of the blurred image of Jacko sitting alone in the customized rear of the stretch Cadillac, his face caked white, his mouth a red-lipstick gash, a grey fedora slanted over his shades, his emaciated body almost a designed-in feature of the car's ergonomics as it finned its way into the Regent Street traffic.

He took the image with him into the Underground, that of a biologically re-created megastar, reputably £240 million in debt, alienated in London without a contract but pursuing the illusion of becoming its monarch and taking over as the latest pretender to the throne in the now deserted halls and corridors of a bomb-devastated Buckingham Palace.

13

Kit was immediately suspicious at Nick's readiness to come over to his flat and talk. Kit had called him in the morning and suggested four o'clock as a time that suited him, and Nick had agreed, arriving promptly at the appointed hour, a bottle of Evian in one hand and his blue-and-white Nokia in the other.

Kit was immediately struck by just how much of Ingram Frizer's influence had rubbed off on Nick. Like Robert, he appeared to have become his clone, incorporating the obligatory Lou Reed-style wraparounds, black leather jacket and skinny-leg jeans into the reinvention of his image. He looked suitably wasted, as though he had also picked up Ingram's habit and was to his detriment metabolizing smack instead of a quotient of vitamins.

Nick came in and took up a chair in the kitchen, the marginally skewed one placed in front of the laptop on which Kit had been writing. The new Nick exuded implacable cool. He placed his phone down and picked at rearranging a long-stemmed scarlet anemone that had looped out on a snaky stem like an inquisitive radar dish.

'What's the news?' he said, casually pushing back into the chair and thrusting out his legs that terminated in sharply pointed boots.

'I need to talk to you seriously,' Kit said. 'It's important, and I promise you it's not about us or our past.'

'Cool,' Nick said, readdressing the rogue anemone that had escaped from its arrangement.

Kit switched on the kettle to make coffee, at the same time offering juice or a beer from the fridge. He had the disconcerting feeling that he was really speaking to Ingram instead of Nick and that in addressing the latter he was engaged in a filter process, a sort of psychic osmosis. He made himself coffee in a mug labelled 'Saint Morrissey' and stared briefly at the minimal contents of the fridge. When he returned to Nick it was to be confronted by the same glacially unnerving stare. Nick could have been asleep behind his shades, but he wasn't.

Kit opened a packet of plain-chocolate digestives and furtively bit a half-moon in one before placing the packet on the table.

'It's Wriothesley I want to talk to you about,' he said as a helicopter slashed over, the blades reverberating with a force that threatened to blow out the windows. Through the window Kit could see the co-pilot leaning right over to his left, straining to look out, as though searching for some clue in the ramified, built-up urban jungle below.

Kit came and sat down on the same side of the table as Nick. He wanted to appear relaxed even if he wasn't. He took another biscuit from the pack and searched for a suitable way into the conversation.

'Look,' he said, 'I assume from Robert that we're all in this together, so I can speak openly.'

'Sure,' Nick said, doing an Ingram with his designer shades and pushing his legs out further from under him.

'I take it that Billy's my gateway to Wriothesley?' Kit said, firming up his territory.

'He's your man,' Nick affirmed. 'He's helped me out on a number of occasions, buying studio time and the like . . .'

Kit realized as he listened to Nick that nothing had changed in his life. He was still rent despite his attempts to reform. He was still adept at using people in return for having been used. When he did make changes in his life, they were short lived and insignificant, like altering the line of a hair parting.

'Do you know who Billy really is?' Kit asked.

'Shakespeare, of course. I've never liked his work – and who needs it? In the past he was too speculative, too sane to destroy himself like you. Do you remember that black prostitute from Turnmill Street who he used to write sonnets to with such cold feelings? What was her name? Emilia Lanier?'

'I do,' Kit laughed. 'She was the young mistress of Lord Hunsdon who had been the patron of the Lord Chamberlain's Men. She was a poet, too, and slept around, got pregnant from some playboy and was married off to a musician called Alphonse Lanier. I always thought I was a better poet than Shakespeare and still do. But, more to the point, Wriothesley and his connection with arms? Do you know the links?'

'I wouldn't touch that,' Nick said. 'If you go down that road you're a dead man.'

'Is it that bad?' Kit asked, snapping at another chocolate digestive.

'Billy might talk to you, though,' Nick added as a cautious footnote.

Kit had no illusions that Nick was going to make it easy for him. He backed off from his line of questioning and walked over to the window, hands buried deep in his pockets, wondering if Nick hadn't come over with such alacrity simply to relay news back to Robert and Ingram – or, worse, to Wriothesley himself. He felt uncomfortable about the whole matter, but he had committed himself too far to go back.

'What's in it for you if I go ahead?' he asked Nick, hoping to dent his façade by appealing to his baser instincts.

'Money,' he said predictably.

'So you mean it's a simple practice of extortion and nothing else? Wriothesley gets blackmailed, and Strange ends up the winner? It all sounds too clear cut for me.'

'It's sort of like that,' Nick asserted evasively, pulling on his Evian bottle and repositioning his legs with attitude.

Deep in thought, Kit came back from the window with its scenic overview of tower blocks and slow-moving clouds and sat down. 'Anything I need to know that's going to cause me big problems?' he asked.

'I'm not here to brief you. Ingram's the one who does that.

All I'm saying is keep clear of Wriothesley's arms links. Anyhow, he's got big-time security. Billy's your man. He drinks at the Admiral Duncan.'

'Thanks for the tip,' Kit said as Nick got up and walked round the kitchen, taking in the posters of Morrissey, Venice, a Howard Hodgkin retrospective at the Hayward Gallery, a Cocteau exhibition from the Pompidou, a few postcards and flyers pinned to a noticeboard before taking up a position at the window. He stood there looking out over the skyline, cold, shot-up and deliberately cultivating the wasted image of the aspiring pop star with his sights set on the charts.

'It's a shame we lost it,' he said, 'but things would never have worked out between us long term. We've both got too much to hide . . .'

Kit watched him look out at the tumbling grey clouds forming smudgy convoys on the horizon. London to his eyes looked like a prime target for kamikaze terrorist reprisals, its obtrusively high-rise architecture waiting for a repeat 9/11 offensive to atomize Canary Wharf or the Swiss Re 'Gherkin' or any number of the prominent Westway towers at Paddington Basin.

'I'd better make tracks,' Nick said, keeping a wide berth of Kit. 'I've got to be somewhere for six.'

Kit, in his confused state, accompanied him to the door. The chemical in Nick's cells had taken away his characteristic fizz. He looked methadone-flat and worked on by the city's equally tired and degenerative chemistry.

'Seeing somebody nice?' Kit asked as a parting shot.

'Ingram,' Nick said abruptly, before quickly walking away without once turning round.

Kit went back inside and poured himself a large Chivas Regal. He was glad to have Nick's druggy aura out of the flat and wondered out of morbid curiosity if Nick had left particles of himself behind as dead skin. With Nick gone Kit felt restless, and he played with the idea of going into Soho that night and searching for Billy at the Admiral Duncan. The need for a proper meeting seemed additionally strong given that he had recently spent time researching their past histories at the British Library to ratify his findings at the Grid. That so much time had been devoted to the academic theory that he and Shakespeare were the same person, at least after 1593, left him feeling that a certain area of academic scholarship was little more than a redundant exercise aimed at generating dead books written in a prose as sterile as its subject matter.

From the research he had done on the subject it seemed there was no actual documentation stating that he and Shakespeare had ever met, only the speculation that because they had arrived in London in the same year, had both written for the same theatre companies and had been only two months apart in age that their paths would inevitably have crossed. There was, in addition, the scholarly theory that the first part of *Henry VII*, usually attributed to Shakespeare alone, was most probably a Shakespeare–Marlowe collaboration and that there were likely to have been other shared projects. That both men had pursued the patronage of Henry Wriothesley and Lord Strange – and had most likely competed for same-sex relations with their sponsors – implied in the footnotes of biography a rivalry for a common love, which was supported by textual readings of Shakespeare's Sonnets 78–86.

History, he knew from experience, was a notoriously unreliable source. He remembered his meetings with Shakespeare only too well, the times they had fallen for the same boy within the limited circle available to them and, before their final falling-out, the occasions on which they had discussed poetry with the intensity of two people willing to cut their fingers on the edge of a knife to prove a point. Theirs had been almost a back-alley brawl of dissension over how to kick maximum impact into the line. They had both believed in using a rev-counter to up the ante of the line, and that was still Kit's practice today in employing the hyperactive image to document action. Either poetry was something to die for or it was nothing at all. He hated the tendency to make the ordinary into the one viable poetic currency. Most poetry was too constrained for his taste, and he expected that Billy was similarly bored by its more quotidian aspects. Pop music could do it so much better and with real energy. When a song was good it cleaned the palate like mint.

Kit was beginning to find through his ongoing sessions at the Grid that he had easy access to whole areas of his past that included Billy. He thought about Billy's attempt to go straight with Emilia Lanier, the half-Italian mistress discarded by Henry Carey, the Queen's Chamberlain. They had met frequently, mostly in pubs, at the time of this major crisis in Billy's life. Billy was chiefly frightened of losing Wriothesley's patronage if he continued his affair with Emilia. Billy had been all nerves, unable to cope with Emilia's emotional storms and voracious sexual appetite, but was at the same time incapable of letting go. He had made an attempt to jump into the river one night as a way of getting out. He had been wrestled back from the glutinous black mud by a sailor and dragged to shore coated with effluent and shaking from the shock and cold. Kit had been a witness to Billy's attempted suicide and had never forgotten it.

Kit was aware, too, how much Billy had stolen from him as a role model, particularly his style of iambics – the blank verse that was to liberate poetry from the necessity to rhyme and give it a pitch every bit as contagious then as the hook in a modern pop song. His plays, particularly *Tamburlaine* and *Edward II*, had been the blueprint for Billy's cycle of historical tragedies. But they were not the same man, and attempts to fuse their work into one life were wholly aberrant. Billy had been overawed by Kit's big line and the irreverence he showed in his work, and he had taken Kit's method and succeeded in making it into a formula so commercial that its architecture continued to dominate the literary skyline just as the pyramid at Canary Wharf did the modern city skyline.

The Billy who now drove a Ferrari 550 WSR had been his understudy not his clone. He had also been his lover, casually, desperately and mostly inconsiderately. Billy had thrown himself at him like someone trying to break into a black-box recorder. Their sex had mostly been quick desperate encounters under the river stairs. There had been nothing in it but the quick attempt to mind-fuck and the soapy taste of semen in his mouth. Billy had wanted fame and quickly, as youth does. They had so often sat, backs to the river, watching the sunset bleed. Neither could have imagined they would meet again centuries later, genes intact, to continue a dialogue that should have ended at Deptford in 1593.

That they had been rivals then and still were now had been evident right from the start. Kit recalled how they had raced each other across the broken shore at Shad Thames, drunk and maniacal, and how, after Kit had tripped, Billy had wrestled him into the tide as though he was going to hold him under in a thrashing vortex of spray.

But more than that, he had realized through his regression hypnotherapy the true part that Billy had played in the events contributing to his death at Eleanor Bull's house at Deptford. He knew the lines that referred to him in *As You Like It*, no matter how cryptic their allusion, word by word: 'When a man's verses cannot be understood, nor a man's good wit seconded with the forward child understanding, it strikes a man more dead than a great reckoning in a small room.'

The idea of his death as a great reckoning had begun there with Billy's phrase. Kit had read in Garry O'Connor's biography, *William Shakespeare: A Popular Life*, how Billy was supposed to have been at Deptford on the night of the murder expressly to view the body and say his last farewells. It was all part of the speculative Marlowe apocrypha and for once dangerously close to the nerve. In another account he had read how Billy had prised the blood-soaked shirt off his back and worn it as a trophy in front of his players, as a reminder that he had not only outlived his rival but would add his blood to his own in a new show of poetic strength.

Despite the apparent myth-making in these accounts, Kit

still needed additional evidence to support his growing belief that Billy was his killer. It was this, as much as the need to investigate Wriothesley, that had him determined to go out and find Billy in Soho tonight. Billy, with his unusually spaced wide eyes and restructured features, had suddenly become the key witness to his past. This platinum man with the Botox boy's makeover wasn't going to own to having tucks. Billy, for all he knew, was probably into grow-your-own-cell shots to create tissue rather than 'short-scar' facelifts as part of his rejuvenation plan.

To keep on the case Kit busied himself with notes at the kitchen table. It was a fact that between the years 1592 and 1594 nearly all of Billy's rivals had been fortuitously eliminated, at a time when he most needed a clear field for the development of his genius. Of his contemporaries Greene had died in 1592, Kyd in 1594, Lodge had abandoned literature for medicine, Lyly was used up, Peele too dissipated to write and he, Kit Marlowe, was presumed dead. In fact, from 1593 to almost the close of the century, Billy had had the spotlight to himself.

The idea of Billy being a serial killer who systematically eliminated all rivals was an entertaining thought but lacked credibility to Kit's mind other than as a conspiracy theory. But people did strange things in the interests of fame, including kill off those who appeared a threat to their ambition. Billy's attraction to him all along had been undoubtedly fired by jealousy. That's what their emotional storms had been about – their fights, their cold sex forced by a desire to gain the ascendant. And, despite Billy's amazing 25,000-word vocabulary, Kit believed that his own gift at the time had burnt brighter and continued in its own way to do so. If Billy had used madness as a psychological tool for his writing, then his knowledge of it was secondhand, whereas, for Kit, madness with its variant pathologies had been a natural form of expression. Billy had analysed motives, hardwired them to psychology, whereas Kit had lived recklessly out of the immediacy of experience that, in turn, became his writing. Today he had decommissioned his big line like Concorde and broken its design down into fragments.

Kit opened a bottle of wine and drank a glass off quickly, his nerves jumping to the instant sugar hit. He had by now decided firmly on going to the Admiral Duncan in the hope that it would be one of Billy's drop-in nights. A traditional gay bar in Old Compton Street that had been the target of David Copeland's nail-bomb in 1999, Kit knew its crowd to be regular clones and druggy superannuated queens. It wasn't a place he used when he went out on the scene, and he couldn't somehow imagine Billy becoming a slave to its pick-up ethic.

He poured a second glass of red to feed his alcohol habit. Kit could drink a bottle dead in fifteen minutes and quickly graduate to a second and third. He drank off a third glass and a fourth in quick succession to get right. Outside the window he could see and hear a hooded gang smashing the CCTV cameras that monitored the building. They had torched a black BMW, and two of the youths dressed in balaclavas were doing a ritual dance round the car – having turned the volume up to maximum on the in-car stereo – and daring each other to dance on the potentially explosive bonnet. It was a madness conducted to the noise of Radiohead sounding like they had survived a nuclear catastrophe on 'Paranoid Android'.

Kit finished the bottle while attacking the page. Writing was like driving – you accelerated on the hard shoulder, re-entered the stream and got caught at the lights. He had discovered that the more he drank the better he could green-light a sentence. The high-octane energy needed for the pursuit was like the blazing BMW out in the street, destructing to a soundtrack of guitars, techno bassline and jerky drums.

He uncorked a second bottle of Bordeaux and felt his head lift. Billy had always had it so much easier in everything. He had married, bought property and become, in time, an institution. What he was writing now didn't matter; it could add little to his fame, although Kit was naturally curious about the new work. Kit's literary reputation, on the other hand, had been slashed on by the uric acid of his detractors. He was viewed as dodgy, lugubrious, hugely gifted but ultimately flawed; his life and work coming to an inspired but bad end. So much had been written on the Elizabethans and subsequently posted on the web that he was able to avail himself of it as a biographical topology to his past. But there were obvious omissions, and he found himself wondering about such old friends as the book-sellers Thomas Thorpe and Edward Blount who had published his work posthumously and cared for his reputation. Were they, too, out there in the London streets as born-again rein-ventions of themselves, rereading his work and connecting with a signal from the past? There had also been a lawyer on the fringes of the literary set, John Marston, the satirist, whose plays were no longer read, with whom Kit had been close in the 1590s. He remembered him now as a saturnine man who read people's characters like a doctor a diagnosis. These were shadow people in his life whom he suspected of having disap-peared for good from the circle.

Ignoring Scott Diamond's persistent calls and the flashing of his voicemail light Kit played with the disquieting prospect that perhaps certain people, including himself, were too indi-viduated to die. Their personalities appeared to have survived the biological fact of death with only partial memory loss.

It was growing dark already. Kit watched a slash of red-and-pink sky unzip over West London, livid as the showroom paintwork of a Jaguar. He played an old Stones CD com-pilation to accompany the raft of his thoughts and listened to the dirty, skewed rhythms of 'Brown Sugar', the driving Richards riff to which Jagger nailed his cocky vocal sounding hot as a beach in Malibu. There were songs, and 'Brown Sugar' was one of them, that had entered so deeply into the collective conscious that their qualities appeared tribal.

Kit filtered the Stones in and out of his writing. Their raw energies cooked a drive that contemporary poetry lacked. Most British poetry left him cold – its lack of shape-shifting imagery appearing like the symptom-formation of mild depression. The absence of risk, tempo or engagement with whole aspects of the technological world, as well as the exclusion of pop culture from its menu, made it without significance to him. This sort of retro-looking, totally unimaginative writing lacked the colour and excitement he needed. It could no more create altered states than Coca-Cola could. It simply wasn't on Kit's map. By way of comparison, even pop's essentially bubblegum lyrics appeared to communicate a carbonated jumpiness more relevant to the times.

Kit killed the music in order to concentrate more fully on writing down a particularly enduring memory of Billy that had come to mind from his past, determined after that to head off to the Admiral Duncan. The event, as he remembered it, had happened several weeks before the murder at Deptford. He had been walking around in a heavy fog near the Inns of Court when he had almost collided with someone who had turned out to be Billy. Not the blond boy he was now but someone with unexceptional brown hair, a Chinese pencil-line moustache and the furtive look of being found out doing wrong. They had squared up to each other over some comment exchanged, some rivalry over box-office takings, with the playfulness of shadow boxing, only Billy had poked him hard, vindictively and with the intention to hurt. Although they had laughed it off and parted as abruptly as they had met, his feelings had been hurt, and he had been left with a bruise above the ribs that had flowered overnight into a deep-violet blotch.

Kit stopped writing, hurriedly pinned a note on to the kitchen noticeboard for Yukio, should he return later, finished his glass of wine, checked he had his phone, keys and urban-survival kit and left the building fast.

It wasn't dark yet, and a broad cerise stripe lit up the sky. The torched BMW emitted a drizzling plume of smoke, and the gang, having lost interest, had grouped in the centre of the road with their attention turned on one of their hooded members who appeared to be about to base-jump from the roof of an adjacent block. Ever since the skyscrapers at Canary Wharf had become a high-rise magnet for a band of extreme-thrill seekers specializing in leaping from tall buildings, base-jumping had grown into a cult in west London, with jumps of 360 feet recorded on security cameras. Kit could make out the hooded figure of a youth attached to a parachute clapping along to a ghetto-blasted 'Kid A' as he psyched himself up to tip over the edge. Kit stared up at the diminutive figure back-lit by a strawberry-coloured sky, jerkily contorting himself to Radiohead's icy electronica. The whole thing appeared to him like a death rite being performed to a cerebral soundtrack. A group of spectators had gathered despite the gang's menacing presence and stood staring up from the street, transfixed by the youth's vacillating bravura. Kit knew that out of fear of losing face there was no way in which the boy could return to the gang without jumping. The point reached now was irrevocable. There was no turning back, no matter how long the youth played for time. At some point his crazy, probably drug-induced momentum would carry him over the edge for an impacted and possibly fatal encounter with concrete.

Kit broke free of the group and walked up the road in the direction of the Underground, the city's collective madness feeding the amygdala in his brain with jerky hallucinated imagery. He half expected to see tanks rolling down Portobello Road and knew it was only a matter of time before the army was called in to rule London in the war of the dispossessed. Soon people wouldn't need homes – the mobile would become an inclusive studio, a digital microcosm dispensing with the need for a permanent address and workplace.

Kit's paranoia on the street created the effects of surround-sound and surround-vision. Dangerous as it was, he still travelled on foot across large areas of the city rather than risk a dys-functional Underground terrorized by urban guerrillas. Tonight he had a gut feeling about avoiding the Tube and decided to bus it over to the West End. He imagined fire raking through the city's arteries – an orange wall of flame licking round the Circle Line like a demented, self-destructing snake.

He jumped on a bus headed for Piccadilly and found a place

upstairs. Seats had been ripped out and not replaced, and the top-deck lighting didn't work. Graffiti was looped across every possible surface so that the aisle looked like a lexical Pollock done in crazily disassembled characters. Kit looked out at the ambassadorial façades of the hotels along Bayswater Road – their lounges empty for lack of tourists and their suites used largely on an hourly basis by Japanese executives and their Eastern European prostitutes, selected from the repertoire that the hotels provided.

There were robopoliced urban nomads living in bubble tents all over Hyde Park. They looked like a crowd on the evening of a giant rock festival, gathered there in anticipation of the revived dinosaur acts.

No matter the dangers of street life, Soho still attracted its reckless quota of clubbers and gay desperadoes who did drugs and stayed out on the scene until dawn. When Kit entered the village via Brewer Street he was immediately approached by a pretty Japanese boy with a red mop of hair, his eyes black with smudged mascara. Clearly high on substances, the boy tailed him down the street before finally turning round and heading back in the direction of Piccadilly.

The Admiral Duncan was already full to exploding when Kit arrived at seven. There were two minders on the door, muscled custodians of a pub under constant threat. Kit squeezed inside and did his best to negotiate a way to the bar through the jostle of leather guys and solitary drinkers there to chill and explore the boundaries of a gay man alone in London over several ruminative hours spent on a bar stool.

Kit always found ghetto bars uniformly depressing. Despite the dance remixes played as statements of clubby euphoria, the largely disillusioned customers sat at the bar or stood in groups vacantly staring out at the street. Kit ordered a large glass of wine so as not to lose his established feel-good peak and went and stood by himself in a space by the door. Two guys standing next to him wearing black T-shirts were exchanging tongues in a protracted kiss. Another couple near by were slipping hands down the back of each other's jeans. Kit was still amazed that expressions of same-sex relations were still only sanctioned within the ghetto and that outside the village prejudice and brute hostility ruled. He disliked being segregated in this way. It was like racism. He would have liked to have kissed a man openly, while queuing at a Waitrose check-out or standing in the middle of the crowds trafficking along Regent Street.

The Japanese boy who had accosted him earlier came into the pub, poppy-red hair collapsed over his eyes, his nerves clearly full of chemicals. He was evidently known to the bar staff, who straight away mixed him a Campari and soda in a tall glass with a cryogenic base of ice. The boy, after scrutinizing the crowd, sat down unsteadily on the knee of a charcoal-grey-Dior-suited exec, clearly a regular, and superficially smooched his ear. Kit found the Japanese boy at the same time sexy and repellent, engagingly *louche* and vulgarly available. He couldn't take his eyes off him, but he had the instinctual feeling that the boy knew he was being watched and at some point would look across and make direct eye contact. The boy had a tooth missing in the front and a twinkle in his eyes like diamonds. His evident devotion to getting wasted suggested the recklessness of somebody self-destructing with a vengeance. He was being fondled by three or four different men at the bar and seemed to delight in the attention. His recurrent bursts of laughter could be heard across the room as he sipped at his drink.

Kit continued to watch his exhibitionistic behaviour, fascinated by the boy's hold on his circle of admirers. It was as if he was being passed around for use later, his lack of inhibition a common knowledge shared by his circle. The executive's hand was on his crotch, while another admirer tracked a finger along his spine. The boy took it all on, as though it was expected of him that he should behave in this way. The music had now changed from dance and electro to torchy sob sisters giving dramatic colour to unrequited love, and Kit took up the impassioned theme of Dusty Springfield's 'I Just Don't Know What to Do with Myself' as a way of empathizing with the woman's broken heart – something that featured so strongly in him and his circle of friends. Dusty's smoky inflections and desperately needy voice rinsed the bar with waves of sustained heartbreak.

Kit finished his drink and looked over again at the boy, a sort of oriental Tadzio, who had exchanged St Mark's Square and the black canals of Venice for the meat racks of the London scene.

Kit could feel the pain behind his right eye start to flicker. He had at one time considered having an implanted electrical stimulator placed on the occipital lobe to help manage the pain but after discussing the treatment with a neurosurgeon at the National Hospital for Neurology had decided against the operation.

Kit was careful to keep his distance from the other drinkers. He wondered how long he would have to wait before Billy showed up – if he did. His attention, meanwhile, remained polarized to the red-haired attraction at the bar. The boy had the full-on drama of a Shirley Bassey in his histrionic response to whatever was said amongst his chosen group. He would throw his head back and open his arms wide as he hammed for the spotlight.

Kit stayed with his drink in a corner. The music was starting to feed his migraine and make him edgy. A stranger came up to him, but he stonewalled his advances. He didn't even want to speak to the good-looking guy with the obligatory cropped hair, finding his approaches too stereotypical.

He was about to give up and go when Billy walked in, dressed simply in a grey cashmere jumper and white jeans, his retrospex pushed up into his hair for effect. Billy made a straight line for the Japanese boy, stood behind him with a hand on each shoulder and kissed him as he turned round like someone intimate with his body. Billy seemed on good terms with the crowd at the bar and was quickly draped in admiring arms. The executive in the dark-grey flannel suit promptly bought Billy a drink and in return had his hair teased by the oriental boy.

Kit bided his time. He wanted Billy to sight him accidentally through the crowd – see him and come over, surprised at his being there – rather than walk up to the bar and introduce himself.

The music had changed again and this time it was the Pet Shop Boys singing 'Rent', which came up as an electronic anthem. The guy standing next to him in the pick-up area was wearing a black muscle-back tank top and dancing along to the music. He recognized the man's scent as Aqua di Parma, an exclusive cologne whose fans had included Cary Grant, Lana Turner and Ava Gardner.

Kit didn't have to wait long. Billy took in the radius of the bar with one searching look, as though his eye was shooting a video. The little imperceptible click of recognition was handled by Billy with the consummate know-how of the professional. His contact with Kit confided nothing to his immediate circle while at the same time clearly signalling that he would be over. Billy had his arm round the Japanese boy's neck, and he was speaking across him to the executive in a way that took them both into his confidence.

Kit watched Billy slip away from his fired-up group to the toilet, and when he returned he came straight over to Kit. 'Let's go somewhere,' he shot at him over the music. 'I'm sick of this place. Come on, quick. Let's get out of this hole.'

14

Billy, with Kit in pursuit, led the way rapidly out of the Admiral Duncan into Old Compton Street and took a quick left into Dean Street at an urgent lick.

'He'll follow if we don't get out of here fast,' Billy said, anxiously looking over his shoulder and steering Kit into the narrow alley of Meard Street as a detour. The night had turned foggy, and Kit followed hot on Billy's heels as they rapped through the alley, once a notorious location for cheap brothels, slackening their pace as they connected with Wardour Street. Billy crossed over the road knowingly, direct into Peter Street, and took a sharp right, at the same time punching buttons on his mobile.

The air was autumnally smoky, and fins of blue mist stood out all along the street. Billy continued to lead the way, the smell of the market leftovers adding a raw, vegetable stench to the damp air. The Soho night was thick with fog like fur. Billy turned left into Broadwick Street and aimed for the black-and-gold gates of the public toilet there, a notorious under-the-street cottage that was closed at night by the council on the pretext of lack of public funding. Billy, who was out of breath from the walk, rattled the locked gates with his hands and then stood with his back to them, his eyes full on Kit.

'Fuck it,' he said. 'I forgot they close at seven-thirty. I thought it would be the best place to talk – inside a cubicle, like the old days, Kit, only now the place is painted Med-blue.'

The toilet was islanded in the middle of the road, and with the fog coming on in cold waves like vaporous surf Kit had the impression they were locked in an isolated space–time in the middle of Soho.

'Who's the oriental guy?' Kit asked, expecting at any moment to see his skewed figure come out of the fog with sopping red hair.

'A friend of Ray's, one of Strange's lot. He lives on a barge at the Reeds Wharf moorings, just downriver from Tower Bridge. The tail end of what we knew in our time as the Neckinger. He's dangerous, I warn you.'

Kit shivered from the cold fog. He didn't know why, but standing there with Billy seemed to invite the same sort of trouble as he had found himself in that time in September 1589 when he had got involved in a fight in Hog Lane with his friend Thomas Watson, and a man called William Bradley had been brutally run through by a sword.

'What is it you want to tell me?' Kit asked Billy, who was staring at him with those inimitably restructured wide-spaced eyes.

'That it was you I always loved and not Wriothesley. The way it worked out at the time made it impossible. I needed his patronage, his money, and I cut you in the process. And now it's happened all over again. I'm back with the wrong man when it's really you I want.'

Kit felt the confession go in like a bullet, activating a whole neural network of associations. He wanted simultaneously to shake Billy away and to bruise him with his mouth as a statement of brutal passion.

'But you chose Wriothesley,' Kit said coldly. 'He not only had the money but the looks. Don't think I've forgotten.' For a moment he hated Billy but sensed he could work the situation to his advantage. 'You shock me. I need time to think about what you're saying. And what about Wriothesley? He wouldn't just let you go?'

'I've got too much on him,' Billy said. 'I don't mean that callously. Of course I have feelings for him. But his profession, his unscrupulous arms deals, get to me. He uses his nuclear bunker under Eaton Square as a conference room. The Commissar used to be there all the time for power breakfasts with his entourage of thugs in suits.'

'And he doesn't emotionally involve you?'

'Never. I'm left to write. Of course, there's a price to pay in that he demands sex. You should know that from your dealings with him in the past.'

'And you oblige, of course, like you always did.'

Billy gave him a hard stare, an angry self-appraisal that he projected on to Kit. 'You have ultimately to defend your gift,' Billy said. 'That's how I see it. Nobody ever pays writers. You know that. Nobody wants to give us the necessary time in which to work.'

Kit laughed. 'You think that's news to me? As if I've ever had it easy.'

'Quick,' Billy said, pushing Kit up against the gate and covering him. 'Over there, it's him, Shusako.'

Kit shot a look through the luminous vertebrae of opalescent fog and saw the Japanese boy with his weird shuffling walk searching the doorways along the street, stopping and starting again with jerky uncoordinated movements.

They stood there, the two of them, flat up against each other, and Kit could feel Billy's erection in contact with his crotch, the testosterone sluicing through his blood. The moment for Kit was independent of everything, pure poetry: the homoerotic union of gestating lyric and desire celebrated in that instant in the smoky Soho fog.

'Thank God he's gone,' Billy said, letting go his hold of Kit. 'He's always on some weird substance – crystal meth, crack cocaine. Strange pays for him and the barge. The mooring fees are £500 a month. It stinks of diesel, and the cabin's a wreck. There'll be a fire on board one day.'

'I can see you've done your homework,' Kit said.

'Mmm. It's a dangerous way of living. There's a thirty-foot tidal fall twice a day, plus the danger of infection from sewage and the hostility of Southwark Borough Council. Shusako will end up in the river one day, like a dog.'

A City of Westminster refuse-truck tunnelled past, followed in quick succession by two Space Cruiser taxis, bright-yellow lights pushing amber beams through the floaty skeins of fog. Normal life was going on all around them, Kit presumed, and he felt oddly reassured by the idea of some form of social continuity.

'Let's go somewhere and fuck,' Billy said with real desperation.

'I'm not ready. I need time to think about this. Don't rush me.'

Billy grabbed him by the shoulders. 'Don't think too long. I can't wait.'

Kit manoeuvred himself free of Billy's hold and negotiated his own space. His head was buzzing with electrical activity as the suppressed migraine building up in his frontal lobes threatened to come on again.

'When can I see you again?' Billy asked. 'What about tomorrow?'

'Don't push me,' Kit said, alarmed by Billy's desperation. 'Give me time.'

The fog was snowing big fluffy puffballs as they continued standing outside the toilet, like two conspirators plotting to subvert history.

'All right,' Kit said shaken, 'I'll meet you tomorrow at five.'

'Where?' Billy said importunately.

'Right here. I'll be here.'

'You're serious?' Billy said, the worry of being let down showing like television in his eyes.

'Deadly,' Kit replied, wanting at any cost to be out of the foggy cold that had turned the night the colour of a blue moonstone.

He buried his hands in his pockets as a signal he wanted to go, hunched his shoulders for attitude, like James Dean standing under a lamppost circa 1950, and started off in the direction of Regent Street.

'See you,' Billy said, disappointed, briefly placing a hand on his shoulder before heading back in the direction of the gay village.

Kit stopped there a moment with his back to the black-and-gold railings, stunned by what had happened. If Billy had appeared reckless, then instinct told him that his impulsiveness was deliberately exaggerated so as to hide its opposite – a slow-burning, calculated duplicity. It wasn't for nothing that he was Wriothesley's boy and always had been, Kit told himself, alive to the prospect, as if he had just been told that he had tested positive.

Kit immediately headed off into the night, chasing a new menu of possibilities in his mind as to what to do, like reading the efficacy data on the label of a prescribed pharmaceutical. For some reason, and perhaps because he was islanded in William Blake's old precinct of Soho, he had a blinding flash of the psychotically hallucinating poet sleepwalking his way through the fog with an orange halo surrounding his punkishly stuck-up hair.

Kit felt the desperate need to talk to somebody, anybody, about what had just happened. He thought for a moment of calling Nick, but his involvement in the same deepening conspiracy ruled him out. London in the fog appeared like the white amnesiac face of a giant sleeping pill, its entire population coded into a barbiturate blank. He couldn't at that moment retrieve a single name that would be of help amongst the millions crouched to their monitors and plasma screens all over the city. There was just an intrinsic numbness in his head, as if the power to his brain had been cut.

Kit crossed the road tentatively, feeling as though his legs were about to give way. There wasn't anybody around, although it was still early, and the fog continued to airbrush familiar Soho landmarks.

He wasn't sure what to do or where to go. His mental signposting was temporarily suspended. He deliberately took the opposite direction to Billy – his head painful but stone-cold sober – and made his way to the corner of a fogged-out Poland Street. He badly needed a drink for his shot nerves. What sounded like a BMW bike roared through on an urgent trajectory, the courier jockeying the alleys with an important dispatch for one of the film-production companies on Wardour Street.

Kit stood there shaking on the corner when a hand grabbed him tightly by the wrist and locked. Unable to free himself, he spun round face to face with Shusako. He was shivering from the cold and dressed in nothing but the tropically coloured cotton shirt he had been wearing in the bar. His red hair had collapsed, and his eyes cooked mania.

'Gotcha,' he said, in a menacing tone that dissolved into hysterically inflected laughter. 'Where did you go, man? I've been looking all over for you and Billy . . .'

Kit tried desperately to free himself from Shusako's implacable grip. Although the boy weighed next to nothing, whatever he was wired on chemically gave him an exaggerated, unnatural strength.

'I need to speak to you,' Shusako continued, still not relaxing his hold. 'Like it or not, you're going to come back with me. My friend has a place near here.'

'Let go of my hand,' Kit said. 'You're hurting.'

'Not till you say you'll come with me,' the boy said, at the same time increasing the pressure.

'Look, you're obstructing me. I'm on my way somewhere, and you're preventing me.'

'Come with me,' the boy repeated. 'You're quite safe. Nobody's going to harm you.'

A couple hurried by, features almost imperceptible in the smoky chiaroscuro, the girl's high heels creating a staccato click on the pavement. Nobody ever stopped in London, Kit knew that, not even if you were flat out on the pavement in a pool of blood. Any appeal for help would create instant paranoia in strangers.

Kit knew there was no way out of the situation but to accede to the boy's demands. He was, in effect, being abducted, and although he carried an automatic in his blue leather shoulder-bag he had no intention of waving it at a potentially dangerous psycho. The weapon was part of his compact survival kit, a recent addition in the light of the threat he felt from the notorious bovver boys – Nick, Robert and Ingram.

'OK,' Kit said, affecting cool. 'But it'll have to be short. I don't have much time.'

'My friend lives in Ingestre Place,' the boy said. 'Two minutes' walk. I call . . . Don't move.'

Kit watched him pull a Nokia from his pocket and punch buttons. 'Hi, Thom,' he said. 'I need flat for one hour. I come over?'

The boy laughed, and it occurred to Kit that this was possibly an apartment to which Shusako took punters for sex. Kit was suspicious and on the defensive. He had just heard it from Billy that this boy was not only attached to Lord Strange but that his obvious promiscuity made his character highly dubious. He was clearly rent and known for it on the Soho scene.

'My friend says we can use flat,' Shusako said. 'Very nice place.'

Kit didn't like being coerced into anything and certainly not by the physical threat of a Japanese pillhead in Strange's pay. He knew as well that Billy hadn't told him the truth about his relations with Shusako, which, he suspected, were sexual from the intimacy with which he had French-kissed him on entering the bar.

'You cold?' Shusako asked. 'Me, too. Let's go. Friend's flat warm. Five minutes.'

Kit was only too familiar with Ingestre Place and Silver Place branching off it as sidestreets dominated by 1960s residential blocks and office conversions – the usual trendy Soho hybrid of minimally furnished floors for Saatchi aficionados and media-occupied workspaces for employees who biked in on state-of-the-art silver-framed Raleighs.

Shusako insisted on placing his arm through Kit's as a token of control as they walked into a bottleneck of fog from which people emerged like the survivors of a catastrophe that had occurred somewhere deep in the city. Kit could smell the liquor on Shusako's breath – a metabolized residue of an exhaustive round of Soho's gay bars that tracked him as raw scent.

After a few minutes' walk Shusako stopped dead outside a building and jerkily thumbed a touch-sensitive keypad for entry to the numbered flat. Kit followed him inside, and they went up a floor on foot to a silver door that was already open anticipating their arrival.

'Hi, Shusako,' a voice called from inside. 'Come on in.'

Kit followed reluctantly and trailed Shusako into a clinical steel kitchen that looked like a film-set design for Stanley Kubrick's *2001*. All the paintwork was white, except for a pale-pink wall resembling a big slice of ice cream and the odd plastic android-like creature placed in strategic positions like space invaders. A fortysomething man, dressed casually in a white cable-knit jumper and bleached jeans, sat at a table busy leafing through a sheaf of foil-wrapped documents.

'Ever seen these?' he asked Shusako, looking up at the same time to smile at Kit. 'They're ownership certificates for an acre of land on the bright side of the moon. I've gone and bought forty moon plots at £12.99 each from Morrisons.'

'Crazy,' Shusako said, his body still shivering from the cold.

'Not that crazy,' the man said. 'The fact is there is a loophole in international legislation governing commercial exploitation of the moon. The 1967 Outer Space Treaty, which stops national governments claiming the moon, omits to mention individuals. I've done my background research into this.'

'Here. Have a plot for yourself,' the man said, handing Shusako a foil sheaf. 'Open it, and you'll see a lunar map that pinpoints your plot. The moon, for what it's worth, is actually owned by Dennis Hope, a Californian businessman who filed a claim for ownership in 1980. He runs a company called Lunar Embassy.'

The man's slightly pedantic factoring of data made Kit wonder if he was by profession a lecturer, an observation reinforced by the pile of books stacked on the steel table, most of which related to Shakespeare and Marlowe.

'By the way, I'm Thom,' the man said, holding out his hand to Kit. 'The place looks repurposed post-modern with its infra-bits, and that's how it's intended to be.'

Kit instantly warmed to the man. There was no hint of entrepreneurial sex about him, no suggestion that he collabo-rated in securing punters for Shusako. The flat, like its owner, looked undeniably glacial and cerebral.

'You can use the study if you like,' Thom motioned to Shusako. 'You look like you could do with some coffee.'

Kit tried his best to figure out what the relationship between the two could be if it wasn't sexual. The one was so manifestly controlling and refined, the other dissolute and obviously street. They didn't seem to belong on this level of intimacy if there wasn't gain for both parties. Or was Thom the impeccable purveyor of a double life, Kit wondered, the academic dissimulating a propensity for sleaze?

'Or stay in the kitchen, by all means,' Thom added as an afterthought. 'I can move next door. Just make yourself com-fortable.' He walked purposefully over to an Automatic Coffee Centre, a German model that looked like it had once belonged to the Apollo mission.

'It speaks eight languages,' he said. 'It not only stores and grinds coffee beans but it employs a new fast-brewing process designed to ensure every grain of coffee makes contact with the water. For what it's worth, I have a fascination with these things. I used to have a La Pavoni Professional Lever – a 1960s design – but this one is better. The advantage, though, with the old one was that you could vary the strength of the espresso according to the speed at which you dropped the lever.'

Kit and Shusako sat down on clear Perspex chairs under a lamp shaped like a nose cone. There was a rounded open-ing in the wall giving access to the living area, and Thom busied himself in there, selecting a number of books from the stack.

'What is this about?' Kit shot at Shusako. 'Why have you brought me here? I demand to know.'

Shusako smiled and placed a finger over his lips. 'I need the hair dryer,' he said to Thom petulantly. 'My hair's gone flat from the fog.'

Thom proceeded to make coffee with the domestic thoroughness of a housewife and placed a bowl of nougat pieces wrapped in foil on the table.

'I'll leave you to talk,' he said indifferently, heading off towards the port that gave on to a living-room, a book under each arm and a coffee cup in his right hand. His brown hair was cropped, making him look like every gay middle-aged man who worked out, cloned to the dream of perpetual youth.

Kit wondered, briefly, if the affability and air of complete confidentiality exuded by Thom weren't a sham, designed simply to encourage him to talk. He was, for all Kit knew, part of Strange's world – the pornographer Ray's friend – and wasn't at all to be trusted.

'I sorry I forced you here,' Shusako said, sipping his coffee. 'I need to talk and not on the street. Too dangerous. Police think I'm rent.'

'Are you?'

Shusako burst into laughter. 'Sometimes,' he said, 'but mostly on the barge and not here.'

'What do you want?' Kit said. 'And make it quick. I'm expected somewhere, and you're detaining me.'

Shusako's hunted eyes appeared to be trying to refocus the world when he got up suddenly, lurched off at a tangent to an industrial fridge with a model astronaut placed on top and came back to the table carrying a frosty bottle of Smirnoff.

'You friend of Billy's?' he asked.

'You mean James's friend?' Kit said.

'Yeah. Rich boy. Eaton Square. He lives with businessman.'

'I've seen him around in bars. We've spoken. I wouldn't say we were friends.'

'You know Mr Waters?' Shusako asked, his eye-whites stringy with red blood vessels.

'What if I do?'

'It's important,' Shusako said, uncapping the bottle. 'I need contact with this man. He's dangerous.'

'What do you mean?' Kit asked. 'Dangerous? In what way and how does this concern me?'

'Weapons systems,' Shusako said, filling his coffee cup with vodka. 'Predator drones, Global Hawks, B-2 stealth bombers. He supplies weapons.'

'Why are you telling me this? I've got nothing to do with the arms trade.'

'You know Mr Waters?' Shusako repeated, the method in his madness chilling to diamond point.

'Look, for all it's got to do with you, I'm a screenplay writer. I've got nothing to do with British firms on the front-line.'

'This Billy,' Shusako continued. 'He part of Control Risks Group.'

'Who are they? You're wasting my time.'

'They hire armed guards to protect officials from Whitehall,' Shusako replied.

Kit could feel his incipient migraine doing serious brain pro-gramming. The wine he had drunk before leaving home didn't help, and he was confused by Shusako's increasing lucidity, despite his excessive drink-and-drugs cosh.

'I'm not your man,' Kit stated flatly.

'You are a spy,' Shusako said. 'Intelligence. You visit Mr Waters at his home.'

'What do you want?' Kit asked, certain now that Thom, whom he could hear moving around in the living area, was not the benign, eccentric academic he appeared to be but most probably a secret agent in government employ.

'Robert Poley. He connected with Mr Waters,' Shusako said with staccato malice. 'He, too, is friend of yours.'

'I wouldn't call him that,' Kit retorted, angry the association had been made between himself and Robert.

'Matter very simple,' Shusako continued. 'Mr Waters, he dead soon. Billy, he dangerous. He has knowledge we want.'

Thom rather abruptly came back into the kitchen to fix another coffee and pick up one of the cutely wrapped Torrone Nougat candies in a bowl. He busied himself efficiently in the steel lab, threw a brief smile at Kit and retained the apologetic air of someone intruding in his own kitchen. He diligently prepared a coffee and distractedly headed off at a tangent through the port giving on to his study, as though still puzzling some virtualized theorem in his head.

'Look, I need to go,' Kit said, getting up from his chair.

'You go,' Shusako smiled. 'We know where to find you.'

As Kit stood up Thom came in again smiling, ostensibly to select another book, and beamed him an artificially inflected smile exuding a sense of false bonhomie. 'Going so soon?' he asked, as if Kit's visit had been a social one rather than the unnerving interrogation into which he had been coerced.

Kit didn't reply. He was anxious to be gone, and he walked quickly over to the steel entry-door. As a snoop he was used to having his defences stripped, but he resented the way in which this had happened. He knew as he went out, with Shusako's eyes doubtless marking him like a contract killer, that he would never now in his life be free of these people. There was something in him, and it was there in his poetry, too, that was irremediably attracted to the underworld. One reality seamlessly translated into another, he reminded himself warningly as he took the stairs down to the street.

The fog was still heavy as he came outside. It reminded him of a cool sauna, a chilling bath-house in which the steam had vapourized into cold, tangible sculptures. He struck into it like a swimmer pushing his way through imaginary obstacles. He couldn't remember a fog like this in London, at least not in his current lifetime. Its smoky shape-shifting muscle was more a throwback to the city he had known in 1590, when dank oppressive fogs had rolled in from the river with an almost suffocating insistency, fogs that had rubbed bacteria into the skin from their polluted source and stayed on the winter river like a bad hangover.

As Kit headed back towards Broadwick Street he almost collided with a couple having sex in a doorway. A tall dark-suited businessman had lifted his tiny Japanese partner off the ground, and with her legs wrapped around him and her voice deliriously orgasmic he was forcefully pumping her towards climax. The act was blatant and unsparingly brutal, in the way that gay men territorialized parks and cemeteries for sexual encounters. It wasn't the first time Kit had come across hetero-sex in the Soho alleys and yards, and he wondered if straight couples hadn't hijacked the unlawful practice for their own and if they weren't now emulating the gay community in risking arrest for their adrenalin-fuelled public transgressions.

Kit was overtaken by the urgent need to write a poem, despite the turmoil in his nerves. His mind was suddenly full on with it. He could feel the neural connections in his brain organizing themselves into clusters of words. It was always a high like nothing else in his life: the formation of the image as a moment of total fusion between right- and left-side brain activities, a synthesis of cooperation between the hemispheres peculiar to poets. It was the neurochemical state for which he lived, the process that when it came up roared like traffic in his veins. He knew it was the same with Billy and that, no matter how much each pretended indifference to their art, at heart it meant everything. It was the big moment, the ballistic lift-off in the neurochemistry – the poem going through its rocket-rejection phases *en route* to Mars.

He tentatively retraced his steps through the atomized fog to the luminous sign at Broadwick Street toilets. There was never a truly quiet place in which to write. Poets were intruded upon everywhere by noise pollution and by the general con-sensus of opinion that people shouldn't be allowed to stay silent with their thoughts for too long. A lover he remembered had once called him an alien, and that was in part how he thought of himself, as an extraterrestrial networking with altered states.

The one genuinely writer-friendly café he knew in the West

End was First Out. It was his refuge at times when words caught him out and he was faced with no other option but to cut off from the crowd and write. That it brought Nick into his mind was inevitable, given the associations the place had with their past.

The poem was there as brain noise accompanying him through the streets. The fog reminded him of an ice lolly – it was tinted orange and frozen. He walked in a trance along Great Chapel Street, dazed by the exploding fall-out of his poem. He made his way forward as best he could, collided with a helmeted biker searching for his bike in Soho Square and picked up on the incongruously loud drone of an aircraft right down low over Oxford Street. He couldn't believe that anyone was flying in this soapy visibility, let alone doing it at rooftop level. He tried to imagine the Boeing's nose cone slicing through the opaque freezing air – the pilots working off radar, their violation of aviation law ending in predictable flame-out. Kit had always imagined that a kamikaze would select Centre Point as his high-rise target. He looked up instinctively but could see nothing in the blanked-out white-on-white sky. Everything vibrated from the sonic roar of engines overhead. The aircraft appeared to be circling, coming back on itself, as though searching to align with its target.

Kit panicked, imagining Centre Point exploding into an orange cone of fire. The aircraft came in shatteringly low again, only this time it went off after completing its circle, the vibration of its engines receding into a corridor of luminous fog.

The poem hadn't gone away. It was still coming on in his head as, shaken, he made his way across the square in the direction of First Out. There wasn't the least sign of the fog lifting as he came out on to Charing Cross Road. The traffic was dead, and a smackhead was shooting up in the doorway to the Astoria Theatre. Some people were using their portable fuel cells to light a way through the silent fog.

First Out shone a yellow window in the dark. The place was

like a second home, and Kit welcomed the relaxed atmosphere in which he felt at ease. He went straight to the counter and ordered a large glass of red wine. He saw familiar faces sitting at tables, talking together or reading the freebie magazines *Boyz* or *QX*, the fog outside looking like it was going to stop at nothing short of asphyxiating the city's inhabitants.

Kit found a seat at a table near the window, opposite someone who was screened by an open copy of *Boyz*, the front-cover image of Marc Almond confronting him as a reminder of the inseparable relationship established between pop divas and pink culture. Kit sipped at his glass of Merlot and let the poem come up. There was nobody alive qualified to teach the weird pursuit of building poetry out of molecular blocks in the head. What he knew about poetry came from hard experience and was too generically impractical to be of use to anyone. The responsibility was huge, unshareable in its commitment and totally self-created in origin. But it was sheer defiance that drove him to pursue his particular art as a singular obsession that took precedence over all other activities in his life.

He thought of these things as he made progressive tracks in his notebook. Writing a poem, while at the same time observing Marc Almond's pop-diva image, gave him the sort of accidentally simultaneous hold on the work that he relished. He wondered why the person opposite him remained so totally fixated by the double-spread of the magazine, to the point of appearing to have disappeared into the contents. The poem he had going was coming to him fast in its initial explosive form, and he knew intuitively from long experience that he had started something that would rapidly take on its own fluid autonomy.

He could, as he sipped his wine, feel the bite of the work in his nerves. He remembered how the last of his Elizabethan poems, the unfinished 'Hero and Leander' – a Neoplatonic fable about desire, derived from Marcus Musurus' Latin translation of Musaeus, a Greek poet who had lived in the fifth or sixth century AD – had been written in similar bursts of hyperactivity, interrupted only by his death. George Chapman, the friend of the poet Matthew Roydon, to whom Chapman had dedicated the occultist rhapsody 'The Shadow of Night' in 1594, had continued the work. He had started the poem at Thomas Walsingham's country house at Scadbury, near Chislehurst, in the dazzling effulgence of the Kentish spring-time. He had intended it to be the great poem of his age, and to make it into a hard one for Billy to follow. He had written it at first in a sunny interlude, just prior to the warrant issued for his arrest on 18 May 1593. The warrant had been delivered by Henry Maunder, a messenger of Her Majesty's Chamber, who had ridden down to Scadbury empowered to summon the help of the police if required. He could remember clearly the pink fists of apple and cherry blossom on the trees on the day of Maunder's arrival and how his writing window looked out on a sunken garden with a maze. He saw the poem he had begun now as a continuation of that fragment, an update of its theme, a radical remix dictated by the language tools at his disposal. Poetry, as he had rediscovered it this time round, lacked excitement. Nobody went out and bought a new book of poetry with the same excitement as purchasing a pop CD. Neither he nor Billy writing today had any purchase on a general readership. He wondered, as he wrote of his past, if that could ever be turned round and whether poetry couldn't again become as contagiously exciting as a dance remix.

When he looked up from writing he was shocked to find that it was Ingram who was sitting staring at him from behind the lowered magazine. The man still had the same methadone-project blankness, the same black shades, the same stick-insect body, the same indomitably disquieting aura. Kit didn't want to acknowledge him or give him any purchase on his inner space. He continued writing, aware of nothing but the speed at which he was neurally gunning words across the page. Ingram stared at him with the same white-out blank as the fog outside. Kit kept his eyes resolutely down and his defences up as one line followed directly from another with amazing clarity. He was determined not to be disturbed and conceded nothing in his pursuit of words and to his relief looked up after what seemed an interminable period of time to see Ingram disappear out of the door and head directly towards the white Ford Transit van dispensing free consignments of needles to junkies.

15

K it was early for his meeting with Billy and, not wishing to draw attention to himself by loitering under the street in the public toilet, he went instead to browse in Cowling and Wilcox, the artists' materials supplier. From there he could monitor the stream of people visiting his favourite cottage, with its bright Mediterranean-blue paintwork and tiles inside and the in-toilet hygiene scrupulously maintained by a Westminster Council attendant.

The site was a landmark cottage, one of Soho's oldest and busiest subterranean meeting places, where everyone from hoodies to couriers, pop stars, film industry execs and rough trade hung out together in a state of sexual complicity. Kit had regularly picked up there, and the chance nature of such encounters had often proved the configurative blueprint to having sex in apartments all over the city. He still found the danger and risk of going down those steps hugely stimulating, together with the fact that potentially he could meet anyone in that confined precinct under one of Soho's busiest streets. So many of the men he had met there were closet gays, married or constrained by their careers into living a double life. They came there to be themselves, independent of social status, and out of desperation often got beaten up, humiliated or mugged but invariably returned to the arena, their urgent libidos air-brushing the prospect of repeat gay-bashing or arrest for propositioning.

Kit occupied himself as he waited by appearing to pretend interest in the weight of handmade papers, while all the time checking the window for Billy's arrival. His eye had singled out a butch-looking black kid who kept coming and going at regular intervals, clearly frightened of being apprehended on CCTV if he stayed too long beneath the street.

Kit looked up and punched buttons on his phone. It was ten to five. The West End sky-ceiling was slashed with pyrotechnical pinks and reds. The light would fade in an hour, and he could feel the apprehension inside himself – the gut thrill that came with twilight. He didn't know what to expect of his meeting with Billy. Sex? Blackmail? Arrest? A spaghetti plate of ramifications? A bullet through the hippocampus?

He kept his eye on the casually dressed black boy who had come back into view and was debating whether to go down again to his subterranean niche. Kit felt existentially frozen in the peculiar space of overlapping lives from which there was no apparent release. He really wasn't sure if there was a way out that would allow him liberation from his past or if time could somehow be overdubbed and resequenced. He remembered, as he distracted himself by looking at pencils, the weird tricks that mescaline played on time and how on one recreational occasion with Yumiko he had experienced the events of three-thirty before those of three o'clock and the events of two o'clock after those of quarter to three, as though the chemical had remixed all conception of linear time.

He was thinking about this when he caught sight of Billy approaching the toilet, this time dressed in a cerise V-neck jumper and skinny blue jeans. He approached the place cautiously, looking round as if he expected Kit to be waiting for him outside Tiscal or Marlom Gray PL. Kit watched Billy hesitate at the entrance, and the poet in him throw his head up to take in the dramatic strawberry sunset.

Kit decided to give it a few minutes before joining Billy under the street. There was something about Billy's face, he observed, that invited endless speculation as to its reconstruction. Billy never looked the same twice, and Kit found it hard to memorize his features. It occurred to him from his knowledge of these treatments that Billy could be having New-Fill, Perlane or Restylane injected into the skin to combat the effects of HIV atrophy, but then perhaps it was just ordinary Botox or even plastic surgery.

Downstairs the place was busy, and Kit could see Billy standing at the far end of the five urinals, his eyes focused on the cock girth of the well-hung youth next to him who was surreptitiously masturbating. Billy was too intensely concentrated on this activity to notice that Kit had joined the short queue of clones standing at the entrance to the bunker-sized brutally hygienic space scoured by detergents.

Kit watched as Billy placed a hand round the side of the blue painted partition and squeezed the youth's erection, as part of the preliminary rituals entertained by serious cottagers. Billy's intrepidity surprised Kit. It was much more pronounced than that of the young Shakespeare he had known in these parts centuries ago, almost guiltily picking up street boys in rags and going with them into rat-infested yards, knowing all the time that he was being watched by Strange's intelligence or Robert Cecil's spies. Billy's libido was powerfully directed at this slim, ordinary-looking boy, whose short brown hair, glasses and insignificant body contrasted with the dynamics of his oversized cock.

Beaming in on him, Kit attracted Billy's attention, with Billy making eye contact but showing no sign of letting up in his pursuit. Encouraged by Billy's audacity, two other men began openly masturbating, as though the ritual was contagious, no matter that the CCTV cameras had been set up precisely to monitor such illicit activities. Recklessly sure that there were no straights present, Billy went down briefly on the boy, who stood back proudly displaying his size, eyes shut, hands on his hips, as Billy gagged on the length.

The act was quick, and at a signal of newly arriving feet on the stairs Billy dodged back to his upright position at the stalls. Kit watched Billy and the stranger exchange numbers on their phones, an act almost as fugitive as the way in which they had made sexual contact.

Billy winked conspiratorially at Kit, as if suggesting they

share the pick-up another time. Kit's nostrils were full of the abrasive smell of cleaners and detergents – an anthology of irritant associations that brought to mind cottages all over the city.

When the boy with the muscled sex made his exit, his place next to Billy was taken by a Japanese youth, the rotating action making it possible for everyone in the toilet to get sexually acquainted. Kit was still a spectator to the action, as were the other four men waiting at the bottom of the stairs to enter the chain.

Billy was clearly a regular at this, his movements conducted with the authority that came of experience. Kit could see that, like all fugitives, Billy had the trust of a thief that he wouldn't be caught. He showed the same adventurousness with the Japanese boy as he had done with his previous partner. It was literally sex in the ghetto – a transgressive community playing with the law and claiming violation as a social right. Kit could feel his erection tugging at his fly. He knew very well that Billy was trying to provoke him into action in a way that was both impersonal and compromising.

When the option came up to get in on the act Kit passed. He gave his place in the queue to what looked like a biker boy, dressed all in leather with buckled boots and spiky orange hair, who took the place of the Japanese boy who had clearly been frightened off by Billy's menacing intensity.

Billy showed no discrimination about coming on to the new stranger. Having trapped the biker's eyes, his hand went in search of his cock. The alacrity of Billy's know-how shocked Kit. This was a poet, the official poet of Britain's literary heritage, whose flagrant cottaging skills suggested he did it regularly all over the city with an obsessive's compulsion.

Kit continued to huddle at the bottom of the stairs, trying unsuccessfully to catch Billy's eyes and signal that it was time to go. Obviously stimulated by danger, Billy and the biker boy were busy teasing one another's erections.

Impatient to get away, Kit let go his position in the queue

and went back up the stairs to wait outside in the street. The sky had changed colour once more and was now a volatile cocktail of tomato-red, hot-pink and ultramarine. He threw his eyes up to the dramatic blocks of colour posted on the widescreen sky – colours that never failed to distract him, no matter his mood.

He hoped his disappearance would bring Billy back above ground, as he went and positioned himself outside Cowling and Wilcox again. Two Japanese girls, probably students at Central St Martins, went into the shop, faces made up like androgynous hybrids, strawberry-blonde bobs conspicuous by their standout, manga-influenced oddity.

Kit had almost given up on Billy when he appeared at the top of the stairs, his YSL glasses repositioned in his hair and his eyes making a rapid scan of the street before encountering Kit's.

'You missed out on something hot down there,' he said excitedly and without apology as he came over and embraced Kit, as if wanting to claim him while at the same time making clear his right to sexual freedom.

'Where do you want to go?' Kit asked, anxious now to get away from the place. He glanced up as he spoke at a final broad stripe of cerise sky disappearing over Liberty.

'Your place,' Billy said, 'if that's OK. We'll be safe there, and anyhow, I'm curious to see where you live. I know it's going to be very different from the place you had at Norton Folgate, near Bedlam, when we first met, soon after you had left Cambridge.'

'Cool,' Kit said, knowing that Yukio was working tonight and wasn't expected back until the early hours. He wasn't happy about the prospect of taking Billy back to his place but decided to stay with the idea. It seemed a bizarre concept to him – the incongruity of the reinvented poets, after four centuries, heading off together in the direction of the Tube station under a suitably dramatic red-and-navy-blue sky.

Kit suggested they take a bus to avoid the rush-hour overspill on the Tube, with its toxic-particle dust clouding the air on the platforms. They picked one up at Oxford Circus, and by the time they got to Notting Hill it was already dark. They matched each other step for step, hardly speaking, in the ten-minute walk to Colville Gardens. There was a recently spray-painted rash of graffiti tags over the walls to the gated entrance, a cut-up dialectic given a glitter finish. The lexicon continued as a spontaneous form of tribal calligraphy over the paintwork of a midnight-blue Lexus, transformed by loopy flourishes into something resembling a pop-art exhibit salvaged from the psychedelic era of the 1960s. It wasn't until they were in the lift going up to Kit's apartment that Billy thawed enough to say, 'I've been waiting for this a long time. It seems like for ever.'

Kit showed Billy into the kitchen on letting them in and watched him sit down, jeaned legs creating a V-shape on one of the wooden, microfibre-covered chairs. The kitchen table still showed vestiges of Yukio's unfinished breakfast: a Pantone mug, a tumbler of half-drunk orange juice, a toast rack with roundels of toast burnt at the edges and Yukio's second phone – a Marc Newson-designed Talby mobile with large green buttons, a gift from a Japanese friend – left discarded amongst a raft of junk mail and pots of marmalade on the tabletop.

'Want a beer?' Kit asked testily, instantly taking two cans of Stella out of the fridge. He threw a cold can for Billy to catch and drank at the spill of his flipped-open ring-top. He felt uncomfortable about having Billy in his personal space and did his best to disguise the edginess he felt. Sitting there, confident, Billy seemed too solid, too sure of himself, too full on and up front. Looking at him Kit was struck with the idea of how hard it is to dispose of the body when dead, a thought that often came to him when he felt unduly panicky.

Billy drew on his can and looked up. 'I know it's probably weird,' he said, 'my wanting to come here, but the whole scenario's crazy. I mean, the fact that we're still living and how our lives have intersected again.'

'You mean our unfinished business?' Kit said, more as a way of thinking out loud.

'You could call it that,' Billy replied, toying with his can. 'But I believe it's love that's brought us together again. We never had time to get truly close the first time round. And all that rivalry over Wriothesley's and Strange's patronage didn't help. At least that's what I feel.'

'And Wriothesley?' Kit said. 'What part does he play in all this now?'

'You ask me? He keeps me. But no, that's not entirely fair. It's naturally more complex than that. I guess there's always a bond, even in the most unequal relationship. You start out using someone only to discover you've grown attached to them. It seems to me that emotions feed as much on negative states as they do on positive ones.'

'We've all encountered that along the way,' Kit said. 'The knife that turns soft on entry; what's called a melting blade.'

'It's not what you really want to know, is it?'

'No, although I'm curious. Wriothesley's an arms dealer isn't he?'

'Mega.'

'And as a poet, you're not bothered?' Kit asked.

'Poets don't have moral scruples, at least not in their work,' Billy said with conviction. 'You of all people should know that.'

'But what about in their lives?'

'I'm not concerned with ethics, only with experience. If you act freely, conscience doesn't play a part. Guilt belongs to those who keep on comparing their actions to some redundantly false ideal.'

'I'd go along with that entirely, but I don't approve of gun trafficking.'

'The new ones shoot round corners,' Billy said defiantly. 'They're a £3,000 platform into which standard military pistols are slotted at the barrel end.'

'Aren't they being used by Yardies?'

'Wriothesley largely supplies them to the UF,' Billy said, 'the Underground Factor. Have you heard of them? They're a cell dedicated to liquidating Whitehall in one sting.'

'Tell me more about the guns,' Kit said. 'I've a contact who is interested.'

'Dodgy area. I know the facts but little else. Wriothesley's your man. He'll tell you what you need.'

'Aren't you running a real danger?'

'Wriothesley's got top security,' Billy said nonchalantly. 'He never takes a step outside without an SAS minder.'

'And you? Aren't you under a similar threat?'

'Yes, but I live with it. My way is to carry on naturally. If I'm his shadow – his accomplice, if you like – then I expose myself to the light. Being open is the best way of avoiding detection.'

Kit watched as Billy dropped a hand to his crotch and stroked the outline of a configuring erection. If the movement was a clear invitation to sex then it had the openness Billy claimed as part of his new, unrestrained psychological make-up. Kit pulled on his Stella and took another two cans out of the bright-pink fridge with its planetary magnets constellating the door.

'If I was to let you in on Wriothesley, then I'd want something in return,' Billy said speculatively.

'Like what?' Kit asked, feeling the alcohol at last starting to kick in. As they spoke there was an explosion somewhere deep in the traffic-canyoned city – another corporate losing its mirror-clad glass fascia in a detonating column of smoke – but Billy hardly looked up as the dull reverberation fanned out through the airwaves. Terrorist acts had become so commonplace of late that they were designed into big-city life as a regular occurrence. People had developed their own psychological immunity to violence, and Kit noticed it in Billy's apparent indifference to this new atrocity.

'Our relationship goes back a long way,' Billy said, straightening up. 'There are things I need to tell you. Like I was there on the night you were stabbed in Deptford. I don't know how much you have learnt from your regressions at the Grid – since we've become, for want of another term, modified humans – but I was a witness to your murder.'

'Go on, tell me,' Kit said. 'Who murdered me, and how did it happen? I'm still confused by the exact nature of events that night. I suppose it's because I was so drunk that the memory of it proves so hard to retrieve.'

'I wouldn't use the term murder,' Billy said, cracking open his second can to a nipple of escaped froth. 'As I remember it you jumped into the river and swam off towards Greenwich Reach. I can still see the red streak of blood in the water, as though you'd been sliced open by a shark.'

'Carry on,' Kit said, feeling a visceral tightening of his gut.

'You disappeared. You were officially pronounced dead and buried in the graveyard of St Nicholas's. At least that was contemporary rumour. You must have been back there often.'

'Is this really what happened?'

'Someone didn't do the job properly,' Billy said with a clinical detachment that shocked Kit in its brutal objectivity.

'And you were there?' Kit said. 'I've read speculative biography on the subject but always presumed it was no more than that.'

'I know only what I can remember. I'd heard rumours for months at Southampton House that there was a contract out on you, and I assumed that was why you were staying with Walsingham at Scadbury. Shall I go on?'

'Yes,' Kit said, turning his can of beer reflectively.

'It wasn't Strange who wanted you dead; it was Wriothesley – partly because you had rejected him, and partly because he considered you dangerous and a rival to his investment in me. Nothing antagonizes like success, particularly when it appears to owe its origins to depravity. The self-loathing that Wriothesley felt for his own sexuality was turned on you. Like most men who create an enemy, he needed a friend to compensate. He assigned us each a role, and the pattern continues, remarkably, to this day.'

'Are you saying Wriothesley was responsible for what happened to me?' Kit asked.

'He was one of its brokers,' Billy replied. 'He had you monitored everywhere you went. Ingram Frizer was one of his hit-men, and he was hired to work as a member of Thomas Walsingham's staff, ostensibly to help him acquire and manage properties during your last weeks there in 1593. Frizer had also been one of Wriothesley's pick-ups when he was rent. His criminal dealings were fingerprinted all over London, largely at the instigation of the Secretary of State. He formed a close friendship with Lady Audrey Walsingham, who doubtless you remember as Thomas's wife, and she set him up with a house at Eltham in Kent as a reward for his dodgy services to the family.'

'So it was Ingram Frizer who stabbed me?' Kit questioned, getting sucked into the plot.

'I haven't finished yet,' Billy said promptly. 'It depends on how much you want to know.'

'Everything, of course,' Kit said emphatically.

Billy sat with his legs invitingly open as he refocused the past, emptying his second can before he spoke. 'Frizer and Nick Skeres were both told to make themselves sexually available to you and to set up a meeting at Eleanor Bull's house. It was Wriothesley who provided the money and masterplan for the enterprise. Frizer kept raising his price, and Wriothesley, who was frightened of being blackmailed by him, had no option but to agree. He was in it so deep there was no way he could pull out. The plan had been to kill you earlier in the year at the instigation of what was called the Baines Note, but Frizer got cold feet. You doubtless remember Richard Baines only too well, as another insidious spy hired by the Privy Council as a projector and assassin. He, too, was one of your Cambridge lot, a rich undergraduate at Christ's College in 1586. Baines, more than anyone, persistently blackened your character. He was the one who accused you of atheism and homosexual practices. But he, like everyone involved in the plot to kill you, had to be careful. You weren't just anyone, after all. You were somebody, a popular playwright, and your disappearance would have attracted attention.'

'And you sat in on all this?'

'Wriothesley was by this time totally in love with me. He wanted to clear the way of competition and invest in my plays. His patronage made me rich and able to buy property. You were an obstacle to his dream of making me England's greatest poet. He wanted you dead and Lord Strange, too, as your backer, whom he arranged to have poisoned. He disliked you for being openly gay and for your controversial views that placed the value of the individual above that of the State. He saw you as a threat to the class system and as generally subverting the privileges from which he benefited. He also feared you for your occult connections – and the same with Strange. The idea was to throw your weighted body into the Thames, substituting it at burial with that of a recently hanged man procured from the mortuary. Everyone in the corridors of power involved in your death was in Wriothesley's pay, even the vicar Thomas Macander of St Nicholas's who gave you burial.'

'What I still want to know is who killed me?' Kit said, his whole body signalling an urgent testosterone charge. 'Fuck you, just tell me.'

'Wriothesley came with me to Deptford the day before you were due there,' Billy continued. 'He wanted to oversee every detail of his plan. Unknown to you, and I'm not discrediting your own abilities as a spy, Ingram Frizer had in your last weeks attached himself to you like a virus. He was invasive as HIV. He had taken to policing your cells in preparation for the contract and had the protection not only of Wriothesley but of Baines and Walsingham, too. He was already in Deptford waiting for us on the 29th of May. He took us to a closed house near the naval yards where there were boys, mostly young sailors who had jumped ship. There was some sort of protection racket that meant it was never raided. I remember Wriothesley went with an Asian boy. He'd never seen an Asian before, let alone fucked one. Frizer knew every trick in town and where to go for sex.'

'He doesn't seem to have changed much,' Kit said, 'except he's got a methadone habit.'

'He still comes to see us at Eaton Square,' Billy said, 'but I'm digressing. We did the necessary preliminaries, like checking out Eleanor Bull's house. It was a place used by the government for planned assassinations. People disappeared there, and Wriothesley had the green light from the Privy Council to proceed.'

'And what about Robert Poley and Nicholas Skeres?' Kit asked. 'What was the role assigned to them?'

'They're probably better known to you than me,' Billy replied. 'To my knowledge it was rumoured you were having sex with both of them at the time – or at least with Nick. Nick was your boyfriend again up until quite recently, wasn't he? I'm still in touch with both. Nick's got something going with Wriothesley. I see him when he comes over for casual sex. It doesn't bother me. To my mind he's always been rent. Back then, he and Robert were part of an extortion racket with Frizer. They all had too much on the government to be done.'

'Rather like us,' Kit said, aware that Billy, too, had been part of intelligence.

'Wriothesley, as you may have guessed, got you to Deptford by linking the world of espionage to the fugitive homosexual underground. It was the right magnet. We knew you weren't going to refuse either. There was the additional lure of sailors and the naval yards.'

'Go on,' Kit said inquisitively.

'We all drank too much that night. We stayed at Eleanor Bull's, and there were boys there, too. I remember the acute feeling of apprehension in the air. It hadn't been decided yet who was to kill you, and the tension showed. Wriothesley claimed at one point that he would do it himself, but it was bravura talking, and he quickly lost his nerve. It was sort of accepted that Frizer would do it, although nothing was said.'

'And what about Nick's involvement?' Kit asked tentatively. 'What was his part in all this?'

'You made a bad choice in him,' Billy sneered. 'If you'd paid more attention to me, none of this would have happened. I'd have given up Wriothesley's patronage on the spot for you. But Nick – no, you're lucky. He lacked the psychological makeup for murder. He knew how to trade off Frizer and Poley without ever committing himself to their extremes. They were a team, but when it came to ripping someone Nick wasn't to be found.'

Kit got two more cans of Stella out of the fridge and again threw the cold metal for Billy to field. 'I'm relieved to hear that,' he said. 'I dreaded the thought that the man I loved was my killer.'

Billy laughed in a protracted way and drew on his can. He placed his hand squarely on his crotch, massaging the taut diagram of an erection. 'We're narrowing in on our choices, aren't we?' he said, 'assuming that it really was one of our intimate circle. It wasn't Robert Poley, I can assure you. Again, like Nick, he lacked the conviction to kill. He was and still is, I suspect, criminal. Diamonds and drugs are his scene, according to what I hear: anything's that's compact and lucrative and that can be concealed inside the resewn lining of a Paul Smith jacket. Robert's clean when it comes to blood. His dodginess fits more with an anthology of marketing tricks than with punching a blade through an eye. I never liked him, and I still don't.'

'It was Frizer then,' Kit said, nervous as though the experience was about to be re-enacted. The intense colour of Billy's cerise jumper was starting to activate weird electronic signals in Kit's brain, and he looked away for respite out of the window at a black cube of night sky lit up over Hammersmith.

'It doesn't have to be,' Billy said precisely. 'Ingram Frizer's criminal profile best fits the bill – I heard he was up on a manslaughter charge two years ago for a drug-related death in his flat – but he's not the only option, even now that I've eliminated Nick and Robert.'

'From what you're telling me, the only other people directly involved were Wriothesley, yourself – and I'm assuming Eleanor Bull was present at the time.'

'And what do you remember?' Billy asked, turning on the pressure.

'I've never followed the regression right through to the end, for obvious reasons. What I've reconstructed mostly is the journey there, the atmospherics of the place: how the day was thundery, the raw smell of sailors hanging out in the alleys, the sex I had with one of them, both of us blind for the moment on a shared bottle of rum, my checking out Eleanor Bull's house before going off again to sit and reflect by the river. I've avoided going right in there because I've never wanted to see my killer face to face.'

Billy turned his head to the left and sat facing a fridge that colour-coded his jumper. Kit could see the strain in him increasing proportionately to the events he was narrating, as if the impacted past was being painfully reconstructed in plastinated DNA.

'Wriothesley was under the spotlight,' he continued. 'He had been brought up as a Catholic, was too precocious for his own good and was under suspicion anyhow for endlessly delaying his marriage to Lady Elizabeth Vere – who you may remember was Lord Burghley's granddaughter. Wriothesley was determined to resist as long as possible any marriage designed to save face. If he'd killed you they would have dragged him by his long blond hair all the way to the block. It wasn't something he could risk, honey. The rich employ others to do their killings.'

'But he initiated it?'

'He would have liked to have done it and perhaps still regrets he didn't, but he needed to keep his delicate fingers clean. He was under surveillance by his detractors at court for being a fag.'

'Was it Eleanor Bull?'

Billy continued to look away and appeared to be internally

editing his sequence of thoughts. 'She was a dark horse all right,' he said. 'We checked her out, of course. She was the widow of Richard Bull, a sub-bailiff at Sayes Court, the manor house in Deptford. Her husband's boss was Sir George Howard, a relative of the Lord Admiral, whose house stood on Deptford Green. She was a woman of considerable means and pathologically cold in a scary, psycho way – a sort of Myra Hindley but without the compulsion to kill. The government paid her for helping facilitate State-planned killings. She was there all right when you were stabbed but upstairs, out of the way; an accomplice to murder but not a murderer. She was a glacial bitch, icy as one of Pluto's moons. Somebody told me she's living at Vauxhall now, running an online poker parlour. We should pay her a visit one day and see what she remembers.'

'Then it must be Ingram Frizer,' Kit said. 'I was right all along, unless you brought somebody else in.'

'Think of it,' Billy said. 'Frizer had been snooping on you the entire time you were staying with Thom Walsingham at Scadbury. Every time you went out into the garden to write he searched your papers and personal effects. He was always the person in the space you had just occupied. Now is that hate or love – or are the two emotions inseparable?'

'I don't quite follow you.'

'I think Frizer was secretly in love with you. He certainly had no reason to hate you – like Wriothesley did, for instance. He'd got your smell that summer and may have been fixated by your reckless lifestyle and genius. He was, in effect, your shadow for the two months you stayed with Thom. He may have accepted the contract to kill you, but that didn't mean that he had to follow it through. Frizer and his lowlifers are generally hardened company but, to my knowledge, not killers. Frizer's always been dependent on a habit. He was back then in his need for pot and is all over again. It's his way of distancing himself from reality. He's frightened to love, so methadone kills the urge. Like Robert and Nick he's essentially into mind games and, in his case, particularly vicious ones.

Frizer breaks people psychologically, and others clean up after him.'

'I'd like to believe that, but I don't,' Kit said. 'His name has gone down in history as my murderer, and he was instantly reprieved.'

'History is nothing but an elaborately devised lie,' Billy countered. 'It's a fiction, like the historical characters we created in our plays. You don't believe any more than I do in the linear reconstruction of time. Events don't fall chronologically, at least not in the way historians factor them. Who will ever know what's really happening in this particular moment in our lives? You and I will have forgotten completely by tomorrow.'

'What are you trying to tell me?' Kit asked, toying with his empty can.

'That I killed you,' Billy said outright, 'although it's not quite that simple. Wriothesley wanted you dead at any cost and placed the knife in my hand while the others held you down. It was partly an accident. Frizer knelt on your chest in the struggle, Poley had one of your arms, but none of them would put the knife in. Skeres backed off, scared. Wriothesley put the weapon in my hand and shouted, "Now." I did it on impulse and ran out into the streets . . .'

Kit went over to Billy and placed his hands gently on his shoulders. He could feel the sexual energy building up between them like two jets on a collision course. His jeans were packed with gonadal explosive as he met Billy's kiss with a correspondingly urgent probe. He could sense the two of them meshing in a force powerful as the polluted river that linked their past to the present, its inexorable current rolling everything before it into a vast estuarial mortuary. Kit ran an exploratory hand over Billy's straining cock. Billy forced his tongue in deeper by way of response, and Kit felt sucked into a dizzying vortex of conflicting sensations. He knew there was no stopping now and that only through sex could they hope to find a way of liberating themselves from the past. They were bonded, he sensed, by intense love and hate, a volatile cocktail that could lead to murder again.

Kit took hold of Billy's shoulders and steered him towards the bedroom in a skewed geometry of colliding bodies. The bed still formed a frothy wreckage of sheets from the sex he had enjoyed with Yukio the previous night. The room had a musty smell of apples and semen, the intimacy of two people whose scents were blended into a common mix.

The only light came from a low-angled reading lamp. They both struggled out of their jeans, oblivious to the how and why of it all, their instincts taking the lead as Kit quickly depressed the switch on the lamp, plunging the room into total darkness.

16

A song about itself, an anthology of clichés programmed into the commercial likeability of a great pop song, Kit listened to the abstract postmodernism of Kylie Minogue's 'Can't Get You Out of My Head' with the same incurable compulsion with which he drank. As he sat at the kitchen table, laptop on, struggling to finish his screenplay, he tried to imagine Cathy Dennis writing the song's lyrics, which were so banal and yet so compelling in a pop-referential format that they appeared to be saying something new to the listener. It was a trick that left poets behind and one he couldn't match for instant appeal, and it had to do with losing self-consciousness about language and dissolving words into signs. That the listener shared much the same vocabulary – and could probably have written it, too – increased the song's popularity. It was a subject he intended to raise with Billy at the planned get-together of the Deptford cast later in the day. Their own plays had been written in a language so organically rich that they had seemed to create it in the process of writing, from a continuously inexhaustible imaginative source. There had seemed to be as much of it as there is dark matter in the universe. Over the centuries that extraordinarily rich pool had shrunk to the size of Kylie's black microdress. The heroic line had been bleached out and language made transparent. It was largely why the job of a poet had become so meaningless to him in the twenty-first century. A good pop lyric needed to be as see-through as a pair of turquoise Agent Provocateur panties. Cathy Dennis could write unselfconsciously to that prescription and so had made one of the most readily communicable statements of language in her time.

Kit knew that he and Billy would be hard pushed to make

poetry stick this time round – he had the feeling that language was no longer something intended for the page – but, if it was to have meaning, like a pop song it needed to be an expression that came at you out of the air. Words had to appear natural, like the style imparted to Kylie's hair by FX toss-lotion, or the nude L'Oréal makeup she used on her face. Reading had become a minority occupation and serious books a depressingly small cult thing. Kit struggled with the prospect not only of cultural devolution but also with the eventual disappearance of the book altogether. Syntactical and semantic systems, with their enlarged repertoires stored in various parts of the cortex, were losing their function in people's lives. He needed to learn from this degradable process and kept Kylie on repeat as he worked on converting his personally expansive recollections of life as the sixteenth-century wild boy and untamed poet Christopher Marlowe into the final draft of his screenplay.

According to the news on television, the explosion that had occurred in the city the previous night had been caused by a dirty bomb. A massive exclusion zone had been set up near Whitehall, monitored by armed police with permission to kill anyone trying to enter the precinct. This shoot-to-kill policy had reportedly been taken up by gangs armed with SA80 assault rifles pretending to be members of the security forces. A cabinet minister had apparently been shot through the head ten times by a rogue colleague in the lift down to the secure bunkers under Whitehall.

Kit had learnt to live with the threat of evacuation but was secretly resolved never to leave the city. He would go underground if necessary and become one of the dispossessed living in London's dendritic network of subterranean corridors. He had only recently bought on the internet a three-volume edition of his own works with dark-green cloth boards, edited by F.S. Boas, for the pleasure of torching a little piece of history. A late-nineteenth-century edition, he had broken the spines on the books by jumping on them repeatedly and then taken them down to the canal where he had made a fire with them on the concrete towpath. Watching the fierce, compressed blaze had given him the sort of catharsis he usually associated with random sexual encounters: brief, incandescent and self-annihilative. The books had subsided to a smoking glow, a red disc of fire the size of an orange in black crinkly sleeves of ash. He had trodden the residue flat before leaving, and, oddly, the sensation had been like a little death, a finality in which he took bittersweet pleasure.

He had agreed, somewhat reluctantly, to meet Billy, Ingram, Nick and Robert at Thom's flat at Ingestre Place in Soho. Getting the major players in the Deptford conspiracy together was to be an attempt to pool information and settle any hostilities that remained from the past. Although Kit was at heart suspicious of the proposal, which had come from Billy, he welcomed any lead, no matter how tenuous, that would help facilitate release from the double lives they all appeared to be living. In his fantasies he imagined his psychic life somehow magnetized to videotape before being electronically digitized as a projection into a deathless future. He wondered if Billy and the others were all visited by the same obsessive fantasy, one in which their lives appeared virtual, like the clinically provocative Kylie in the video to accompany the scorching 'Can't Get You Out of My Head'.

Kit's failure to observe still another deadline had placed his contract in serious jeopardy. He wasn't in a position to pay back his sizeable advance and was now committed to finishing the work in a week. He had already brain-mapped his rewrite and was confident he could get it done according to schedule. He was staying up nights and feeding his writing with pop: a confection of Kylie Minogue, the Velvet Underground, Leonard Cohen and solo Lou Reed. In between manic bursts of writing he was constantly distracted by the now autonomous recollection of whole slabs of his past, which had now become the direct subject of his work. Most of the time, and particularly after his sessions at the Grid, he lived in a parallel reality in which his past and present lives belonged to a single character.

Of late he had been forced by his deadline to stop his nocturnal visits to Deptford, and while he missed the thrill of contact with the dark he took comfort in looking out over West London from his top-floor window at a city that looked increasingly like a computer-generated image. Sometimes, late at night, he really believed that Jacko was going to reveal himself as the new Messiah and be crucified spectacularly on a neon-lit gantry overlooking the Westway. That the eccentric pop star had ordered his raft of customized limos to adopt a cross-shaped formation whenever road space permitted and had changed to dressing exclusively in white only confirmed his assessment of the mutant celebrity's incurable Messiah complex.

To distract him from the traumas of writing so directly about his past Kit went and reacquainted himself with the Mikro House environment that Yukio had assembled for recreation on the kitchen table. The product of the British designer Sam Buxton, it had been painstakingly unfolded by Yukio from a skinny sliver of stainless steel into an intricate 3-D sculpture. As relief from his concentrated hours of writing Kit liked to look at the dress hanging in the wardrobe, the water in the bath and mineral water in the fridge that were part of the ingenious construct, and to imagine a London mapped out in a similarly minimal 3-D architecture in the future.

Kit was always slow to get into his work in the morning. He would endlessly delay taking it up again, as though a considerable repair process was necessary before he reconnected with the source. He occupied himself in the meantime with channel-surfing for pop programmes, eventually finding one in which a Japanese girl-band dressed in black hot pants were doing a synthetic remake of Lee Hazlewood's 'Sugar Town'. The four girls all had lipstick-pink hair, like manga cartoon characters, and lip-synced their way superficially through a song originally written for Nancy Sinatra.

The video was interrupted by an urgent news bulletin stating that the Commissar had been shot in the underground car-park at Whitehall after returning there from a secret rendezvous. He had, prior to this, been off-message for an unprecedented three hours, and not until his movements had been minutely analysed would there be any significant lead on the crime. The gunman, wearing a balaclava, had shot both the Commissar and his driver from a distance of three metres before getting away through an exit tunnel in the labyrinthine warren under Whitehall. More details were expected imminently from the crime room.

For a few minutes Kit felt immense relief, but he was suspicious that the event could be still another instance of manipulative spin. Earlier in the year the media had announced the possible death of the Commissar and his wife, only to report hours later that, in fact, it had apparently been two government-paid lookalikes who had been killed. He knew it would take time to verify the facts and that it was still possible that yet another double had been shot, but the idea of being liberated from the despotic regime of an inveterately megalomaniacal autocrat was something he and his friends had been longing to celebrate. The Commissar had stood as an affront to all humanitarian values, and he had infected democratic principles with a ruthless totalitarianism. He had entered the political system as a pathogen and left it irreparably toxic. For Kit he had come to assume the metaphor of a swimming pool in which the water had been substituted by thousands of gallons of blood.

Already Kit, half believing the news to be true, imagined himself able to breathe easier, as if a storm had dispersed over the city, ionizing the air. He could feel megatonnes of oppression lifting off central London, as though the Commissar's aura, heavy as reinforced concrete, was rapidly breaking up in the hours after his death. This man's psyche, Kit imagined, with his international war crimes and the rivers of blood he had shed unnecessarily, was now possibly decoding itself in death into a stream of psychically relived atrocities.

In case Yukio hadn't heard, Kit texted the welcome news of the event to him, and he then emailed Scott Diamond to assure him the screenplay would be with him by the end of the week.

Scott, in his usual manic way, was already creating deadlines for the screenplay of a proposed Derek Jarman biopic as well as looking to green-light a Cocteau project. Kit wanted to be involved in both and fired his email off with renewed confidence in his abilities to meet the final deadline.

The update from the crime room came through ten minutes later. According to selective information given out by the police, the Commissar and his driver had been forced to kneel inside a circle drawn with their own blood before being shot. The police were confident that CCTV cameras had picked up high-resolution images of the masked gunman at work in the high-security parking space. However, Kit still anticipated a rewrite of the story with DNA tests confirming that it was one of the Commissar's innumerable clones who had been murdered as part of a security plan to assist his escape from the threatened capital.

Kit did his best to refocus his screenplay and thought, too, of the disquieting prospect of his appointment in Soho later at the flat of his one-time friend Thomas Walsingham – who had reinvented himself as Shakespearian scholar Thom Davenport. The clinical stainless-steel surfaces in Thom's kitchen had for some unknown reason left Kit with the overriding impression that sadism was a dominant feature of Thom's personality. It was a feeling he had instinctively come away with and one that had stuck. He had the idea that there was an unrestrained and outwardly suppressed violence shared by Thom and Shusako in their clearly unequal relationship. The flat, as he remembered it, observed few domestic comforts, and Kit wondered if it hadn't originally been the home of a Soho film director who had modelled it on an extraterrestrial theme. Stanley Kubrick would doubtless have mistaken the place for a model of his imagination, and Kit was relieved at having emerged safely from the anonymous and – outwardly – forensically hygienic flat.

He saved to disk the corrections he had made to his draft and prepared once again to cross London's network of gang-ruled apocalyptic boroughs on the Tube, this time in the hope of finally finding a solution to the unresolved issues that he and the group had re-encountered.

Kit particularly didn't relish meeting either Nick or Ingram in Billy's company. He knew in advance that he would feel inhibited speaking to Nick in the presence of people who knew them both. He was still fiercely protective of the relationship they had shared, and he wanted to sit on it as some sort of valued security deposit from the past. He also feared being exposed to aspects of Nick's character that might cause him pain and of discovering, in the company of others, that he had never truly known him. Meeting somebody out of context, particularly a lover, was always a risk, and he was afraid of the long-term consequences.

Kit continued to hope that the meeting would lead to his being somehow liberated from the past. He wanted nothing more than to move on and be free of associations that not only held him back but which, over time, would clearly threaten his sanity. He could feel the subtext of a headache starting up somewhere mid-brain, a signal that came on like a referent whenever he felt himself placed under intense pressure.

Kit placed his automatic in his survival kit preparatory to going out and, reluctant to leave the safety of his flat, stayed on in the kitchen as though fearing he wouldn't ever return. He kept on delaying his departure, his eyes fixed on the crowded skyline as he surveyed it from his window like a film director wired for a take on real-time apocalypse. His eye scanned the imposing concrete towers at random, wondering which one amongst the corporate giants on the City skyline would be the first to be hit by a kamikaze pilot. The horizon looked for the moment like his idea of an imaginary city on Mars, the red smudge on the horizon superimposing a Martian sky on the ruptured interzones of a digitized London urban jungle.

Kit finally went out into the day, feeling more like a gun-carrying mercenary than a civilian in a major city. Although the social fabric had outwardly collapsed he still went about his life adopting some of the social values that were part of his conditioning. He continued for the moment to treat people and their possessions with respect, unlike the widespread marauding guerrillas, whose tactics were to loot under the banner of virulent anarchy. There were rumours of unauthorized paramilitary tribunals having been set up in various parts of London and of illegal executions of suspected terrorists taking place in Westminster yards. Kit knew it was only a matter of time before they came for him and Yukio, as they would for all same-sex couples.

When he got to Soho he stopped off at the underground toilet in Broadwick Street. It was quarter to four, and the place was empty. He couldn't get Kylie's song out of his brain as he waited, fired up for a possible sexual encounter.

When nobody showed he walked the short distance over to Ingestre Place for his four o'clock appointment. The sky was still extraterrestrial red, waiting to change to deep blue. Somebody drove by in a crash-damaged Lexus, the in-car stereo playing 'Can't Get You Out of My Head' as a synchronistic piece of consummately infectious pop.

On arriving he depressed the buzzer on the entryphone and heard Thom's voice quietly instruct him to come up. When he got to the first floor the heavy security door had been expectantly left off the latch, and Kit walked directly into the kitchen's state-of-the-art steel fixtures, with the pink-and-white walls coloured like confectionery. The first person he saw on walking into the room was Billy, busy scrutinizing the Siemens Coffee Centre, as though the steel cube was a demanding robopet. His defiant stare met Kit with an unexpected cool that seemed to deny any knowledge of past sexual involvement. Ingram, Nick and Robert were already there, too, sitting round the kitchen table talking to Thom. Ingram was sprawled with customary disdain for the company on a Perspex chair, screened by black wraparounds, the rolled-up sleeve of an old army shirt showing a fleur-de-lys tattoo inked in purple and red on his forearm.

'Hi,' Thom said breezily, making the unnatural meeting of lives all in some ways tenuously connected seem perfectly natural. 'We were expecting you. Come in and sit down.'

Kit heard the conspiratorial noise in the room go dead, as if the conversation had been immediately unplugged when he entered. Somebody – and he guessed it was Billy – had brought along an architecturally leaved plant that he recognized as a phormium, its multitoned leaves making it look like a species of rainforest tropicana transposed to a postmodern interior. It was evidently a gift for Thom.

Billy continued to ignore him, standing alone by the fridge, deep in thought, his mind quite obviously elsewhere. He was drinking a can of Japanese Sapporo beer and appeared oblivious to the others conferring at a table in the room.

Kit sat down, his mind incongruously occupied by the schema for a new poem, as if he was being vitally recalled, at this moment of crisis, to what was most important in his life. The poem was in the process of being brain-mapped, independent of him, as a psychic diagram, its molecular building blocks patterned into imagery. In his vision he could see Michael Jackson, arms open wide, dancing on the roof of a Canary Wharf skyscraper as a Boeing, piloted by a naked psychopath, narrowed in on a collision course with the thirty-second floor.

'Have some coffee or a drink,' Thom said solicitously, with perfectly formal manners. 'If you'd prefer tea then I've got some Fortnum's lapsang.'

Kit asked for tea, and while Thom busied himself with preparing it he sat down at the kitchen table. His *Collected Works*, compressed into one red clothbound Oxford University Press volume, had been placed conspicuously above Billy's plays on top of the fridge.

'Glad you could make it, man,' Ingram drawled, the methadone fixing his inertia like a polymer.

'It's been a long time,' Robert said testily. 'We thought you weren't coming.'

Kit glanced over at Nick, who didn't return his stare. Nick

seemed to have aged dramatically in just a few weeks. He was no longer the boyish image of a blond-haired pop star but someone who looked ill and ten years older than his actual age. He had his eyes directed towards Billy, who continued to pull on his frosty aluminium-plated can by the imposingly industrial fridge.

'I think you know why we're here,' Robert said without any preamble, as Kit poured out a cup of the evocatively smoky lapsang souchong tea that Thom had so efficiently prepared.

'I assume, naturally, it's got to do with our double lives,' Kit said, sensing that Nick's eyes were suddenly turned full on him.

'Too fucking right,' Ingram replied in a blankly concurring voice.

'It's time you came round to our way of thinking,' Nick said. 'You're always the odd one out.'

'The real loner,' Robert added, 'with far too many secrets for our liking.'

'Isn't that something we all have in common?' Kit said, determined to keep his cool.

'I'm not sure we trust you any longer,' Robert continued. 'What if you were to let the secret of our reconstructed lives out? What if you were to talk about the Grid?'

'What do you fear most coming out?' Kit asked.

'That we're all still alive,' Robert answered, 'and looking for the solution.'

'The solution to what?' Kit enquired.

'To breaking the pattern,' Billy said, coming in unexpectedly without turning round.

'It's a case of one of us needing to die so that the rest are set free,' Robert said.

Kit looked at Thom, dressed in a charcoal cashmere Jaeger jumper, who once again appeared totally dissociated from what was happening in his flat. His impassive stare gave nothing away. He seemed unconsciously to stonewall all involvement in the conversation.

'Maybe everybody's dead and we're the only fuckers who are alive,' Ingram said.

'You can reverse any state,' Billy said impatiently. 'But this isn't a philosophical debate, it's a situation the reality of which is confirmed by the Grid. None of us has ever died in the sense of letting go the past. We're a bunch of weirdos who can't detach from the events in our lives that belong to a particular time and place, namely the events that occupied us all at Deptford and specifically on 29 May 1593.'

'It's fucked my head,' Nick said, angrily glowering across at Kit. 'It's stopped me getting ahead. I could have been Number One in the charts by now.'

'Don't delude yourself, chicken,' Ingram sneered. 'You've had the chance like everybody else.'

'And you're just a good-for-nothing smackhead,' Nick retorted.

Ingram, by way of response, fitted himself deeper into his shades, like someone taking their place in the back of a car. He appeared to position Nick's comment dead centre in his user's brain before he broke into a derisory laugh. 'That's all I've ever wanted to be, jerk,' he said. 'Drugs are like space travel inside your head. I've been there and you haven't, so shut up.'

'You shut up,' Nick said, his anger fizzing. 'Methadone's a dumb planet to live on.'

'Cool it,' Robert interjected, sensing the situation was growing ugly.

'Don't come at me with that,' Ingram said, ignoring Robert's intervention. 'Didn't you used to score for me in Soho, you bitch? It was good when I was a smackhead then, wasn't it? You were the pusher, and I, as the user, always had to find the money.'

'You're a liar,' Nick said. 'You'd say anything to justify your habit. Me deal? You should be so lucky – at least not for a street rat like you.'

'Robert and Billy both know you deal,' Ingram said, starting to lose his composure. 'You've always fingered dirty money.'

'Cut it out, you two,' Billy warned.

'You stay out of it,' Nick said, showing something of the nastiness that Kit had always suspected of being there but never fully observed. 'What have you ever done? Written all that eloquent-sounding poetry in the past to end up sucking an arms-dealer's cock?'

'Shut up,' Billy snapped. 'We're here to discuss matters intelligently and not to trade insults.'

'You're all fuckers,' Nick said, balling the fingers of his right hand into a compacted fist. 'Dodgy criminals like the people in the music industry. The boys I worked with on the rack at Piccadilly were far more honest.'

Ingram laughed derisively without producing a smile line on his brain-fade features. 'You're a fine one to talk,' he said. 'There's no one dodgier in this city. Your soul's the colour of the Dilly pavement.'

'Stop it, both of you,' Robert ordered outright, his anger concentrated in a groove centred above his nasal bridge.

Kit felt Thom's hand unexpectedly come to rest on his thigh under the table before being almost instantly withdrawn. The concealed action brought to mind his very first meeting with Thom Walsingham and how he had made a similarly furtive gesture to establish illicit contact and as a sign of what was to come, despite his wife Audrey being present.

Nick stood up from his chair by way of retaliation and pointed directly at Ingram. 'You're a leach on intelligence,' he said maliciously. 'You're brain-dead, and you're paid to get people on drugs. Isn't that what you do? Build up a habit in someone and then do their head in with your mind games?'

'It was you who shopped Kit,' Ingram said accusingly. 'You were the last one who went to Wriothesley.'

'Liar,' Nick shot at him. 'You don't know anything.'

'You'd be surprised,' Ingram said. 'I've been tracking you under your pores for centuries. Liars belong to a certain blood type, don't they, Nick?'

Billy turned around and faced the two full on. Kit for the first time noticed the flaws in his reconstructed cheeks and how the makeover couldn't fully hide the biological age that was coded into his features. For a moment, as he walked indignantly over to the table, he looked like two people competing for one face. 'Stop this now,' he said authoritatively without raising his voice. 'We're here to try to reverse the past, not to re-create its animosity.'

'Don't threaten me,' Nick said, his confrontational stance enforced by his refusal to sit down.

'Hasn't the Grid taught you the need for self-reflection?' Billy said. 'Anger prevents clear thinking. It enforces prejudice in the place of truth. These things are rudimentary and should have been a part of your training.'

'You're a right one to talk,' Nick replied. 'You're as fucked up as the rest.'

'Am I?' Billy laughed. 'But at least I'm articulate.'

Kit again felt unsettled by finding Thom's hand pinnacled on his knee. This time the pressure seemed to communicate reassurance rather than the attempt to possess. Kit didn't know what Thom's role was in all this, other than that he seemed to be remaining impartial to the events happening round him in his home. Whether or not it was a façade aimed at airbrushing his true role in proceedings, it worked.

'You're dead,' Nick spat at Ingram, 'if you say another word.'

Ingram leant back into himself, as if he was looking for resources, and repositioned his shades like his inner balance depended on their alignment, then he folded his arms and kicked out his legs in a nonchalantly disrespectful V. 'You threatening me, man?' he asked in a measured drawl, each syllable measured to effect.

For a moment Kit thought Nick was going to hit Ingram. It was then that he saw the flash of a blade issue from Nick's hand to be withdrawn almost instantly. It happened so fast that Kit wondered if it was actually just a trick of the light on the stainless-steel fixtures.

'Yup, I am,' Nick said, his words power-pointed with anger.

'Don't think I'm alone in what I have on you,' Ingram said with unfazed cool. 'Robert and Kit have stitched you up and so has Billy, although he'd never admit it.'

'Lying smackhead,' Nick said. 'You're the pits.'

Ingram didn't falter. His almost reptilian response to events had Kit imagine the slowed-down metabolism of a lunar tourist sitting in a moon-hotel atrium contemplating the mountains outside.

'Get out, you two,' Billy said. 'If you can't discuss things without animosity, then go outside and brawl in the yard. We're trying to move on, but you keep pulling us back. If you want to remain hot-headed impetuous Elizabethans then go carve each other up in the alley.'

Billy stormed over to the window and gestured to the street. 'Silver Place. It's the perfect killing field, isn't it, Nick?'

Kit watched Billy return to his fixed place by the fridge, as though he had stationed himself there as a custodial outrider to events.

'How many people did you infect with the virus when you were positive?' Nick fired at Ingram.

'Not as many as you at the Dilly,' Ingram shot back, inspecting his blackened fingernails.

'That's enough,' Robert said. 'It's time we looked seriously at why none of us can escape the past. What was the great reckoning in a small room that Billy refers to in his play?'

'It means you got rid of a bad lot,' Nick said, pointing at Ingram.

'I think it means he killed Kit,' Ingram replied, returning Nick's gesture by pointing at him with an accusatory finger.

'Liar,' Nick said. 'Everyone knows it was you. It's public knowledge that you were convicted of the crime even though your sentence was repealed. It's entered the history books.'

'Bullshitter,' Ingram said, still concentrating on the state of his nails and how the last coat of black nail varnish to be applied had turned flaky. 'Ask Robert if it was me who stabbed Kit.'

'You're all liars, the whole lot of you,' Nick declared. 'Robert saw you do it, and so did Billy.'

'No I didn't,' Robert said. 'I don't have any clear memory of Ingram knifing Kit. It hasn't come up in any of my sessions at the Grid. Not in years of going through painfully re-enacted regression and sorting out the facts of what really happened.'

Kit looked across at the expensive Philips LCD television, blank and switched off in a corner, as though the dead screen somehow concurred with the end of time. He felt acutely nervous of how things were turning out between Nick and Ingram, and he tried to defuse the tension between the two by appealing to Billy with his eyes.

'Billy was there. He saw you do it,' Nick said with increased desperation. 'Didn't you, Billy?'

Billy remained silent, rooted to his spot, his downturned eyes giving nothing away. He looked to Kit like someone on a mental treadmill, totally concentrated into its rhythm.

'I'm not getting drawn into this,' he said after a time. 'But, no, Ingram didn't kill Kit Marlowe. He was simply an accomplice – if being in the room implied we were all agreed on one thing, his murder.'

'You're covering up for him,' Nick remonstrated. 'You all know he did it . . .'

'You're the only person claiming to be innocent,' Robert said. 'Wouldn't that be better coming from someone else?'

'What are you trying to say?' Nick questioned. 'That you believe Ingram rather than me?'

'Anybody would,' Ingram sneered, his methadone sedation lifting a fraction with each renewed run-in.

'Can we look at what really happened, the best we can reconstruct it?' Billy said. 'May the 29th 1593, we were all there at Deptford Creek on that day, including Thom, but, more importantly, so was Wriothesley. We had all gone south of the river to meet Kit as intelligence, some of us salaried by Wriothesley, who hoped to join us later, and some of us in the pay of Thom here or Lord Strange. I had arrived the night before with Wriothesley and had gone with him to discuss certain things with Eleanor Bull. These are facts that have stayed clear in me for four centuries. The allure of the place was, of course, sexual, if we're honest. There was, as you know, a thunderstorm on the night of the 28th. I remember sailors dancing naked in the street holding bottles of black rum. Wriothesley had a plan that I'll come to later. It was designated Plan A. Plan B was known only to ourselves, as an expedient should A fail.'

'Ingram killed him,' Nick interrupted. 'You're wasting your time with this explanation.'

'Shut up,' Robert said. 'Let Billy speak.'

Kit felt the tension in the room go stratospheric. It seemed to him that at that moment they were all connected to a neural circuit wired to a speedtrack.

Billy didn't move. He looked as if he was attempting to repair the flaw in a defective space–time in order to rehabilitate some sort of continuity. 'As I remember,' he went on, 'Ingram and Robert arrived together early the next day and started drinking in a pub call the Black Bear. Nick was already in Deptford so must, like us, have arrived the previous night.'

'What are you getting at?' Nick asked, his body looking as wasted as Ingram's waistless figure.

'Nothing,' Billy said. 'I'm concerned with facts, and to me they're as clear as vodka. Don't keep trying to confuse the issue by adding mixers. A fact is like a vodka shot, Nick. You take it in as absolute truth, and it burns.'

'Don't give us that poetic crap,' Nick said, taking off his leather jacket to reveal a newly inked tattoo on his bare left arm. Kit stared at the whiplashed loop of an olive-green snake swallowing its own tail, positioned marginally below the shoulder of an immaculately laundered white T-shirt.

'Go on,' Robert said, clearly squaring up to Nick psychologically.

Billy walked over to the table with alacrity and picked two books off the stack. He opened one and went straight to the place he intended. '"It strikes a man more dead than a great reckoning in a little room,"' he read out loud before returning to his place deep in thought. 'The collected works of both Marlowe and Shakespeare,' he said, toying with the books. 'And who would believe that we're still here today in a little room in Soho in Thom Walsingham's flat!'

Billy placed the books disdainfully on the fridge top. 'I wish I'd never written a word of it. Language corrodes like an industrial fixture that won't degrade. All of this,' he said, slapping the book hard, 'has followed me down the centuries. I'm stuck with it for ever. What I wrote fast and expendably is, amazingly, still being read. I intended it to be disposable. Writing passed the time and was, in my case, a lucrative profession that got me some money, but that's all. What I wrote was never intended for posterity.'

'I feel the same,' Kit said, showing no outward resistance to Thom's exploratory hand moving like a mole beneath the table.

'I'm stuck with the legacy of ideas in which I never properly believed. I wrote partly out of sexual frustration and partly because I wanted to kick the establishment in the balls. When I see my old books in Borders or Waterstone's I buy them up and trash them. Anything to reduce the weight of the legacy I carry.'

'You're crazy,' Nick said. 'But who cares about poetry? Let's get back to the facts.'

'They're what I'm giving you,' Billy said. 'This little aside is all part of the great reckoning. It helps explain why we're still here. There were things that Kit, in particular, wrote that offended everyone at the time. Language was powerful then. It burnt in like radiation fall-out. It could also come back on its user and incriminate.'

Ingram massaged his shades to effect and said, 'Books, man. I was one of the addicts who shoplifted books for Ronald Jordan. He employed a gang of about ten shoplifters to steal from high-street chains like Waterstone's and W.H. Smith's.

We were paid a pound for every book we stole. I don't remember stealing yours, though. Crazy, man, I can tell you. The cat was selling about a hundred stolen books a day and making a profit on each of about ten pounds. I did forty for him in one afternoon. He had two stalls, one in Dominion Street in the City and the other at Waterloo Station.'

'Good for him,' Billy said. 'Books may have been the essential building blocks of civilization, but they're through now. Eventually even Kit and I will be airbrushed from syllabuses. Language is the reason people cling to the past. Get rid of it and we're free.'

'If only it was that easy,' Kit said sardonically. 'Every generation naturally alternates between the belief that it is either the last or the first. As it is, the present offers very few clues.'

'Except,' said Billy, 'that we've all experienced the Grid. We've known what it's like to live with an insider's knowledge of death and to regress to whatever started it all on that night in Deptford.'

'How can you be sure the Grid doesn't lie?' Nick asked. 'It's the reason, after all, that we're all in this state.'

'It's you who lies,' Ingram said.

'The Grid's the only way of making sense of it all,' Kit said, expecting Nick at any moment to explode. 'It's our instructor. It's as much responsible for our biological repair as it is for our mental rehab. It's cleaned the virus out of our cells, and now it's time for us to let go the past by reconstructing what really happened.'

'I'm with you,' Billy said, posting his eyes towards the window on the street. 'Honest reconstruction of the facts is our only possible way forward. We've probably all convinced ourselves at some stage we did it or else lived in denial of what really happened.'

'Too right,' Robert agreed. 'Some of the sessions at the Grid have brought the issue that close I thought it was staring at me.'

'It's always the same in my sessions,' Thom said, breaking his silence. 'It's almost like the murderer and the victim have reversed their roles. The dead man's always running at me with the knife he's pulled out of his eye.'

'The closest I get is seeing the room,' Robert said. 'Eleanor Bull's closed room with its heavy brown hangings. We're all sitting there heatedly discussing politics with our own peculiar spin. There's no row, no heated falling out, but it happens. I see blood pooling and leaking from the table. That's all. Then everything freezes . . .'

'It's cool when I go in there, man,' Ingram said. 'The sessions never freak me. I look at it all in slow motion like I'm doing smack. We've all been walking in the garden and come back inside and take up our places round the table, just like we are now. The only person missing from the original group at present is Wriothesley.'

'He should be here soon,' Billy said. 'It's not like him to be late.'

'Doing business, man,' Ingram said.

'Dirty as yours,' Nick added. 'Drugs and arms. Don't they both make you sick?'

Ingram's laugh sounded to Kit like a distorted fade-out somewhere under the city rather than something issuing from his larynx.

Kit was again conscious of a flash, a trick of the light that came from Nick, confirming Kit's belief that he could be toying with a blade kept in his pocket.

'Will anyone confess to the killing,' Billy asked with gravity, 'or should we wait for Wriothesley before answering the question?'

Kit listened to the silence in the room, which was like the space inside sleep. It was like everyone present was locked into a window on the past, and outwardly, too, the city seemed to stand still for a moment, its ubiquitous sonic hum receding to something indistinct.

'Well?' Billy asked. 'Anyone care to own up? Now's your chance.'

Kit felt the silence intensify. It seemed to have deepened to a temporarily shared catatonia. What came up most memorably in his free-associated thoughts of the past were the green scales of a sailor's snake tattoo that had impressed itself on him that Deptford afternoon. The lime-green, crudely inked serpent mapped out on the iron shoulder of a man who would have died almost four centuries ago . . .

The silence continued until it was shot through by the noise of the buzzer. Thom walked over to the entryphone, as though he was in the process of unplugging the collective current in the room, and Kit knew instinctively that Wriothesley had arrived. He watched Thom go over to a front door that looked like it had been made out of Boeing panels and show Wriothesley in.

He came into the room quietly, discreetly dressed in a black roll-neck jumper worn under a grey Dior Homme suit jacket. This time there was no doubt in Kit's mind that James Waters was none other than the one-time Earl of Southampton. The distinct oval-shaped face, the arrogant hauteur of the man, the little giveaway scar above the nose gained in a childhood fight and, pertinently, the air of moneyed presumption implicit in his character, all these were the individual hallmarks of the Wriothesley he had known, now given a contemporary makeover by his genes.

As he entered, Wriothesley's eyes went directly to Billy's, before he took up a place opposite Kit. An understated smile did little to compensate for the inflexible manner with which he carried himself, and something of his dubious reputation seemed to have preceded him, given that the company maintained a brooding, stony silence. Only Nick looked up and smiled.

Wriothesley immediately dominated the room with his powerful gravitas. He was by nature imposing, an aristocrat linked to a dodgy profession and with enough plastic in his wallet to make things happen globally. Kit avoided his cold, disinterested stare – the look of a man who treated others as subordinates – and instead looked over at Ingram who alone appeared unperturbed by Wriothesley, continuing to sprawl with his legs triangled open. Ingram was chewing gum with the sort of disrespect natural to him.

'Don't let me spoil the conversation,' Wriothesley said with cutting irony.

'As it happens,' Billy said, 'I was asking a question which, now that you're here, I'll repeat. It applies as much to you as the others. Who killed Kit Marlowe on that evening in Deptford? One of you did, and now is the time to confess.'

Kit felt the silence return and build. Even Wriothesley appeared thrown by the directness of the question. Nobody answered. Kit could feel ice crawl through the room, like the beginnings of the big freeze. For a moment it occurred to him that guilt was a form of cryogenics. Whatever the individual was unwilling to shift stayed programmed in some neural recess of the unconscious. He imagined the confession being dragged up by someone with the same shattering as that from the body emerging from a liquid-nitrogen unit, the cells immediately splintering on contact with the air.

Kit felt the tension up its ante. He had the impression he was at the wheel of a car that was about to spin out of control, like a Jimmy Dean or Princess Diana Big Bang at optimal speed.

'Own up, you fucker,' Nick said, pointing his finger at Ingram, who continued nonchalantly chewing and staring into his black-outs.

'Think on it hard, all of you,' Billy said, still holding his position by the fridge.

'I did it,' Wriothesley announced, his measured voice breaking the silence like a stone smashing a window. 'I did it with you, Billy. And what's more, I'd do it again,' he said, rising from his seat and levelling an automatic at Kit.

'Put that gun down, James,' Billy shouted, turning to face him full on.

'He was always your rival, Billy, never your friend. It was you who were the great one. The idea that he wrote your work is contemptible.'

'Drop that gun, James,' Billy repeated, his voice dead level. 'Put it on the table and sit down.'

'Don't think I don't know that the two of you have something going,' Wriothesley said. 'I had you followed, Billy. You went to his flat and fucked.'

'Kill me instead,' Billy said. 'I don't care. I love him.'

'You love him,' Wriothesley repeated, shifting the aim of the gun to Billy before bringing it back level with Kit's eyes. 'You little shit.'

Kit didn't move.

'Give me that gun,' Billy repeated, walking slowly towards Wriothesley and looking him straight in the eyes.

'Get back,' Wriothesley ordered Billy. 'If you come any closer I'll shoot him.'

Kit could hear his heart beating with the amplified thud of someone running for their life through an underpass. He watched Billy freeze, the smile dropping from his face as he conceded to Wriothesley's demand.

For a moment nothing happened. Kit kept expecting Wriothesley to lower the gun and admit to its being a replica. He was waiting for Wriothesley to back off and laugh, but he didn't.

'You, Billy, over there next to Kit,' he ordered. 'Move, or I'll blast you both.'

Kit watched Billy's face drain of colour as he walked mechanically across the room. He noted the line of the thin gold chain he was wearing round his neck.

'Look at me, both of you,' Wriothesley commanded. 'So you're an item are you? Is his hole big enough for you, Billy? You've contaminated your place in history.'

Kit saw an obscene smile flash across Nick's face, as though something in him felt suitably vindicated by the insult.

'You can have him,' Wriothesley continued. 'I've got Nick now. You can marry each other in death.'

'Calm down,' Billy tried. 'Drop the gun, and we can talk about it.'

Kit looked at the inflexibility in Wriothesley's face. It was the look of arrogance inflected with unscrupulousness, of aristocratic demeanour turned corrupt, the sort of expression that treated others as natural-born losers to its innate superiority. Wriothesley tightened his grip on the gun. There were runnels of sweat showing on either side of his forehead, and the rim of his black roll-neck jumper had a line of foundation caught from his chin.

'Put the shooter down, man,' Ingram said, by way of unexpected back-up.

'You shut up,' Wriothesley snapped, turning his eyes and his gun briefly on Ingram.

'Shoot him,' Nick commanded with impulsive malice.

Neither Wriothesley nor Ingram moved. Ingram was still chewing his gum like he hadn't a care in the world. Kit admired his cool out of the corner of his eye, amazed at his sass in the middle of a potential flame-out.

'That'd be a pleasure,' Wriothesley said, 'but not before he's crawled.'

Kit caught sight of Nick revealing the knife he had been toying with under the table and pointing it derisively at Ingram. 'One word and I'll stick you,' Nick said.

Kit kept his eyes on the gun barrel pointing at him, magnetized to its snout, as though death would somehow be easier if he kept on looking at its source.

Suddenly, he saw Robert dive to the right, bringing Wriothesley down by his legs, so that he was pulled backwards on to the floor. It all happened so quickly that it was like fast-tracking film. Nick jumped into the ensuing skirmish to pull Robert off, and, electrified into action, Ingram came down on top of Nick, his hands locked in a stranglehold round his neck.

There wasn't time for Kit to act. He heard Nick scream that he'd been stabbed and saw him jump up, a ketchup-slew of blood running down his left arm from the shoulder. He looked at Kit imploringly and then bolted from the room like someone exiting a burning building. Wriothesley followed hard in pursuit, his voice calling after Nick, the gun left lying on the floor. He could hear them all the way down the stairs, the one clattering after the other and out of the building into Silver Place.

Ingram and Robert got up, shaken, and dusted themselves down, visibly shattered by the unexpected violence and ensuing carve-up.

'What happened?' Thom asked, seemingly impervious to the knifing that had just taken place in his kitchen, his voice expressing characteristic detachment from all human involvement despite the overturned chairs and livid blood trail leaking from Nick's stab wound. 'Who stabbed Nick?'

'He did it to himself,' Ingram replied, equally cold. 'The knife pointed back on him in the fight. He was trying to stab Robert when I grabbed him. I forced his arm up and it happened . . .'

'There won't be any enquiries here,' Thom said, his voice ruthlessly matter-of-fact. 'Wriothesley's connections rule it out. It's a closed affair. Shusako will clean the place up later. With Wriothesley everything gets processed as disinformation.'

Thom's cold pragmatism seemed brutally glacial to Kit in view of what had just occurred and with blood all over the kitchen floor.

'I suggest we get out of here and go to a café. There's one just over the road,' Thom said pedantically. 'I'll call Shusako in to do the necessary.'

'What about Nick?' Kit asked, his mind frantically shooting films of him leaving a graffiti trail of blood all over the Soho alleys with the distraught Wriothesley in desperate pursuit. 'I can't leave him to die. We've got to find him. That man was a huge part of my life.'

'He'll live,' Thom said in a totally dispassionate voice, 'providing he gets patched up privately. Wriothesley will call someone in to stitch him up, and there'll be no questions asked.'

'What do you mean, there'll be no questions?' Ingram levelled, repositioning his shades with attitude and promptly sitting down to regain his breath.

'Just what I told you,' Thom said. 'Wriothesley is too well connected with the Commissar's cabinet for there to be any police follow-up. He's regularly in on their power breakfasts.'

'Let's get out of here,' Ingram said to Robert, who was dusting himself down. 'Come on, man, let's split. There could be trouble.'

'See ya,' Ingram said as a parting shot, taking Robert with him, clearly unconvinced that the law wouldn't come looking for him. 'Nothing's changed, has it?' he added. 'A bit of blood, but we're still left with the Grid and the legacy of the past.'

'Wait and see,' Thom called after them. 'I think you'll find yourselves pleasantly surprised. What began in blood may have ended in blood.'

Kit looked at Billy. 'Let's go over the road,' he said. 'I need to get out of here fast. Somebody I loved is out there, possibly bleeding to death, and nobody will do anything about it. I'm shattered.'

Epilogue:
London Burning

The air reeked of kerosene. Kit could still hear the sub-sonic vibrations of a decommissioned Boeing that had been circling London on and off for the past half-hour, the pilot coming in low and jockeying over Tower 42, the Stock Exchange and the 'Gherkin', as though about to make a direct kamikaze hit, before pulling out in a deliberate sonic shattering. He wondered why the airliner hadn't been shot down yet, as its engine rumble receded east into dense cumulus rafts of smoky cloud.

Kit could instinctively sense the chemical change that had taken place in him overnight. It wasn't the MDMA that he had done with Billy bringing about the usual alteration in his serotonin levels but something deeper than that, some fundamental change that seemed to make him much more alert and attentive to the present.

He could hear Billy in the bathroom doing a post-shower cardiovascular workout with the Orbit Competition, an elliptical trainer with six pre-set programs allowing for full-body exercise, a smart gadget he and Yukio had recklessly purchased as part of a scheme intended to turn the bathroom into a home gym.

Kit busied himself preparing breakfast in the kitchen. He wondered if today would be the anticipated day, the one when toxic-site clean-up crews, kitted out in their Demron hazmat suits, would be called on to attend some irreversible rupture in the city's matrix. He found himself straining, listening for the aircraft's return through floating continents of cloud and audio-hallucinating the roar of engines thrusting an insane flight path over the city's skyscrapers.

The information had long ago been coded in his cells that London would burn and that troops who had prepared for the catastrophe through repeated trials would gather at the disaster site dressed in protective nuclear-biological-chemical suits. The expectation of apocalypse was big in him now, and he anticipated its imminent arrival almost as a form of perverse joy. He had the crazy notion that he wanted to link arms with Billy and walk out into the roaring orange flames.

When Billy emerged from the bathroom, his hair was slicked back, dripping wet. He was wearing a flame-orange T-shirt and black jeans distressed at the knees from continuous wear. Their sex the night before had been good, but Kit still felt it necessary to stand back from Billy's emotional demands. He was like someone who had lived out the fantasy of a relationship for so long that he had deceived himself into thinking it was a reality. He expected Kit to be similarly committed and made no allowance for his attachment to Yukio, no matter how casual that might be.

Kit broke away from Billy's kiss, holding him off with the spread palms of his hands. 'Did you hear that aircraft?' he asked. 'It's a Boeing, and the pilot's looking to ditch it on Tower 42 or some other skyscraper. It's going to happen this time.'

'This really is apocalypse,' Billy said, apparently without fear, 'although it's just an update of the one we wrote about in our plays, the end we always anticipated.'

'What would you want to do right at the end?' Kit asked.

'Have you fuck me on a rooftop while the city burns,' Billy replied without hesitation.

'I feel so different today,' Kit said. 'There's more space inside me. I don't know how to describe it, other than that I feel I'm living now, in the present, instead of panning in and out of the past.'

'Me, too. I don't feel bilocated any longer, as though I'm about to be flashbacked into my past with the onerous responsibility of having been Will Shakespeare.'

'There's an *Independent* on the table,' Kit said as he went back to the toaster. 'I haven't had time to look at it yet. It's probably full of the latest updates on CancerVax, terrorism and what the Commissar had stored in his refurbished Whitehall bunker.'

Billy picked the paper up as the airwaves roared with the Boeing's return, the rogue plane blasting its way back into a terror orbit of the City's towers.

'The pilot must be on acid to do this loop,' Kit called out as the whole skyline was whipped by catastrophic turboblast. The flat vibrated from engine roar, with plates and hanging fixtures dislodged from walls and splintering on the floor.

'Sounds like he's gone off again,' Billy said, his eyes bumped out huge, as the volume of noise pollution diminished behind a white cumulus formation resembling an exploded meringue.

Kit fetched a jar of peanut butter from a cupboard and remoted Billie Holiday into singing 'On the Sunny Side of the Street', the vulnerability in her small highly personalized voice forming an acute contrast with the subsonic thunder of the Boeing lurching through the airways on its simulated terrorist attack.

Billie's voice reminded Kit of a post-mortem low now, as she phrased 'The Man I Love' from an impossible distance behind the beat. He moved in on the song as a form of redemption. For this brief moment in time it was all that he had, a little pivot on which to rest his sanity before the deranged pilot returned looking for his corporate target.

'He's dead,' Billy said from behind the paper he had picked up from the table, his voice dropping an octave as he looked up at Kit. 'Nick's dead. He was shot outside a building in Silver Place, and Wriothesley, it seems, is critical in intensive care. Double shooting. What the . . .' Billy said, his voice faltering. 'Police have arrested a 46-year-old man called Ray on suspicion of murder.'

Kit had let a cup fall as the news hit. Now his hands continued to go through the motions with the breakfast things.

'That's why we're free,' Billy said. 'Somebody's paid the price of my great reckoning in a little room. It's unbelievable. We've both lost a lover . . . just like that. Strange has gunned them down. Nick and Wriothesley. It can't be real.'

Kit, in a state of shocked disbelief, walked over to the table and held Billy. They fell on each other in an attempt to cancel out something of their pain and the extraordinary events connected to their pasts. They struggled desperately to find comfort in their embrace while the loopy Boeing pilot blasted in again on his mission to terrorize the city's high-rise corporates into evacuating their towers in a panicked exodus of hysterically driven staff.

'What was it Thom said? "What began in blood may have ended in blood"? Do you remember that?' Billy said, lifting his head on to Kit's shoulder.

Kit thought of Nick dead. He couldn't locate him anywhere tangible now, only in imaginary space; the living person's image kept breaking up inside his head. It didn't seem real or possible to him that Nick, with his pop-star aspirations and rent-boy attitude, was gone from the London scene. He had beaten Aids only to die as the fall guy for the group in a shoot-out between two equally power-mad men, Wriothesley and Strange.

There was no question now about what time this was. Kit occupied the present directly, like he had never done before. Despite the impacted shock of death on him and Billy, and despite each having lost a lover, they were free of the past. He was convinced of that. He could feel the urgency of the present, without mediation from the past, register like helium in his blood.

He space-walked in a daze back to the fridge and dug out the bottle of champagne he was keeping on hold to celebrate the completion of his screenplay. He handled the bottle, a frosty-walled Veuve Clicquot, as though it contained all the compressed, fizzy euphoria he was longing to release into his chemistry. It was the chilled liquid explosive that he and Billy needed exactly at this moment in time.

He released the cork to a Niagara of fizz, pulled on the gushing bottleneck and handed it to Billy. The idea of using glasses at this time seemed superfluous, and Kit watched Billy draw deep on the shaken-up contents.

Kit felt the champagne kick in on his empty stomach immediately. He fed his tongue into Billy's mouth and savoured the taste of the wine. It was like cold sunlight coating the palate. It was like tangoing with a corridor of bubbles.

Billy grabbed Kit's swollen crotch as the kitchen filled with Boeing roar. This time the plane had dropped height and could be seen low over Paddington Basin and the disco-ball glitter of the mirror-clad Westway towers. The sun breaking through the cloud ceiling had lit up London's skyscrapers like a species of vertically cut blue diamonds.

'Let's go up on the roof,' Billy said, cradling the bottle. 'Now's the time.'

Kit led the way out on to the narrow strip of balcony and up a short blue-painted ladder to the roof terrace. His abortive attempts to grow heather, geraniums and resilient evergreens had largely failed because of a lack of application. But from that platform they could see the rogue Boeing pursue its wonky trajectory of the London skies. Kit knew it would be only a matter of minutes before the pilot self-destructed in a volcanic roar of detonating kerosene.

Billy stood on the rooftop in his appropriately flame-orange-coloured T-shirt, arms wide open, saluting the sun. He had unzipped his jeans and was already fully erect. His blond hair made him look like an Aryan android, frame-grabbed by secondhand interplanetary light.

Kit unzipped and went down on all fours, facing east into a dusty red sun. He knew that whatever configuration their bodies took was to be a form of death rite. The sky stank of aviation fuel. He had the mad thought that the pilot might be a nude woman, sitting at the computer, blonde hair tied back, her black aviator sunglasses protecting her from refracted glare.

'Now,' Kit said, impulsively. The Boeing had tracked east with its throttle fully open, and now the pilot rammed the nose cone through his selected target in a detonating thunder of urban apocalypse. Kit caught the blinding orange blaze of an explosive impact like the Big Bang as the jet ripped into the tower. The whole sky shook as their bodies created a twisted lexicon of poetry under a black mushrooming scroll of smoke driven upwards from the hit. Kit continued facing east as the devastation set off a chain of explosions and corresponding emergency sirens. London was burning, and the city was being partially airbrushed by towering columns of acrid smoke. He thrilled at his union with Billy in the light of the nuclear sun. They were one body, the first and the last poets, and he intended to keep it that way.

If you have enjoyed this Jeremy Reed title, you may like to read some of his other books also published by Peter Owen. To order books or a free catalogue or for further information on these or any other Peter Owen titles, please contact:

Sales Department, Peter Owen Publishers
73 Kenway Road, London SW5 0RE, UK
tel: + 44 (0)20 7373 5628 / 7370 6093 fax: + 44 (0)20 7373 6760
e-mail: sales@peterowen.com
www.peterowen.com

Angels, Divas and Blacklisted Heroes
    978-07206-1052-9   £10.95
Bitter Blue: Tranquillizers, Creativity, Breakdown
    978-07206-0892-2   £15.99
Black Sugar: Gay, Lesbian and Heterosexual Love Poems
    978-07206-0871-7   £10.95
Boy Caesar
    978-07206-1193-9   £11.95
Chasing Black Rainbows: A Novel Based on the Life of Artaud
    978-07206-1008-6   £9.95
    978-07206-0924-0   £14.95
Delirium: An Interpretation of Arthur Rimbaud
    978-07206-0825-0   £15.50
Diamond Nebula
    978-07206-0922-6   £9.95
    978-07206-0891-5   £14.95
Dorian: A Sequel to *The Picture of Dorian Gray*
    978-07206-1012-3   £14.95
Inhabiting Shadows
    978-07206-0787-1   £13.95
Isidore: A Fictional Re-creation of the Life of Lautréamont
    978-07206-0831-1   £13.99
Lipstick, Sex and Poetry
    978-07206-0817-5   £14.95
Madness – the Price of Poetry
    978-07206-0744-4   £17.95
Red Hot Lipstick
    978-07206-0943-1   £9.95
    978-07206-0988-2   £14.95
A Stranger on Earth: The Life and Work of Anna Kavan
    978-07206-1273-8   £13.99
When the Whip Comes Down: A Novel About de Sade
    978-07206-0858-8   £9.75

Also published by Peter Owen

BOY CAESAR
Jeremy Reed
978-0-7206-1193-9 • paperback • 219 pp • £11.95

'Full of delicate and beautiful conceits, and deeply erudite' – *Independent on Sunday*

'Baroque time-travelling reading thrills . . . Reed's tale tackles control and being out-of-control in virtuoso style.' – *Scotsman*

'A brilliant and original talent whose writing occupies a unique landscape.' – J.G. Ballard

AD 218, Rome. Heliogabalus becomes emperor of Rome at the age of fourteen, beginning a reign of legendary decadence that ends with his murder in the palace latrines. AD 20??, London. Jim has been researching the life of the little-known boy emperor. But he is disturbed. His boyfriend Danny has started spending a lot of time on Hampstead Heath at night. Slut is the messiah of the Heath, the saintly figure at bizarre sexual rituals who sacrifices himself to numbers on the orgy-tree. He doesn't like Jim at all. Masako, Jim's friend, is a psychic. While on a visit to Rome with Masako Jim has visions of a blond youth, while Masako dreams of Heliogabalus alive and residing in the Eternal City under the name of Antonio – and Antonio's face is strangely familiar . . . In Jeremy Reed's novel contemporary Soho seeps into Heliogabalus' Rome. As the Roman army marches through the city after the emperor's blood, boundaries of time, gender and space break down in a thrilling conclusion as original as it is electrifying.

Peter Owen books can be purchased from:
Central Books, 99 Wallis Road, London E9 5LN, UK
Tel: +44 (0) 845 458 9911 Fax: + 44 (0) 845 458 9912
e-mail: orders@centralbooks.com

www.peterowen.com

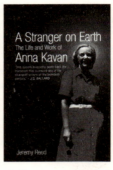
Peter Owen books can be purchased from:
Central Books, 99 Wallis Road, London E9 5LN, UK
Tel: +44 (0) 845 458 9911 Fax: + 44 (0) 845 458 9912
e-mail: orders@centralbooks.com

www.peterowen.com

Also published by Peter Owen

ICE
Anna Kavan
978-0-7206-1268-4 • paperback • 158 pp • £9.95
Peter Owen Modern Classic

'A classic, a vision of unremitting intensity which combines some remarkable imaginative writing with what amounts to a love-song to the end of the world. Not a word is wasted, not an image is out of place.'
– *Times Literary Supplement*

'One can only admire the strength and courage of this visionary.' – *The Times*

'Few contemporary novelists could match the intensity of her vision.' – J.G. Ballard

In this haunting and surreal novel, the narrator and a man known as 'the warden' search for an elusive girl in a frozen, seemingly post-nuclear, apocalyptic landscape. The country has been invaded and is being governed by a secret organization. There is destruction everywhere; great walls of ice overrun the world. Together with the narrator, the reader is swept into a hallucinatory quest for this strange and fragile creature with albino hair. Acclaimed by Brian Aldiss on its publication in 1967 as the best science fiction book of the year, this extraordinary and innovative novel has subsequently been recognized as a major work of literature in any genre.

There is nothing else like it . . . This *Ice* is not psychological ice or metaphysical ice; here the loneliness of childhood has been magicked into a physical reality as hallucinatory as the Ancient Mariner's.' – Doris Lessing

Peter Owen books can be purchased from:
Central Books, 99 Wallis Road, London E9 5LN, UK
Tel: +44 (0) 845 458 9911 Fax: + 44 (0) 845 458 9912
e-mail: orders@centralbooks.com

www.peterowen.com

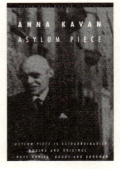